BY FIRE
ABOVE

TOR BOOKS BY ROBYN BENNIS

The Guns Above
By Fire Above

BY FIRE ABOVE

Robyn Bennis

TOR

A Tom Doherty Associates Book

NEW YORK

BY FIRE ABOVE

A Tor Book
Published by Tom Doherty Associates
175 Fifth Avenue
New York, NY 10010

www.tor-forge.com

Tor® is a registered trademark of Macmillan Publishing Group, LLC.

The Library of Congress Cataloging-in-Publication
Data is available upon request.

ISBN 978-0-7653-8879-7 (hardcover)
ISBN 978-0-7653-8880-3 (ebook)

Our books may be purchased in bulk for promotional, educational, or business use. Please contact your local bookseller or the Macmillan Corporate and Premium Sales Department at 1-800-221-7945, extension 5442, or by email at MacmillanSpecialMarkets@macmillan.com.

First Edition: May 2018

Printed in the United States of America

0 9 8 7 6 5 4 3 2 1

BY FIRE ABOVE

THE MISTRAL
of the Aerial Signal Corps

Captain's Cabin

Secondary Condensers

Sleeping Compartments

Officers

Crew

Boiler

Steamjack Turbine

Gearbox

Hurricane Deck

Fuel

Water Ballast

Auxiliary Control

Reservoirs

Primary Condenser

Carrier Pigeons

The Hurricane Deck of
THE MISTRAL

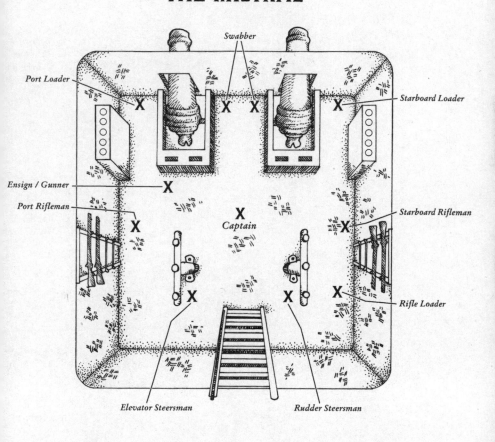

Swabber

Port Loader

Starboard Loader

Ensign / Gunner

Starboard Rifleman

Port Rifleman

Captain

Rifle Loader

Elevator Steersman

Rudder Steersman

1

"Up ship!"

At the word of command, His Majesty's Signal Airship *Mistral* rose above the cratered, blood-spattered fields of Canard. The ship's condition was little better than the field's, with her wicker decks stained red, her envelope in tatters, and half her gas bags filled with inflammable air.

Josette Dupre, *Mistral*'s captain, stood in the center of the hurricane deck, enjoying the nearest thing to quiet she'd had in days. The only flaws in this rare moment of peace were the wicker creaking underfoot and the soft burble of paraffin running through fuel lines above.

The usual din would resume when the ship rose to her cruising altitude, but until then Josette basked in the silence. By unspoken, common consent, the crew went about their work without the usual racket, as if in appreciation of so precious and unusual an event as this.

"Good God, it's quiet!" cried Lord Bernat Manatio Jebrit Aoue Hinkal, who stood to Josette's right and who did not, it seemed, subscribe to such whimsical notions as common consent. "What say we all sing a song to liven things up? Does everyone know the words to 'The Merry Monks of Melatina'?"

The crew met Bernat's comment with the less enjoyable class of silence—the sort that hangs awkwardly in the air, hoping against all odds that true peace will return in a moment.

"No one?" Bernat asked, quite oblivious. "What about 'The Sotrian Lady'? Everyone knows that."

The crew made not a sound.

Josette set her eyes on the horizon, where a broad but ill-maintained road disappeared into the Magdalene Fens. She could just make out, rising above the morning haze, gun smoke from the Vinzhalian army's desperate rearguard action as they retreated toward the border town of Durum, pursued by Garnian cavalry. The cavalry would not pursue them as far as Durum, however. Durum—the town where Josette was born, and the town where her mother now lived under Vin occupation—would remain in enemy hands.

She put it out of her mind, and looked to the instrument panel above her station as the ship climbed. High above the wicker gondola of the hurricane deck, above the instruments, above the catwalk and the keel, *Mistral*'s nine enormous gas bags puffed out, growing larger as the pressure dropped with altitude. To Josette's right, the much smaller gas bag who went by the name of Bernat said, "So, no one's even talking to me, now?"

At just under five thousand feet, Sergeant Jutes reported that the bags were nearly at their full size, and would have to be vented if the ship rose much higher, to prevent them from bursting.

"Rigging crews will make one last check for leaks, now that the bags are fully inflated," Josette ordered. "Then we'll spin up the steamjack."

Sergeant Jutes repeated the order, shouting it back along the keel from his station at the top of the companionway. In the narrow spaces between gas bags, riggers crept like spiders across a web of lines and plywood box girders. Between frames, they climbed out onto longitudinal girders of questionable integrity, their backs squeezed against the inside of the canvas envelope as they checked the outer faces of the bags.

Such a thorough inspection prior to starting up the steamjack was not routine, but neither was carrying inflammable air. As the name implied, it had the nasty habit of igniting at the slightest pretext.

"Five-inch hole in bag three, Sarge!" a feminine voice called from the other side of the ship's canvas skin, directly above the hurricane deck. Jutes repeated the report, shouting it down the companionway and swapping in a "sir" at the end.

Josette heard another report from far aft, but couldn't make it out. Jutes relayed it as, "Foot-long tear in bag eight, sir."

"Multiple holes in four!" called a masculine yet strangely high-pitched voice from amidships.

"Is that bad?" Bernat asked.

"The furnace is under bag four," Josette answered, turning to face aft.

Bernat tapped his chin, as he made a show of thinking about it. "The furnace? You mean that lumpy tangle of metal beneath the boiler? The one with all the bullet holes in it?"

"The same." Josette said. "Ensign Kember, you have the deck. Ballast coming aft!" She started up the companionway.

Bernat followed her up the companionway and called, "Two ballasts coming aft!"

She thought his voice had a slightly higher pitch inside the keel than in the open air of the hurricane deck.

She turned and cast an inquiring look at him. "Is it my imagination, or . . ."

"Oh dear," he said, clearly recognizing the change in pitch of her voice, too. "Does that mean what I think it does?"

"I'm afraid it does. We're soaking in inflammable air." She looked to Private Grey, the mechanic's mate. "Quench the boiler fire. Riggers recheck all fire screens and tarps. Make sure they're tied securely." The riggers hardly needed telling. They were already on their way down, and as they arrived they set to inspecting the fabric screens that separated the keel, at the very bottom of the superstructure, from the gas bags above it.

Josette knelt by the boiler and inspected its furnace. The smaller punctures had been patched with clay, but half a dozen holes were too big for that, and so were covered by a protective wire mesh held in place with solder. She peered through a mesh screen. Inside the furnace, the paraffin flame sputtered out, but the fuel nozzle remained red hot, and the forest of tubes that ran up through the furnace to feed water into the steam drum were speckled with burning embers.

And it wasn't only the furnace that could ignite the ship. Here, a mile in the air aboard a floating powder keg, a dozen possible ignition sources occurred to her, all of which had seemed insignificant on the ground. There were the loose flints in the small arms locker, the metal tools used on the steamjack, the rigging lines run through blocks with iron bearings. Even Bernat's frippery might cause a static spark that was quite sufficient to blow them all to hell—all the more reason for him to start dressing sensibly.

"Don't take off your jacket," she said, looking up at him.

Bernat beamed a smile and said, "It's quite stylish, isn't it? I didn't think you'd notice." He ran his hands across the green velvet and filigreed buttons.

"Don't ruffle it, either. You could cause a spark."

As Bernat recognized her meaning, the disappointment rose on his face in proportion to his earlier joy. "I'm sorry to inform you that I can't help causing sparks," he said. "It's in my nature."

But it was not to be Bernat or his clothing which would ignite the inflammable air. The chain of disaster began where Josette had first suspected it: inside the furnace, where inflammable air was slowly seeping through the mesh. Even as she contemplated the glowing embers, one of them ignited the thin gas inside, the boiler clanged like a bell under the sudden increase in pressure, and the mesh-covered holes flashed with a flame so bright it left purple spots in Josette's vision. Along the keel, crewmen froze in place and held their breaths, while the riggers ceased their work and swung gently on their safety lines—all waiting to see if the entire ship would follow the example of its furnace.

But the wire mesh did its job. It kept the brief flare-up from penetrating beyond the boiler housing, so that the initial explosion was contained safely inside. But inside the furnace, the air was now swirling with glowing flecks of soot, glowing all the brighter when eddies brought them near the mesh-patched holes. But as bright as these embers burned, they couldn't pass through the mesh to ignite the gas outside.

"Good God!" Bernat cried. "That nearly stopped my heart. It's a good thing for you, Dupre, that you don't have one."

Josette began to breathe, and was just about to answer his quip, when she saw that one of the mesh patches was damaged. A corner had been bent outward, the solder cracked by the blast. It wasn't much of a gap, but perhaps it was just enough to let an ember out. She struck out instantly to press her hand over the gap, grimacing as the heat of the furnace blistered her skin. For all that, she was not in time to keep a single glowing wisp of soot from whirling out and dancing past her head.

"Spark!" she cried, as she followed the minute, deadly ember with her eyes. "All hands lie flat!"

Everyone along the keel dropped to the wicker catwalk in a moment, save for Bernat, who only stood there, bewildered. Josette had to grab his safety harness and yank him down with her free hand. She'd barely got him to the deck when the entire keel went up in flame.

MINUTES BEFORE THE disaster, Auxiliary Ensign Sabrine Kember stood in the captain's station at the center of the hurricane deck. It wasn't the first time she'd stood the deck, aboard *Mistral* or her previous ship, but she always felt as if she hadn't yet earned the right to occupy that hallowed spot. She wondered if she shouldn't stand a pace or two to the left, out of consideration.

Above her, the captain and Lord Hinkal were at it again. They bickered with an odd mix of venomous spite and grudging affection that Kember had previously only seen in elderly married couples. For a while she'd thought there was something to that, but the scuttlebutt said that Lord Hinkal was actually enthralled by the captain's mother. Kember was skeptical, not only because Lord Hinkal couldn't possibly be that stupid, but because she was doubtful that Captain Dupre had a mother.

She looked up to check the aneroid altimeter and pneumatic thermoscope, and a twinge of pain shot through her wounded neck. She winced and sucked air through her teeth.

"You okay, sir?" a nearby crewman asked.

Being called "sir" had long since ceased to bother her. Army regulations provided no other form of address for women officers, probably because no one had bothered to update those regulations when they started letting women in. When in civilian company, she was occasionally called "ma'am" or even "Sabrine." In the latter case, it invariably took her several seconds to remember who that was, for no one had called Kember by her first name in so long that she'd almost forgotten it.

She rubbed her neck around the sore spot and said to the crewman, "I'm fine. It hardly even hurts any—"

"Spark!" In the keel above, that one word stood out from the rest.

"Down!" Kember shouted to the deck crew at the top of her voice, despite the stabbing pain it caused in her throat.

As she dropped flat herself, she saw the explosion's flash reflected on the deck. The concussion of the blast hit her, thumping into her like she'd just been punched in the back.

A wave of heat followed. As it passed, she looked up to see the deck crew alive and well, save for one dazed man who'd had his safety line clipped onto a rope above, and so couldn't lie flat.

"All hands to fight fire!" she called. As a mere auxiliary ensign, she wasn't sure she had the authority to call all hands, but the captain and Lieutenant Martel might already be dead, so there was hardly time to worry about it.

She turned and ran to the companionway ladder, passing between the steersmen, who were still getting to their feet after the blast. She dashed up to the keel, taking three stairs at a time.

The smell of charred hair and burnt varnish filled the atmosphere inside the ship. Canvas ports were blown out all along the keel, so that daylight streamed into the usually gloomy space, catching the floating ash as it swirled through the ship. The keel girders were intact, but above them the fabric fire screen between keel and gas bags had been thrown upward in several places, and there were gaping holes in its coverage, most particularly over the boiler. As soon as the next wave of seeping inflammable air reached any of the small secondary fires still smoldering along the keel, there would be nothing to stop the flash from penetrating into the superstructure and igniting the bags.

In frame six, the monkey rigger was already at work in the spiderweb of girders above, trying to repair a gap in the fire barrier. "Never mind that," Kember called. "There's no time." She grabbed a bucket from the gunnery supplies and tossed it up to her. "Fill it from the water ballast and wet the canvas. Wet everything, from the top down."

Kember continued aft, to frame four, where the captain was lying insensible on her back, her hair smoldering at the ends. "Apologies, sir," Kember said, as she snatched a fire blanket and unceremoniously wrapped her captain's head in it.

Fore and aft, the few lucid crewmen were at work on the fires, but here in the engine frames, where the danger was greatest, everyone was either unconscious, flash-blind, or spouting delirious babble. Worse, frame four was absolutely swimming in embers, floating in the air or settled onto the deck. Fragments of canvas smoldered along the envelope, while hot ashes dropped from the safety screen above. And every moment, an invisible cloud of inflammable air was spreading toward the fires.

Even if she brought the entire crew into this frame, she couldn't quench every possible source of ignition in time. She needed to quench all of it at once, but even if she had a fire hose, she wasn't sure she could do it in time.

Her eyes turned to the boiler, and she knew in a moment what she had to do. She reached up and pulled the manual release on the steam drum's safety valve. The drum roared as the pressure inside dropped and a geyser of wet steam vented from the side of the keel out into the open air, where it did her no good at all. She took a wrench from the mechanics' toolbox and took careful aim at the vent pipe, just above the valve. If she damaged the safety valve, half an inch below her target, the pressure inside the drum would fall instantly to zero and the whole thing would explode, killing them all in a slightly different but equally effective manner.

She swung and the wrench connected, knocking the pipe from its valve. A jet of scalding steam whistled out, burning Kember's arm up to the elbow before she could duck out of its way.

She looked up to see the frame filling with steam—hot, choking, but blessedly moist steam. The burning canvas above sizzled and sputtered, and the smoldering ash along the keel was soon coated with a fuzzy layer of dew.

At her feet, Captain Dupre was just regaining her senses. She sat up and pulled the fire blanket off her head. Something about her face seemed even more dour and angry than usual, and it took Ensign Kember a few seconds to realize that the captain's eyebrows had been the first casualty of the accident.

"Ensign?" she asked. And then, quite suddenly, she seemed to remember the circumstances that had led to her being face-up under a fire blanket. She rose unsteadily. "What's our status?"

"Fires are out amidships, sir. They're working on them fore and aft. Not sure about casualties, but I haven't seen anything serious. Mostly just stunned, sir."

She looked up at the jet of steam overhead, now tapering off as the boiler pressure fell. "Perhaps not what I would have done, but novel nonetheless."

"Thank you, sir."

Lieutenant Martel came forward from his station near the tail. "Ballast coming forward," he called toward the nose. He saluted the captain. "Fires are out aft, sir, but the riggers are wetting everything to be sure."

"It's a steam bath in here," Lord Hinkal said, as he sat up on the deck. "If there weren't ladies present, I might strip down to better enjoy it."

"As if that's ever stopped you," the captain said.

And so the bickering began again, just moments after the crisis had passed. Ensign Kember had to use all of her will-power to keep from rolling her eyes.

2

ALL TOLD, THE voyage to Arle might have been more pleasant. Besides the possibility that the ship might explode at any moment and send them plunging all aflame to the earth below, the bird cages had fallen over during the first incident and set a dozen homing pigeons loose inside the superstructure. Some had escaped through holes in the envelope, but most of them were still up there, darting around in the narrow spaces between the outer canvas skin and the inner gas bags.

For reasons Bernat could not fathom, they seemed to prefer the aft portion of the ship, above the officer and supernumerary bunks, where Bernat woke in the morning to find his baggage covered in bird shit. Stowed in the netting above his bunk, it had at least shielded him from the nocturnal bombardment, but this seemed small consolation when he discovered that the moist guano had spoiled his store of breakfast foods.

He was thus forced, quite against his will, to breakfast on ship's provisions: a soppy mess of hard biscuit and hot water, referred to by the fanciful term "porridge." He ate a bowl of it, spoonful by dreadful spoonful, leaning on the rail in his habitual spot on the hurricane deck. The porridge sat like a lump in his belly and tacked up his mouth, making speech difficult. But paradoxically, despite his inability to converse with them, the deck crew was unusually cheerful this morning.

The annoyance was all the greater because these days Bernat didn't like where his mind went when unoccupied. It followed his eyes now to the northeast, where Durum lay far over the horizon. Somewhere in that war-ravaged town, Elise Dupre was trying to survive under the bootheel of the Vins.

He shoved another lump of porridge into his mouth and swallowed without chewing. Stale, sharp bits of hardtack scratched the back of his throat and hurt all the way down his gullet, but he found the pain a welcome distraction.

"Coming up on the Knees, sir," Ensign Kember reported from the forward rail, her voice hoarser than the day before. The bandage around her neck rode a little higher this morning, and Bernat hoped the girl wasn't hiking it up to conceal spreading putrefaction. There'd already been quite enough death aboard this ship.

"That's about a third of the way to Arle," Josette said, apparently for his benefit.

He tried to speak but found his words blocked by porridge. He spent some time clearing the obstruction, then said, "Is that all? It's taking longer than the trip out."

"The wind was fair on the trip out," Josette said. "Now it's fighting us, and we with a damaged steamjack, limping along at a quarter power."

He looked over the side, gauging their speed by the passage of the fields below, where stalks of winter wheat bent under a wind in direct opposition to *Mistral*'s movement. The ship was hardly making headway against that chill breeze. "Rather different from an oceangoing vessel," he said.

Josette shrugged. "They live by the wind. We live in it."

It seemed to Bernat that her "we" had a more inclusive tone than he remembered, the last time she'd explained something about airship life to him.

"What are you smiling at?" she asked.

He hadn't realized he was. He looked away, abashed. "Just a joke I heard."

IN HER NEAR-CRIPPLED state, it took another two days and most of a night to bring *Mistral* to Arle. Apart from the delay itself, always anathema to an airship captain, it meant there was no hope of seeing Gears alive. *Mistral*'s chief engineer had been hit with canister shot over Canard and had almost as many holes in him as the steamjack. He'd been loaded onto a wagon bound for Arle with the rest of the wounded, and if he hadn't died on the way, might have lingered in the hospital long enough for a final goodbye, if only *Mistral* had made better time. As it was, he was surely already in the grave, and if not already covered by earth, then covered by those who'd died after him.

Josette focused on the beacon atop the airship shed, only a few minutes out. Dawn was still hours away, and that beacon was their only guide as they steamed toward the signal base's landing circle.

Mistral slid through the dark sky, slicing down toward the mooring mast until she was so close that the monkey rigger in the airship's nose could reach out and take a line from the yardsman stationed atop the mast. The approach was so well-timed, despite the variable winds heaving the ship about, that the nose and mast did not make contact, but hung inches from each other until the monkey rigger drew in the line and tied on. With the ship secured forward, the ground crews clapped onto lines and kept a tight hold to keep *Mistral* from flopping like a fish in the blustery weather.

They were reasonably successful, until *Mistral* was halfway into the shed. In that position, with her forward half shielded from the wind, but her great tailfins exposed to it and acting like a weathervane, a sudden gust blew the ship's stern sharply to port, where there were only a few yards of clearance with the massive shed door. Josette called to the yardsmen, but before she could get an order out, she heard the crunch of plywood girders as the ship impacted at frame five.

She ran to the port rail and took the measure of the situation in a fraction of a second, noting the angle of the ship, the relative positions of the door and starboard airscrews, the depth to which the superstructure was impaled, and the reactions of the men on the ground. She ran then to starboard, where the yardsmen were hauling on their ropes to yank *Mistral* off the door.

"Hold!" she called. "Don't pull! Watch for the rebound! Eyes on the tail!"

In a rare display, and perhaps only due to the confusion of the moment, the yardsmen actually obeyed her orders. And well they did, for in another second the wind reversed, wrenching *Mistral* off the door, and threatened to swing her to port with equal force, where she would impact *Ibis,* the chasseur in the next berth. But the yardsmen were ready for it, and brought her back into alignment with little fuss.

Josette looked back along the envelope to assess the damage. Girders were stove in and canvas ripped in a vertical line that stretched fifty feet up *Mistral*'s superstructure. The hurricane deck crew were utterly silent, waiting for her to explode into a frothing rage. But she only sighed and shook her head as *Mistral* was secured into her berth.

Lieutenant Martel came forward from his station in the keel. Josette asked him, "Eager to get away from us?"

"Not as such, Captain," he said with a grin. "But I would like to get a start on securing spare planks and girders from the warehouse, before the quartermaster wakes up."

Josette had rarely won a battle with the quartermaster, but Martel seemed to have a knack for outmaneuvering her. "Then go, by all means," Josette said. "Come back with our girders, or on them."

Martel went over the side, but was immediately stopped by a signal lieutenant, who said to him, "Congratulations, Captain."

This was not the first time someone had called *Mistral*'s first officer "captain." Josette, in fact, had sometimes encouraged him to indulge the mistake, since the sort of person who made it was invariably someone she didn't want to deal with. But alas, Martel answered, "You're mistaken. The captain is still aboard ship, if you'd like to hail her."

"No mistake, Captain Martel," the lieutenant said, handing over a folded piece of paper. Martel's face lit up as he read it.

Josette didn't have to ask. She called down to him, "Well done, Captain." He was still technically a lieutenant, as was she, but the Aerial Signal Corps had borrowed the navy's manner of referring to any ship's commander as its captain. "What ship did you get?"

"*Goose.*"

Goose was a semi-rigid, moored two berths over from *Mistral*. She was a reliable ship, if a bit on the sluggish side, even for a high-altitude scout. Josette had heard that *Goose*'s commander was leaving the air corps and joining the regular army after promotion to the rank of major, which was how it usually went with airship officers. An air officer with even the smallest measure of talent could advance from ensign to major in under ten years—or they could become a twisted, charred corpse in under a month. But for men who didn't possess connections or family influence, the air corps might be their only chance at promotion.

It was then that Bernat came down the companionway ladder to the hurricane deck, yawning, dabs of shaving powder still stuck to his jaw.

"You're not usually up this early," Josette said. "It's not even light out."

"I couldn't sleep with the engine off." He looked over the rail. "What's going on down there?"

"Martel has gotten the *Goose*," Josette said. She hadn't realized how it would sound until that moment.

Bernat gave a sleepy smile. "I'm happy for him, of course, but I must ask: how many of Garnia's airships are named in the service of some inane pun or un-clever turn of phrase?"

Josette thought about it. "A little over half, I'd say."

"Captain." Martel's voice came from over the side. "About those girders . . ."

"You must see to your ship, Captain," Josette called back. "We'll manage."

"Thank you, sir," Martel said. "I mean . . . thank you." He saluted her and, before she could even return it, had spun on his heels and was heading for *Goose*.

"So," Bernat said, watching him go, "if Martel gets the *Goose*, what do you get?"

"The goose egg, probably."

Bernat flashed a triumphant smile, as if he'd asked with the particular hope of receiving that very response. When she eyed him, the smile faded to an expression of innocence, pure but for a small undercurrent of resentment at the unspoken accusation.

She shook her head and called out, "Ensign Kember."

The girl appeared almost instantly.

"Ensign, you will act as first officer until a replacement is appointed."

Kember first beamed, then went pale with a sudden fear. "Does that mean I have to deal with the quartermaster, sir?"

Josette was about to answer in the affirmative, when she happened to glance down at the girl's bandage. Every day, Ensign Kember had worn it a little higher, until it now covered not only her neck but her jaw and half her cheek on the right side. "No," Josette said instead, "you will proceed without delay to the flight surgeon, to have that wound checked."

At this, Kember turned even more pale. "Sir, I'm sure I can help with—"

"Without delay, Ensign."

"It hardly hurts," Kember said. "Ow!" She recoiled from the flight surgeon's metal probe, convinced he had pricked the tender edge of the wound deliberately.

Eyes stern, he continued to prod at the wound without speaking, and to tug at the stitches one of the riggers had sewn it shut with. Now and then he would press a square of gauze against the wound, then sniff at it. After each sniff, he cast his eyes up and shook his head in silent accusation.

"It was only a graze," she said. "It just tore the skin away."

"And you went back to work afterward?" It was the first time he'd opened his mouth since he began his examination.

"Light duty," Kember lied.

He only grunted as he palpated the splotchy bruise on her face, which had grown upward from the wound over the past few days. Kember stared sidelong at him and tried to keep from squirming.

He let go with a final snort. "I'll have to have a word with your captain," he said, in the same tone her schoolmasters had once used on her. "If you'd been resting instead of traipsing around, or if it wasn't sewn up so tight, perhaps there'd be hope."

Kember's eyes went wide at that last word.

"It's gone putrid, and there's nothing I can do about it, so you'll have to go to the hospital."

Her eyes went even wider at the thought of being sent to the hospital, where so many soldiers emerged in pieces, if they emerged at all.

"If it weren't so close to the artery, I'd only have to cut one or two ligatures and let it drain. As it is, they'll have to slice halfway up your face and lay the skin open, so the corruption suppurates in the open air." He shook his head once more, unwilling to look at her. "I'm sorry to say, you'll never be pretty."

Never in her life had it occurred to Kember that she would be, nor did she expect it to ever be relevant, but now she faced the possibility that she'd end up hideous. Even so, her most immediate worry was that she'd cry out under the knife and make a fool of herself, and this was what occupied her thoughts as she made her way through the streets of Arle. Or, at least, it occupied her thoughts until she came within a block of the hospital, and the smell of that place nearly overwhelmed her. It wasn't only the smell of corruption, of putrefying limbs and gangrenous flesh. Blended with those were the smell of an open latrine and the general reek of unwashed humanity. This stench came not from the hospital itself but from the camp that had grown up around it, occupied by soldiers maimed in recent battles.

By law and custom, these men ought to have been shipped back to their hometowns, where they would have been dumped just as unceremoniously onto streets that would at least be familiar to them, but something must have gone wrong with the paperwork.

As she moved through the camp, their resentful eyes followed her, peering out from what little shelter they'd managed to cobble together in the streets. "S'one of them lady officers," a legless man said, for the benefit of his blinded companion.

She had half a block to go, and picked up her pace. She passed a man whose shelter was covered by a broadsheet with the headline, "GARNIA'S HEROES!" She wondered if he'd chosen this for his roof out of a sense of pride or a sense of irony. That was assuming, of course, that he could read it at all.

After a final dash past a score of Garnia's heroes engaged in searching for their breakfast in a pile of fresh garbage from a nearby inn, Kember reached the hospital. It was more crowded than the street, with men packed into every square of floor save for a narrow corridor through the middle of the central hallway.

Toward the back of the hospital, she found the officer's ward only half full. The atmosphere was, if anything, jovial. Wounded officers hobbled about, or sat up in bed, chatting with each other. When she stepped inside, a major with a pencil-thin mustache stood up from a stool next to one of the beds, plucked the loosely rolled cigarette from between his lips, and asked, "Looking for something, Ensign?"

She snapped to attention and saluted. "Flight surgeon sent me over to find a physician, sir."

"That'd be me." Looking annoyed, the major stuck the cigarette back into the corner of his mouth. He walked right up to her, took her jaw in his hands, and turned it left and right, examining her wound as if it were an interesting trinket.

A lieutenant in a nearby bed piped up, "Take care not to cry, Ensign. They treat officers like horses. If they think you're in pain, they shoot you to put you out of your misery."

The major snorted and blew smoke into her face. "That'd be a waste of a goddamn bullet," he said. Then he let her go. "You'll be fine, but it'll have to be cut open. Stay here."

The nearby lieutenant grinned and said, "Don't worry, girl, I was only joking. The doctors here are the best in the army. They'll have that head off so fast, you'll hardly even feel it."

"Yes, sir," was all Kember could think to respond, and this inspired a roar of laughter among the wounded officers. She didn't get the joke, but she was glad she could serve as entertainment.

The major returned, along with an assistant carrying a case of equipment. They sat her down on the edge of a bed.

"Am I going to be hideous?" she asked.

The major didn't meet her eyes, keeping his attention on her bandages as he removed them. "Kid," he said, "this morning I had to stretch the skin of a man's ass cheek out and sew it over the bloody hole where his leg and his genitals used to be."

Ensign Kember was duly impressed, but she didn't see how that answered her question. Still, she was too nervous to ask another, as the medical personnel began their work. The process was surprisingly painless, for the major began by making Kember swallow so much tincture of laudanum that she hardly knew what was going on. She gathered from their conversation that they were slicing into her face, laying the flesh open to ulcerate, and applying a bread poultice. But she was so dull and mellow that they really might have attempted to amputate her head, and she wouldn't have raised more than a fuss over it.

When it was finished, they led her to a small, solitary room. She remained there for the rest of the day and another night, of which she retained very little coherent memory, except for the vague impression of dogs scratching and growling outside her window.

In the dark of the pre-dawn morning on the second day, the major visited her, examined the wound, and declared it to be weeping with "laudable pus." What was laudable about it, Kember didn't know. Perhaps it gave to charity. In any event, its appearance was sufficient to have her dismissed. Kember was pleased to hear it, for by now the effects of the laudanum were well behind her, and she had regained sense enough to fear the hospital.

On her way out, she passed just as many men as she had on her way in, the hospital having made no real headway between admissions and discharges. So she moved carefully through the space between them, stepping precisely so as not to squash someone's hand or, God forbid, step on the stump of an amputation.

But then, halfway down the hall, she saw a ghost. She ran the rest of the way, and didn't slow down until she reached *Mistral*.

ALONE IN THE darkness of the shed, Josette and the mechanic's mate stood on the hurricane deck of the scout airship *Smew*, surveying the instrument panel above them. The panel was suspended by stout springs between two girders, the better to preserve delicate instruments against the shocks and concussions of battle. Josette hauled herself up, set her back against one girder, snaked a leg around the other, and so suspended herself above the deck, within easy reach of the instruments.

She reached down. Private Grey slapped a small wrench into her palm, then held up a lantern. As Josette went to work, Grey cleared her throat and said, "Are you sure this is okay, sir? Taking Captain Daumac's instruments?"

"Of course it is," Josette said, without looking away from her work. "Captain Daumac and his ship are bound for Imix in Quah-Halach, where there will be plenty of spare instruments. *Mistral* is stuck here, where the quartermaster swears there are none. So all we're doing, really, is helping to sort out the army's logistics problems."

"I follow you, sir, but this isn't exactly regular, is it? Pulling instruments out of another ship, in the dark, while everyone else is asleep?"

Josette looked down from the panel and waved a greasy wrench at her. "Private Grey, in the Royal Aerial Signal Corps we stand as one. In both manpower and material, what belongs to one ship belongs to them all. We all pull together for the good of the service."

"I understand that, sir. My only question is, does Captain Daumac understand it?"

"He will when he finds his chronometer missing." With that, Josette freed the instrument and handed it down to Grey. "Install it in our panel. Don't forget to add some dents and scratches, and blacken it with candle smoke so it matches the others."

Grey took the pilfered instrument and ran to her duty. When she was aboard *Mistral,* she lit the deck lanterns, turning the wide wicker gondola of the hurricane deck into an island of light within the dark shed. The reflection off the deck lit the whole curved underside of *Mistral*'s superstructure from frame six all the way up to the nose. The once-white canvas envelope was pockmarked with holes, many charred around the edges. It was a wonder the ship held together.

Josette disentangled herself from *Smew* and strolled to the edge of the shed, where she stood looking up at her battered airship. She remembered back to something Captain Tobel had told her, again and again, when she was first officer aboard *Osprey*: "Love a ship and she'll treat you kindly."

She certainly loved *Mistral,* though *Mistral* had been anything but kind. She was an accident-prone ship. No doubt she was fast and turned tighter than any two-gun airship Josette had ever known, but she was liable to become suddenly unwieldy if mishandled in the slightest. It seemed now that Captain Tobel had been describing a certain species of domesticated airship, whereas *Mistral* was an untamed creature that longed for blood, and made up its own fun when denied it.

Yet she was still a damn fine ship, for all that. Josette stood admiring her for so long that dawn broke outside, and light began to creep in through spaces in the shed roof. Josette craned her neck to look at the full height of *Mistral*'s superstructure, towering above her in the upper reaches of the shed. Yes, she was a damn fine ship, for all that. Josette only wished she could get her hands on the parts to set her right.

Dawn meant that the yardsmen would be coming to

continue repairs, and that realization finally snapped Josette out of her reverie. She went to one of the smaller, man-sized doors inlaid into larger shed doors, and there met Sergeant Jutes leading the three dozen men of the repair crews on their way in.

"Captain," he said, touching a knuckle to his forelock.

"Morning, Sergeant. Please remind the yardsmen, as some of them seemed to forget yesterday, that our priority is replacing sprung girders. Not merely charred girders. Replacing them is a luxury, considering how few spare girders we have. So sprung girders only for now. Not charred girders, and certainly not 'whatever girders are easiest to get at.'"

"I'll see to it, sir," Jutes said, and led the repair crews over to *Mistral*.

Only half the men were aboard when Ensign Kember came running out of the morning mist, a poultice wrapped against her cheek. "What the hell happened to you?" Josette asked, when the girl was within earshot.

Kember clopped to a halt in front of Josette, saluted, and spoke in a hoarse and breathless voice. "Gears is alive, sir."

"Good God!" Josette spun about and shouted, "Sergeant!"

But Jutes had heard and was already hobbling toward them, his eyes wide and hopeful.

BERNAT WAS ON his way back to the signal base when he saw Josette, Kember, Grey, and Jutes go past. They did not see him, however, because in this case, "on his way back to the signal base" meant that he was in a tavern, where he'd stopped to refresh himself six hours earlier. But as the tavern was undeniably on his way, he considered the trip still in progress.

He left his mug on the table and followed after them. He had trouble closing the distance, for they were walking briskly and he, entirely apart from the effects of his libations, was having trouble with the ground. Apart from the recent, disconcerting addition of bright white dog shit to Arle's byways, no street could have the comfortable give of a wicker catwalk, nor the gentle sway of the hurricane deck. He thought it an injustice that he'd already had to walk on this flawed surface for so much of his life.

"You look better with most of your hair burned off, you should keep it that way," he said, when he finally caught up.

Josette glanced back at him and asked, "How much have you drunk this morning?"

"Just enough," he answered. "What's going on?"

Josette kept her eyes forward. "Gears is alive."

Bernat thought he'd misheard, or that it was some of the captain's black humor, taken too far this time. But when she looked at him, her face equal parts hope and worry, he knew she was serious. "You told me no one ever recovered from a gutshot," he said, "and Gears had half a dozen."

"It wasn't that many," Josette said, her voice flat and cold, her face tightening back into its usual stony expression. "And I have heard of soldiers surviving, in some rare cases."

Bernat wasn't sure what it was about Gears that made his survival seem so important, compared to all the others who had died aboard *Mistral*. Perhaps it was that Sergeant Jutes was so fond of him, and Jutes being fond of hardly anyone.

They reached the hospital, where wounded soldiers had erected a shanty town in which to convalesce. Bernat couldn't help but stop to admire their industry. The conditions would never do for someone of his birth, of course, but for men accustomed to hardship it must certainly have been comfortable enough. He did wonder, though, why they hadn't been put to work on some civic project in exchange for inhabiting the avenue rent-free.

When he caught up to the others, they were gathered just inside a long ward off the main hall. Bernat expected an argument over visiting hours, but he was surprised to find only one nurse in the entire ward, to attend to perhaps two hundred men. She moved to intercept them, but was cowed when she got a look at Josette's scowling, eyebrow-less face.

Gears was near the door, resting in a proper bed, thank God. And he wasn't comatose, as half the men in this ward were. As Bernat looked around, he saw that they all had the most terrible wounds. Blood soaked through their bandages to stain bedclothes. Some weren't even bandaged. Their flesh, pierced by bullets, laid open by sword and bayonet wounds, was left to fester unimpeded. Few had surgical amputations, but many bore limbs that ended in a tattered mass of shredded meat, left to bleed and to rot with little medical attention.

Surely this was only a momentary oversight. Perhaps these men had come in recently, just when the shifts were changing, and there was no one to give them proper care. Soon, no doubt, there would be a dozen doctors and nurses swarming the ward.

Jutes knelt beside the bed and asked, "How you doing, you old arsehole?"

Bernat couldn't follow the chief mechanic's reply, but it was something about superheating and steam injectors.

Private Grey reached out to take his hand, and said, "Don't worry. As soon as we have the parts, we'll be giving it a complete overhaul."

They went back and forth like that for some time, Gears giving instructions or making inquiries about the state of the ship—sometimes the very same series of instructions and inquiries, repeated several times in the same order—and Grey or Jutes giving reassuring answers. After perhaps half an hour, Gears settled into a light sleep, still speaking from time to time, but seeming to rest in spite of it.

It was then that Bernat noticed his earlier prediction had

not come true. No company of medical men had come in to see to the wounded here. It was only the same nurse as before, and she doing precious little to treat injuries. Rather, she only adjusted the positions of those who had contorted in their sleep, fluffed the pillows of those who were awake, and spoke softly to those who were crying out in pain, until they quieted. In a flash, Bernat understood why.

"This is a death ward!" he cried out.

Faces throughout the ward turned to him, and the single nurse fixed him with an acid glare.

"Calm yourself," Josette said, quite softly. "He's as well here as anywhere. The doctors won't bother with a gut wound, which is all the better. It isn't up to them to cure him, now. It's up to him to survive."

"He'll survive," Sergeant Jutes said. "He survives."

"Come on," Josette said to Kember and Bernat. "Let's leave them to it."

Bernat put a hand on Jutes's shoulder—it seemed the right thing to do—and left him with Grey, to watch over their chief mechanic.

In the days that followed, Sergeant Jutes and Private Grey split their time between repairs to *Mistral* and their vigil at the hospital, with precious little left over for sleep. Bernat visited when he could, when he was sober enough and when he had the stomach for it—conditions which were, for the most part, exclusive of each other. But when he did attend, he found the watchers to be as attentive as the most diligent nursemaid. They spoke to Gears, whether he was awake or not. They held his hand and wiped the sweat from his fevered brow. They spoon-fed him broth, and more than a little brandy.

In a week's time, the fever was subsiding and Gears could speak lucidly, though he still slept through most of the day. As he improved, and as the hospital discharged its wounded by one way or the other, room was made for him in one of the sick wards, where he was attended to by proper doctors and nurses. He was well on his way to recovery.

And so it seemed to Bernat that it was all the greater an injustice when Sergeant Jutes returned from the hospital one morning and told them Gears was dead—gone in the night.

"It's not how it's supposed to go," Bernat said to Josette.

She only shook her head and replied, "It's exactly how it's supposed to go, as a point of fact."

REPAIRS CONTINUED AT a steady, slow pace, with the yardsmen often sitting idle for want of materials. Even when trains came in with fresh girders, luftgas, or goldbeater's skin, the quartermaster would only let a little out at a time, and kept the balance in the warehouse. Josette was by now convinced that the quartermaster thought it was her job to amass as much stock as possible, until the warehouse was filled to the rafters and no airship could fly.

In the case of the goldbeater's, the situation was particularly dire. Made from the intestines of oxen, it was becoming more and more scarce. You only got a few square feet of goldbeater's per ox, and the bags were several layers thick, which meant the guts of tens of thousands of animals went into just one chasseur. With more and more chasseurs in the sky, and so many of them the larger two-gun ships, the service was having trouble finding enough oxen willing to die for their country.

Josette didn't need an entire airship's worth of goldbeater's. She only needed enough to repair the damage to *Mistral*'s bags, but she couldn't get her hands on even that much. She'd have to sacrifice one bag to repair the rest, and rebuild the sacrificial bag out of rubberized silk, which was cheaper and easier to obtain than goldbeater's, despite its two components being shipped from opposite sides of the world. It was also heavier and leakier than goldbeater's, and had an unfortunate tendency to spark if torn—a particularly frightening prospect, since there wasn't enough luftgas to replace the inflammable air, either.

Even that wasn't the end of her problems. Half the damaged girders still hadn't been replaced. The steamjack turbine was a mess, the primary condenser in shambles. Private Grey was working on them, but she didn't have the material to do a proper overhaul. *Mistral*'s steamjack was a prototype design, so the logistics office hadn't planned on needing spare parts for it so soon.

So Josette's airship remained very much a wounded bird on the drizzling, cold afternoon when her orders came in. Heading to open them, she passed Kember's berth, and saw the girl inside, hastily pulling a blanket over a package wrapped in waxed paper.

No sooner had Josette closed the curtain on her cabin than Bernat pushed it open again and followed her in. He'd been sleeping aboard ship, and hung about even during his waking hours, when he wasn't off carousing.

Josette pulled the curtain closed behind him. "Bernie, you haven't gotten a look at what's in those packages our ensign has been bringing aboard, have you?"

"No," he said, "but I recognize the watermark on the wax paper. It's from a cosmetics shop in the Septenian quarter. I get a discount there, which I offered to share with her last week, but she only sputtered, apologized to me—for what offence, I can't imagine—and ran off, tripping over her own feet on the way."

Josette peeked around the edge of her curtain, arched a stubbly eyebrow, and said, "She's an odd girl." She turned her attention back to her orders, breaking the wax seal with her fingers.

"Something from the general?" Bernat asked, referring to his uncle. Bernat had somehow gained the impression that

General Lord Fieren Hinkal handled every single detail of the operation of the army. "A promotion perhaps? A decoration?"

"More likely an order sending us up north, to the Meat Grinder. I only hope they leave us a few more weeks to finish repairs, and see to it that we get some goddamned luftgas."

Bernat settled into the hammock chair across from Josette, the small cabin table between them. He parted his lips to speak, hesitated, wet them, and then finally went on, "Meat Grinder? I take that to be one of those fanciful names you airmen give to distinctive landmarks, yes?" When she gave no answer, but only ignored him and began to read, he went on, "I have of course heard of the Knuckle. The Fingers. The Nose. The Knees. I've been taking note of them all, and have nearly enough body parts to construct an entire person. I only lack a torso, though I've amassed several superfluous sets of genitalia—many of them from saints." He laughed nervously, and when she still didn't answer him, his mouth continued to run on. "So, I can only conclude that this 'Meat Grinder' is some such memorable piece of terrain. Perhaps a natural chimney or a bluff?" She said nothing. "I have even heard tell of a geological phenomenon called a kopje, and have always wanted to see one." Silence. "If that's it, I'm quite looking forward to it."

She looked up after reading to find him pallid and sweating. "We've been ordered to Kuchin, to overfly the city on a goddamn publicity tour."

"Oh thank God," he said.

She did not share in his relief. "Next week," she said. "We have to be underway by next week!" She hit the table in frustration.

Bernat was not in the least perturbed by this. "At least the citizens of Kuchin won't be shooting at us," he said, "as I imagine might happen, were we to go to that other place you mentioned, which I take it is not a kopje."

She stared at him so hard that he recoiled. "Properly

repaired and manned, this ship might make a difference. The war needs us, but they're sending us to show off in front of a bunch of fops and bankers." She leaned across the table, wagging her finger, and Bernat leaned away. "This ship and a single battalion could retake . . ." She trailed off, hit the table with her fist again, and slumped in her chair.

"Durum?" Bernat asked.

She didn't give an answer, but only looked out at the shed floor through an open port.

3

THE PACE OF repairs picked up, and in a week's time *Mistral* looked like a brand-new ship. At least, she looked like a new ship from the outside, white-clad and gleaming in her pristine outer envelope. Inside, even Bernat could see that she was hiding a greater sickness. Along the keel, many of the box girders were still braced with rope to shore up battle damage. Up in the superstructure, it was even worse. There, cracked girders were tied precariously to other cracked girders, for lack of a sound girder near enough to secure them to. In areas, this pattern repeated itself several times, with three or even four damaged girders strung together in a line before the last was secured to a sound one, in a configuration with all the structural integrity of a ball of yarn.

The steamjack was in even worse condition, if that could be believed. Every time Grey dared to push it past half power, it spewed smoke and noxious gases into the keel. At full power, it shook so hard it threatened to tear itself out of the keel entirely, and made sharp plinking sounds at irregular intervals, each of which made Grey freeze up, as if she expected it to explode in the next moment. On the single occasion when it was tested at emergency power, it caught fire after five minutes, and the crew had to scramble to keep it from burning the ship at her moorings.

The state of the crew wasn't much better. A little over half of the fire-forged veterans of *Mistral*'s recent actions remained, with the other half made of new volunteers with little airship experience between them. Still absent were a chief mechanic—sorely missed, given the state of the steamjack—and a first officer. Bernat attempted to make up the deficit by volunteering his own natural leadership, but was not met with the enthusiastic gratitude he'd expected.

So it was not a sound or a happy ship that took off from Arle, but it was a beautiful one, with her envelope so bright it dazzled the eye. The trip, at least, went off without incident, which is to say that nothing exploded.

For two days, they had fair winds and made quick progress despite their ramshackle steamjack. From dawn to dusk, the bountiful fields of eastern Garnia whipped past below. In the evenings, Ensign Kember came onto the hurricane deck to stand her watches, each time wearing a new beauty product to conceal the scars on her face and neck. One evening it might be something from Pekstrom's Terra Cotta Princess Palette, while another might find her wearing a thick smear of their lead-based Golden Goddess Foundation—an absolutely ill-conceived idea, because it was from the summer collection.

Bernat dined with Josette most nights, and even talked her into playing a few hands of cards with him. On the third day, the fields thinned and turned to grassland in the morning, grassland turned to rocky wastes in the afternoon, and mountains rose over the horizon at evening. *Mistral* passed over them in the night, and the next dawn found her struggling against blustery headwinds, with terraced hills barely moving under her keel. They had covered two-thirds of the distance to Kuchin already, but the winds were so strong during the last third that *Mistral* was often reduced to an absolute standstill for hours at a time, hovering in a slow wobble over the same patch of ground, her airspeed entirely cancelled out by the wind. It was even worse on the afternoon of the seventh day, when *Mistral* had to turn around and run back the way she'd come, to dodge the first of the big winter storms sweeping down from the north.

"Slow going at this time of year," Bernat said to Josette, on the eighth day of travel. *Mistral* had just passed the same bend in the Secana River, and Bernat had just waved to the very same rice farmer for the third time in twenty-four hours. "Will we be very late getting in?"

Josette looked insulted. "As long as we don't get another storm tomorrow, we'll arrive in the afternoon, with time to spare."

The winds conspired to prove her wrong, but not by much, and they arrived above Kuchin just after dark, which was all the better. Dazzling, sun-bright quicklime lamps illuminated the great glass dome of the National Museum and the decorative cherry trees in the gardens surrounding it—though their lovely blossoms were out of season—and gaslights along the Ager Beatus cast that broad avenue in a softer but still-beautiful light. Couples strolled down the riverfront as if in broad daylight, with ripples in the water twinkling behind them. And that splendor was only the crowning jewel of Kuchin's network of gas street lamps, which formed a great constellation of stars below, rivaling those above.

Josette stepped to the rail next to him, resting her hands on it. She stood there so long that he had to ask, "Let me guess: you're calculating how much luftgas we could purchase for the cost of running those lights?"

She swallowed and shook her head. "No," she said, just loud enough to be heard over the steamjack and airscrews. "Only looking at them. It is a goddamn waste—you're right about that—but it's also quite beautiful."

He began to laugh, until she silenced him with a glare. "My apologies," he said. "But this is so unexpected. I'm proud of you."

"I am capable of appreciating beauty," she said harshly, "when leisure permits."

He struck a pose and ran his fingers through his hair. "And yet you can't seem to appreciate the beauty that's right in front of you." He undid a button on his jacket. "Won't you come to my berth, when leisure permits, so that we may appreciate my beauty together?"

He was only trying to make her blush, of course, but by the light of the quicklime it was clear he hadn't succeeded. She stood watching the ground for a while, before finally asking, "Are you clipped on quite securely, Bernie?"

He glanced at the clip connecting his harness to the overhead jack line. "Well, yes, why do you—" That was all he managed say before she gave him a quick shove that sent him tumbling over the rail. He fell a short but harrowing couple of feet before the jack line caught him short and hung him by the shoulders, a hundred feet over the ground.

He looked up to see Josette leaning over the railing. She shot him a rare smile and said, "It would be selfish of me to not share your beauty with the entire city."

"That was not funny!" he called, but the deck crew disagreed. They howled with delight, and Josette did nothing to stop them. The ship was just descending over the Ager Beatus, where crowds who had gathered to watch the airship now pointed up at him. Bernat waved, and they replied with cheers and applause.

Once everyone had had their fun, he pulled himself up to the railing and Josette helped him the rest of the way. By the time he had his clothes smoothed out, the ship was all but landed. It only remained for the mooring mast to winch them in snugly, and the ground crews to walk them into the shed.

"I suppose your family has a house in town?" Josette asked.

"We usually stay at the palace when we're here."

"I'm surprised the king allows that."

"Oh, he quite encourages it," Bernat said. "All the better for keeping us in order, but don't tell anyone I said that." He craned his neck, to see if the ship was secure.

Josette gestured over the side, with a flick of her head. "Off you go. I know there's debauchery out there with your name on it. Just be back by dawn."

Bernat grinned back and did his best imitation of standing at attention. He unclipped his harness and hopped over the side, calling out for the benefit of ballasting, "A hundred and fifty pounds of prime lady-killer, going ashore!"

He skipped and trotted his way along the length of the ship, rounded the tailfin, and then came to a dead stop. He recognized, just outside the shed, the most insipid man he'd ever met. He tried to duck back, but it was too late. He'd already been made. Even as he groaned inwardly, he put on a smile and walked over to the twit, saying, "Hello, Roland."

The muttonhead smiled back and said, "Hello, little brother." Instead of taking Bernat's outstretched hand, Roland put his arms around him and wrapped him up in a tight embrace.

"Oh good, hugging," Bernat said, his voice a study in polite resignation. When Roland finally let him go, he added, "I don't suppose Mother is about?"

Roland shook his head. "No. When she found out you were coming, she left town in a rush, cursing your name and the day you were born."

"I'm sure she was talking about someone else."

Beaming a false smile at him, Roland said, "Yes, I'm sure she was referring to an entirely different 'scheming, goony-eyed, sap-headed mollycoddle.'"

Bernat smiled fondly. "I miss her."

"Who the hell is this?" The question came from behind him.

Bernat heaved a great sigh and turned to face Josette, who

was standing with her bag over her shoulder. "Josette," he said. "I'd like you to meet my brother, Roland. Roland, this is Josette. Captain Dupre to the likes of you."

Roland's face brightened to rival the limelight of the Ager Beatus. "Never!" he cried, looking to Josette. "The stories say you're ten feet tall."

"As usual," she said, "the stories are just about half right." She shifted her baggage to the opposite shoulder and stuck out her hand. Roland clearly meant to kiss it, but she recoiled and he quickly substituted a handshake.

"Half right! Ha!" Though he had been foiled in kissing her hand, Roland couldn't stop shaking it. "And she's a wit, too," he said to Bernat. "The papers don't mention that."

"Wit?" Bernat asked, frowning. "Oh, don't be such a fawning yokel, Roland. I've wiped superior wit out of the crack of my—" In light of the nasty looks they shot him, he stopped short to consider his next word. He finally settled on, "Intellect."

Roland was still shaking hands with an increasingly flabbergasted Josette, and the look in his eyes told the rest of the story. If only most of her eyebrows hadn't grown back already, perhaps there might have been a chance he'd be put off by her. In all her life she had surely faced no greater danger than Roland's interest. The man was boredom brought to life, and that was among the least of his faults.

Roland finally let go of her and offered to carry her baggage, and she—the damn fool—accepted. Roland flung the flight bag over his shoulder, assuming the most insidiously casual pose. As they turned to walk off together, Roland flashed a grin at Josette and asked, "I wonder, may I show you the waterfront sometime?"

She was just working up to rejection. Bernat could see it in her face. But then she spotted Bernat emphatically shaking his head, and she grinned. Grinned twice in two seconds, actually, in what might have been a personal best for her: one grin for Bernat and another for Roland.

And, no doubt just to spite Bernat, she said to his brother, "I'd like that. When leisure permits."

"I KNOW YOU didn't sleep with him."

As *Mistral* cruised at rooftop level over the city, Josette ignored him and kept her mind on her duty, for what little it was worth aboard an airship turned into flying scenery.

"No," he said, in reply to unspoken words. "No. I don't believe you."

She said nothing. Indeed, she hadn't said a single word about Roland all morning—not since they'd returned to the ship an hour before dawn, and she'd said goodnight to him right below Bernat's sleeping berth.

"I know what you're doing," Bernat said. "But I can see right through you. Nothing happened between you two. Nothing at all."

She glanced at him and shifted the smirk to the other side of her mouth.

"You expect me to believe that? How credulous do I look?"

She only shrugged.

"It defies all reason. You may each be desperate in your own manner, but that would hardly result in anything happening between you."

"Up three degrees," she ordered, though she wished she could remain mute and go on teasing him with the full force of her silence. "And bring her around when we're over the river."

"Do you know why I'm sure?" Bernat asked.

She looked at him with polite and amiable attention.

"I'm sure, because you would never do that to me."

As much as she wanted to keep the game alive, that was just

too much. "And why not?" she asked, stepping to the rail and lowering her voice. "You slept with my mother, after all."

"That was different!" Only then did he remember himself and add hastily, "I mean, no I didn't."

She only shook her head at him. "I knew it."

"So what? You bedded my brother as retribution?"

"No, of course not. He showed me the waterfront, then we strolled through the Low District to the Sumida Temple."

Bernat eyeballed her. "That's the one with the great big paper lantern under the gate?"

She eyeballed him right back. "Yes."

"Ah," he said, looking away with a dour face. "It's tradition for lovers to kiss under it, you know."

"That tricky son of a bitch," Josette muttered, neither cross nor surprised. "Well, we didn't kiss, if you're wondering. We talked and saw the sights. That's all."

Bernat was not consoled. "Yes, of course. That's where it always begins."

"That's where it'll end, too. And not because I have too much respect for you, if that's what you think. Tell me, why do you dislike him so?"

"You might as well ask the farmer why he hates the vermin that ravage his harvest," Bernat said, waving a hand about with irritation. "My brother—if indeed he is even legitimate, on which subject I have my doubts—will one day become the Marquis of Copia Lugon. Why? Not because he is wise, which he is not. Not because he has dignity, which he does not. Not because he can politick or even hold up an interesting conversation, which he most certainly cannot. No, he will be marquis because of an accident of birth. As a commoner, you couldn't possibly understand how frustrating that is."

"Surely, I can't even begin to understand," Josette said, looking straight ahead.

Mistral steamed along the river for a while, running up and down until the crowds of morning watchers thinned. Josette then took the ship over the Tellurian Quarter, where students at the university rushed from their classes to gawk skyward. From there, she turned across the Secana to buzz the greater of the Kuchin's two pagodas, and proceeded through a wide sweep across the city.

At eleven in the morning, crowds swelled again on both banks of the river, many of them with picnic lunches. *Mistral* entertained them with a few circuits over each bank, then resumed her meandering loops about the city.

At three in the afternoon, the mild westerly headwind suddenly increased and turned quite chilly. The more experienced crewmen looked at the western horizon. The sky there was blue, and contained nothing more fearsome than a few fluffy, white clouds, but Josette didn't trust its benign appearance. She looked up at the aneroid barometer, whose mercury was falling steadily.

"Sergeant," she called up the companionway, "let's rig the signal lamp and call for a weather report."

The call, flashed to the semaphore station atop City Hall, was promptly returned with a report of clear skies from every station in the hundred-odd miles between Kuchin and the coast.

"I still don't like it," she said, and several of the airmen on deck nodded their assent. "Steersmen, bring her to west northwest, a quarter west. Steamjack to half power."

Mistral steered straight down the Secana River, but between the force of the headwind and her much-reduced airspeed, *Mistral* was being overtaken by steam barges on the river below, and by some of the faster donkeys on the road beside it. One donkey cart ahead of them matched the ship's ground speed almost exactly, and the driver kept looking back over his shoulder at the airship, as if he suspected it of pursuing him.

By five o'clock, Josette's weather instinct was confirmed. The western horizon boiled with darkening clouds as they came within sight of the air base. Before they could even rig the signal lamp, however, a message was flashed to them, asking why they were off station.

Josette, manning the signal lamp herself, dearly wanted to signal them back with a request to look out a goddamn window. Instead, she sent, *Mistral request landing due to worsening weather.*

The answering message was: *Clear weather expected. City officials have complained your absence. Mistral return to station.*

Now she really wanted to send her preferred signal, but by a heroic exertion of self-control, she refrained. She only acknowledged the message, stowed the signal lamp, and ordered *Mistral* about.

"If I die because some goddamn paper-pusher can't be bothered to glance at the fucking horizon," she said, "I will wait patiently for his arrival at the gates of hell, and then he'll be in for it."

Bernat looked up from the rail. "Do you suppose they allow that in hell?" he asked. "I would expect them to have a stricter policy as regards loitering."

Corporal Luc Lupien replied before Josette could. "No need to worry about that," he said. "Give the captain a week in hell, and she'll be running the place."

With the wind at her tail, *Mistral* sprinted back to Kuchin, making her station in under a quarter of an hour. She turned into the wind and went to one-third power, just enough to hold her practically motionless, three hundred feet above the river. From there, Josette watched the storm brewing.

Every quarter of an hour, she requested a weather report. Most of them came back identical, down to the exact wind speed at each weather station, which gave away the game: the semaphore network was backed up, and the weather reports were coming in hours behind schedule. The staff at base either hadn't noticed, didn't understand the implications, or never looked at weather reports unless they were marked urgent.

She flashed a message to the signal base via the city hall semaphore tower, explaining the situation and requesting new orders. She didn't wait for the message to make it through the clogged network, but immediately ordered, "Steamjack to maximum safe power. Let's bring her home ahead of the storm. Perhaps orders to that effect will make it to us by the time we arrive."

As *Mistral* struggled upwind, the first line of clouds blew in over the city, peppering them with stinging rain and obscuring further developments in the weather. Josette lowered her goggles to keep the needle-drops out of her eyes. The headwind had lessened somewhat with the coming of the rain, but what it lost in raw speed, it made up for in turbulence. To maintain course and trim, the steersmen had to swing their wheels first one way and then the other to adjust for the changing winds. Worse, the wind didn't shift all at once, across the entire length of the ship. Josette had to grab an overhead girder as a sudden lateral gust hit the tail while the nose was still in a headwind, yanking the ship through forty degrees on the compass before the gust blew its way forward and the ship stabilized onto a steady but sideways course.

She looked back to her steersmen, who remained calm and controlled. To her right, however, Bernat held so fast to his safety line that he was practically dangling from it, his feet barely touching the deck. As the gust blew itself out and the headwind returned, he swung inward due to the tilt of the deck, until his feet were nearly touching Josette's knee. He looked desperately at her, as if hoping for rescue.

"Steady, Bernie. Steady." She thought about sending him up into the keel, but judged it better to leave him where she could keep an eye on him. The ship stabilized and Bernat swung back to his customary place on the deck. "Let's get a double frapping on those bref guns," she said to the deck crew.

As the crew lashed the guns, *Mistral* clawed her way downriver. No donkeys passed her this time, but only because they'd all been driven to shelter by the rain. The thunder had started by the time they came within sight of the signal base—or rather, within sight of the beacon lamp shining through the haze. This time, permission to land came without fuss or delay, and the landing circle below was marked off by flares. The ship drove down toward it, and the ground crews became visible through the mist of rain.

They disappeared again as Mistral was flung nose-high by a sudden updraft. "Emergency power!" Josette ordered, despite the risk of fire. "Elevators down full!" For if the nose was rising, it meant the tail was pivoting toward the ground. If the rudder hit and was damaged, they'd be lost in the storm.

At the top of the companionway, Jutes was thrown to the deck by the sudden heave. But he kept his eyes pointed aft, and as the ship leveled off, he called, "Tail's clear!"

"How close?" Josette asked.

Jutes relayed the question, then relayed the answer. "Private Davies reports that he shared a moment of meaningful eye contact with a 'very alarmed ground squirrel, or possibly a marmot.'"

"God be with it," Josette said. "Steamjack to half power. Let's try that again."

By the time *Mistral* came around again, fat drops of heavier rain were pattering at the top of the envelope, hitting so hard it was audible even on the hurricane deck. As it soaked into the envelope, the rain weighed the ship down, so that the elevator man had to put an extra half turn on the wheel just to keep her in trim.

"Half a point to starboard," Josette ordered, making her

best guess as to where the mooring mast lay, for the yardsmen's flares, patented and warranted to work in all weather,
were sputtering out under the downpour.

"Set gears to reverse!" she ordered, when she thought she
heard the nosecone connect with the mooring mast.

"Monkey rigger reports we're tied off to the mooring
cable," Jutes said.

Soon she could feel the deck jerking underfoot as the ground
crew began to winch *Mistral* out of the sky. She was pulled
in, turn by turn, fighting it all the way as the wind played on
her, twisting her about like a fish flopping at the end of the
line.

"Increase steamjack to full power," Josette ordered.

"Full power, sir?" Jutes asked.

"Full power, Sergeant. We may catch fire, we may even
steam straight into the ground, but if we don't get down soon,
they're going to reel in half a ship."

Bernat, in the calmest voice he could muster, asked, "We're
not in peril, are we?"

"Of course not," she said, without looking at him.

"Good, good," Bernat said. "Only, you seem to be in a
particular hurry to be on the ground."

"I have opera tickets."

A moment later, a hard pull on the mooring cable coincided
with a heavy gale, and the sudden force wrenched at *Mistral*'s
nosecone, where a cleat held the mooring line secure. The cleat
held, and the girder the cleat was attached to held—that girder
was specially reinforced for exactly this contingency—but the
girders in the frame behind the nosecone had been cracked in
battle and never replaced, and those began to sheer off by ones
and twos.

"Emergency power forward! Elevators down!"

Her order brought strain off the line, but it was too late.
The damage was already too great, and what was left of the

forwardmost frame could no longer take the stress. When it came apart, it pulled the bottom third of the nosecone with it, which in turn peeled away a string of longitudinal girders from the underside of the superstructure, running halfway back to the hurricane deck.

The ship lurched, throwing everyone forward who wasn't clipped on, Josette among them. She let the lurch take her to the forward rail, where she grabbed on, steadied herself, tore off her goggles, and squinted through the storm. She could just make out the silhouette of a person—the monkey rigger, she thought—dangling from the bow, clinging to nothing but a narrow strip of torn envelope. The strip grew longer as it peeled from the underside of the ship, so that even as the rigger climbed hand over hand up it, she was losing ground. When it seemed she could not but plummet, an arm came down from the bow and held the fabric in place until she could clamber up to safety.

Josette took a breath. But for that flap of canvas, yet another member of her crew would be dead.

Above, she could hear Chips running along the keel, heading forward to inspect the damage. But she didn't need his report to know it would take at least an hour to shore up the nose for another landing attempt. With the storm growing worse by the minute, they didn't have that kind of time.

As a flash of lightning outlined the shed, she called out, "Steamjack to half power. Bring the wind on her tail, up angle three degrees. Quench lanterns. We're running for it."

MISTRAL'S STARBOARD RAIL might have been the wettest place on the hurricane deck, if not the entire world, but Bernat clung to it with one hand as tightly as he held his safety line in the other. Apart from drawing some small comfort from the familiar place, he felt a vague sense that this was his station, and as important a station as any other aboard the ship— the pesky fact that he had no official function notwithstanding. Besides which, he wasn't sure he'd be able to make his way anywhere else in the dark, with the ship being buffeted and the deck swinging randomly underfoot.

Below, the streetlights of Kuchin were just visible through the clouds, still lit inside their ornate glass casings. They went by at a fantastic speed, and rather more sideways than Bernat would have preferred. "Are we meant to be moving right to left?" he asked.

"Yes, actually." Josette must have seen his incredulous expression in a flash of lightning, for she went on, "With our steamjack in the condition it's in, it's too late to run straight away from the storm. It'll only sweep us in. So we're going to use the storm's own vortex to slingshot around the worst of it and come out the back."

Her unrattled confidence made him feel quite a bit better. "So you've done this before?"

She didn't answer, but only looked briefly toward him in the darkness, and he hoped to God she was rolling her eyes, or at least shooting him a nasty expression. Anything, really, but the cocky smirk he was imagining—the one that said she was learning as she went.

Jutes descended the companionway ladder, his arms full of pea jackets. Even the sure-footed sergeant lurched across the deck as he distributed them to the deck crew. Bernat donned a jacket, just as lightning struck the spire atop the Pagoda of the Luminous Sky, half a mile ahead of them and not very far below. Five heartbeats later, with the ghostly image of the bolt still burned into Bernat's eyes, the whole ship rattled from a thunderclap. He tried not to think of the great mass of inflammable air just yards above his head, of the whole ship lit up like a lantern if the bags should take fire.

The ship's canvas skin, already taut before the damp

stretched it even tighter, beat like a drum in the buffeting winds. Near the nose, a strip of envelope flapped spastically, tearing more and more of itself clear of the ship, until it was only held on by a corner. The whole strip, perhaps three feet by ten, gyrated around its single remaining anchor for several seconds, then came loose and flew toward him.

He ducked, but it didn't go over his head. When he came up, he saw it had caught around one of the suspension cables holding the hurricane deck gondola to the ship. He felt a hand tapping him on the shoulder, and Josette was pulling him forward. He stopped only to adjust his safety clip on the jack line, and joined the captain and two crewmen at the forward rail.

"If it tangles in the airscrews, it'll be the end of us," she shouted through wind and rain.

Bernat grabbed a sopping fold of it in each hand and held tight, bracing his feet against the bottom of the railing as wet fabric slapped him painfully in the face. Over his shoulder, he could hear the thrum of the airscrews even over the storm. He rocked back, hauling on the fabric until it slid aboard, leaving half its weight in water wrung out into the suspension cable.

THE SHIP EMERGED into a pocket of calm air between thunderclouds. Over the rail, Bernat had a fine view of Kuchinites going about their business in the streets below, bent into the wind and either soaked to the bone or holding tight to their umbrellas. For a moment it struck him that they were unusually stout and ascetic to be out in this weather. But then he realized, as the ship slipped back into rain and cloud, that the cyclone tearing *Mistral* apart was no more than an ordinary winter storm. He'd seen a thousand of them, and hardly noticed when he was on the ground. It was only from the inside and aboard a ship made of plywood and canvas that this ordinary storm seemed the great tempest of the world.

There were fewer streetlights to judge by, as the ship skimmed the outskirts of the city, but it seemed to Bernat that *Mistral* was taking a truer course now, her nose pointing closer to the actual direction of travel. In ten minutes' time, his suspicion was confirmed when *Mistral* burst out into clear air, leaving the cloud and rain away to port.

"We made it!" he called out, in the relative quiet. Even in the darkness of the deck, he could tell that everyone was looking at him. "Sorry, is it bad luck to say that?"

"More like premature," Josette said, and pointed forward.

A wall of cloud lay ahead, alive and crackling with lightning. He looked backward, where the air was untroubled. "Why, uh, why don't we head off in that direction?" he asked, pointing toward open skies.

"Because it's a trap," she said. "If we went that way, the storm would roll right over us and we'd be sucked up into the heart of it. Forward's the way—a quick jump up and over the edge. That's the shortest path to clear air." She reached up to clip on to the nearest jack line. Apart from the times she'd intentionally leapt over the side to inspect something, this was the very first time he could remember seeing her clipped on. He rechecked his own line five times, to make sure it was secure.

Ahead, the storm front was coming up fast. "Pass the word," Josette called through the companionway, "hold tight and don't panic." Then to the rudder and elevator steersmen, she said, "Don't overcorrect. Be careful of lash in the control cables. Above all, remain calm. Ready?"

Bernat was expecting some stalwart quip from Corporal Lupien, the most relentlessly cheerful of *Mistral*'s crew, but he and the elevator steersman only nodded gravely back at their captain.

"Full power!" she called. From amidships, the steamjack began to shake and rattle, and gave a keening sound that nearly matched the wind for volume.

The bow hit the squall head on, dipped for an instant, then kicked up so fast and so far that it seemed *Mistral* was standing on her tail, with all the waters of heaven pouring down her throat. Bernat clutched the rail for dear life, and instantly abandoned Josette's advice to remain calm. In complete darkness, with the thunder crashing all around, with so much water hitting him in the face that he couldn't breathe, with the hurricane deck thrashing so violently that it seemed it could not possibly remain attached to the ship, all he could do was clap on and pray.

He spat out a mouthful of water and gasped for breath, and after a few moments found that the deluge had diminished enough for him to breathe regularly, if not easily. He realized that his eyes were closed, and opened them to find himself staring backward, toward the stern, with no idea how he'd come to be turned around. In the darkness, he could hear girders straining, popping, and grinding all along the length of the ship.

A flash of lightning outlined the superstructure, which was bent left in a curve that had to be at least twenty degrees. The lightning died and total darkness returned, until another bolt lit the clouds, revealing the ship was bent at least twenty degrees in the other direction. After a few moments' intervening darkness, another flash showed *Mistral* bent in the first direction again. All along the envelope, fabric which had been pristine this morning was torn open and flapping in the wind.

He looked away from it, not wishing to see what state the ship would be in by the next lightning flash, whether it might be bent double this time and going down. When the next flash came, he was looking across the hurricane deck. He saw a moment captured in time, the steersmen holding white-knuckled and straining against their wheels, Josette with one hand on a girder and the other hauling on emergency pull ropes. In the next flash, he saw her shouting to him, but he couldn't hear a word of it over the fury of the storm.

Without taking his hands off the rail, he raised a thumb at her, until the next flash illuminated the signal. The lightning's last dying flicker showed her nodding gravely back to him. The thunder followed a moment later, and at the next flash he found that his eyes were closed again.

Soaked to the bone and holding on for his life, he gradually slipped into a strange state of detachment. The thunder became distant, the rain and cold insignificant, the stabbing pain in his ears a mere nothing, and the promise of death irrelevant.

Sometime later—he couldn't say how long—a voice by his ear whispered out of a perfect silence. In the quiet, motionless air, it said nothing more than, "Bernie, look."

He opened his eyes to find Josette leaning next to him, staring over the side, and wearing the most disconcerting smile. He looked out over the rail.

Clouds stretched far below them, running away to the north like a snow-covered mountain range. The storm was lit from above by the moon and stars, and intermittently from within by flashes of lightning. Bernat's breath fogged the icy but untroubled air. Soft, calming moonlight illuminated the deck. *Mistral*'s superstructure did not bend. The envelope was still, the girders unperturbed.

And everything was perfectly quiet. Even the steamjack had stopped.

"We've gone up two miles in ten minutes," Josette said, still whispering. "We're so high, we had to vent a quarter of the gas so the bags wouldn't burst in the low pressure."

The serenity he'd been cultivating for the past few seconds evaporated. "Isn't that quite a long way up? How will we get down again, after losing all that gas?"

"Less gas makes it quite a bit easier to get down, actually."

"I mean, without crashing."

She shrugged. "We have ten thousand feet to think of something."

"Oh God," he said, closing his eyes again.

"Not so loud. We're so high he might hear."

Bernat held tight to his safety line and said, "And it's obvious he hates us."

SHE DIDN'T HAVE the heart to tell him they were already falling.

If she dropped enough ballast, the steamjack might have the power to hold them to a steady altitude, but the bearings had overheated while fighting the updraft. All Josette could do was wait for them to cool, and hope the ship didn't hit another updraft that forced her to vent even more gas.

She heard someone coming down the companionway, and turned to find Kember. The girl stepped to Josette's right and said in a quiet voice, "Bags two, seven, and eight are losing gas. Friction tears, we think, from the frames twisting around so much in the storm. Riggers are having a hard time getting to them. And number six had a vent stuck open, but we've repaired it now."

Josette lit a mesh-enclosed lantern to have a look at the aneroid altimeter. Their fall was definitely accelerating. "Drop five hundred in sand ballast," she told Kember. "Make sure they pour it out, or we might accidentally drop sandbags on the goddamn palace. And make sure the keel is well ventilated."

Sand was dropped in short order, but *Mistral*'s descent was still accelerating. She ordered another five hundred pounds dropped, which brought them to a steady rate of fall.

They were fast running out of disposable ballast, and coming up on the turbulent top side of the storm, with the steamjack still inoperable. Josette ordered three hundred pounds of galloping ballast—that is to say, two crewmen—into the forward frames to bring *Mistral* down by the nose. In that attitude, the ship did not fall straight into the storm, but slid along the air currents of its rear-facing slope, like a toboggan riding the sky.

Halfway down, the welcome sound of the steamjack's whine cut the silence. "Private Grey says she can give you one-third power," Sergeant Jutes reported.

"One-third power it is. Steer northwest, and we'll try to get a bearing on the signal base."

They were behind the storm, but the leaking bags still ate away at their buoyancy. Within an hour, *Mistral* was flying with the bow up ten degrees just to maintain altitude, enough pitch to tire the crew out from standing at an angle. After another hour they were still at ten degrees, and falling, even though the steamjack had been brought back to half power against Private Grey's advice. Half an hour after that, with the sand ballast gone, the cannonballs and shot went over the side, with dearest hope they didn't land on anyone important. After that it was the reserve fuel and all the ship's stores that went by the board.

Mistral still fell. There was nothing left to drop but the bref guns and the water ballast, and Josette wanted to reserve water ballast for landing. So she had hatchets distributed, and together with the deck crew hacked away the lines and supports holding the cannons, letting them fall, with the dearest hope that they'd land on someone soft.

With that dismal task finished, she called landing stations and had Jutes hand out knives. When Bernat took his, he blinked at it a few times and said, "Oh, thank you."

"If you end up inside a bag after we've landed," Josette said, "use that to cut your way out. Don't tarry, or you'll drown in the gas."

He looked at her in disbelief, and then suddenly cried, "Why in hell do I come aboard this deathtrap?"

She smirked and looked forward. "Same reason the rest of us do: irredeemable insanity."

They slipped into cloud cover behind the storm, and the turbulence began again, though not so bad as on the leading side. Then again, *Mistral* had been in better shape on the leading side, with a more capable steamjack and ballast to spare.

She leaned over and said, "We might die in a minute, Bernie. Anything left to say?"

He spent a few moments staring contemplatively into the lightning-lit clouds. Finally, he said, "I'm not the slightest bit sorry I slept with your mother."

Josette considered this, and answered, "Neither am I."

She might have said more, but the next flash showed them clear of the clouds. In the flickering lightning, the hills and treetops outside the city appeared no more than a hundred feet below.

At the next flash, they were noticeably closer to the ground. So low, in fact, that in the next moment the tail caught on a copse of trees. Now anchored aft, the rest of the ship pivoted down like a flail threshing wheat, so fast that anyone on the hurricane deck would surely be squashed between it and the keel.

"Everyone into the keel, now!" Josette screamed. "Bernie, up! Someone quench the boiler fire!"

Josette was the only one not scrambling for the companionway. Instead, she leapt for the ballast controls and put all her weight on the pull-ropes. Another lightning flash showed ballast water pouring from ports forward—every second reducing the force of the inevitable crash. The hurricane deck now lay forty feet above the treetops, which were arrayed like a pit of spikes below. At the next flash, it was only twenty feet.

"Where the hell's the captain?" she heard Jutes ask, a second before the hurricane deck hit the tallest pine.

She yanked herself up by the pull cords and slipped between two keel girders just as the deck came up into the space she'd been occupying. She heard the companionway snap into pieces, felt branches slap her body as a pine tree tore through the deck, inches from her head. Somewhere aft, she could hear the buzz of the airscrews clipping branches.

Finally, the ship ceased its descent. The buzz of airscrews sawing through lumber turned into irregular thumps, then went silent. Girders above still creaked and the force of the wind against the envelope still rocked *Mistral* back and forth. Up in the superstructure, girders cracked and lines snapped in the darkness. Josette's hiding place was not unaffected. The movement of the ship might bring the girders together to crush her at any moment, so she took the knife from her harness and cut her way up into the keel. In the darkness there, she called out, "Is the boiler fire quenched?"

No answer from inside the ship.

"Anyone amidships, check the boiler fire!"

Still no answer.

She nearly wept, the tremor clear enough in her voice when she called, "Is anyone still alive?"

Bernat groaned and said, "I am. I think."

"Boiler fire's out, sir," Grey called back.

"Deck crew's all accounted for," Jutes reported.

The riggers began to report in, the last reporting that Chips was out cold, but breathing.

"Where's Ensign Kember?" Josette called, as she clawed her way up the incline of the keel catwalk, past the companionway, to where Jutes and the deck crew were clustered. She tried to make her way farther back, but another tree had pierced the keel there and was blocking the way.

"Sabrine?" Private Grey called aft.

"Make sure a bag didn't come down on her!" Josette called. "Check frame two!"

"I'm here!" Kember called. "I was out on the tail. You can see the beacon at Kuchin Signal Base from here. It can't be more than five miles away. Can you believe that? Half the night spent spinning around in the storm, and we land five miles from base!" She was practically giddy. "It'll be nothing to get her back, once we refloat her."

"That's wonderful, Ensign," Josette said. "Now could you see to opening the top vents on all the bags containing inflammable air, so we don't explode between now and then?"

"Er, yes, sir. Sorry, sir."

And with that, Josette sat in the crook made by a snapped-off stub of a branch and a keel girder, to catch her breath.

"You okay?" Bernat asked through the darkness, a few feet away.

"Fine," she said. "I think I saw Davies's marmot, though. How about you? Hurt?"

"Only my pride. Ow! And my leg."

"Sorry, my lord," Jutes said, from somewhere on the far side of Bernat's voice. There was some rustling as Jutes checked him over, then the sergeant said, "Knee's out of joint."

She heard Bernat heave a sigh of relief. "Well, that doesn't sound so bad." He laughed. "I was afraid it was broken, and you'd have to grab hold of the leg and yank on it to reset the bone."

"Jutes, now!" Josette said, reaching over and clapping onto Bernat's thigh.

Whereupon Jutes grabbed hold of Bernat's leg below the knee and yanked on it, not to reset the bone—which was indeed unbroken—but to pull the dislocated knee back into place. This procedure required less medical expertise than resetting a bone, but was by far the more painful operation. It had to go on longer, to boot, since the sinews as well as the muscles around the joint all conspired to oppose the necessary adjustment.

All of which could be deduced by the pitch of Bernat's screaming. He cried out so long and loud that he wore his voice ragged. As he wailed on, Josette had to fight him off and keep hold of his thigh, a task made all the more difficult by its writhing, as the muscles twisted into unnatural shapes.

Finally, though, Jutes let go and Bernat's voice quieted into a long moan.

"Got it?" Josette asked.

"Almost," Jutes said.

"Almost?" Bernat asked in a whimper.

"Never you fret, my lord," Jutes said, "It'll only hurt . . ."

Bernat screamed out again as Jutes gave one last, hard pull.

" . . . for the rest of your life," the sergeant concluded.

BERNAT WAS IN more pain than anyone in history, as near as he could determine. And yet these people, ostensibly his friends, were carrying on as if everything was perfectly ordinary. If anything, some of them were more cheerful than usual, now that *Mistral* was safely back in the shed.

Kember and Grey stood under the bow, laughing and sharing stories about the crash—and both of them stationed on the same keel, where the tale could hardly be different. Then there was Davies, leaning against a sawed-off tree trunk still impaled into the ship, describing to a gathered crowd of yardsmen—and for the hundredth time—the expression a marmot made when in shock. And of course there was Josette, speaking to some officer or another as they both strolled around the ship, inspecting the damage. All of them lavished concern and attention on the wounded ship, but none on the wounded gentleman.

"Never mind this," he said to the yardsman carrying the front end of his jury-rigged palanquin chair. "Take me back to the medical building. No, on second thought, take me to the nearest tavern and leave me there."

"How will you get back, my lord?" the man in back asked.

"How is not the issue. Who is the issue. Who will carry me up the stairs to her bedroom? But I will handle that business on my own."

On the way out of the shed, however, he spotted Roland

coming the other way. He nearly sprang out of his chair before the pain shot through his leg and pinned him back.

"Follow that man!" he commanded his carriers. "No, the one to the left! Left, damn you, left! Do they not have left where you come from?"

They eventually managed to steer him toward Roland, and by much calling and shouting, he managed to get the twit's attention. Roland turned about just inside the shed, and stood transfixed by the sight of Bernat on the palanquin. He greeted him with, "Bernie! I didn't know you'd been made Emperor of Utarma. Congratulations."

Bernat sneered and said, "My knee is dislocated, you insufferable fribble."

Roland only smirked. "A shame. That will put a damper on the coronation." He looked over at the men carrying Bernat's palanquin. "Can't be too hard for them to hold you up, though. You're filled with more hot air than the balloon."

"It's an airship!" Bernat corrected. "And it is not filled with hot air!"

"We mustn't be picky," Josette said, as she approached from behind Roland. This was, as far as Bernat knew, the first time in her life that Josette had chosen not to be picky about aerostatic terminology.

Roland turned around, and judging by the look reflected in Josette's face, he must have been beaming. "Thank goodness you're well," he said. "I rushed over as soon as I heard about the crash."

She walked to the other side of Bernat, putting him and his palanquin between her and Roland. "The only injury was to my career prospects."

"Indeed," Bernat said, feeling venomous. "How many airships is it that you've crashed?"

"Two," she said. "Which is actually about average for an

airship captain, but somehow I don't expect that to be taken into account at my court martial."

"Oh, you needn't worry about that," Roland said. "The city councilor who complained that you were off station has resigned and will be taking full responsibility. He'll have a letter in all the papers tomorrow morning, admitting his guilt and praising your superior foresight." He removed a letter from his coat and handed it to Josette.

Bernat caught a glimpse of it and called out, "That letter's in your handwriting!"

"Yes," Roland said, "but it's his signature. I convinced him to come clean."

Josette arched an eyebrow. "You're telling me you charmed him?"

"No, you have it backward," Bernat said. "Roland isn't the charmer, he's the snake."

"Never in my life," Roland said. "We only chatted for a while. He was admittedly reluctant at first, but after I inquired into the health and safety of his family members living in Copia Lugon, which I will one day be marquis of . . . Well, I suppose he must have felt a certain fraternity, as he became suddenly quite amenable."

Bernat snorted so vigorously, it sent a renewed spasm of pain through his leg. " 'Will one day be marquis of through a simple accident of birth,' you mean. And here you are, already scheming and abusing your power."

Josette didn't acknowledge these salient points, but only smirked as she read. "I like the bit about his everlasting shame and sorrow, that he endangered such a fine collection of national treasures as *Mistral,* her officers, and crew."

"Do you?" Roland asked. "I was worried it might be a bit over the top."

"Not at all."

"Does no one care about the fate of the poor city councilor?" Bernat asked.

"Your concern is touching, Bernie," Roland said. He looked at Josette. "Did he ever tell you how he reacted, when he found out I was sole heir?"

"Oh, for the love of heaven, are you still whining about that?"

"You tried to hire someone to have me assassinated!"

That, finally, brought Josette's attention up from the letter. "Good God!" she cried. "Bernie, how could you?"

Bernat waved the matter away. "I was six years old and the 'assassin' was our nursemaid." He looked thoughtfully into the distance. "She might have taken the job, too, if I'd made a better offer than my hobbyhorse and a couple of hawk feathers."

"Next time you'll know," Josette said, handing the letter back to Roland.

"And do you know how he responded?" Bernat asked.

"Proportionally," Roland said in a flat tone.

"He tried to smother me in my sleep that night!"

"I was never trying to smother you."

"He held a pillow over my face for five full minutes!"

"Yes, but you're still here, aren't you?"

"You could have caused permanent damage!"

"But I didn't. Well . . . I suppose there's some room for debate on that matter." He spoke an aside to Josette. "I was barely eleven, by the way."

"And mature enough to know what you were doing, unlike a six-year-old."

"Boys?" Josette said. "This is becoming less cute and more irritating by the moment."

Roland grinned and said, "Then it will cease immediately." He cast a sidelong glance at Bernat. "At least, it will on my end. Oh, and there'll be a reception in your honor this evening. The king won't be there, unfortunately, but we may be able to arrange an audience in the coming weeks. And I've managed to get rooms at the palace for you and your officers, for the duration of your stay in Kuchin." He looked up at *Mistral,* ragged and pierced through with pine trees. "Which I imagine will be some time."

Josette just made eyes at Roland for a while, a sight which brought bile into Bernat's throat, before she called out, "Ensign!"

Kember was there in a moment, standing at attention. "Sir?"

"Are you interested in having a room at the palace, while we're here?"

Kember's eyes widened in surprise. She swallowed, causing her still-raw scar to twitch. "Sure!" she said.

Josette looked back to Roland. "We accept." She turned to Kember. "Let's give the crew leave to enjoy the city. You too, Ensign. I'd say you've earned a day off."

Kember looked back at *Mistral*'s crew, already tending toward the rowdy side, and they hadn't even been given leave yet. "How, uh, how much should they enjoy themselves, sir?"

Josette considered it, and said, "Let's keep it to wanton drunkenness and petty vandalism. No fights. We start repairs as soon as the surveyors finish cataloging the damage, so we want everyone intact."

Kember saluted smartly, then ran back to the ship, where her announcement of leave was answered with raucous cheers.

Roland shot her his snakiest grin. "Will you also be taking the day off, Captain?"

" 'Off' is not quite how I would describe it," she said.

"But it's close? What would it take to get you the rest of the way, perhaps so far as to allow me to show you the Tellurian Quarter?"

Bernat tried to warn her away with his expression, but it only seemed to buoy her resolve. She gave Roland a smile—a genuine smile, which always spelled trouble—and asked him, "Am I detecting an attempt to bribe an officer of the Royal Aerial Signal Corps?"

Roland only grinned. "I was worried you wouldn't pick up on my meaning, Captain Dupre."

She smiled. "You needn't have worried. Signals are our business, Lord Hinkal."

Bernat couldn't take it anymore. "Oh good God!" he cried. "Is tincture of ipecac the new thing for out-of-joint legs? If it is, I fear I've been overdosed."

"It's amazing," Roland said, speaking as if he only had just noticed Bernat there. "Your injury has actually worsened your demeanor. I wouldn't have believed it possible."

"Oh, I'm just getting started, Brother."

"If you two will excuse me," Josette said, "I have to change into a uniform with less sap on it." With that, she set off for the ship.

"No! Stop! Josette, it's a trick!" Bernat kicked with his good leg at the yardsmen carrying the front corners of the palanquin. "Follow her!"

The yardsmen carrying Bernat leapt to action, running after, but Josette looked over her shoulder and stopped their progress by turning them both to stone—or near enough.

"You're making a terrible mistake!" Bernat called after her. "You don't know him like I do!"

But Josette ignored him entirely. On her way to the ship, she stopped only long enough to remind Ensign Kember of her solemn duty to keep the crew from brawling.

"But who threw the first punch?" Josette asked.

"The girl, Ensign Kember," the lieutenant of police said. "But I'm prepared to release her to your supervision, if you can promise she'll never return to the Upper Park, or any other area of Kuchin which has been set aside for peaceful civic enjoyment."

Josette signed a paper to that effect, and then accompanied the lieutenant to the detention building. As he was unlocking Kember's cell, a voice from behind said, "Afternoon, Captain."

She turned to see Luc Lupien leaning with his hands on the bars of the opposite cell, and six other bruised and bedraggled Mistrals sprawled on the floor or on benches. In the next cell over, Private Grey made brief eye contact and then lowered her gaze. "And I'll take this lot, too," Josette said to the policeman. "Can you wrap them up for me?"

Outside, she helped Kember into a covered carriage. Some of the crewmen were about to climb in themselves, but a single look from Josette told them they'd be finding their own transportation.

Half the ride went by in silence, with Kember staring at the split skin on her knuckles and looking like she might die of shame at any moment. When they were on the outskirts of town, Josette finally asked, "Who won?"

Kember perked up at the comment. "Well, sir, if you consider that there were more of them, and the navy doesn't pay extra to people who weigh less—"

"Both of which are customarily taken into account when deciding the winner of an inter-service brawl."

"—I'd say it was about a draw."

"And how did this fight—which ended in a draw if all extenuating conditions are considered—begin in the first place?"

Kember gave the reason. And, in all fairness, navy enlisted uniforms were indeed very tawdry and did, in fact, feature an idiotic pommel on the cap. Any rational gang of sailors should have therefore taken no offence from the perfectly accurate comments Private Davies had directed toward them, and should have peacefully accepted the truth of the matter, and certainly not returned comments of their own regarding the air corps.

"This will go down in your service record," Josette said. "We couldn't keep it out if we tried. And it will therefore make it more difficult for you to be promoted to lieutenant. Promotion comes hard enough already, for an auxiliary officer. You needn't make it any harder."

"Yes, sir."

After a moment's consideration, Josette added, "You're the most promising ensign I've ever served with. It would be a damn shame if your impulsiveness and stupidity robbed the country of a good officer, which we need now more than ever."

Kember was struck silent. When she finally regained the power of speech, she only asked in a meek little voice, "The most promising, sir?"

Josette was beginning to regret saying it. "Don't let it go to your head."

The carriage continued on through the countryside, until finally coming within sight of the palace. It could be seen from a great way off, though it was only three floors tall, because the ground for miles around had been flattened to leave an unimpeded view, and the palace itself was constructed on the raised bailey of a much earlier castle, so that its entire 850-acre grounds lay forty feet above the surrounding countryside.

The driver took them across the famous Reflecting Bridge over what used to be the moat, through the Ministers' Court, past the royal menagerie, to the Nobles' Court, and skirted the edge of the King's Court before going around the palace and dropping them off at the back.

An attendant came out to meet them, and led them through the east-wing apartments, where they passed Bernat. He sat in a wheeled chair pushed by a servant, with his leg cast in plaster and held horizontal by a board. "You're not ready yet?" he asked, sitting up.

"We shall be there on time," Josette said, hurrying past.

The attendant first showed Kember into her room, but the girl paused in the doorway, examining it. The room was no more than ten paces to a side, with decent if not opulent furnishings. "Is this it?" she asked. "I thought a room at the palace would be bigger. With more . . . gold things."

"I shall file a complaint with the management," Josette said, as the attendant showed her to her own room, next door.

They met again outside the ballroom, both wearing dress uniforms, which were similar to their deck uniforms, but featured a cravat around the neck and epaulettes on the shoulders. Josette's hair, still too short for the servants to do much with it, had been brushed flat against her head with boar bristles dipped in almond oil, and the scent at least covered the faint burnt smell that still lingered around her head.

"I'm not sure I want to do this, sir," Kember said, as they waited for the courtier attending the door to let them in.

"Then you have the advantage of me," Josette answered. "I'm certain I don't want to do it."

"Only . . . do I look ugly?" In response to Josette's sudden gaze, Kember added, "With the scar? The medical officer said I'd never be pretty."

"As to that," Josette said, "you should have thought of it before you let someone shoot you."

Ensign Kember looked forward and said, "Yes, sir."

The courtier nodded to the servants on either side of the ornate double doors, which were thrown open and held wide. "Ladies and gentlemen," he said, quieting the room. "I present Captain Josette Dupre, of His Majesty's Signal Airship, *Mistral*."

The gathered nobility, perhaps a hundred of them clustered by the dozen throughout the gilded, candlelit room, paused in chewing on their hors d'oeuvres to politely clap. When the clapping subsided, Josette steeled herself and drew a long breath.

Of the speech she had prepared, she got as far as, "Th—" before Roland appeared at her side, quieted her with a quick shake of his head, and led her by the shoulder to a group of noblemen in the middle of the room. Bernat was among them, looking at her like she was an idiot.

"You told me I had to say a few words," she said, leaning over and speaking in a quiet hiss.

"Yes, but obviously not the moment you enter the room," Bernat said. "What in hell were you thinking?"

She rolled her eyes. "My apologies. Where I come from, formal dress receptions are conducted along different lines."

"No harm done," Roland said, leaning in to join the conspiracy. "But it might be wise to look to one of us for guidance, in the future."

She was about to offer a biting reply, but in the candlelight Roland looked nothing like his brother, and this softened her mood considerably. His dark hair was longer, but kept neat and parted at the side. His features were softer, his expressions hardly sanctimonious at all. And he cut a fine figure in his tailed coat, woolen breeches, and obi sash—which were not quite the fashion. The loose, pleated hakama seemed more popular among Kuchin's upper crust, but she judged Roland correct in eschewing it for breeches. The tighter woolen garment better flattered his . . . qualities.

"Captain?" he asked.

She shook her head, smiled, and said, "Sorry. Just gathering wool." She looked about the ballroom. "Where's Kember gotten to?"

Josette had been ushered away so quickly that she'd had no chance to help her young ensign become situated. She imagined the girl, lingering adrift and alone near the door, trying not to look bewildered in this sea of nobility.

Bernat quietly indicated a group of young noblemen off to

the right. Kember was among them, partly hidden by their numbers, and by how closely they crowded around her. For her part, the ensign was grinning as she pointed to her scars, and through the greater buzz of conversation, could be heard to say in a cheerful tone, "No, no. The bullet only hit my neck. They cut open the face to keep me from dying of inflammation. Here, help me wipe the makeup away, so you can get a better look at it." She laughed as her concealer came off. "It's just hideous, isn't it?" This was met with such an expression of admiration and denial from the young noblemen that Josette couldn't make out anything else Kember said.

"Now, come on," Roland said. "I'm sorry, but we must mingle."

"God preserve me," she said.

"Courage, Captain. Courage!"

IT WAS GOING well until Count Morishita asked, "Does your family go back very far, Captain?"

Josette stood thinking about it—not a good sign at all—and said, "To the beginning, I suppose. Same as everyone else's."

Bernat waited for disaster to result, but the remark drew friendly laughter from Count and Countess Morishita, and their hangers-on joined in as soon as they knew it was safe to do so.

Josette, however, reddened and went on. "Or did you think, your lordship, that—"

Bernat cut in with, "That any of our lineages could be a match for yours. Your line descends from the Ashkaitian Dynasty, does it not? And I believe the family of Countess Morishita, née Hada, goes back to the Almurab Dynasty of ancient Mauratia." He looked up at Josette. "Did you know that, Captain?"

"I did not," she said, and returned to clenching her jaw.

"Then you have all the more reason to admire an already admirable couple," Roland said.

"And now we must see to Duke Prevot's party," Bernat said. "If you'll excuse us." He bowed as far as he could in his chair, and directed his servant toward another cluster of guests.

Josette and Roland followed, and as their little party made its way across the ballroom, Roland whispered instructions to her. "For God's sake, try to be nice to these ones, they're more important. The man in the plume is Duke Prevot and the woman next to him is his mistress. Address him as 'Your Grace' and her as 'Your Ladyship.' If she likes you, she'll ask you to call her Evette. Do not do so the first time she asks, or they'll think you've acceded too readily, but do not fail to do so the second time, or they'll think you're being insolent. Do not under any circumstances call her Duchess—his wife's title—or they'll both be mortified. Especially considering that his wife is here as well. See her flirting with the Minister of Correspondence? Oh, and there's Lady Evette's husband over there, pouting in the corner. It's unlikely they'll come over while we're chatting, but if one of them does, the other will certainly follow. If they stand next to their respective spouses, you must address each pair as you would any other husband and wife. If either does not stand with their spouse, you must address each as if the spouse were not there at all, but be sure to give each of them equal attention, so as not to favor one spouse over the other. Understood?"

She nodded her head, but her eyes were fixed on him in a blank stare. "What in hell goes on in this place?" she asked.

"The management of the Kingdom of Garnia, of course," Bernat said with a smile.

"That explains so very much about the state of the country."

Roland shook his head. "That is exactly the sort of comment you must bury deep within yourself, if you're to get through this evening. Ready?"

"No."

"That's a shame, because here we are. Ah, Your Grace ..."

This encounter went better. Josette was, to her credit, learning to remain silent and show appreciation for the paltry wit of her betters. It helped, certainly, that everyone here wanted to be seen with her, and to be seen on friendly terms with her, as she was quite the celebrity. Bernat's contribution to the recent victory at Canard did not go unmentioned either, least of all by himself.

Trouble only arose when one Mr. Dagan Lemerre walked into their circle and invited Josette to dinner with his family. Josette handled it in the best manner possible, by standing mute and paralyzed, while Bernat and Roland took charge of the situation.

"Captain Dupre," Roland said, "As much as I'm certain you'd like to dine with Mr. Lemerre's family, I believe you've already committed yourself to attending Baron Guisset's ball tomorrow evening."

Mr. Lemerre would not be dissuaded so easily, however, and went on, "Perhaps you could join us for a riverfront picnic on Wednesday?"

Josette helpfully stalled by making an uncertain, rolling trill, much as a mental defective would under similar circumstances.

"I believe," Bernat said, leaping to her aid, "that you'll be in the country that day."

"Oh," she said, finding her brains at last. "What rotten luck."

Mr. Lemerre kept trying for some time, suggesting half a dozen events on various dates, but the brothers found a matching event that excused Josette from every single invitation, until he finally got the message and gave up.

When they had a moment's privacy, Josette asked, "How did I manage to get such a crowded social calendar, without ever noticing?"

"Oh, don't worry about that," Bernat said. "We just had to keep Lemerre at bay. You couldn't very well go to dinner with his family. It would be the end of you."

She frowned. "What, are they cannibals?"

"Worse yet: merchants."

"I see," she said. "Shall I spit on him, the next time he comes over, or is it enough to turn my back and harrumph?"

Bernat looked positively alarmed. "No, no. You mustn't offend him! That would be the end of you."

Josette tried to form a question, but found that she possessed so little understanding that she didn't even know how to start. She only stood there, with her mouth popping open and closed, like a gasping fish.

Seeing her confusion, Roland said, "Half the nobles here have an interest in his enterprises, and draw much of their income from him. If he were to sour on them, he could see to it that they were utterly ruined. Likewise, if they were to sour on him, then by the very slightest adjustments to the laws governing trade, they could see to it that he was utterly ruined. And then again, he's a *merchant*. If they were seen to keep friendly company with him, their standing in the court would diminish, they would no longer have sufficient influence upon the trade laws, and *everyone* would be ruined."

This enlightened her only a little. "And . . . how do I fit into all that?"

"Good God!" Bernat said, in an annoyed whisper. "How can you be such a damn fool?"

"More easily than I'd ever imagined," she said, staring contemplatively into space.

Roland remained patient. "You're the man of the hour, as

it were, the conduit through which their alliances and petty grievances alike will flow. You must step delicately."

A servant came by with a drink for Josette, which she took eagerly. After some time had passed with her saying nothing, Bernat finally looked up from his chair and asked, "Is everything all right?"

"Have you ever had a dream," she said, looking over the rim of her champagne glass and off into space, "where you're in a play, but you can't remember any of your lines, and everything that's going on is a complete mystery to you?"

"Of course," Bernat said cheerfully, "but I improvise and the audience loves me."

"It's only another few hours," Roland said.

"Though I think," Bernat said, "we should make a sally to rescue one of our stranded compatriots." He motioned to Ensign Kember, still surrounded by a group of young noblemen, but no longer seeming to enjoy it. Indeed, as they crowded in around her no matter which way she walked, all vying for her attention, she looked rather like she was being slowly pecked to death by hens. "Good God. Have they been at her all this time?"

"It's no wonder they're fascinated by such an exotic creature as a battle-scarred young lady," Roland said. "They're all of an age to join the army, and none with duties so vital as to prevent it, and yet here they are, lounging in the palace instead of out fighting the war."

Josette rolled her eyes, though Bernat couldn't tell why. She asked, "Can she be saved, do you think?"

"Let us at least make the attempt," Roland said, nodding to Bernat.

Bernat nodded back, as he showed his servant which way to push his chair.

They managed, by appealing for some bit of military trivia

that only Ensign Kember would know, to finally extract her from amid the gang of nobles. But, though heady with victory, they had a nasty shock when they returned triumphant, for Josette was nowhere to be found.

"Oh dear," Roland said, "We've lost the guest of honor."

JOSETTE WAS ALREADY outside when she realized she could have brought a glass of champagne and a tray of hors d'oeuvres with her, or at least a coat to keep away the evening chill. She couldn't risk returning, though, lest she be captured again.

She strolled over well-manicured lawns and gravel paths, with little regard for any particular route, but always moving farther away from the palace itself. Skirting the fence around the palace menagerie, which was more easily smelled than seen in the evening dusk, she looked up to see a child peering out at her from the gap in a nearby hedgerow. He was so still that she first mistook him for a statue in the gloom, and thought nothing of walking straight toward him to get a better look.

She was just close enough to doubt her initial assessment when he suddenly said, "I'm hiding from my guardians. What are you doing?" He spoke with an accent she couldn't quite place.

Josette considered it for a moment, then said, "The same, actually."

She could see now that he was perhaps six years old and dressed in expensive finery. "Can we hide together?" he asked.

"Certainly," she said, not knowing how else to reply.

He beckoned her past the hedgerow. On the other side, a bench faced the bear cage, though the bears were not much entertainment. All they did was lie still, making great furry lumps in the shadows. She sat down, and he next to her.

He looked her up and down, seeming confused. "Are you married to someone in the army?" he finally asked.

She smirked. "And I got my clothes mixed up with my husband's? No. I'm not married."

He spent some time digesting this, then asked, "Do you want to get married?"

She smirked all the more. "Is that a proposal?"

"Not married to me!" At his exclamation, one of the bears raised its head and eyed them. "Not to me," the boy repeated, at a whisper.

Josette put her nose in the air. "Oh," she said, affecting resentment. "I see. I misunderstood."

The child's face grew mournful, and he said, "I didn't mean to hurt your feelings. I'm sorry."

"Well, if you're sorry, I suppose I can forgive you." That's when she saw Roland standing by the gap in the hedgerow, attempting to stifle his mirth.

Once caught at spying, he walked up to them, bowed, and said to the little boy, "I think, sir, you should return to your apartment. It's dark out."

The boy looked to Josette for salvation, but she only shrugged her shoulders. "You had your chance with me," she said. Abandoned, he marched with his eyes downcast, until he'd turned the corner heading back to the palace.

Once he was out of sight, she asked Roland, "How long have you been watching?"

"Just long enough," he said, sitting next to her.

"And who was that child?"

He looked surprised. "You didn't know? That was His Royal Highness, the Crown Prince of Sotra. He's being tutored here."

When she realized at last that Roland was not playing on her credulity, but was indeed being perfectly serious, she asked, "Are the tutors here so much superior to the ones in Sotra?"

Roland laughed softly and said, "I couldn't say. But arrangements such as this strengthen our relationship with Sotra, and may bring them into the war on our side."

"So the people of Kuchin do know there's a war on." She was mildly impressed, by virtue of low expectations. "I was beginning to wonder."

"They appreciate that their interests—most of their interests, anyway—are served somewhat better by victory than defeat."

"Well, how can we lose, with spirit like that?"

He had no answer, but only stared at the ground.

"I didn't mean to discomfit you," she said. "I suppose you've come to bring me back?"

He brightened a bit at that, and said, "That was my purpose, but we can certainly stay out a while longer, if you don't mind my company."

She arched an eyebrow. "Won't someone come looking for us?"

In answer to that, he chuckled. "If it were only one or the other of us, yes. But as long as we've both gone missing, no one will think twice of it."

"Why would that . . ." The words hardly left her lips before the answer occurred to her. "Ah."

"Does that bother you?" he asked.

She hadn't thought she'd need to consider the answer, but she did, and finally concluded, "Less than I imagined it would."

5

"WE MIGHT HAVE won, too, if you'd made an effort," Josette said, on a crisp morning several weeks later.

Bernat shot her a disgusted look from the other side of the enclosed carriage. "I was making every effort to not win, obviously. That's enough of a feat against Duke Royama, without having to drag you down as well. Don't they teach you how to take a goddamn hint, in the army? Why must you be so competitive at all times?"

"Ha!" She appealed to Roland, saying, "When your brother came aboard my airship, the first thing he did was challenge me to a test of marksmanship, and humiliated me in front of my crew. And now he calls me too competitive."

Roland had pushed himself into the back corner of the carriage, which was as far as he could get from both of them without climbing out the window. "Indeed?" he asked, noncommittal.

"I did not humiliate you!" Bernat said. For a moment, such an intensity of wrath flashed across his face that Josette thought she had never seen him so angry outside of combat. He cooled presently, though, and added in a calmer tone, "Not as much as I could have. In any event, that was to a purpose. Losing today was also to a purpose."

"Which was?"

"To not win." He looked at her as he might a particularly slow child. "You've been immersed in palace life for over a month and you still don't understand? These people have been coddled all their lives. They're not like you and me."

Josette had quite a bit to say about Bernat not being coddled, but she was too stunned by the audacity of the claim to compose a response.

Bernat went on. "They fancy themselves the best at everything—so if you beat them fairly, they think it persecution. And how can you expect their beneficence when you're persecuting them?"

"I don't want their beneficence!"

"Well, why the hell not?"

Roland finally spoke up, saying, "I have rare enough occasion to say this, but my brother is correct. It is well known that you have enemies in abundance among the army's upper echelons. You would do well to have friends with similar influence."

"Perhaps you wouldn't have to lose at shooting," Bernat said, in the manner of a lecture, "if you went to more dinners and excursions. And you *will* be going on the duke's hunt next month, in case there was any question of it in your mind."

"Oh, give it a rest, Bernie," Roland said. When Bernat looked away in furious disgust, Roland leaned in and told Josette in a hushed tone, "Although, you will certainly be going on the hunt. When Duke Royama invites you to anything, you go—unless you've died prior to the appointed date, and perhaps even then, if the funeral hasn't happened yet. The man owns a fifth of the country, including Quah, which gives him particular influence over the affairs of the army. He's second only to the king himself, in power and wealth."

"I'd heard," Josette said, twisting around to look out the window. "From everyone. Multiple times, usually." Outside, the first snow of the year—which had begun in the middle of their shooting match—was just tapering off into tiny flakes, drifting about on the wind.

The carriage rode on in uncomfortable silence, until Roland spoke softly. "Did your father teach you to shoot?" he asked. "You do it well."

Josette watched the snow-dusted countryside as it went past. "My mother, actually." Her breath fogged the glass. "Best goddamn hunter in the county. She would go out into the woods, in the freezing cold, for days at a time, ranging across Garnian and Vinzhalian territory like she didn't know there was a war on. She kept the town fed almost by herself, during the worst of the winter. Not to mention, she brought in enough money to purchase a commission in the army for me. My father, on the other hand, was an assistant miller until he was conscripted into the Garnian army."

Roland's eyes sparkled. "What a family you must make. Do you see them often?"

Josette arched an eyebrow as she turned to him. Roland's expression betrayed nothing but innocence. She asked Bernat, "You didn't tell him?"

But Bernat was asleep, or pretending to be.

"My father's dead and my mother still lives in Durum," Josette said.

After he'd thought about it, Roland frowned. "You mean the town the Vins took on their way to Canard? Is she well?"

"She's alive," Josette said, and did not mention that she'd been made homeless by the new government. And in Durum, the snows would be coming thicker and colder than in Kuchin.

Roland's voice became cheerful. "Then you'll see her again, after we've retaken Durum. Tell me, do people in Durum speak in one of those delightful border dialects? You know, the ones that are sort of half Vin, half Garnian?"

She snorted. "They do not, and haven't for hundreds of years. Not since Garnia first conquered the town and the new government started looking very hard at anyone with Vin leanings. And I don't know why you expect us to retake

Durum. The way things are going, we won't be retaking anything at all, and Duke Royama will have to scrape by with
one less duchy to his name. When the war ends, we could ask
for Durum back at the bargaining table, passing it off as a
mere pittance—a charity for the vanquished—but no one will
bother to ask. No one will remember to."

Roland was less cheerful now. In fact, he was well on the
way toward incensed. "We haven't lost a war in three generations," he said. "You can't imagine we're losing this one, can
you?"

She turned to look at him, and laughed. "You imagine that
we're winning?"

"We're wearing the Vins down," he said, with so much
assurance that she nearly believed him over her own experience. "It won't be long now before they crack. Everyone knows
that."

"Do they?" she asked. "Did they read about it in the papers?"
She laughed. "I honor their bravery, in daring to read the news.
They're courageously risking an upset stomach."

Opposite her, Bernat stirred. "What the hell is going on?"

Roland rolled his eyes and said, "We've lost the war."

Bernat frowned and said, "Good God, I was only asleep for
a minute."

They were at the gates of the signal base now, and Josette
banged on the roof to remind the driver to drop her off there,
well away from the eyes of her men. But, as the driver had
done three times this week, he turned the carriage and went
on through the gates, taking them straight to the shed.

She sighed. "I've told him not to do that. What will the crew
think of me, if they see me being ferried everywhere in a
carriage?"

Bernat and Roland looked at each other, perplexed. "That
you're a person of importance?" Roland suggested.

"That you're yet more terrifying than they imagined?" Bernat added.

Josette only grunted in response. They were coming up on the shed now. When they stopped, she opened the door, letting in a burst of cold air that had Bernat hurrying to get his coat on. She stepped out and said to the coachman, "Only to the gate next time, please. I've told you that."

"Ma'am," he said, touching a rein to his hat.

"Will someone help me?" Bernat asked, trying to pull his crutches out from under the bench.

She ignored him and headed for the flatbed railcar she spotted, parked between *Mistral* and *Shearwater*. She walked around the car, unwilling to touch its cargo lest it prove an illusion. As she wondered at it, Roland strolled up and said, "Ah. I was hoping it would arrive today. It was supposed to be here three days ago, but you know how these things go."

She eyed first the cargo of spare box girders, then Roland. "I'm not sure I do. I've been trying to obtain the girders I need for weeks, and getting stonewalled at every turn."

Roland rested a hand on the corner of the flat car and leaned against it. "They've been sent over from Laurent Yards, where they're building *Levante* and *Ostro*. Only, I heard a rumor that their construction has been delayed by a redesign of their tails or some such. And I thought, all those materials must be sitting idle. So I suggested, over dinner with a Mr. Laurent— you may know of him—that those materials could be put to good use elsewhere. And I may have suggested that, upon inheriting, I may make an investment in his enterprises, though of course we shall have to see where things stand at that time."

"Of course," Josette said, too stunned to say more.

"I believe we can find canvas, too." He went on walking along the length of the flat car, dragging his hand across its dusty top. "As to luftgas and steamjack parts, I've had less luck. Laurent is hoarding his luftgas, and I don't blame him. If he had to purchase it at the current prices, he'd never make a profit on the ships he's building now. And they've reallocated the spare steamjack parts that were meant for *Mistral* to *Levante* and *Ostro,* to save money on construction."

She looked up at her ship, its superstructure looming above, shored up and empty of gas, tied to the ceiling to keep it from collapsing in on itself. "Well," she said, "they won't send a chasseur into battle filled with inflammable air. I don't think we're quite that desperate."

Roland grinned. "Then, it would appear, you'll be stuck here until sufficient luftgas becomes available, and who knows when that'll be?"

As much as she appreciated the material, Roland was taking a bit too much glee in the fact that she was stuck on the ground with him. Besides which, she could not help but think of what he might want in return for his generosity. This was shaping up a bit too much like that conversation under the kissing lantern—a clumsy attempt at a shortcut on the path to her affections. She said, "To be frank, Lord Hinkal, I see you expending a great deal of other people's resources on my behalf, but none of your own."

In an instant, his expression shifted to that of a child who'd been scolded. "To be frank, Captain Dupre, I haven't many of my own resources to expend." He laughed ironically, growing less petulant and more stern by degrees. "And if this doesn't impress you, then I can't imagine any expenditure that would, nor any within the power of mortal men. Perhaps if I went out this evening and won the war myself, and carried Durum here on my back, and laid it at your feet, that might merit a 'thank you.'"

Damn. She had only meant to check his expectation, not bring him that far down. "Pray leave Durum where it is," she said, in a soothing tone. "The smell would attract notice."

When this did nothing to lighten the mood, she sighed and added, "And you'd have me think it's the dukes who must be coddled."

With that, she stepped along the breadth of the flat car and hopped to sit on the corner of it. Her eyes now level with his, she pulled him toward her by his necktie and kissed him.

Roland's grim countenance came down like a falling curtain. As he leaned into the kiss, however, Josette noticed a strange silence behind her, where seconds before yardsmen had been busy along *Mistral*'s keel. She leaned back, turned her head just aside, and bellowed past Roland's ear, "Back to work, you lazy bastards! This isn't a goddamn peep show!" Activity aboard *Mistral* resumed instantly, and with even greater bustle than before.

Roland was no less alarmed than they. He stood frozen in the precise manner and expression he'd had a moment before, except that his eyes were wide in alarm. She wiped a bit of spittle off of his cheek. "Thank you," she said. "This is, perhaps, the most thoughtful gift anyone has ever given me."

He finally blinked, and his face relaxed. "Oh, don't thank me. I did it for *Mistral*." He looked up at the ship, a devilish smile growing on his lips. "A true beauty, though not everyone has the eyes to see it." He spared a quick sidelong glance at Josette, apparently wary that she might assault him. But she only sat with her arms folded across her chest, smirking.

"Elegant lines," he said. "An unwavering protector to her crew. Relentless in pursuit of her nation's enemies. A warrior through and through, and all the more deadly for having such an unexpected form."

Though the subtext was clear enough, as Roland ran his eyes over *Mistral* from bow to stern, it was obvious that his words weren't merely subtext. Surely, he couldn't love this strange, misshapen airship as she did—who could?—but there was real admiration in his eyes when he looked at *Mistral*. In that moment, she wondered for the first time whether she might really be able to love this man. Not as much as she loved her ship, of course, but perhaps only a little less.

"Her only flaw, perhaps, is being a bit too eager to attack." His eyes returned to Josette. "I wish I could know her better."

She couldn't see anyone looking out at them through the keel ports, but that only meant that her resourceful crew had found better hiding spots to watch from. So she resisted the urge to reach out and take his hand—and resisted a few other urges atop that.

"In fact," Roland said, returning to his examination of *Mistral,* "While she's here, I'd like to go aboard her every night, if that could be arran—" He got no farther before she tackled him to the shed floor. "Help!" he cried, squealing in giddy mirth. "Do you airmen know nothing but violence?"

BERNAT HAD JUST managed to put his feet on the ground and sort out his crutches with the help of the coachman, when Roland returned, looking strangely pleased with himself. While Bernat stood there, Roland hopped up the carriage steps with a sprightly gait and settled himself.

"Are you going to help me up?" Bernat asked.

Roland looked down at him. "Why did you get out in the first place?"

"I thought we were staying," he said. "Neither of you thought to tell me otherwise. Her, I understand. She's too distracted by her goddamn flying machine to notice the concerns of a mere human being. You, I thought better of—more fool me. Now, will you help me get up? And try not to bang my leg, like last time."

"Oh, is there something wrong with it?" Roland asked with a smile. "Sorry, I find I'm a bit distracted, myself." He reached down to help Bernat up, while the coachman supported him on the other side.

Between the two of them, they hauled Bernat back into the carriage. He settled onto the front seat with his leg propped on the rear, but the operation left him out of breath and in agony. "Good God," he said. "Do you suppose we could stop for a drink on the way back?"

Roland climbed in, reached under the seat, and came up with a wine bottle, which he handed to his brother. "Aren't you going to ask what I meant, when I said I was a bit distracted?"

"I know exactly what you meant," Bernat said, and took a drink. "It's my leg that's faulty, not my senses."

"Do you need help mounting your horse?"

Josette eyed the mare suspiciously. The animal looked back at her with big, innocent, dark eyes, and whinnied. "No," Josette said. "I only want to be sure it isn't planning any mischief, before I make the attempt."

Roland, already mounted, walked his own horse alongside, and reached over to stroke the mare's head. "You needn't worry. The duke's head groom assures me that she's the sweetest, most thoroughly friendly creature yet bred."

Josette was unconvinced. "The beast may only be biding its time."

Roland chuckled. "If so, then she has maintained the fiction without interruption for this long, and will certainly not reveal her true nature to the likes of us."

While Josette was still working up the nerve to mount, Bernat rode up, wincing all the way until his horse clopped to a rest. "What the hell are you doing still at the stables?" he asked, as he adjusted his plastered leg in the stirrup. "They're about to cast the hounds."

"Are you sure your leg is well enough to ride?" Roland asked him.

"I'll be just fine," Bernat snapped, more testy than usual this morning.

Josette mounted her horse without incident, much to her surprise. She settled into the saddle and patted the side of the mare's neck, more in gratitude than affection. A servant handed up a hunting spear, which she slid into its holster behind the saddle.

Bernat began, "Now to get her going, you must—"

"I know how to ride," she said. This was, if not a lie, then the nearest thing. It would have been more truthful to say that she knew how one was *supposed* to ride. The actual execution had always eluded her. But this horse really was as docile as Roland claimed, and certainly an experienced hunter, for it set off at a canter toward the sound of the horn, a moment ahead of Josette's kick. Josette attempted to convince herself that the horse's presumption was not a commentary on her skill as a rider, but found that it took a conscious effort to not resent the animal.

"Nicely done," Roland said, joining her on her left.

"Indeed," said Bernat, coming up on the right. "My compliments to the cargo."

Together, they crested a hill to find the rest of the hunt spread out across the landscape ahead. The pack of shikoku hounds was halfway up the next hill, and the majority of the horsemen just reaching the valley behind them. The pack suddenly veered to the right, began howling madly, and entered the woods. The horsemen skirted the edge of the trees, galloping through the snow as they steered a course around.

"I'm not sure I entirely understand this sport," Josette called, reining in to keep her mount from speeding to a gallop. "The dogs catch the scent of the deer?"

"Yes," Roland called back.

"And the dogs catch the deer?"

"When possible," Bernat said.

"And they kill the deer?"

"They often do, though it's considered an honor to get to the prey before they're finished with it, and land the killing blow." He patted the spear holstered against his horse's flank.

They were in the valley now, with the other riders out of sight, and her mount champing in distress at being left so far behind the field. "Then it seems to me," Josette said, once she was reasonably convinced that the animal was under control, "that the dogs are doing all the work. Why are we here at all? Do the duke's hounds not know the way home?"

"You're missing a critical component," Roland said, laughing. "After the hounds have done all the work, we take the carcass away before they can eat it."

She wrinkled her nose. "This is truly the perfect sport for the aristocracy."

BERNAT WAS HAPPY to have Josette along, as her timidity in the saddle left him an excuse to ride smoothly and not over-tax his leg. If it were only Roland along, the swine would surely have pushed ahead to taunt him. As it was, they rode at an even pace and took no shortcuts over fences or difficult terrain, and Bernat's leg was merely in agony—nothing more—by the time a spotted deer was scented, caught, and killed amid a thick wood.

The antlers were awarded to Duke Royama, who had finished the quarry off with a spear thrust through the heart. He had been first to reach the quarry by virtue of everyone in his way suffering simultaneous confusion as to whether the deer could be found at bay amidst the pack of barking shikokus, or off in some other direction entirely.

As Bernat's little party of three approached the rest of the field, slowing to a walk, Josette stood in the stirrups to see what was happening. "Is that it?" she asked, as servants retrieved the deer carcass and hoisted it onto a horse.

"You hoped for more?" Bernat asked.

"I only thought it would go on longer. We spent more time waiting than we did chasing."

"It will be more engaging," Roland explained, "once you become more comfortable on a horse. Then it's a wonderful ride: all gallop and leap and tally-ho. Quite invigorating, really."

"I'm sorry we held you back from it," she said.

"We?" Bernat asked, but was ignored as usual.

"Don't apologize," Roland said. "I wouldn't have traded this ride for the world."

Bernat flashed a sly smile and said, "For, I dare say, he has in mind a different sort of gallop and leap and tally-ho. Though it's every bit as invigorating, I'm sure."

Josette turned in the saddle, but Bernat stepped his horse neatly to the side, so that she wouldn't be able to hurt him. True to his expectations, she tried to hit him with her riding crop, but being unable to coax her horse into sidestepping, she only managed to slash at the air.

Ignoring her feeble attempts, with his glee concealed under an impassive expression, Bernat said blithely to Roland, "Shall we follow the rest of the field to breakfast, or just mill about in the woods like idiots?"

Roland circled his horse around and broke into a trot, using his hand to smack Bernat across the back of the head on his way past.

BY THE TIME the hunting party returned to the duke's chateau, his men had set two long tables topped with sumptuous pastries, sweetmeats, spiced juices, and sparkling wine. The servants ran about, wearing black riding vests and red horo cloaks that puffed out into a balloon shape when they were moving fast enough. Until now, Josette had only seen the horo cloak in old paintings, where it denoted an elite warrior, but to Duke Royama it apparently denoted the men who fetched his morning meal. It was undeniable, however, that they were elite among breakfast-fetchers. Everything set on the tables was fresh and delicious, and it would have been a truly lovely breakfast if there weren't a bunch of horses shitting on the lawn, only a dozen paces away.

Josette was biting into a small tamarind pie and looking pointedly away from the creatures when Bernat hobbled up to her and set his cane against the table. He stood there, catching his breath.

"You really shouldn't be exerting yourself so much," Josette said, glancing at the cane and wondering if he shouldn't still be on crutches. "You'll only make it worse."

"I appreciate the concern," he said, with apparent sincerity, though you could never really know with him. "But we must offer our congratulations to the duke. Where the hell is Roland? The villain ought to be helping you through this."

"Roland tried to bring me over, but before we could say a word, the duke sent him to check on the coffee. There were half a dozen servants within arm's reach and he sent the heir to Copia Lugon."

Bernat was not offended, but rather terrified. "Tell me you didn't speak to the duke by yourself."

"No," Josette said, not meeting his eyes. "I ran and hid."

He drew a deep breath and laid a hand on her shoulder. "You did the right thing. But now that I'm here, we must introduce you at once, before the coffee does come out."

She arched an eyebrow at him.

"Duke Royama becomes irascible under its influence."

Josette sighed and tossed the other half of her pie to the horses. "You people are a goddamn mess," she said.

He smiled back to her, wiping sweat from his forehead, though it was quite chilly. "And yet you must humor us, if you wish to make something of your time here."

They approached the duke at Bernat's best pace, which was not considerable, so Josette had plenty of time to remember the proper form of address. When they arrived, she said, "Congratulations, Your Grace. The antlers—"

"Trophy," Bernat said.

"The trophy was well won."

The duke studied them both. He was a rotund man, tall and imposing in his black hunting jacket. He wore two blades at his waist, a rapier and a dirk—a long and a short weapon, in the style that for centuries of Garnian history was allowed only to the aristocracy. He didn't quite ignore her, but only flashed a wide grin that seemed to say he was setting her aside. To Bernat, he said in a deep, gravelly voice, "You're one of the Hinkal boys?"

"Bernat, Your Grace," he said.

"The younger one, yes." The duke worked his jaw for a while, as if chewing cud. With a grunt and a nod, he indicated that he was finished with Bernat for the moment, and turned his attention back to Josette. "I noticed you took no risk of showing me up, this time. Stuck well to the rear, no doubt on the wise council of your two advisors."

She opened her mouth to speak, but couldn't find the words.

The duke went on, regardless. "I'm not quite as stupid as they think me. Though I am every bit as impatient, so I wonder at seeing you still here, and not out fighting the war."

This was the first time anyone had mentioned the war at such an outing, and Josette was taken off guard. She stumbled and stuttered, and began to speak three times, but managed nothing coherent.

Again, the duke went on, as if he hadn't been expecting a

reply at all, and indeed wouldn't have welcomed one, but was only pausing to think of the next thing he wished to say. "That's my land you're defending. Did you know that? The king's father fought for my claim on that land. I fought. My sons fought." Josette wondered what the duke meant by "fought," for she didn't imagine that it involved being shot at overmuch. "And now it's being dribbled away, piece by piece, by incompetents and cowards. We may not have lost a war in three generations, but our present king is doing his best to break with tradition."

At this, the duke looked at Bernat, who only bowed and said, "As you say, Your Grace."

His gaze swung back to Josette. "And you on the ground, going on hunts. Why aren't you in the air?"

She very much wanted to remind him that he'd invited her to this hunt, and that such an invitation could not be refused. But Bernat helpfully whacked her in the ankle with his cane, to indicate the foolishness of such a course. "*Mistral* has six weeks of repairs ahead of her," she said instead. "And that fig-ure assumes we'll have luftgas enough to float her, and spare parts to overhaul the steamjack."

He grunted. "Six weeks, eh?"

Josette looked him straight in the eyes. "If not longer. Apart from the crash, we took quite a thumping over Canard."

It seemed at first that he would grow angry, but then he grinned and said, "I hear that you also gave quite a thumping. In Vinzhalia, they're calling you 'The Shark,' because you always get in close to bite. Did you know that?"

It occurred to Josette that any animal must get in close to bite—that, indeed, was practically part of the definition of biting. But she spoke respectfully. "I did not know that, Your Grace. By their fear, they honor me."

"Ha! I only wish that our idiot king—may God preserve

him—had half the spirit of a goddamn woman." He looked over the top of her head and his eyes brightened. "Ah, finally, the coffee."

Josette had already resolved to hold her tongue, so the sting of Bernat's cane against her leg went to waste. Roland appeared next to her, off the opposite shoulder to Bernat, and said to the duke, "The coffee, Your Grace."

Josette took the cup that Roland offered next to her, and sipped quietly at the rim.

"Now," the duke said, taking a gulp from his steaming cup and ignoring Roland entirely, "we'll soon be going on the offensive up north, and throwing everything we have into a winter campaign that ought to catch the Vins off guard. That took some doing, let me tell you. The generals, the rest of the king's council? They're not as bold as you and me. And that's why I want your ship to be up there, if not for the opening moves of the campaign, then at least screening the advance following our initial success. The sooner the better. Your ship's technological edge won't last forever."

"Indeed," Josette said. "The Vins' aeronautical engineers are as talented as ours, God help them. Now that they've seen *Mistral* in action, they'll soon appreciate the principles behind her, and have ships like her within a year or two. That's assuming one of their spies hasn't stolen the plans already. But I'm afraid that, without enough luftgas, *Mistral* will be wasted even if deployed. With inflammable air, we'd go up like a sulfur match the first time they threw a shell or a carcass round at us. In those circumstances, a blimp would fight as effectively as Garnia's most advanced airship." She received another whack from Bernat's cane, and a kick from Roland on the other leg, and added a hasty, "Your Grace."

In response to the duke's peevish, skeptical glare, Bernat leapt in with, "If anything, Captain Dupre understates the danger of flying with inflammable air. I traveled aboard *Mistral* for not more than a month, Your Grace, and in that time she suffered . . ." He began counting on his fingers, but soon ran out. "Somewhere above ten separate fires."

The duke looked no less skeptical. "I think you need to take better care of your ship, Captain."

Josette held her ground. "Your Grace, that sentiment is not always compatible with the needs of the army."

He lifted his cup and took another sip. When he lowered it again, it revealed a wide, toothy grin pointing down at her. "I do like your spirit, Captain. I'll purchase the luftgas your ship needs, and get Laurent working on your spare steamjack parts. And, in return, you will help to ensure that this offensive succeeds. I want to read reports saying that the skies over Quah have been swept clean of Vin airships, that our army advances without risk of observation, while the enemy's every move is known from the moment they make it. And I want to start reading those reports as early as possible."

It took real strength to keep herself from throwing her arms around the duke and declaring him the finest gentleman in all creation. By an admirable exertion, she limited herself to saying, "I will make every effort, Your Grace."

"Good, good," he said, looking toward the other guests, as if picking out the next item on his list of chores.

Bernat slapped her lightly on the shoulder by way of congratulations. She expected much the same from Roland, but when she looked at him, he had to draw up a smile to cover the warring feelings underneath. She had no eye for emotions, but she could see the regret in him—and if not regret, then outright self-reproach—for setting her on the path that would see her ship restored and herself leaving Kuchin.

But this was merely a momentary weakness, she was certain. She set the matter aside, and turned to something more pressing. "And, if I may ask Your Grace's indulgence for only a moment more," she said to the duke, "what are your thoughts on retaking Durum?"

"What?" he asked. And then he seemed to remember the subject. He snorted. "No. Durum would be a fatal distraction." With that he simply walked away from them without another word, or even a glance.

"You nearly pressed your luck too far," Roland said, when the duke was gone. "It's fortunate he paid hardly any attention to that question. It means he'll likely forget you ever asked it."

Bernat gave her another friendly slap on the shoulder, and smiled proudly. "You've made an ally of a very powerful man. Don't think it'll end with luftgas and engine parts. Perhaps, if you do well up north, he might even offer one of his less important sons to you. That would be nice, wouldn't it? A trade up, certainly, from the fool who's courting you now."

She waved the notion away, but nothing could sour her mood—not even Bernat's attitude, or the fight that seemed to be brewing between him and Roland. "The Vins are calling me 'The Shark,'" she mused. "Because I always get in close to bite. Had you heard that, Roland?"

"The Shark," Roland repeated, with a grin. "I like the sound of it. Very menacing."

"I had not heard it before now," Bernat said, then frowned. "But doesn't any animal have to get in close to bite? It's not as if that's unique to sharks."

She rolled her eyes and asked, "Must you always be so contrary?"

6

For two weeks, Bernat avoided the air base, lest he run into his insufferable brother visiting Josette. By the third week, however, the weather had taken a hard turn toward a cold winter, and he had to go back to *Mistral* for his russet kariginu robe, which would pair so well with his white cravat and red pantaloons, matching this season's winter fashions in Kuchin—and the warm wool lining would, incidentally, keep him from freezing to death.

He'd snuck onto the ship stealthily enough, confirming by the pale morning light that no one was working on the keel, and that the ship was perfectly silent. But when he retrieved his robe and turned to leave, Josette was standing behind him.

"Gah!" he screamed, throwing his bundle into the air and nearly falling backward onto the wicker catwalk.

She stood, impassive, and put a hand on her hip. "You startle too easily. People will think you have soldier's heart."

He looked up into the superstructure of the ship, a wide, empty cavern crisscrossed by lines now that the luftgas bags were deflated. Had she descended from one of them like a spider?

He calmed himself and asked, "Soldier's heart?"

"Something soldiers sometimes get when they've seen too much. Where do you suppose my luftgas is?"

"I'm just going to see it now. It's invited me for breakfast." He squeezed past her and walked toward the companionway—in no particular hurry, lest running away invoke some deep predatory instinct in Josette, inciting her to wrap him in silk and hang him from the girders for later consumption.

"Haven't seen you around in a while," she said, following.

"I would have been by earlier, but I was detained on state business."

Josette snorted, and he could hear the smirk in her voice when she asked, "And this state business, what's her name?"

"Lidia," he said, grinning wide. "And she can put her legs behind her head."

Another snort. "I'm sure she has a rich career in dance ahead of her."

"Oh, I hope not. She's a diplomat from Sotra. You've met her, now that I think of it. At Count Stoger's luncheon. Remember?"

Josette only muttered, "The things you people get up to, I cannot understand."

He laughed. "Not everyone finds pleasure lamentable, Josette. A brave few are actually quite fond of it."

"You say that, of course, but what would you think of me if I went off and bedded some limber Sotrian diplomat?"

They had reached the top of the companionway steps, so he paused and turned to her. "I'd be happy for you, of course, because I am not a jackass." He laughed again at the absurdity of the question.

"And if I bedded your brother?"

His laughter ceased in an instant. "That is a different matter entirely." He grew anxious, and a chill cut through him despite the relative warmth inside the ship. "You're not actually thinking of it, are you?"

She shrugged. "We're seeing each other tonight and . . . it's not impossible."

"Good God!" It took him a little while to adjust to this grim new reality. "Do you love him?" he asked.

She did not meet his gaze, even for a second. "It's not as simple as that."

He made his best impression of Josette's indignant snort. "It is that simple, actually. It's a very simple question, in fact, made complex only by fear of the answer." When she said nothing, he went on, "What could possibly drive you to consider this? The man's a twit! And I knew he was a twit even when I was a twit!"

"You're still a twit."

"Then think of how much more of a twit he must be!" He tried to calm himself. "And an oblivious twit, at that. He and the rest of that pack of idiots have constructed their opulent façade, their illusion of peace. They've all built a throne of delusion, and they sit upon it, up to their heads in champagne and optimism, while outside the country is going to hell. We've seen men with their guts ripped open and their brains spilled out, while he thinks the war is a delightful little distraction—something cheerful to read about in the morning newspaper, though only when one is in the proper mood for it, of course."

"That is true," she said, so quiet he could hardly hear.

"Then what on Earth do you see in him?"

She faced him, flashing a peculiar little smile. "I was wondering myself, until you hit upon it."

He stood perplexed.

"I mean, don't you think I've earned it?"

"Earned what?" he asked, growing impatient.

"A moment's peace, however illusory it may be."

He looked at her sympathetically. "Surely there are enough oblivious twits in this town that it doesn't have to be him. Give me a day—give me an hour!—and I'll bring you a baker's dozen to pick from. Why does it have to be *him*?"

"And why not him?" she asked. "Is it only that you wish he were lonely and miserable?"

"Not primarily," he said. "My chief concern is your well-being, though of course I want my brother to be lonely and miserable. Does that make me such a bad person?"

"That, among other things."

Bernat tried to think of an argument that might sway her, but if he couldn't sway her with the simple fact that his brother was a no-good vermin—as was plainly obvious to all—then what else could he possibly say? "If you won't listen to reason, at least let me give you the address of a good apothecary. If you're going to sleep with my brother, you'll require protection against a whole host of sexual diseases."

"I have girders to inspect." She gave him a curt nod. Without another word she hauled herself up by an overhead girder, and climbed into the vast superstructure.

SHE HADN'T NOTICED how dark it had become, nor how quiet. Up in the superstructure of frame one, just ahead of the tail, she squeezed through a gap in the web of rigging cables and wedged herself in. With lantern in hand, its light flickering upon the keel thirty feet below, she inspected the joints of a newly installed longitudinal girder. They were sound, as all had been so far, and there were only two hundred and seventy-eight left to check.

She climbed farther up, one hand on the rigging and one on the lantern, weaving through the network of cables, until she came to the next longitudinal box girder. As she held up the lantern to inspect it, she heard from below, "Hello up there! Permission to come aboard?" It was Roland.

Despite needing a lantern, it was only now that she became truly cognizant of the darkness outside the ship's canvas skin, and the quiet in the shed now that everyone else had left for the night. "No, don't come aboard," she called, shouting through the canvas. "I'll come down to you. What time is it?"

"After eight," Roland called back.

"Hell." She slid down one of the transverse cables that cut athwartships from port to starboard, then down another going the other way, and from there it was a short hop down to the keel girders and then to catwalk.

Roland was waiting for her on the shed floor, near the hurricane deck. They embraced and, after a quick glance toward the shed door to be sure the carriage driver couldn't see, she kissed him. Indeed, she went on kissing him for quite some time, with brief interruptions to check for voyeurs. Despite the awkwardness commensurate with so much caution, the impulse to inspect girders for the rest of the night gradually abated, until it was hardly noticeable at all.

When they finally leaned apart, Roland asked, "Where would you like to have dinner?"

"Wherever is farthest from the palace and politics and the war," she answered.

"I know just the place," he said, snapping his fingers. "It's in Utarma, so we'll have to take a ship to the other side of the world. But if we leave now, and skip dessert, we can be back in only two or three years."

"Wonderful," she said with a smile. "Let's go."

He seemed almost to consider it, or at least something along the same vein. She had heard talk of establishing an aerial signal base in Utarma, and it wasn't unheard of for noblemen to travel there with the aim of securing property, so the thought was not quite as absurd as it had first seemed. It was still rather absurd, however, and he seemed to realize this at the same moment she did. They both laughed.

"Perhaps someplace a bit closer for this evening?" he said. "I know a place just outside the city. Excellent food, private rooms upstairs, and a variety of dishes to choose from every night, prepared individually. But the restaurant has no name, which is not quite the fashion in gastronomy these days, so it's been left pretty much alone by the palace set."

"That sounds perfect," she said, offering her arm.

He took it, and they strolled down the length of *Mistral*, he tilting his head back the whole way and marveling at the ship, while she kept her eyes ahead. A burst of chill air met them outside the shed, which didn't concern Josette until she saw that the carriage had no roof.

"An open carriage?" Josette asked.

"I expected it to be warmer," Roland said. "It was warmer when I made the arrangements for the carriage. But we have plenty of warm blankets. I saw to that before I left the palace."

"Aha," she said, smirking. "You saw to warm blankets, but regrettably couldn't find a warmer carriage?"

He smirked back. "They're in great demand, you know. Hard to get one on short notice."

He helped her up. The blankets lay folded on the rear seat, which was just wide enough for both of them to fit. Her smirk grew, and threatened to turn into an outright smile. "And harder yet," she said, "to get a carriage wide enough for two people to sit next to each other with any space left between them."

"Oh, indeed," he said, stepping up and lifting the blanket. He slid down next to her, hip to hip, with not an inch to spare, and spread the blanket across them. "Practically impossible, with the demand so high at this time of year." And then to the driver, he instructed, "Down the Ager Beatus and across town, please. I'll direct you from there."

In the air service, Josette had long since grown accustomed

to the cold, but she pretended a chill and said, "I wouldn't say it's very warm under here."

"Give it a minute," he said.

AT THE SAME moment, Bernat was also giving directions to a palace coachman—or rather, relaying them. The coach had stopped in front of a man dressed in the smudged white trousers and gray shirt of a signal base yardsman, and the yardsman was telling Bernat how to reach the closest tavern. Bernat, with half his body stuck out the carriage window, was relaying those directions up to the carriage driver, who—being only a couple of feet away—was in as good a position as Bernat to hear what the yardsman was saying.

Despite hearing the directions twice, however, it took him a surprising amount of time to find the destination. This, as it turned out, was not a fault in the directions, but a fault in the tavern itself. Instead of facing the street and presenting signage like any sensible establishment, this tavern was hidden behind a bakery, its entrance tucked into a narrow side street that was hardly wide enough for two men to walk side by side. Bernat stepped down the alley and into the tavern, and leaned on his cane to have a rest while he looked about the place.

The unvarnished wooden floorboards were warped and cracked, with splinters sticking out of them at odd angles. The three long tables were fairly falling apart, held together by makeshift repairs, and none of them quite level. The only thing this place had over the dives in Arle was that the windows weren't blackened by soot from the manufactories, so the patrons had a clear view of the snow-covered trash pile in the alley outside. But at least Bernat's knee, which had begun to ache from the cold the minute he left his carriage, was now only aching from the muggy warmth, which was an altogether superior sort of pain.

"My lord, back here," came a familiar voice from the rear corner. It was Sergeant Jutes—the last person Bernat expected to give him such an enthusiastic welcome. Though he had never tested the proposition before now, he'd always thought that Jutes would casually hide his face if he saw Bernat come into a tavern where he was drinking.

He made his way to the back, where Jutes was alone and brooding, and had a third of a table to himself. "Good to see you here, Sergeant," Bernat said, as he sat and removed his gloves. "Do you expect any other Mistrals tonight?"

"Likely not," Jutes said, motioning to the serving girl for another drink. "The lads have switched to Heloise's, a few blocks over. I think they find this place a bit too swanky for their tastes."

Bernat took a ceramic mug from the serving girl and sipped at the frothy head. It tasted like horse piss and turpentine. "And you don't?" he asked, once he got his tongue working again.

"Don't know about that, sir," Jutes said. "But I gotta maintain some distance, as their sergeant. Can't rightly go frolicking around with them at night, and call them a bunch of lazy slugs in the morning. Ain't proper."

"Didn't I hear tales of the captain drinking with the crew, in Durum?"

Jutes sucked on his front teeth and stared into his drink. "Mayhap that ain't the best idea she's ever had."

"Well, I'm going to be very honest with you, Sergeant," Bernat said, and swallowed a mouthful of his beer so fast he hardly had to taste it going down. "I plan to spend the night getting drunk and moaning about how rotten the world has become."

Jutes considered this in silence, over the course of several swigs of beer. Finally, he set his mug down on the table and said, "It just so happens that was my plan for the evening, too. With maybe a game of darts for variety."

They had passed half a game of darts in silence before Bernat said, "You don't talk much." He threw the last dart of his set, and missed the twenty he needed to win the game. "Blast."

"I have a rich inner life," Jutes said, taking his place on the line.

Bernat plucked the darts from the board, handed them over, and stepped out of the way. "Then you must have spent time reflecting upon the unnatural proclivities of your captain."

Jutes hit a bullseye, bringing him within striking distance of victory, though none would have known it from his expressionless look of concentration. "I didn't even know she was unnatural," Jutes said, calm as a millpond. "Plenty of men in the service are, but she must be the first woman I've met. Funny, I'd have taken Ensign Kember for one a' them, a'fore the captain."

"No, I mean," Bernat said, but was interrupted by Jutes making another throw. "I mean, what madness compels her to seek comfort in the arms of my idiot brother?"

Jutes, though he didn't bat an eye at him, seemed more surprised by this news than by his initial impression. "Couldn't speak to anything specific, my lord," he said, "but it's the air corps. If a person wasn't half mad, at least, they wouldn't be in it."

Bernat made a frustrated groan that drew a sidelong glance from Jutes, just as the man was lining up his third throw. "So what am I supposed to do?" Bernat asked. "Just stand by and let him . . . ooze his way into her heart?"

"Well, sir," Jutes said, rocking the dart rhythmically back and forth as he aimed, "whatever else one might say about the captain's heart, however much it may take to open it up, I dare say there's room in there for more than one sort of ooze."

He tossed his dart, hit the three dead center, and so won the game. His only celebration was a mute little nod.

"That is not what I'm worried about," Bernat said. "My only concern is for her well-being."

Jutes turned to look at him, and the sergeant's studious stare made Bernat uncomfortable almost immediately. "Can't see how her well-being's in danger," Jutes said. "Though I would warn you, my lord: the air corps ain't the place to look, if you need a friend. Not because they ain't good people, mind you, but because they're so apt to die on you."

Bernat muttered, "Which is . . . neither here nor there. I'm only concerned about her welfare. That's all."

"Just as you say, my lord." Jutes collected the darts and wiped the scores off of the slate. Four men, seeing the game over, were already queued up, waiting to play.

Bernat stood at the line and held his hand out for the darts. "We're going again," he said.

Jutes looked past him and said, "I think these fellows might be waiting on the board."

"Let them wait," Bernat said, without looking at them. "Say, Jutes? What do you know about soldier's heart?"

While Bernat lined up his first shot, the sergeant responded to his question with a long, thoughtful sigh.

THEY HAD A cozy table in the large salon room, not too far from the hearth fire, with a window looking out into the snow-caked woods. Roland had asked for a private room, but the restaurateur refused him, ostensibly on the grounds that there were none available. It was obvious, however, from the way he looked between Roland and Josette before answering, that this was not the reason.

"What was that about?" she asked, when they were seated.

Roland shook his head. "I must have mentioned to him that

I'm not married, on one of my previous visits. Some people look down on an unmarried couple dining together in a private room. I have to remember to be more discrete in the future."

"Indeed. Think of the scandal, if word got out that you were dining alone with a woman, without marrying her first. Why, all your peers would hold you in contempt, and their mistresses likewise."

He smirked back. "Surely. I think we've also hit upon the real reason this establishment is unpopular among the gentry." He looked over at the day's menu, written on a slate hanging on the far wall. "They do a superb herb-stuffed duckling here. Do you care at all for marjoram?"

"Hmm?"

"Marjoram herb. Do you care for it? It's only that there's quite a lot in the duckling."

"Is it imported or hot-house marjoram?" she asked.

"Hot-house, and picked this morning, I'm sure. Nothing less, at a place like this."

She scrunched her lips and furrowed her brow. "Minced or ground?"

"Ground," Roland said. "They grind it fresh for every dish, I believe."

Josette stroked her chin in contemplation. "Leaf only, or stems included?"

"Leaf only."

"Oh," she said, putting a hint of disappointment in her voice. "Well, in that case, I have no idea what the hell marjoram is."

Roland laughed in soft little gasps, no doubt to avoid drawing stares, as she fixed a grin on him.

She leaned across the table, and spoke in a mirthful whisper. "Now I'm sure, around here, they start you on marjoram from the moment you're weaned. But, where I'm from . . ." She trailed off and joined him in demure laughter. The glee didn't last, however, as the thought of Durum soured her mood. Her laugh trailed away as she looked back to the window, adding only, ". . . things are simpler."

She steeled herself for the sympathetic reassurances that must inevitably follow such a foolish moment of weakness. But somehow he knew better, reached across the table to squeeze her hand, and said nothing as she leaned toward the window to look out into the woods behind the restaurant.

The silence drew the neatly dressed serving boy over. "Ma'am?" he asked.

Josette leaned back from the window, and the alabaster woods disappeared behind her own reflection in the glass. "Suckling duck, was it?" she asked Roland.

"Stuffed duckling," he corrected.

She looked at the boy and said, "Stuffed duckling, for two."

"And a magnum of Gebyl," Roland added. "The '98, please."

"Gears had soldier's heart," Jutes said, standing off to the side and staring straight across the path of the darts, at a blank wall. "He used to scream out in the night, aboard ship."

Bernat swallowed hard. "He never did it aboard *Mistral*."

"Only 'cause, a couple years back, he noticed he clenched his fists before the screaming started. So he took to tying a sharp piece of wire around the end of one finger before he went to sleep, and if he clenched his fists in the night, it'd wake him up." He frowned. "What makes you ask about it?"

"No particular reason," Bernat said, staring at his feet. He looked up. "Was Gears hurt badly, in the airship crashes he survived? It must take a grievous wound to produce such dread."

"That's the bloody thing," Jutes said, laughing without

humor. "He came away from every one without a bloody scratch, just to die like that."

At the line, with a dart in his hand, Bernat said, "He was a good man."

Jutes laughed. "He was a scoundrel and a lecher."

"Just as I said." Bernat tossed the dart and hit his mark. He rested a moment before throwing the next, leaning on his cane. It had never occurred to him before, that the legs were the slightest bit involved in throwing darts, but it was occurring to him now with every galvanic spasm that wracked his poor knee.

"How's that leg doing, my lord?" Jutes asked.

"Better," Bernat said. "Yours?"

"Still gives me trouble, now and again, but most days I hardly notice it. Just a twinge when I walk, really. Nothing more."

Bernat stood straight, letting his cane lean against his hip. He threw and hit a five—not very detrimental to his current game, but not what he was aiming for. "Goddamn it," he muttered, as he hobbled off to sit nearby, leaving Jutes to retrieve the darts.

"Yer just having an off night, is all. Happens to the best of us, my lord, and likewise to such as you."

Bernat couldn't help but grin. "Sergeant Jutes, you've insulted me," he said, and saw the man tense in response. "I'm touched."

"Well, you're one of us now, sir," Jutes said, relaxing. "As much as you may come to regret it." He threw and hit a twenty.

Bernat drained half a pint of rancid beer. "I already regret it. The air corps wrecks your body, tears your friends away, makes you stare into the face of death every day you're aloft, and what does it ever give back?"

Jutes threw another twenty, which put him nineteen away from winning the game. "Not rightly sure, sir. If you ever do work it out, be sure to let me know."

"You'll be the first."

And with that, Jutes threw a nineteen to win.

"Damn it, man! How do you do it?" Bernat asked, more in wonder than irritation.

"For one thing, sir, I drink about half as much as you do."

Bernat could hardly deny it, for the evidence was pouring down his throat at that very moment. He held up his finger to beg patience as he finished off the pint, slapped the mug down on the table, and answered Jutes with a loud and vulgar belch. "That may be so," he finally concluded.

A quartet of rough men rose from their seats and approached the board, looking a threatening question at Bernat. They were not the same men who wanted to play earlier, he thought, though they shared a similar odor. Perhaps they were related.

"Another game!" Bernat said, sparing them the briefest glance before rising, cane in hand. "We're going to play until I win one, Jutes."

Jutes looked serenely from the men to Bernat. "Is that fair, sir?"

Bernat grinned. "Fair? Not a bit, but what the hell's the point of being an aristocrat, if things are going to be fair?" He stood and walked toward the four rather large ruffians, ignoring the pain in his leg so he could keep his cane tight in his hand, ready to use as a club. "If these fellows have a problem with that, then we shall set them back in their place using the method historically preferred by the aristocracy: overwhelming violence."

The apparent leader of the little group, or at least the cleanest of them and the one with the most teeth, brought his face near Bernat's and said, "Now just calm down there, my fancy boy, and let us take our turn at the board."

"I am calm," Bernat said, and it wasn't a lie. "And if you don't turn around and walk away, you're going to be calm, too. The 'he looks so peaceful' sort of calm."

Bernat was about to add to his reply, when Jutes pulled him back by the collar and whispered, "This ain't like you, sir."

Bernat was perplexed. "But it must be like me, Jutes. I'm the one doing it."

"And what would 'it' be, exactly, sir? Just what the hell are you doing?"

He considered for a second. "I may be a smidge too drunk to be certain, but I believe I'm picking a fight with the nastiest sons of bitches in the room, because I don't like the way they looked at me. I'm perfectly content to continue alone, if the affair doesn't suit you."

Jutes sighed. "Ain't got nothing else to do, I suppose."

And so the brawling began.

"Did you enjoy dinner?"

As she settled into the carriage seat, Josette said, "It was superb, but . . ."

He raised a concerned eyebrow. "What is it?"

"Oh, I'm just wondering, what do you suppose first inspired someone to eat stuffed duckling?"

"Impatience?" he suggested.

She laughed. "And you, Lord Hinkal? Are you a very impatient man?"

He looked forward and feigned resentment. "That is a personal matter, between myself and the ducklings." Ahead of them, the carriage driver cleared his throat in a phlegmy rasp. Roland looked back to Josette and asked, "Where to now?"

"Where to?" It had to be at least ten o'clock. What did people do in this town at ten o'clock at night? She wanted to ask, but she was afraid of the answer. "I thought we'd head back to the palace."

With only the glow from the restaurant windows to light Roland's face, she couldn't be sure she'd seen disappointment in it, but it was clear when he spoke. "Forgive me my selfishness. It's just that you're only here for a few more weeks, if that. I'm trying to fit too much into what little of your time I have left."

She allowed herself a smirk only because she knew he wouldn't see it in the dark. In a quiet voice, she said, "In that case, Duckling, what would you say to returning to your room in the palace?"

The nerve-wracking silence lasted mere seconds, but she had ample time to imagine that she'd gone too far, and would be forever shamed by that one moment's impertinence. So it threw her when he answered, "Is yours not comfortably furnished?"

"It's very comfortable," she said, perhaps a little too hastily. She forced herself to slow down and think, and finally concluded the thought with, "but the night is very cold, isn't it?"

"And you suppose I have some secret artifice for warming myself?" he asked.

She could only chuckle and say, "I couldn't speak to that. But I'm sure we could collaborate on some scheme or another."

He leaned in and dropped his voice even lower. "Is it to be a scheme, then?"

"Lord Hinkal," she said, "you torment me with your refusal to catch my meaning."

He leaned back, just a bit. "Oh, I catch it, sure as anything," he said, "but I also worry that, should you change your mind on the way back, the rest of the ride will become rather awkward."

She smiled. "I wouldn't worry about that."

"Indeed?" he asked.

"Indeed."

7

Josette woke to a kiss on the cheek. She blinked away sleep, as the fuzzy blur in front of her resolved into Roland. "Good morning, Lord Hinkal," she said with a grin.

"And good morning to you, Lady Dupre," he said, returning a wider grin.

She laughed, and scooted over until her forehead and the tip of her nose were pressed to his. Looking into his eyes, she said, "It's still just 'Dupre.'"

He shook his head, rolling her head along with the motion, until his nose slipped and he took the opportunity to steal a kiss. "You see, that's why you don't do well with courtly life. If you're mistaken for a higher station, you should use that to your advantage. Who can ever be sure of their lineage, in any case?"

Entwining one leg with his, she said, "I can, and it isn't the sort of lineage that gets away with that sort of gambit. Anyway, what possible advantage would I need with you?"

He smirked. "Hardly any, it would seem."

She slid across the silk sheets, closing what little distance remained between them, and was just about to speak when a knock on the apartment door froze her solid.

"It's only the servant bringing breakfast," Roland said.

This did not assuage her worry. "You don't suppose any of them saw us coming in together?" she asked.

"Even if they did, they're known for their discretion."

But she couldn't take her eyes off the door, watching it as

if it might burst open at any moment, and all her most judgmental acquaintances pile through.

He sighed and rolled away. "Go check, if you're worried. All you'll find is a cheese and olive plate, the newspaper, and—if we're lucky—some mutton dumplings. They make wonderful mutton dumplings."

"You should go and check," she protested. "People expect this sort of thing from your sort."

He stuck his nose in the air and pushed out his lips in imitation of a pout. "I refuse. I'd rather my dumplings get cold, than indulge your paranoia and class-envy."

"With that attitude, I can assure you that your dumplings will be cold either way."

He tried to look hurt, by all appearances, but couldn't stop himself from chuckling. "Then I have even less incentive to check the door, don't I?"

She groaned with frustration, rolled over, and sat at the edge of the bed, looking for her clothes. Roland propped himself up on one elbow and laid there, admiring her as she dressed.

When she noticed him staring, she rolled her eyes. "There's nothing worth leering at."

"That's where you're wrong." He went on watching, and she pretended to ignore him. "You know," he said, "you do have a Vin tinge to your accent. It's quite subtle, but it comes out when you're . . ."

She narrowed her eyes at him.

He grinned and said, "Lively."

Shaking her head, she tiptoed to the door, cracked it open, and peeked out. There was, indeed, a breakfast tray sitting on the floor outside, and the servant who'd delivered it was just returning to bring a similar tray to the next apartment down the hall. His eyes flashed up, but before he could spot her, she ducked back into the room.

Still, she thought, if he saw the door open but didn't notice the tray disappear, he might come by to inquire about the problem. The safest possible course, therefore, was to retrieve the breakfast tray, including its plate of delicious-smelling dumplings. She stuck her bare foot out, hooked her big toe around the handle, and dragged the entire thing into the apartment. The carpet was thicker than she realized, however, and caused the silver plate to advance in little jerks, with the plates clattering all the way. The metallic racket was so loud it echoed up and down the hall.

"Masterful obfuscation," Roland said, even as she shushed him and closed the door. "You should have been a spy."

"It would have worked on a wicker deck," she said. She locked the door, picked up the tray and set it down on the bed, then sat on the corner. In addition to the newspaper—one of the broadsheets most sympathetic to the government, naturally, and bearing some melodramatic headline cut in half by the fold—there was a slip of paper with a handwritten reminder about a social affair in the afternoon. She read the latter reflexively, not quite meaning to snoop, but she lost all interest in it when she took her first bite of a dumpling. It was easily the best mutton dumpling she had ever tasted. She swallowed and asked, "Do you get these most days? They only leave me the cheese and olives."

Roland sat up, resting his shoulders against the headboard. "Once every few days, but you have to ask for them. You know, there's a table in the other room, if you prefer to eat breakfast like a civilized person."

"Who told you I'm civilized?" she asked, taking another bite and chewing. "Bring me the slanderous bastard, and I'll set him to rights."

She put the last of the dumpling in her mouth and reached for another before she'd even swallowed it. As she chewed, something about the newspaper caught her eye. Even with the headline folded over and unreadable, the top half of the line seemed strangely familiar. With her free hand, she unfolded the paper, and froze with a dumpling held in the air and a quarter of another between her teeth.

"You're not going to eat all my dumplings, are you?"

She didn't answer, didn't even acknowledge the question, but it snapped her out of her paralysis. She swallowed what was in her mouth and dropped the other dumpling onto the bedsheets in her haste to unfold the paper.

"Oh, come now," Roland said. "I was only teasing. Don't be cross. You know, it's the washer ladies who have to clean the sheets, so it's really only the small folk who'll be harmed by this little dumpling rebellion of yours."

"Shut up" was all she said, running her eyes across the front page.

It was only then that Roland realized something was wrong. He sat up straight, reached for his clothes, and asked, "What is it?"

She threw the paper at him and growled. "Your uncle has been defeated in Triese, in the very first battle of his vaunted winter offensive." She took a deep breath. "The army is falling back in shambles. Four thousand men are dead, wounded, or missing, and we're on the retreat again." She picked up the handwritten note that had accompanied the tray, made a show of reading it, and then added bitterly, "Oh, and Countess Miguelena would like to know if you'll be attending her luncheon party this afternoon."

Roland looked over the news. "Four thousand casualties," he said, "but nearly as many casualties inflicted on the Vins. See? In the greater picture, nothing has changed. We're still wearing them down."

"That is, I suppose, General Hinkal's one redeeming virtue: he doesn't lose an entire army all in one go. He portions it out to the Vins a few regiments at a time."

"But we're still wearing them down," Roland said again. "We haven't—"

"If you remind me that we haven't lost a war in three generations," Josette interrupted, shooting him a glare, "I cannot be held responsible for what I do to you." Her eyes unfocused. "My God, what have I been doing with myself? I have to see to my ship." She went to the floor and began looking for her missing boot.

Roland, not half dressed, stood and looked down at her. "What are you on about? You're not going north any sooner that you would have. The battle's already lost. Celerity, however admirable in appearance, can't change that now."

"Have we lost the battle?" she asked bitterly. "I'm told it's all part of a grand strategy to wear them down." She found the boot under the bed, just out of reach. She jammed her shoulder under it, as far as it would go, and stretched her arm to reach. Her fingers just barely touched leather, which she attempted to pull toward her without success.

Roland joined her on the floor and, with his longer arms, easily retrieved the boot. "Please don't be angry at me over something I can't control," he said, handing it to her. "You're not like that."

As she sat on the bed and pulled her boot on, she said, "Lord Hinkal, I am under no obligation to satisfy your notions of what I'm like."

He shook his head and looked at the ceiling. "This must be the side of you my uncle sees."

She began lacing up her boots. "And this must be the side of you that concerns itself with trivial matters in the face of calamity—the side of you that's exactly like every other overgrown child in this palace, the side that spends so much time doing the thinking for other people that you have hardly any left to think for yourself."

"Well, it also happens to be the side that's fallen in love with you." Her startled reaction checked him, and he stammered on, "I mean . . ." But his words trailed off.

Josette was no great judge of motive, but it seemed even to her that this slip was not nearly as spontaneous as it first seemed, that perhaps he had been working up to it before she'd noticed the newspaper, or even that he thought it would serve to calm their bickering—that she might fall promptly into his arms. It was the latest and quite possibly the last in a string of shortcuts he'd attempted to take, on the way to her heart.

"I have to see to my ship," was all she said as she left the apartment, one boot still unlaced.

DAWN CREPT UPON Kuchin, spreading its rosy fingers over quiet streets. Rich, orange sunlight sparkled through icicles hanging above pristine snow. At the edge of the river, a single marsh warbler lifted its voice into the chill air, proclaiming to the earth and sky with its merry trills and chirping notes that the desolation of winter was near its end, and that life would soon return with the coming of spring. And on an avenue near the airfield, suffused with the delectable, yeasty scent of baking bread, the sun crested the adjacent rooftops to pour its warmth onto the face of Lord Bernat Hinkal, who woke to the realization that he'd gone to bed on garbage again.

Sergeant Jutes was already up and, seeing that Bernat was stirring, offered him a hand up. Bernat took it and got to his feet, saying, "Slept well, Jutes?"

"Well enough, sir." Jutes's uniform was covered with stains of revolting origin, but he looked strangely chipper.

"Not too cold, I hope?" With a hand on Jutes to steady himself, Bernat felt his face. It was sore in several places, and his left eye was swollen half shut.

"Not at all. You warmed up the heap quite nicely. Next best thing to having a fire going."

Bernat smiled. "And they say I'm of no use. I, uh, didn't scream out in the night, did I?"

Jutes looked at him with an odd mix of surprise, concern, and helplessness. He shook his head. "Not that I heard."

Bernat nodded back as he looked Jutes over. In contrast to Bernat, Jutes didn't have a single bruise on his face, where even the slightest blemish would be obvious against his ivory skin. "You came off well."

"Tell that to my ribs," Jutes said. And though he grimaced, he seemed relieved to be on another subject. "A little trick of getting into bar fights while you're in the service, sir, is to get yourself hit where it don't show."

"I'll have to remember that for next time. Say, you haven't seen my cane about, have you?"

Jutes leaned over and came up with the mahogany cane. It was broken in several places, held together only by threads of wood fiber. "You came off pretty well yourself, sir," he said. "Compared to the fellows on the other end of this, at least."

"Damn." Bernat tried to take a step without it, and pain shot up his leg. Between the fight and the way he'd slept, his leg had regressed back through several weeks of healing.

"Let me help you to the signal base," Jutes said. "You can get a carriage to the palace from there."

The city woke as they made their way, and it seemed to wake with as big a hangover as theirs. Two carriages nearly ran them over in the street, racing past on their way to the signal base. Then a troop of dragoons, riding at a canter, nearly ran them over going the other way.

Half an hour after the dragoons passed, Bernat thought he heard a musket going off somewhere far down the river, near the heart of the city. He heard another when they were halfway to the base, and he was certain this time, even though they were farther away. More faraway muskets popped off as they walked, until it seemed that someone must have started a riot. At a bend in the river, on the outskirts of town, they had a clear view of the city skyline, and could see smoke rising from the Tellurian Quarter.

Bernat wondered, as they approached the signal base, if it was also experiencing a riot. There was certainly a lot of smoke and dust going up, and panicked yardsmen running in every direction. The place seemed to be on the verge of mayhem, but Jutes pointed out that the smoke was from fires set to clear out brush on the expansive grounds, and the dust from teams of mules dragging logs to level the earth.

Jutes offered to help him to the shed, but Bernat insisted that Jutes use the opportunity presented by this chaos to sneak off and change into a clean uniform. So Bernat was left hobbling along the shed door, until he spotted Josette yelling at some crewmen. He waved her over.

As she came near, she began by berating him about not having his cane, but switched tacks when she approached within reach of his scent. "You smell worse than you look," she said, shaking her head, "and that's saying something."

"What happened was—"

But before he could explain, she waved the matter away. "You're not the first airman to start a brawl." She leaned in and sniffed. "Though you may be the first to do so on a compost heap."

He wondered how she knew that he'd started it, but he didn't want her thinking she had some special insight into the workings of his mind, so he asked instead, "What the hell is going on? We heard muskets in the city."

"Your uncle is what's going on."

Bernat frowned in confusion. "What, have they shot him?"

She snorted. "They ought to." She was about to put an arm

under his to help him walk, but thought better of it and called for a yardsman to bring a plank and a few feet of sailcloth. "He lost four thousand men in Quah, and now they're scrambling to replace them. A quarter of all militia regiments have been activated for regular army service, and the exemption from conscription has been lifted for university students, among others. Soldiers from the city garrison have been trying to round them up before they can flee town—and making a goddamn mess of it, of course. But you'll be pleased to know that palace servants are still on the exempt list."

"That does not please me." Bernat looked out at the parties clearing the grounds. "Are the new conscripts from Kuchin to be trained here, at the signal base?"

"I have no idea, but the levee notice had a bit in it that said, 'national buildings are to be used as barracks, and open spaces as encampments.' I think it was more of a rhetorical flourish than a specific instruction, but Colonel Shihi, the base commander, is taking it seriously." The yardsman had arrived with plank and sailcloth, which Josette assembled into a makeshift crutch.

With some of his mobility restored, Bernat followed Josette as she made a circuit around her ship. "Not as many at work on her as I'd have thought," he said.

"I had to fight for this many," she answered. "The colonel wanted all the yardsmen clearing brush, and the ships' crews on top of them. It's been a goddamn madhouse."

"How did your rendezvous go? As well as the war, I hope."

The embarrassed look, and the pause before answering, told him everything he needed to know. "None of your damn business," she said, far too late.

"So you did sleep with him." It was a statement, not a question. "I find your desperation equal parts tragic and hilarious. You took precautions, of course?"

She still didn't look at him. "Of course, and I should have

taken precautions against his goddamn insincere affectations, as well." When Bernat did not comment on this, she turned to him, looked again to see that no one else was within earshot, and added, "I suppose he lets slip a declaration of true love to all of his conquests, and pretends it was an accident?"

He thought he had misheard her, and stammered through several seconds before he realized that he hadn't. "Yes, of course," he finally spat out. "He's pulled that trick on half the whores in the city. 'Roland's Gambit,' they call it."

She turned toward him, and he could see in her face that she wasn't buying it. "Good God," she muttered. "You don't suppose he means it?"

"Of course he doesn't mean it. How could such an absurd thought even enter your mind? You're usually far too sensible to even consider such nonsense."

"No, he can't possibly mean it." She spoke as if he'd said the exact opposite of his actual words, which perhaps he had by too much insistence. "And my accent does not have any Vin in it! I don't even have an accent!"

Bernat had never noticed any Vin in Josette's slight Durum accent before, but he could hear it now that she'd mentioned it. "No, you certainly don't have an accent, and certainly no trace of Vin," he said, adding a lie to an impossibility. "Perhaps the best thing you can do now is to concentrate on getting the ship ready. There's no better cure for an awkward romance than to literally fly from town."

She mulled it over, then nodded. With a smile, she said, "You're a good friend, Bernie."

"Yes," he said, now that she was finally talking sense. "I am that."

IT WAS AN entire battalion of boys, hardly older than herself. A week ago, they'd been studying at one of the city's prestigious universities. In a few weeks more, they'd be at the front, killing and being killed. More the second than the first, Ensign Kember thought, if they didn't shape up quickly.

One of the battalion's eight infantry companies was at musket practice, and Kember watched them as she ate her lunch of rice, miso, and river char atop a barrel next to the shed. These boys had been training for a week now, but only a handful of the company's hundred soldiers could load and fire their muskets in under a minute. Even Lord Hinkal could beat that, while any half-decent musketeer was expected to fire three aimed shots per minute.

As she watched, one of their muskets hung fire, its priming powder fizzling in the pan. When the fizzling stopped, he held the musket up to inspect it, and it went off a second later, careening into his shoulder and recoiling sharply up to hit him in the face. He was bleeding from the nose and missing a tooth when he stepped off the firing line, leaving his weapon smoking on the grass.

It must have set off the nerves of the other boys, for their firing practice became even more sporadic and clumsy. Flints sparked into empty pans that they'd forgotten to prime. One of them loaded five full cartridges without firing in between. His sergeant stopped him when he raised the gun to shoot, before his suicide could ruin a perfectly good musket.

But with the sergeant occupied in screaming at that boy, another antsy lad managed to fire his musket with the ramrod still in the barrel. The rod flew like an arrow and embedded itself into the grass, twenty paces ahead of the firing line. And, in an apparent effort to multiply his stupidity, the boy ran after it and plucked it out of the green. Only a fool's luck and his compatriots' pathetic rate of fire saved him from being shot by one of them, for God knew their aim wouldn't preserve him.

"Have any of them hit a target yet?" The voice came from her left, where a junior lieutenant had snuck up on her while she was distracted by the clown show on the firing range. The lieutenant was a short, stocky young man with an absurd little beard that came to a point at the bottom of his chin. He took a long, sucking pull from a cigarillo, as if trying to draw as much from it as possible between breaths.

He wasn't in her chain of command, and they weren't so different in rank, so Ensign Kember supposed she was allowed to answer informally. "A few," she said. "By accident, probably."

He let the smoke out of his lungs in a wheezing chuckle. "Well, so much of being a soldier is luck, anyway. The ones that luck picks for survival will harden up soon enough. It all works itself out in the end, whether they get a lot of training or a little."

"If they could be trained longer, perhaps luck would pick more of them to survive and be hardened up," she said, a little angrier than she'd intended. "And they'd be less likely to get others killed, besides."

The bastard laughed at her, took another drag from his cigarillo, and said, "And what the hell would an auxiliary ensign—a little girl—know about that?"

She turned fully toward him, and saw his eyes widen when he noticed her scar. She wore no concealer today—she'd learned the hard way to forego makeup on days when the still-tender wound looked inflamed. The scar was a variegated canyon running up her neck and onto her cheek. His eyes froze on it.

"No smoking within twenty paces of the shed," she said in a calm and even tone.

He looked ready to argue, but her unflinching stare must have cowed him, for he dropped the cigarillo and stamped it out with his foot. "Happy, Ensign?" he asked, putting emphasis on her lower rank.

"Yes, sir," she answered, with as much respect as she judged necessary. Her lunch finished, she returned to the shed without another word.

Mistral, quite unlike the infantry outside, was at least coming along. The rubber gas bag had been replaced with goldbeater's. Most of the new girders were in, the spliced rigging lines replaced with fresh rope, and the new canvas was going up even now. The steamjack was still a mess, but at least it wasn't catching fire quite as often. And structurally, at least, the ship was good as new. Probably better, in fact, with the new modifications the captain was making to the tail.

Kember set to her work of inspecting and aligning the sights on the new cannon. She'd been at it for a while when the captain's voice came from the shed floor. "Kember, is that you up there?"

She stuck her head above the rail of the hurricane deck. "Sir?"

The junior lieutenant from earlier stood now at the captain's side, on the shed floor below. "This is Lieutenant Hanon, our new first officer."

"We've already met," Hanon said, fixing Kember with a wicked grin. "It's going to be a pleasure working with you, Ensign."

"Yes, sir," Ensign Kember said, smiling politely and hoping her thoughts didn't show on her face.

ENSIGN KEMBER HAD seemed rather cold, but perhaps that was to be expected, as Hanon's arrival spelled the end of her stint as acting first officer.

Josette led him to the tail, where the yardsmen were still working on the latest round of modifications. She waited to see Lieutenant Hanon's reaction—whether he appreciated the principles involved or blindly scoffed at the deviation from the ordinary. Perhaps, if he was sharp enough, he might even catch something she had missed.

Hanon was quiet for a while, until the silence of his captain seemed too much for him, and he said simply, "The engineers don't mind you making these changes?"

"Of course they mind," she answered. "They're engineers. Once they've hit upon a clever theory, they believe in it implicitly. They believe in it until it's been positively disproven, and sometimes until it's been disproven by several different methods."

He only nodded along, adding none of his own thoughts on the matter.

"Though I must give them some credit. *Mistral*'s a temperamental bitch, but even with two guns she's as nimble as a single-gun chasseur." Josette grinned with something like pride. "More nimble, if she likes you."

Lieutenant Hanon continued to nod, but remained silent.

She pointed up at the tail cage. "As you can see, my joint modifications borrow quite a bit from the articulated hinges of the old N-3's."

He made an appreciative grunt.

"Have you flown in many rigids?" she asked. Perhaps his experience was all in semi-rigid scouts, whose architecture worked on slightly different principles. She only hoped they hadn't assigned her a goddamn blimp jockey, though that would explain why she'd never heard his name before.

"I've only been up in blimps," he said, smiling apologetically. "But I was captain of them all, so I'll be happy to share the leadership role with you, if ever you feel overburdened with command."

"Thank you, Lieutenant," she said. "I don't expect that it will be necessary." She was only just keeping a lid on the flurry of curses she wanted to aim at him, when she spotted Bernat coming over. "Bernie," she said, as he limped the last few feet and paused to catch his breath. "Let me introduce Lieutenant Egmont Hanon, our new first officer. If you stay for a while, you can meet Warrant Officer Megusi as well. He's taking the chief mechanic post."

Bernat nodded in response to a bow from Hanon.

"Lieutenant Hanon," Josette went on, "this is Lord Bernat . . . Something Something . . . Hinkal. Lord Hinkal is serving as a supernumerary, filling the roles of rifleman and ship's mascot."

"And doing so with great pride," Bernat said, still out of breath. "Captain, may I speak to you privately?"

"If you'll excuse me," she said to Hanon, and strolled off with Bernat. "If it's another message from your goddamn brother, I'm not interested."

"No, it's . . ." He trailed off, peering at her. "Has he been sending you messages?"

"Three a day, on average, and showing up on the base at odd hours, but I've managed to avoid him so far."

Bernat considered this as he strolled along. "If you'd like to write a note letting him know it's over, I can deliver it. I promise I'll only gloat a little."

"I'm composing just such a note." This was true, but she did not add that she was also working on an entirely contrary note, professing her love for Roland and asking his forgiveness for leaving so discourteously. She planned to send whichever seemed the most appropriate, depending on how her feelings settled out in the meantime.

"Let me know as soon as you've finished it," Bernat said. Before she could say anything else about it, he went on, "You have an interview with the king this evening."

She stopped in place and stared mutely at him, thinking she'd misheard.

"You have to get into your best dress uniform, and we have to go," he said, speaking loud and slow. "I'll coach you as to the proper etiquette on the way."

When she'd recovered herself, she said, "I don't have time

for this. By the time we're back and forth between the palace, it'll cost us the rest of the day."

"Then the day will have to make do without us," Bernat said, "for one does not beg an audience with the king and not show up when it's granted."

"I didn't beg an audience! I didn't beg anything!"

"But an audience was begged on your behalf. By myself, by Roland, and apparently by my sister Nina, by way of the post."

This was too much to believe. He had to be playing a joke on her, though she couldn't possibly see the humor in it. "I've never even met your sister."

"No, but I've given accounts of you in several letters, and she quite admires you."

Josette snorted, more convinced than ever that she was being played upon. "You mean to say you've written flatteringly of me?"

"I didn't say that." He held up his hands, palms to the front. "I said that I've given account of you, and that she admires you greatly. How she arrived at one from the other is a mystery."

"All right. I'll play along."

"Yes, yes," he said, urging her toward the officers' quarters, "play along. Only hurry!"

EVEN IN THE carriage to the palace, Bernat was still fussing over the state of her uniform and coaching her on the proper etiquette of court interviews.

"Here's the protocol." he said. "Do not approach closer than the center of the room. Bow when you first enter the room, and then again when you stop. Address him only as 'Your Majesty,' and do so every time you speak. Do not make sudden motions. Do not look him directly in the eye. Do not, at any time, turn your back to him."

She frowned. "My father once gave me much the same list of instructions, in case I ever ran into a rabid dog."

"You are not the first to notice the similarities," he said, picking a speck of dust from one of her epaulettes. "Now hold still. You could use a bit of shadow about the eyes."

In the jostling carriage, she raised her hands to keep Bernat's makeup brush away from her face. "When we've stopped, Bernie."

He didn't resist. "Yes, yes, of course. I'm sorry, it's just . . . I'm just very nervous for you." He sighed. "I know how you can be, and if you're how you can be in front of him, you'll likely be a head on a spike the next time I see you."

She eyed him. "They don't really do that anymore, do they?"

"They haven't in a while," he said, waving his hands in agitation. "It doesn't mean they won't bring it back for the right person."

Josette went on eying him. "And this isn't some attempt at a reconciliation between Roland and me?"

Bernat was appalled. "Good God, no. Why in hell would I ever do something like that?"

"No, of course you wouldn't," she said, and looked out the window, beginning to look as nervous as she ought to be. "We're really going to meet the king, aren't we?"

"Well, of course we are!" he shouted.

"Pray control your voice," she said, low and icy.

"I'm sorry, I'm sorry," he said. He put a hand to his chest, worried he might be having palpitations. "It's only . . . this is a very big day for you."

IT WAS TRUE.

She hadn't quite believed it until she found herself standing in front of an ornately carved door trimmed in gold, waiting to go into the king's audience chamber. Two of the attendants were taking brushes to her uniform, in a manner that she found both too familiar and utterly pointless, as Bernat had already attended to the job with the diligence of one of those little birds that cleans the mouths of crocodiles.

Speaking of which, the man himself had just returned from getting an update on the king's schedule. "Stop, stop," Bernat said, slapping the wrists of the attendants. "Just stop. You're making her nervous. This is her first time seeing the king, for God's sake. You mustn't make her nervous!"

Josette only smirked and kept her eyes ahead.

"Duke Royama is in with him now," Bernat said, at a whisper. "Remember to smile, don't look him in the eye, and don't bring up Durum until he does."

"Why would he bring up Durum?" she asked.

Bernat stared at her a while, his face slowly contorting into a mask of dread and horror. "What do you think this is about? You're here to ask him to keep Durum in mind at the end of the war, when the treaties are being made."

Now she really was nervous. "But how do I do that? What if he doesn't bring it up?"

"He will," Bernat said. "It's all been worked out ahead of time by back channels."

"Then why am I here at all?"

"Well, you have to give the thing the appearance of spontaneity! Good God, how can you be so stupid about politics?"

The attendants took up station on either side of the doors, and slowly pushed them open. Inside, Duke Royama was still speaking to the king, and from far closer than the center of the room. In fact, he was leaning with one hand on the throne, and the two of them were whispering to each other.

Josette took a step forward, but Bernat whipped his cane up to bar her path. "No, stop!" he hissed. "The last one isn't done yet."

She came to a halt, whereupon one of the attendants scowled at her and flicked his head toward the chamber. "Go on," he whispered.

Bernat brought his cane around and gave her a push on the back. "Go on, go!" he said, as if he'd never said anything to the contrary. When she passed the threshold, he added, "Remember to bow!"

Hell, she really had forgotten. She wondered if she should back up, but in the end decided to bow from a few steps inside the chamber and hope the king wouldn't notice. She moved—not too fast, of course—to the center of the room. Duke Royama, still chatting with the king, looked over and nodded to her. She wondered if she ought to bow to him as well, but decided in the end that it must work the same way as saluting superior officers, and she bowed only to the highest in rank. And, amid all her confusion, King Leon the 18th happened to glance toward her and she accidentally looked him in the eyes. Damn. Now she'd done it.

She stood and waited for them to finish, reminding herself to not look impatient. But then, she couldn't remember what that was supposed to look like, and so she only ended up smiling like an idiot.

Mercifully, the duke gave a final nod to the king and turned to leave—turned his back fully on the royal personage, in fact.

"Oh, and Jack," the king said, seeming to remember something when the duke was nearly out of the room, by the back door. "I'm told that the farmers are displeased with the latest round of conscription."

Josette took note of the king's "I." Not the royal "we," which he perhaps withheld for close friends and dukes who owned a fifth of his country.

The duke stopped at the door and looked back. He considered it for a second, then gave a laugh that echoed through the chamber. "Even if that were true," he said, "who would ever know?"

The king scrunched up his face, his bushy gray eyebrows coming together in the middle. He adjusted his wire-rimmed glasses and said, "They would, for a start."

The duke chuckled politely, made a pale imitation of a bow, and said, "Your Majesty," as he left.

The king's gaze swung around to Josette, and she remembered to look slightly away this time. "You go up in one of those balloons?" he asked.

She swallowed, and remembered Bernat's comment about how she could be, and what that might lead to. "Yes, Your Majesty."

"Ah," the king said, running a finger across his mustache. "Though, now that I recall, I believe they are called airships, and not balloons." There was that "I" again.

She looked slightly up. They shared a small, secret smile. "That is correct, Your Majesty," she said.

Moments passed in silence, while he contemplated his next comment. "And how are you faring at it? When I had you made captain of an airship, they told me I was making a mistake. They told me a woman couldn't handle the strain."

She laughed, very softly, and said, "I'm holding up quite well, Your Majesty."

"I hear that you are." He shifted on the throne, leaning an elbow on the armrest. "And what do you think about the latest round of conscription?"

Though the king was being friendlier than she expected, she worried that this question was a trap. "It cannot be denied that the people are displeased," she said, carefully. "But I'm sure they recognize the necessity."

The king sniffed in a rather unkingly manner. "No doubt they do," he said. "It is, as you say, a necessity. But it's the sort of necessity a more dignified nation would at least have the decency to be ashamed of. Did you pass any of my vassals on your way in, who struck you as ashamed?"

She tried to think of something diplomatic to say. "The nobility remain enthusiastic about the prosecution of the war, Your Majesty. As far as I can see."

The king laughed. "Of course they would. They've got people to do their dying for them."

She said nothing, for she had the strangest impression that the king was using her as a means of speaking with himself.

He said, "There's nothing exceptionally bad about the aristocrats of Garnia, you know, except that they're all convinced they're the best of us."

"Yes, Your Majesty."

Her answer, as empty as it was, seemed to give him pause. "But then, I'm one to speak, eh?"

She said nothing, imagining spikes and silver platters.

"I can sit here and pretend to be a noble, civil person, because I have people like you to do all the ignoble, uncivil things that are necessary to carry out my decisions. What do you think about that, Captain Dupre?"

She cleared her dry throat and said, "I'm not sure it's always wise for someone in my position to have an opinion on these things, Your Majesty."

Thank God that tickled him, for otherwise she might be sunk. He chuckled softly and said, "Wise not to speak it, you mean."

She only tipped her head and remained silent, which seemed to tickle him all the more.

"They tell me, Captain, that you wish me to keep Durum in mind during the peace negotiations, after the war is over."

Josette steeled herself. "They are incorrect, Your Majesty."

The king's gray eyebrows rose into wide arches, high on his forehead. "Oh?" was all he said.

She looked him full in the eye, if only for a moment. "I wish you to retake Durum, Your Majesty. By force."

"My, my," he said, strumming his fingers on the throne. "I think someone's going to be very cross at you, when this interview concludes. Indulge me, Captain. Why should we spend blood and resources on an expedition with so little to be gained?"

"There's more to be gained than only the town, Your Majesty." She didn't even say the name, for fear its unfamiliarity would draw attention to its insignificance. "The new battalion training at the signal base is a shambles."

"Is it?" he asked.

She could almost feel the pike sliding into her severed neck. "Yes, Your Majesty. Their training won't do much to help that, either. They don't have the motivation or the mindset to be proper soldiers, and the only way to make something like soldiers out of them is to blood them—to give them a victory, if only a small one. Durum is not a difficult target. It can be taken in a matter of weeks, and the experience will be worth more than any amount of training. We can send one battalion of these boys to the front with a victory, with confidence, and have some good news to put in the papers. Durum has a rich history, Your Majesty. It flourished under . . ." She realized too late the direction she was headed in.

"It flourished under Vinzhalian rule, and withered under ours, as I recall," the king said.

Josette did her best to move on. "Be that as it may, at some point Vinzhalia is likely to try another attack on Arle, and Durum is well-positioned as an outpost."

The king stared at her for a while, and then said, "I'll think on it. Good day, Captain."

"Your Majesty," Josette said, as she bowed and backed out of the room, never turning her back to him.

The doors were closed in front of her, and finally she

could relax. She turned to find Bernat lying on a couch at the back end of the antechamber.

"Why the hell are you lying down, Bernie?"

"We insisted on it, ma'am," one of the attendants explained, "for fear he might hit his head if he fainted."

Indeed, the veins were bulging in Bernat's face, his eyes were wide as dinner plates, and his skin shone with sweat. "Have you lost your mind?" he asked. "I thought you were about to be flayed."

"Your idea was too chancy," she said, shrugging by way of apology. "If we lose after drawing the war out this long, the Vins may be disinclined to give us anything back, no matter how insignificant. They'd keep Durum just to be petty, just because we asked for it. Even if he does decide against my plan, he'll still remember Durum at the bargaining table, as a chance to fulfill the favor he denied me today. So you see, there really wasn't any risk at all."

Bernat was briefly stunned into silence. When he came out of it, he said, "No risk, except that you'd be flayed alive. And the certainty that you'd lose Duke Royama's favor. That man spent a lot of money on you, and now you're asking the king to divert troops from the territory he's desperately trying to hold onto."

She shrugged again. "He can disinvite me from his next social event."

"Oh, Josette. You have no idea what you've done." He looked as if he might go into pulmonary spasms at any moment. "Nothing could possibly make this day any—"

And then Roland walked into the antechamber.

"Oh, at least let me get it out before you run me through with your goddamn irony!" Bernat screamed at his brother, to Roland's absolute perplexity.

"I came as soon as I heard there was a disaster," Roland said, kneeling in front of Bernat's couch. "Who did this to him?"

"She did it!" Bernat cried, pointing an accusing finger at Josette. Roland turned to look at her, though he was more hesitant to meet her eye than she had been to meet the king's.

"I asked the king to retake Durum," she said in a much smaller voice than she'd intended.

Roland nearly had occasion to make use of the fainting couch alongside his brother. "Good God!" he cried. After being politely shushed by one of the attendants, he went on more quietly, "Well, you've lost Duke Royama's favor, and there's no getting it back. You're lucky the luftgas and steamjack parts he promised you haven't arrived yet, or he'd have your skin in payment. How did the king react?"

She took a step toward him, but stopped herself from taking more. "Not . . . angrily. Do you . . . do you suppose there's any hope of an accord?"

Roland's eyes flitted up, finally meeting hers. It seemed to take quite an effort of will, but he kept that contact as he spoke. "I should think that would depend entirely on you." He might have gone on, but he had to step away from the couch, to stop Bernat from hitting him with his cane.

If he had gone on, perhaps in another moment Josette would have begged his forgiveness. As it was, she only cleared her throat and said, "I'll . . . keep that in mind."

With that, Roland bowed and left the room.

8

Mistral's luftgas and steamjack parts never arrived, of course. Bernat had tried to tell her, but she'd held out hope until the matter could no longer be denied, and only then consented to have the bags filled with inflammable air.

And so *Mistral* was as ready to fly as could possibly be arranged, with gas that would explode at a spark, and a steamjack that caught fire if not constantly attended to. She waited only on her orders.

The battalion training at the signal base was in no better condition. The soldiers had completed their abbreviated training and were preparing to board trains for the front the next day, and no word had yet come from the king to change their destination.

Bernat had even less to do than usual, so he walked about the companies as they prepared to leave. Here and there, he recognized the face of a lad who'd entered university the year he graduated, and he simply couldn't resolve the notion that those snotty little pipsqueaks were soldiers now. He could believe it of himself only because he had become so used to violence, and so inclined to use it whenever convenient, and because of the cold sweat he broke into whenever he thought of going back into battle.

But to think of these lads in battle seemed impossible, and simply unfair on top of it all. It was one thing to conscript farmers' sons, who already expected a life of toil, disease, and

early death. It was quite another to pluck a promising boy
from his education and aspirations, and tell him to slay Vins
for three dinars a week. If there were any justice in the world,
a man of learning wouldn't have to get out of bed for such a
meager salary.

But out of bed they were, and making a mess of packing
for their next morning's departure. In fairness to them, Bernat
couldn't comprehend how the army expected them to fit all
of their equipment into their narrow haversacks. By his accounting, the average infantryman was expected to carry a
shaving kit, sewing kit, mess kit, mess tin, oiled overcoat, pipe
clay, shoe polish, belt polish, button polish, button board, pol-
ishing brush, coat brush, grooming brush, toothbrush, towel,
canteen, drinking can, tent rope, tent fabric, tent pegs, bed
roll, cartridge box, forty rounds ball cartridge, forty rounds
loose ball, powder horn, powder flask, musket cleaning and
worming kit, turn-screw, spare flint, practice flint, knife,
bayonet, shovel, shako cover, flintlock cover, two collars, two
linen shirts, two pairs cotton socks, one pair woolen socks, two
pairs knickers, one pair gaiters, one pocket handkerchief,
four days tobacco ration, four days tea ration, four days pick-
led vegetable ration, four days rice and barley ration, two
days meat ration, patent field stove, patent field lamp, patent
self-igniting matches, patent water filter, patent tooth powder,
and patent miracle blister ointment.

On top of that were any personal items the lads wanted to
take with them. In this battalion, that meant books. Indeed,
these must have been the most literate enlisted soldiers in the
entire army, for there wasn't a man among them who couldn't
read and write. This was much to the army's chagrin, for a
large fraction of the boys had already written letters to the
Ministry of the Army, to the newspapers, and even to the governing aristocrats in their home counties, complaining about

the harsh conditions of their training and the ill-treatment by their superiors. By these endeavors, a few had even succeeded in being excused of their service, but most succeeded only in making themselves a nuisance.

And they had opinions. Good God, did they have opinions. It didn't seem proper for a common solider to have opinions, let alone give voice to them, and yet here they were exchanging views, pretending expertise on subjects ranging from Gesshin's treatise on ethical conflict to General Fieren's strategies in Quah.

"You know, this is why these wars are still going on," one of the youngest lads said, pointing to the medley of equipment spread out on the ground before him.

"Because of your lamp?" another asked. "What, is there a genie in it?"

Bernat slowed his stroll, the better to eavesdrop.

The first lad picked up the lamp and said, "No, because some goddamn fat industrialist is making a fortune selling this useless rubbish to the army." He threw the lamp against the ground, where it smashed into his tin of boot polish. "Couldn't make his goddamn fortune if there wasn't a goddamn war on, could he?" He picked up the lamp and threw it again, hard enough to pop open the machine-crimped seam on the paraffin reservoir. When the boy saw the paraffin leaking out, something seemed to break inside of him. He fell over, his face in the grass, and sobbed.

The boy he'd been complaining to put his full attention into fitting the equipment into his haversack. Another boy left his packing work to comfort the crying lad.

Bernat walked on through the encampment all the more briskly, though it was hell on his leg. As he walked, he looked at his feet, but saw only the sobbing face of that blubbering boy—a soldier in the king's army.

* * *

JOSETTE SAT HUNCHED over the desk reserved for her in the administrative offices, just off the main shed. The desk was covered to a depth of five sheets with documents of trivial administrative importance, and atop them all were the beginnings of two handwritten letters. One began, "Roland, I love you and I'm sorry," while the other started off, "Roland, I am sorry to say I don't love you."

These few words constituted everything she'd written thus far. She consoled herself that this was a tricky job that required quality over quantity, and went on staring at the two letters, as she had stared at them for at least an hour out of every day for the past week.

The new chief mechanic walked in on her work, and she wasn't sure whether she was relieved or annoyed. She quickly slid the letters under a stack of paperwork and said, "Ah, Mister Megusi. Anything to report?"

The mechanic had his hat off and crumpled in front of his chest, and made a small deferential bow—which Josette couldn't help but compare to the carefree ways of the late Gears. "I've been over the steamjack a dozen times, sir, and there ain't a lot to do. Your lass did as good a job as is humanly possible, in fixing her up."

"I could have told you that without looking at it, Mister Megusi. Private Grey has proven an invaluable asset."

"Yes, sir. My only reservation is that she'll be aiming for my job." And he laughed heartily—a bit too heartily to be perfectly endearing, truth be told. "Still, I wouldn't recommend running the engine above three-quarters power for any length of time, and not above one-quarter without both of us on duty to keep the steamjack from . . ."

"Blowing us all to hell?"

"Yes, sir, that exactly." He fidgeted, hardly looking up for fear of her reaction. "Without the right parts, there's only so much an overhaul can do. Some of it just needs replacing."

"There are no replacements. Revolutionary new design means not a lot of spare parts floating around. I've already explained to Kember and Hanon that the engine needs to be handled with care. Make sure you talk to them yourself, though. I want them to understand the danger. I don't intend to lose my ship because the officer of the watch gets a notion that our peril has been exaggerated." In truth, she didn't have to worry about Kember, but she could hardly send her chief mechanic out to give a lecture to the first officer alone.

"I'll do my best to make it clear, sir," Megusi said, and left her.

She went back to staring at her letters, waiting on the burst of inspiration that might complete them.

"Right in there, sir," a voice from the corridor said after some minutes, and the last face she expected to see appeared from around the doorframe.

"Captain Emery," she said, leaping to her feet. "Sorry, Major Emery. Congratulations on your promotion."

The now-major laughed and said, "Whichever. Good to see you, Dupre." Even as she started to salute, he shifted a package under his arm and offered her a hand instead, though he was now two full ranks above her.

"What the hell are you doing here?" she asked, shaking his hand. "They haven't thrown you back into the signal corps, have they?"

He looked wistful at the thought. "No, nothing as fortunate as that. They've made me junior major of the 132nd." He lowered his voice, "Not exactly a crack outfit, are they?"

Josette nodded gravely. "They're calling themselves the Fighting Philosophers, though everyone else seems to prefer 'The Fangless Fops.' What does a junior major do, anyway? I've never been entirely clear on that."

Emery chuckled as he reached up to scratch at his neck. "I'm not entirely clear myself. Administrative duties, I suppose, on the colonel's staff. I'm told there's a possibility of independent command, if the battalion is ever divided into thirds or more, though I can't imagine when that would ever happen."

"Well, it's your own fault," Josette said. "If you hadn't been so good at your job, you'd still be commanding *Ibis.*"

"Speaking of being good at one's job . . ." Emery swung the package out from under his arm and presented it to Josette with both hands. "The fellows at the Ministry of the Army said that since I was going this way, and since we'd served together, I ought to have the honor of presenting you with this gift from the king."

Her sudden interest in the oilcloth-wrapped package rivaled only her surprise. It was too short to be a sword, the usual gift for accomplishments in the army. She pushed some papers aside on the desk, laid the package down, and unwrapped it.

It was a pistol, and a finer pistol than any she'd ever used. It had a rifled barrel nearly a foot long, with which it would fire more accurately than any smoothbore pistol—more accurately than a musket, she supposed, though only within the pistol's shorter range. Examining the lock, she found that it took the new percussion caps, which were said to fire reliably in all weather. Grapevines and stags were engraved on the finely stained wooden handle, and hidden among them were the initials of the master craftsman who had made it.

"He gets you," Major Emery said, grinning at her.

"I dare say he does." She found that she couldn't look away from the weapon.

Emery produced an envelope from his jacket. "This is for you, as well. Your orders."

"Thank God," she said. "I've been going mad, stuck on the ground." She frowned. "But why are you delivering them?"

He shrugged. "The fellows at the ministry gave them to me when they handed me the pistol. They said the orders might as well come through me, since none of your goddamn orders ever come through the proper goddamn channels, anyway. Their words."

As she opened the envelope, she said, "Just as well. They're probably only ordering me to escort your battalion up to the Meat Grinder."

Again, he looked wistful. "I promise I'll try not to look too envious, as I stare up at *Mistral* from the train."

But the orders did not send her to the Meat Grinder. She sat down on the edge of the desk, and nearly knocked the pistol to the floor in her distraction. "Good God," she said.

"I take it you won't be escorting us?" he asked.

She turned the orders around, so he could see them. "I am escorting you," she said. "To Durum."

"Durum?" he asked, as if it were the last place he expected his battalion to be going. "Who the hell decided that?"

She laughed softly and said, "The king." In response to Emery's confusion, she added, "I had an audience, and asked him to send a battalion there. My mother lives in Durum, you see."

He was quiet for a second, then said, "I suppose I do see. But good heavens, Dupre, the king himself? That's as far outside the chain of command as you can go, without appealing directly to God."

She grinned at him and said, "Next time."

THEY WERE FOUR days out of Kuchin, and just keeping pace with the troop train, when it disappeared into a fog bank in the middle of the night. Not long after, Josette had gone to bed with no more admonition to Lieutenant Hanon than, "Watch for signs of the wind shifting, and correct our course as best you can."

Bernat, not tired in the slightest, had remained on the hurricane deck. Lieutenant Hanon, for his part, had waited half an hour before he lit a cigarillo and went to the forward rail to smoke it.

Bernat couldn't help but feel a certain sort of admiration, for he'd rarely seen a man so casually risk death, whether by accidentally blowing up the ship—now filled with inflammable air in every bag—or by being caught and pummeled into oblivion by Josette. There were only three other crewmen on deck, one at lookout and the other two on the wheels. Bernat couldn't see who they were, though Hanon must have gained their silence by some means or another.

As Bernat approached the rail, Hanon pulled the cigarillo from his mouth and was ready to throw it over the side. When he saw that it was Bernat, he stopped and put it back between his lips. "Lieutenant Hanon," Bernat said.

Hanon said, "Please, please, call me Egmont."

Bernat nodded, unsure whether the gesture could be seen in the darkness, but not caring very much either, for he was distracted by a sight below. A thousand feet under the keel, there was a beautiful halo of moonlight shimmering off the top of the fog, as iridescent as the inside of an oyster shell. It took him a second to realize that the dark spot in the middle of the halo was *Mistral*'s own shadow. Looking more carefully, he could even see the tailfins in crisp silhouette, surrounded by a ring of pale white light. There was another shadow, a speck near the edge of the halo, which would have been hardly noticeable if Bernat had not been entranced by the entire phenomenon and studying it with all his attention. He didn't know what caused it, but perhaps Hanon would. "Have you ever seen anything like that?" he asked.

Egmont's voice betrayed little animation as he said, "Now and again. Not as often at night, I suppose." He took another pull. "More common in the day."

"It's beautiful." Perhaps it was only the wine from his supper, but Bernat was becoming a little misty at the heavenly sight.

"There's a word for it," Egmont said, his voice not searching but matter-of-fact as he waved his cigarillo about. If he made any effort to recall the word, no one else could have known. He sniffed. "How am I supposed to tell if the wind shifts at night, with this fog?"

Bernat wasn't sure how one was supposed to tell the wind had shifted without this fog, so he only shrugged and said, "She does expect rather a lot from her officers and crew, and from whatever handsome young gentlemen might happen to be aboard."

"Oh. Sorry. I didn't realize you two were . . ."

"Just friends," he said, cheerfully.

Egmont remained cautious, nevertheless. "Well, it's the other one that's the real problem. Probably got that scar falling off a ladder."

It was only this last speculation that let Bernat know who the "other one" was. "I believe, in fact, she was shot in the neck."

Egmont laughed. "Is that what they say?"

Bernat, who was there when it happened, answered, "It is what they say. Though, of course, the truth is so elusive in these cases. Who's to say, amid all the smoke and noise and confusion, whether a ladder wasn't somehow involved?"

"If she got shot in the neck," Egmont went on, seeming to think that Bernat was on his side in the matter, "how come there are scars on her face?"

"Quite, quite." Bernat was in too far to back out now. Besides which, he was rather enjoying himself, for reasons he couldn't quite put a finger on. "On reflection, the story of that scar is not nearly so watertight as it first appears."

"I'm supposed to take my cues from her?" He pointed

two fingers at Bernat, the cigarillo wedged between them. "Some pretentious little girl, whose tits have only just come in the mail?"

Though Bernat desperately wished to inquire further into Egmont's notions of human biology, for they seemed truly fascinating, his attention was caught again by the speck of shadow at the edge of the halo in the fog below. Having watched it now for several minutes, he thought it was moving, ever so gradually, from left to right across the top edge of the glow. Pointing it out, he asked, "Is that typical, in the nature of this phenomenon?"

It took some time for Egmont to find what Bernat was talking about, so subtle was the shadow. But when he did, he only stared at it, peering intently, with the burning end of his cigarillo reflected in his eyes. "Shit," was all he said.

"What is it?"

Egmont didn't answer him, but only tossed the burning cigarillo over the rail and called aft, "Wake the crew! Rig for battle!"

JOSETTE WAS NOT a light sleeper. She did not possess that slumbering awareness that many airship captains had, which allowed them to note every change of the watch, every alteration of trim, and to wake in an instant if anything was the slightest bit out of the ordinary.

But even as she struggled up into lucidity in response to the bustle in the keel, she knew something was amiss, and when she noticed the steep upward inclination of the ship and heard the rudder turn hard over, she knew exactly what it was.

"Where away?" she asked the crewman who'd come to wake her.

"Astern and above," he said.

"Thank you, Private. Carry on."

She had gone to sleep half dressed, and now only had to put on her jacket, harness, and boots. She worked on the boots first, and gave orders as she laced them, "Douse lanterns. Everyone clip on and watch your step."

She had to hold tight to her hammock ropes as the ship's inclination reversed, coming out of its climb and going into a dive instead. The ship went dark, and for a while it seemed that the bustle along the keel had abated, though it was only the crew taking extra care.

Josette laced up her boots and went forward, buttoning up her jacket as she walked, her safety harness slung uselessly over her shoulder. She was still fussing with buttons when she reached the hurricane deck and trotted carelessly down the companionway in the darkness. She heard Jutes's distinctive walk behind her as he took up his station at the top of the steps.

Lieutenant Hanon's voice came out of the pitch black of the hurricane deck. "They almost had us in the dark, but I spotted them in time. We'll get them now." She wasn't sure whether he recognized her coming down the companionway and was making a report, or if he was continuing some conversation started before she arrived.

"Was she a scout or a blimp, Lieutenant?"

Her eyes still hadn't adjusted enough to see him, but she heard Hanon shift his position, as if startled. "Don't know," he said. "She could be a chasseur. We didn't get a good look, before she dove into the fog."

She stepped toward his voice, and found him leaning over the forward rail with Bernat beside him. "A chasseur, finding itself above and behind us, would not dive for the fog," she said. "It would make us pay for our lack of attention."

"A scout then, I suppose. We're lined up on where she disappeared. We only have to follow her in."

She cut him short with an order to the elevatorman of, "Level us off."

Below, the moonlight was reflecting off the fog in a luminous glory, but there was no sign of the other ship. Hanon cried out, "You're letting them get away!"

Josette was glad of the darkness, so the crew couldn't see her look of disdain. It wouldn't do to let them know what she thought of her first officer. "Thank you, Mr. Hanon. If you have nothing else to report, please take your station in the tail." She took her own station at the middle of the deck. "Ensign Kember?"

"Sir." Kember's voice came out of the darkness behind the port gun.

"Keep an eye on that fog. Report any change."

"Yes, sir."

Hanon, meanwhile, had followed Josette and was whispering as he went, speaking only loud enough to be heard over the steamjack. "I ought to stay here. I'm wasted in the tail. You've already messed this up enough. You obviously need me here."

"Mr. Hanon," she said, "your station is in the tail. That is the first officer's station. It is placed as such so that, should the hurricane deck be lost, this ship will still have an officer aboard, such as he is."

Hanon lingered much longer than he ought to have, but Josette took care not to notice; for, if she had noticed, she would have been obliged to bring him up on insubordination charges. Her capacity for not noticing him had almost been expended when finally he stepped up the companionway, pushed roughly past Jutes, and went back along the keel.

"My apologies, sir," Jutes said, with what Josette thought a superhuman degree of respect.

"I think it's turned three points to port," Kember said from the forward rail. "Hard to be sure."

"Three points to port," Josette ordered. "And hope they're within sight when the fog burns off in the morning."

Damn Hanon. They could have doused lamps and come smartly about with a chance of catching the scout as she dove past, if he hadn't turned *Mistral* straight at it the moment he became aware of its presence. And then to dive after it? Did he think he'd be able to see them any better from inside the fog? Did he have any idea how deep it was, and whether a ship as large as *Mistral* could fit into it without hitting the ground? Did the fool think he was still on a blimp?

ENSIGN KEMBER WATCHED the sunrise from the forward rail, saw it burn off the fog, and was the first to spot the scout ahead of them.

Too damn far ahead of them.

The light of day showed it to be an older, slower scout, and running for the safety of clouds to the east. Steam spouted diagonally in two jets pointing down from the enemy ship's keel, evidence that the crew of the scout had disconnected her secondary condensers to squeeze as much speed as possible from their antiquated turbine.

The captain wasn't willing to do the same, wary of the weight of ballast water that would be lost as steam. Nor was she willing to risk fire by running her steamjack above two-thirds power. *Mistral* gained, but so slowly that she likely wouldn't close the distance in time.

Kember wasn't sure she would have made the same decision, though with the benefit of time she had come to the conclusion that it was the right one—not least of all because Lieutenant Hanon had come forward several times, suggesting they go to full power against the mechanics' advice. If that goddamn blimp jockey thought it was a good idea, it had to be a bad one.

But good God! Didn't *Mistral* and her crew deserve this kill? Shouldn't they take a little extra risk, and hope fate could be equitable enough to make up the deficit?

Kember spent a long time watching the scout grow slowly larger as they closed the distance. As *Mistral* eased nearer to a mile from them, their closing speed was so low that she had ample time to prepare her shot.

"Sergeant," the captain called up the companionway ladder as they closed with the enemy, "rig a fearnought screen over the companionway, to be opened only when bringing powder forward. Close the air scoops, and every port along the keel. Leave no opening for an ember from the guns to get through to the bags. And let's wet the martingales again, just in case. I'd rather that little scout didn't return home with an unlikely story about sinking a Garnian chasseur."

As the crew rigged the fearnought screen, Kember's mind positively itched to fire. They could get a long shot in even now, if they pitched the bow up far enough. So far she wouldn't be able to see the target when she fired, now that she thought of it, but that hardly mattered to the flight of the ball. In the end, it was all only math.

But after endless moments, the screen was rigged, the scoops were closed, and the martingales were more thoroughly wetted. "We'll only get a couple of shots, so aim them well," the captain said. "Fire when you're ready."

Kember rechecked everything, and when she was certain that the gun was as perfectly aligned as it could be, she pulled the lanyard and the cannon recoiled with a thunderclap, spitting a spear of fire under the bow and filling the hurricane deck with smoke. The smoke swept aft as Kember ran to the rail and watched the scout. She could just see the momentary, ghostly blur as the roundshot passed to starboard of the scout's envelope.

"Miss," she said. "But not by much."

"Fire starboard when ready. I believe this is the last you'll get before she's in the clouds, Ensign."

As Kember moved to the starboard gun, its swabber was busy putting out the little embers that clung smoldering to the envelope and martingales ahead of the deck. He was in her way, but she didn't resent his thorough attention, with the bags filled with inflammable air.

She spun the elevation screw on the gun through a quarter turn, to account for the small distance closed in the time since the previous shot. "Stand clear!" she shouted, for the swabber was still working on the martingales.

He stepped briskly away as Kember pulled the lanyard. Again she ran forward through the smoke and watched for the fall of the shot.

She saw nothing, for in that moment the scout disappeared. Kember had just resigned herself to misery, when a splintering crack sounded from within the clouds. She'd hit the airscrew, or at least sprung the boom it was mounted on, and the results must have been devastating, with splinters flying out like canister shot.

She waited and listened, expecting at any moment to hear a boiler explosion, a turbine disintegrating, a keel snapping in the middle—any sign that fate had intervened to make up for the aerial kill it had so capriciously taken from them.

Nothing. The scout had lost an airscrew, and maybe a few crewmen, but that was all. It was crippled but alive, and safe now in the clouds, unless Captain Dupre chose to hunt for her.

"Well done!" the captain said. She seemed to mean it, too. It had been a damn fine piece of gunnery, Kember supposed.

"Thank you, sir," she answered, hoping the next order

would put them in the clouds, there perhaps to finish the stricken quarry.

But alas, it wasn't to be. The captain decided to turn back and make their rendezvous with the battalion.

"Sorry about that," she said privately, coming to the forward rail to explain her decision. "Even crippled, we'd have been hours poking around in that soup, trying to track them down. Not worth it, to kill a scout that's likely to be retired soon anyway. But she'll be heading back to base, which means the battalion will have a clear run to Durum without being observed. They owe you thanks for that."

"Yes, sir," Kember said, trying to hide her disappointment. "I understand. It's the same decision I would have made."

Or, rather, it was the same decision she was supposed to make. But in all truth, she knew that if it had been up to her, *Mistral* would now be groping blindly in the clouds for that scout, and the battalion be damned.

For all that, they might have spent as long as they liked hunting the scout, for they arrived at the rendezvous location to find that the battalion hadn't moved an inch. Bernat stated as much, and Josette replied with a nasty look and a comment of, "Well, I'm not a goddamn fortune-teller, am I?"

He was about to point out that such a delay, in a battalion of such qualities, hardly required unnatural foresight, but he wasn't in the mood to be thrown to his death right then.

Two hundred feet below him, the plains were covered with newly budded grass shining a brilliant green, even under sunlight diffused by high cloud cover. The infantry companies had disembarked their train hours ago, and were now milling about on either side of a dirt road which cut the plain clear to the horizon.

It was the cannons that had held them up. The battalion's single artillery company possessed four cannons, and not one had yet been unloaded from the train. There was a positively chatty level of signaling going on between Major Emery below and Josette on deck, he waving flags about and she flashing messages on the ship's signal lamp. From what Josette told Bernat, and from what he'd gathered from her mutterings, the men on the ground lacked some crucial piece of equipment required to haul the cannons off the train and onto their limbers, having accidentally left it behind in Kuchin.

Now that *Mistral* had returned, the artillery captain wanted to rig a rope and pulley from her, and use the airship itself as a crane. Even Bernat could see the idiocy of that idea. It would only pull the ship down on top of them if *Mistral* were to idle her engine, or swing the guns around with deadly abandon if the ship were under power.

Major Emery was the only voice of reason on the ground, but could not convince the artillery captain even by virtue of superior experience and rank. Indeed, all work on moving the guns without *Mistral*'s aid had stopped when she approached, so certain were the artillerists in the soundness of their new plan.

The battalion was stalled with no one doing anything, their train sitting idle and another one—a supply train bound for the front lines—stuck behind it on the track.

"These are the men who are going to retake Durum?" Bernat asked Josette when she put down the signal lamp.

She sighed. "They'll outnumber the garrison by five to one, in all likelihood. And it's apt to be a garrison of old men and convalescents. And we'll be attacking from the city's weakest side. And they'll have airship support. And perhaps even the support of the citizens inside."

"I still don't like our chances," Bernat said.

"There's the next train, sir," Kember reported from the opposite rail. "Right on schedule."

"What a goddamn disaster," Josette said. "It is slowing down, at least? It's not going to crash, is it?"

"It is slowing, sir."

She took some small relief but no particular consolation at this news, still looking as vexed as ever. "Small miracles," Bernat said, to try to cheer her up.

She only shot a nasty look at him and said, "What a goddamn disaster."

IT WAS ALMOST evening before the 1st Battalion of the 132nd Regiment managed to rig a tripod pulley and get the guns onto their limbers. With night coming on, the battalion marched only a couple of miles down the road before they had to stop and make camp.

In the morning, Josette woke to a morning drizzle pattering against the top of the envelope, and riggers collecting the rainwater for extra ballast. After breakfasting on ship's biscuit—was this batch more inedible than usual, or had her palate been ruined by the food in Kuchin?—she went forward and caught Egmont sitting on the companionway instead of standing his watch on the deck as he was meant to.

The rain stopped just after ten, but the weather remained overcast throughout the morning watch, through the afternoon, and into the evening, which suited Josette just fine. It would make observation by enemy airship all the harder, should another ship replace the scout they'd chased off.

On the second morning of the march, she breakfasted on disagreeable ship's biscuit again and came forward to find Hanon sitting on the companionway and an overcast sky. The third day was just the same. It was nominally a three-day march to Durum, but the battalion was making poor time, and the town was still over the horizon.

Only on the fourth day did *Mistral* come near enough to sight the green roof and red woodwork of Durum's single pagoda, standing out against the gray horizon. As they approached, the flat green plains under the keel turned into fenced-in squares of brown farmland, many of them already furrowed for planting.

Once close enough to pick out smaller buildings, she called for the ship's best spyglass and studied Durum in detail. Bernat joined her at the forward rail with a glass of his own.

"What are those things in the town square?" he asked. "Scaffolds? Perhaps they're constructing a pavilion around the pond?"

She'd been studying them for some time, and thought she knew the answer. But she waited until they were closer, and had a clearer view, before she said, "They're gallows."

"But there are scores of them!"

"The Vins have been busy. Oh, look, you can just see Mother's house there in the southwest quarter. Maybe I'll drop by when this is over."

"Leave something on the stove?" Bernat asked.

She laughed. "I've never left anything important in that house. Well, almost anything." She wished she hadn't said that, for she knew his questioning gaze would not let up until she filled in the details. She sighed and lowered her voice. "I did once abandon the Duchess of Almonesia there."

Bernat's eyebrows skewed and pressed together until they nearly touched. "Let me guess . . . buried in the basement?"

"No, no. We didn't have a basement, so I stuffed her into a secret space in the wall of the upstairs room."

Bernat only blinked several times.

"She was a doll," Josette said, giving a self-effacing laugh. "Her name was Duchess Prettyheart."

He seemed no less shocked than when he thought she'd murdered an aristocrat. "You? Played with dolls? And a doll named Duchess Prettyheart, at that?"

"Don't speak her name in that disrespectful tone," Josette said, chiding. "She had to rule her demesne alone from the age of twelve, after her father died heroically in the wars and her mother succumbed to a bite from a rabid horse."

Bernat did not laugh, but only looked at his feet with his hand over his mouth, trying to hide his grin. When he finally recovered the power of speech, he said, "I hope you'll introduce us, after this is over."

"Of course." But then Josette frowned. "Oh. It just occurred to me that she was probably torn to pieces by rats, years ago."

"An ignominious end for such an accomplished young lady."

"She knew the risks going in," Josette said. And then her voice increased in volume, and she called to the steersmen, "Bow angle up three degrees until we're in the clouds. Jutes, pass the word to rig a bucket for low-level observation."

The canvas bucket, made of sailcloth and wicker, and connected by line and pulley to the keel near the tail, was usually used to scoop supplementary ballast from waterways, and occasionally as an anchor to assist in making unlikely landings in the middle of battlefields. But now Josette was using it as an observation platform.

It had been cinched up high enough to put her feet on the bottom and still have her head and shoulders above the lip. It was quite a good platform for spying, she reflected, when the next hour found her occupying it, a hundred feet below *Mistral* and still in the clouds. She only wished the bucket didn't smell of fetid stream water. The smell had seeped into the canvas after its last use, and wouldn't come out no matter how many times it was washed.

Mistral was completely silent, as ordered, with the steamjack shut down as she drifted over Durum on light winds. Josette was only certain she'd plotted the ship's drifting course correctly when she smelled the Vedat family's tannery on the northwest side of town, its pungent odor making the bucket's seem mellow by comparison.

She waited and listened, and could just make out, on the very edge of her hearing, footsteps on cobblestones below. She gave three tugs on the signal line, to tell the crew above to lower her another ten feet. When the pulley above started to creak, it seemed the loudest sound in the world, and she had to remember to breathe as she descended.

The pulley stopped, the bucket ceased its descent, and she was still in the clouds. She should have been just below them, and fifty feet above the ground, but perhaps the cloud cover had dropped while they were positioning *Mistral* for the overflight, or perhaps there was some problem with the winch. Whatever it was, she had to get lower, so she gave three more tugs.

The pulley squeaked above, more hesitant this time, and the bucket slowly descended. She still couldn't see a damn thing. She caught a whiff of wood smoke, and a moment later felt a wash of hot air coming up from below. No sooner had she worked out the significance of this, than she saw, looming out of the thick fog in front of her, a triangular roof. There was a second-floor window near the peak, where a woman—Josette thought she recognized her as Mrs. Malleville—was taking in her laundry. Yes, it was definitely Mrs. Malleville, looking straight at her now, eyes wide and mouth agape.

Josette gave two hard tugs on the line, and the bucket began to ascend almost instantly. But not quite fast enough, for while the drifting bucket closed the short distance in seconds, the canvas caught on the peak of the roof and held fast to a jagged bit of wood left over from some poor repair job. It tore through the side of the bucket, and Josette only avoided being skewered by a quick dodge to the side.

The bucket was not so lucky. It was pierced through and stuck fast, anchored to the rooftop. As the wind continued to carry the ship along, the bucket's supporting line went taut and vibrated like a plucked harp spring. Somewhere above, *Mistral* was being dragged down by the line, and would crash into the town if the bucket wasn't cut free. And if Josette couldn't cut it free below, the crew would have to cut it free above, leaving her stranded inside the city.

She leapt out and onto the roof, cursing herself for not bringing a knife along. A shingle came loose under her foot and slid down the steeply inclined roof, to land on the street below. Taking inspiration from it, she pulled out another loose shingle, tore one of the nails from it, and jabbed at the canvas where it was pierced.

From below, a voice from the window inquired, quite politely, "Is that you, Josie?"

The tension on the fabric helped tear it away, but it was still slow going with only a nail, and every second brought *Mistral* closer to the ground. "Yes it is," Josette said, "but I really don't have time to talk, Mrs. Malleville."

A moment's silence, while she jabbed at the canvas and another few fibers tore away. She was making an unmistakable racket, but it couldn't be helped.

"It's Mrs. Turel now, dear," the woman said.

"Congratulations to you and Mr. Turel," Josette said, and then leaned down to tear at a particularly tough patch of canvas with her teeth. Spitting out rough, rancid-tasting fibers, she added, "And my sympathies about Mr. Malleville."

The lines leading up to *Mistral* were near a forty-five-degree angle now, the ship dragged halfway to the ground already. Soon they'd either have to cut her loose or come crashing down.

"Thank you, sweetie," Mrs. Turel said. "And I hope all is well for you."

Canvas tore under the strain and it seemed for a moment that the bucket would come free, but before Josette could clear the tangle of fabric, the tension on the line sank the jagged edge of the roof into the bucket again, as quickly and firmly as a fisherman sinking his hook.

"I'm quite well," Josette said, as she struggled to cut it free again, "but unless you know the disposition of the Vin garrison, ma'am, I'm afraid I can't stay to chat."

There was a slight bustle below as Mrs. Turel leaned out of her window and looked up and down the street through the fog. Josette stabbed desperately with the nail, poking holes in the canvas, alternately cursing it and begging it to tear. "It's five hundred and eighty-six as of this morning, dear," Mrs. Turel said, with foregone certainty. "From the 64th Fusiliers."

While Josette was staring down in slack-jawed awe at Mrs. Turel, the last of the fabric tore away and the bucket slid away along the roof. "Thank you," she said, saluted her, and ran after it.

"Anytime, dear!" Mrs. Turel called after her. "You know where to find me."

The bucket had slid off the edge of the roof by the time Josette got to it, but she took a running leap and grabbed onto one of its lines over the street, hanging on by her hands alone. She swung straight into the house across the street, but hit feet first and walked her way up its side, clearing the roof and rising into the fog as the line reeled in.

After what seemed a timeless ascent, a hand reached down to help her back aboard. Jutes pulled her up and, holding the tattered remains of the bucket over his other arm, asked, "Eventful trip, Cap'n?"

Josette grinned back. "More than I expected, but no matter. We have the information we need. Durum is being garrisoned by the 64th Fusiliers, who number five hundred and eighty-six, after casualties taken at Canard." She drooped as, in the relative peace of the ship, she finally appreciated the significance of that number. It was too damn many. A fresh Garnian battalion—and most particularly *this* battalion—would need to outnumber the defenders three or four to one to have a chance in the breach. With less than a two-to-one advantage, even with an airship overhead and their superior artillery, the 132nd couldn't retake Durum.

Bernat was looking at her over Jutes's shoulder. "Your observations indicated precisely five hundred and eighty-six soldiers in the garrison? Not five hundred and eighty-five, nor five hundred and eighty-seven, but five hundred and eighty-six, exactly? And you arrived at this remarkable figure from a few minutes peering through fog and being dragged over rooftops?"

She only shrugged and said, "Reconnaissance is as much an art as it is a science, Bernie."

IN THE LATE afternoon, the 132nd arrived outside Durum. The battalion immediately set to work digging entrenchments for the artillery company's guns, and they labored all through the night to extend the trenches within range of the walls. At first light, the cannons began to fire in earnest, waking Bernat only a few hours after he'd gone to bed. He tried to get back to sleep for two more hours, but the cannons didn't stop, so he washed, dressed, and went down to the hurricane deck to watch.

After only a few hours' firing, there was already a great crack in Durum's east wall, about a third of the way from the southwest corner. It occurred to Bernat that what had once been the wall's strength was now its weakness. Its interlocking stones, carefully shaped and fitted by master craftsmen in a bygone age, presented a flat face to cannonballs and so had to absorb the entire force of their impact, rather than deflecting it as a modern slope-faced fortification would. And once a stone near the base of the wall cracked, the incredible weight above would come to the aid of the artillery, and so the wall would conspire with the enemy to shatter itself. Adding to that, the Garnians were firing upon the most dilapidated spot on the western side—the side whose repair had been most neglected over the years.

The Vins were not waiting idly for their walls to come down, however. They had already begun constructing a roof made of thick wooden timbers atop the unbombarded segments of the west wall, as a defense against shells dropped from *Mistral.* They were also returning fire, with old cannons mounted in bulwarks at intervals along the wall, but so far Durum's ancient guns had destroyed nothing but a couple of the rock-filled wicker gabions set up to shield the Garnian batteries. These defensive guns seemed to be the same species of cannon that had failed to protect Durum from the Vins two seasons earlier, and were now continuing their tradition of ineffectual fire.

Mistral landed in the evening, as soon as a stubby, jury-rigged mooring mast was constructed outside of cannon range. When his feet touched the ground, Bernat felt strangely vulnerable. He had left the ship often enough when she was moored in a shed, and once even in the middle of a smoke-clouded melee, but now it felt strangely chancy to leave her moored in the middle of a wide-open field, with Lieutenant Hanon in command and only the 132nd standing in the way of the Vins. It felt something like leaving his clothes on a riverbank while he went in for a swim.

Josette seemed to feel a similar anxiety, for she glanced over her shoulder at *Mistral* the whole way to the command tent. At the entrance, she took one long, final look and then went inside.

Bernat, too, paused to look over that ugly, beautiful ship with a sardine's shape and a shark's reputation, her envelope gleaming white against the gray sky. He stepped inside, finding the tent stuffy and warm, which was a welcome change from the chill of early spring outside. Major Emery was there, along with Colonel Okura and a couple of staff officers Bernat didn't know, huddled around a table with maps strewn over it.

Emery stepped away from the table to approach Josette and Bernat. "There's a slight delay," he said. "We're expecting an envoy from the Vins, to respond to our request for surrender."

"And how is life as a junior major?" Josette asked.

Emery laughed softly. "It leaves plenty of time for gossip. I heard something interesting about your Lieutenant Hanon, from one of the company captains."

Josette and Bernat both leaned in close.

"He led a hope last year, up in Quah, but was never promoted."

The word "hope" apparently meant something to Josette, for she gave a low whistle. Seeing Bernat's confusion, she said softly to him, "A forlorn hope is the first unit to assault a breach. All volunteers, usually, whose only job is to soak up bullets and keep the enemy occupied while other units come up behind. It's not unusual for over half to be killed or wounded." She narrowed her eyes. "The officer leading a hope always gets a promotion. It's automatic, except in cases of extreme cowardice."

"Could that be it?" Bernat asked. "He doesn't have a scratch on him, after all."

Josette shook her head. "No. Our Lieutenant Hanon may be many things, but he doesn't lack courage."

"What about stupidity? Surely an act of true stupidity must exempt the leader of a hope from the usual honors?"

Josette considered it. "Perhaps, but he isn't stupid, either. Not exactly. It's more that he commits himself absolutely to whatever plan his first instincts suggest. I can't imagine that habit counting against you in a hope, though. The entire point is to charge headlong into an unwinnable attack. His habits could only help him in that."

"So he was an unusually old ensign?" Bernat asked. "Or a sergeant?"

Emery shook his head. "Neither. I asked about it. He received no promotion. No badge of honor. No awards, gifts, accolades. And no one knows why, or if they do they don't want to say."

"Something must have gone very wrong in that breach."

"And yet it's hard to imagine what could possibly go wrong enough to . . ." Emery trailed off, distracted by a commotion outside the tent.

The staff officers quickly hid their maps. The tent flap opened and a blindfolded Vin major was led inside by two sergeants. They untied his blindfold at a nod from Colonel Okura.

"Ah," the bright-faced Vin major said, in perfectly accented Garnian. "That's better. Good morning, gentlemen. I do hope the day finds you well."

Okura offered his hand and said, "Quite well, Major Dvakov. Would you like some coffee? Anything to eat?"

Dvakov shook hands and smiled eagerly. "Oh, yes please. I haven't had good, strong Garnian coffee in ages. I'm ashamed to say, my countrymen have never quite gotten the hang of it. It's all in the roast, no? I don't suppose you have any of those wonderful little ginger cakes?"

At a look from Okura, one of the sergeants left the tent, and came back a minute later with a tin of cakes. In the meantime, Okura poured the coffee himself.

The Vin major took a sip, and then a bite of ginger cake, and nearly melted with satisfaction. "Better than I remembered," he said. "I must admit, Garnians understand food and drink as Vinzhalians never will. You even make better dumplings than us, eh?" The officers chuckled politely. Dvakov looked around the tent, from the canvas cover, to the table, to the muddy turf underfoot, and across every face in the room. "How were the roads, coming in?"

"Muddy, but accommodating in the end," Colonel Okura said. With a sly smile, he added, "We only had to bring up four guns, after all."

"Now, now, sir," Major Dvakov said, returning the smile with one yet more sly. "It doesn't do to be boastful. You may have the advantage of firepower, but I slept in a warm, soft bed last night. Alongside a warm, soft woman, to boot. So I ask you, who comes out ahead?"

This evoked more than just polite chuckles from the staff officers. There was real humor in their eyes, alongside a dash of envy.

"As to the question of our business today," Colonel Okura reminded him.

"Indeed. So you've come to blood your battalion, yes?" He grinned into Okura's suddenly stone-faced visage, tossed the last of a ginger cake into his mouth, and spoke as he chewed, "Yes, of course you have. No other reason to commit so many troops to such a useless town. You want to guarantee the outcome. Give the boys an easy victory before they go north, when it becomes not so easy for them. So you bring overwhelming numbers and array them against a severely understrength Vin regiment, depleted and wearied by battle." He looked to Josette. "The airship, I thought, was an ostentatious touch. With every respect to you and your crew, of course."

"Of course," she answered, tipping her head.

"So, to the business at hand." Dvakov reached into his jacket pocket, brought out a sheet of paper, and unfolded it. He read aloud:

To Lt. Colonel Haru Okura
132nd Regiment of Foot, 1st Battalion
Outskirts of Durum

Sir,

   In light of your overwhelming superiority of infantry
and artillery, I find my regiment's position as garrison of
Durum untenable. I salute your mercy and good conduct
in graciously offering to spare the lives of my men. How-
ever, I must, with regret, inform you that my orders at
this time contain no instructions on the subject of surren-
der, and I must therefore decline your kind offer, with
greatest compliment.

> *Yours,*
> *Colonel Checheg Saihan,*
> *64th Fusiliers Regiment*
> *Durum*

"Do you mind if I take another of those cakes back with me?" Dvakov added, without a pause, and only then handed the letter over.

"I, uh," Colonel Okura stammered. "Sergeant? See that the major has a fresh tin of cakes. Major, I'm sorry it has to be this way."

"Not half as sorry as I'm apt to be," Dvakov said, with rather less concern than Bernat expected from the second-in-command of a supposedly doomed regiment.

When Dvakov was gone, Colonel Okura spent a moment staring at the tent flap, then said, "I have the distinct impression that man was toying with us."

"He had two messages with him," Bernat offered, since no one else had noticed. "Did you see the way his hand stopped in his pocket, his fingers feeling around? He was making sure he got the right one."

Emery shook his head. "I'll wager the other was a surrender. But he took one look at us and knew he wouldn't need it."

Okura returned to the table, where one of the staff officers had spread a map out. "Well, Lieutenant Dupre, can they back up their bravado?"

Hearing Josette addressed by her proper rank, rather than her courtesy title of captain, struck a sour chord in Bernat, but she seemed not even to notice. "I believe," she said, "that their garrison numbers between five and six hundred. The entire surviving complement of the 64th Fusiliers."

Major Emery made a dire-sounding whistle.

Another of the staff officers muttered, "Good God."

The colonel looked at her skeptically, then at Bernat. "Do you agree with that assessment, Lord Hinkal?"

Bernat wasn't expecting anyone to ask his opinion, and for a moment he stood dumbstruck. Word must have gotten out about the letter he sent to his uncle, warning of the Vin surprise attack the previous fall. "I do agree with it," he said. "I'd put it closer to the high end. Call it, say, five hundred and eighty fusiliers, give or take half a dozen."

"You were able to count them as precisely as that?" Colonel Okura asked.

Bernat smiled and said, "Reconnaissance is as much an art as a science, you know."

The colonel let out a long sigh. "That's it, then. We have no hope of victory against hardened troops of that number, and there's no contingency for a siege. We were meant to remain here no more than a week, then top off our provisions from the town before heading back."

Josette spoke up. "We might bring their numbers down by aerial bombing, sir, and by setting *Mistral*'s marksmen to picking them off. With some luck, and if we can periodically land and refresh our magazine from the artillery company's stores, we might reduce their numbers significantly in only a few weeks."

The battalion's officers cast wan expressions at each other, and Bernat knew that something had gone wrong. Colonel Okura confirmed it when he said, "There's, uh, been an interesting development. We sent a rider with our dispatches to the nearest semaphore tower, and had him wait for a response. He got back an hour ago." The colonel paused, seeming to consider his words.

Bernat was still at a loss, but Josette's shallow sigh said that she understood. She said, "You gave them the engineers' estimates on how long it would take to open a practical breach, didn't you?" And then she added a hasty, "Sir."

The colonel swallowed. "Yes. General Bellamy congratulated us on our progress and informed us that, as we have enough provisions to see us through the siege, and as we can draw from the town after it's taken, our resupply expedition has been cancelled and sent to the northern front."

"We have scavenging parties combing the countryside," Major Emery said, "but it's just the wrong time of year for it. Taking the return trip into account, we can stay for two or three days, perhaps four if we stretch things and use up the last of our rations. Then we'll be marching home on empty stomachs."

"Sir," Josette said, her eyes suddenly brightening, "I may have an alternate plan."

10

"ARENʼT YOU READY yet?" Josette spoke into the darkness, quietly lest her voice be heard in the town, not a great distance under *Mistral*'s keel. She was in the sleeping berths toward the tail and could hear Bernat stuffing clothes into a bag.

"I'll hardly be a minute," he said. Though he spoke quite softly, shushing sounds replied to him from three different directions. He lowered his voice even further. "I just need a few more things."

"Why the hell are you even coming along?" she asked.

"Because I'm the only person on this ship capable of subtlety," he answered. "As Colonel Okura clearly recognized."

She took a few steps toward his voice, but stopped when her face hit damp fabric. "Damn it," she whispered, "I've told you about hanging your laundry from the control cables. It's bad enough that it could interfere with steering, but consider the weight of ballast lost to evaporation."

"I wrung them out first!" he said, and the same trio of shushes again brought his voice down. "You went off like a cannon the time I hung my laundry on the hurricane deck, so what other choice do I have?"

"You could refrain from washing your clothes while we're in the air, like everyone else."

He made a huffing sound. "When I might be visiting the love of my life? No, I won't be caught in dirty clothes for that."

"This isn't a goddamn vacation in the country. It's an infiltration. Jutes and I are dressed as locals, more or less." Less, on the whole, but at least they'd made the effort. They were both wearing tunics hastily cut and stitched from sailcloth, and closed around the waist with hemp rope rather than a sash. They bore a passing resemblance to the woolen deels commonly worn about Durum, and might be mistaken for the same by anyone who was new to the concept of clothing.

"It isn't luggage," Bernat said. "It's a small bag. Just the essentials. Anyway, your bag is bigger than mine."

Josette's tightly wrapped bundle contained her pistol and two more from the ship's arms locker, along with signal flags, phosphorus flares, rocket flares, rations, three rifles, an infantry pattern musket, various cartridges, and three sharp cutlasses. But there wasn't time to debate the matter of Bernat's luggage, so she said, "Fine, but hurry. We're over the town already."

"Well, why didn't you say so?"

"It shouldn't need to be said. You should be ready on time."

The damp undershirt in front of her was whipped away, and she could hear it being hastily stuffed in with the rest of Bernat's things. He cinched the bag shut and said, "Ready."

"Follow me." She pushed her way past him and went aft, to where the pulley system was rigged. This time, however, it was not a bucket at the end of the line, but a rope ladder specially made for tonight's operation. "Sergeant Jutes first, then you, Bernie. He'll guide you down the ladder. There, give me your cane. I'll put it in with the rifles."

After Jutes descended, Bernat stood at the edge of the keel catwalk, probing for the first rung. Jutes guided his foot from below, but it still took him nearly five minutes to descend a few dozen rungs in the darkness.

Josette followed more swiftly, leaving the warm stuffiness of *Mistral* for the chill damp of the clouds. She felt suddenly very vulnerable, as if she were a knight who'd lost his horse and stood exposed on the battlefield.

She couldn't see *Mistral* above, but thought she could feel it receding into the clouds as the ladder was let down. Whether this was some haptic sense of subtly changing air patterns or merely an anxious imagination, she couldn't say. Below, the bottom rungs dragged over a street and Jutes's feet touched down, but he held firm to the ladder, keeping his weight on it lest the ship ascend and leave him stranded.

Josette held her breath through the torturous seconds it took Bernat to fumble his way from rung to rung. He let out a yelp, and she heard his feet scrambling frantically against the ladder. "Jump!" she hissed down at him. "Jump!"

He didn't have the chance to obey, for Jutes had already pulled him off the ladder, and both landed in a heap in the middle of the street. She climbed down even as the ladder was going back up. She'd only gone down three rungs before the ship's drift pulled the ladder clear across the street, and a house emerged from the fog ahead. She smacked into it a second later. Above, a rung caught at the edge of a shingle.

If left in that state, it would drag the ship down just as it had before. The crew would have to cut the ladder loose from above, leaving the Vins with unambiguous proof that some idiot or idiots had dropped into town during the night.

Josette let go of her bag and climbed up, as fast as she could. She vaulted over the edge of the roof and nearly slid down the slippery, fog-dampened shingles. As soon as she had her footing, she snatched a knife from her belt and cut the snagged rung just as the tension was coming onto it. It came loose and she guided it clear of the roof, following it to the other edge to make sure it wouldn't snag again. As the rope ladder—the only way out of the town—disappeared into darkness above, she remained frozen in that stance, listening and running through the last few seconds in her mind, trying to recall exactly how much noise they'd made.

It was enough, evidently, to wake the residents of the house whose roof she was standing on. She'd hoped it was one of Durum's many abandoned houses, but her luck was not running in that direction tonight, and at least two people were stirring indoors. One of them went to the second-floor window just below, opened it, and whispered something in Vinzhalian.

She heard the click of a pistol being cocked in the window. Someone inside the house lit a lamp, and its light spilled across a narrow alley to the house behind. It projected a rough silhouette of the man with the pistol, leaning out with his head turned upward.

Josette had nothing but her knife for defense. The other weapons were wrapped tight inside her pack, and might as well be a hundred miles away, for all the time and noise it would take to retrieve them.

She leaned back as far as she could, but if spotted she could only run and hope to find a way down before the Vins started shooting. She was about to commit to that very course of action, when from the other side of the house she heard a foppish voice imitating a tomcat's yowl. She winced and clenched her teeth, dead certain that the sound couldn't be mistaken for anything but a foppish voice imitating a tomcat's yowl, but it succeeded in drawing the attention of the men in the room below.

The Vin's silhouette receded and the opposite window was opened. Josette stepped carefully back from the edge and knelt down to make herself as small as possible. She barely breathed while she waited, expecting at any moment to see a pistol pointed at her over the edge of the roof, or to hear her companions being shot.

After a few minutes of whisperings in Vinzhalian, the light of the lamp went out and the windows were pulled closed. A little too soon, she thought. Perhaps they were only trying to lure her out. Perhaps the windows had been left open a crack, and an armed man waited next to each. Jutes and Bernat must have had the same thought, for they made no attempt to signal her.

She knelt on the roof, perfectly still, standing a gargoyle's vigil. While she waited, hardly daring to swallow lest the sound carry below, the fog rolled on through Durum, depositing dew on her clothes and on the tips of her unruly tufts of hair. Such a long time seemed to pass that she was watching for signs of the sunrise when the temple bell tolled one in the morning, revealing the improbable truth that she'd been up there for less than an hour.

But that was all the more reason to wait longer, or risk a bullet for her haste. She had done this before, she reminded herself. She regularly stood deck watches in the windy damp for a dozen hours at a stretch. And it wasn't just deck watches. A far colder, far damper example rose from the distant past, and swelled until it occupied her mind entirely.

The wolf. She hadn't thought of the wolf in years, and across that span of time it had faded into a pale shadow of a memory, as if it were a mere story she'd heard, or perhaps read in a book, but not her own experience.

The wolf had been taking livestock all winter, coming at night and disappearing into the woods by morning. No one could find its lair. It never took the carcasses stuffed with wolfsbane and powdered glass that the townsfolk left for it, preferring instead to kill a live victim every night. Each morning, one of Durum's herdsman woke to find his flock shorter by one. Those who could, drove their livestock into the town, where they inevitably made a nuisance of themselves. Those who couldn't spent sleepless nights watching over their stock, or else saw their meager fortunes diminish night by night.

On reflection, it couldn't have been as bad as it seemed. There were always more sheep and more goats, after all. The wolf might have taken one a night until the end of time, and there would never be a shortage. But at the time, Durum's mood was steeped in dread, and it seemed this predator would eat up the whole town if given the chance. It was all the locals ever spoke of. The war faded into remoteness, the news and gossip about Mehmed Dupre's death were forgotten. Every tavern, street corner, and fireside buzzed with dire predictions of Durum's impending starvation, or with wild notions of how to prevent it.

Josette had remained silent through the talk, spoke barely a word during the entire crisis, but every night she dropped stealthily from her bedroom window and carried her rifle and a dark lantern into the packed snow beyond the walls.

For an entire month, in the very teeth of the winter, she kept to this regimen. And for an entire month she fired not a single shot, for want of a target. Most nights she lay belly-down on the roof of a three-sided shed built to shelter goats, which gave her a slight improvement in elevation and comfort compared to improvising a hunting blind in the snow. Most nights, she detected no trace of the wolf, except that somewhere, out in the darkness of the fields, a sheep or a goat would suddenly scream out in terror before going silent.

Finally, on the longest night of the year, moonless, with the wind blowing hard from the forest, carrying ice that stung her face and eyes, and with the goats stirring restless and alarmed below her, the wind let up just long enough for her to hear the crunch of a footstep in the snow. It was no more than ten yards ahead. The goats in the shed threw themselves against the rear wall, each one pushing for the back. With their bustle serving to cover the sound, she pulled her rifle's hammer back to full cock and put a hand on the shutter of her darkened lantern.

The goats' panic grew, and they climbed atop each other to get away from the smell of death creeping toward them. Josette pulled the shutter and a square of light lit the snow ahead.

For just an instant, she saw the beast's yellow eyes reflecting the glow of the lantern, like windows into the fires of hell. They disappeared as the predator turned to flee, but in that light she could make out its ghostly gray body against the white snow.

She aimed just ahead of it, let out half a breath, and squeezed the trigger.

The temple bell rang out two in the morning, startling her out of her remembrance and pulling her back to the moment.

The Vins must have gone back to bed by now, but she waited another quarter of an hour, in case they too had been roused by the bell. Then she took a tiny, birdlike step down the slope of the roof.

A whisper rose from below, saying, "Jump here." She scooted over, climbed down, hanging by her fingers off the edge of the roof, and dropped. She landed soft as a feather on Bernat's luggage.

"It's a good thing I insisted on taking this," he whispered in her ear, as he helped her down to the street. "It's my instinct for contingencies that Colonel Okura was counting on, when he asked you to take me on this mission."

"I swear to God, Bernie, I will choke you to death with your own spare pantaloons." She tugged the luggage out, handed Bernat his bag, and shouldered hers. "Stay quiet and stay close."

He offered her a dark lantern as they set out, but she refused it. She had navigated the streets of Durum in pitch black a hundred times before. She could tell where she was by the pattern of cobblestones under her feet.

She led them across town. In her head, she worked out the quickest way to Mrs. Turel's house that avoided the barricaded southwest quarter, as well as the town square with its forest of gallows.

As they were skirting the center of town, they saw a Vin patrol coming down the street. They had to duck into a side alley and hide behind a pile of garbage until it passed. They hit another patrol as they turned north, and would have been caught going around the corner if the Vin soldiers weren't in the midst of a heated conversation that revealed their presence from half a block away.

After that close call, Josette slowed and took her party by a more tortuous path, weaving down the most disused alleys and crossing the wider streets only after stopping for minutes at a time to watch for patrols. The caution paid off when three Vinzhalian patrols passed without spotting them, while her little band of infiltrators huddled in stinking alleys.

By the time they approached Mrs. Turel's house, with the reek of the nearby tannery hanging thick in the moist air, the eastern sky was already turning gray. If Mrs. Turel wasn't part of a secret network of loyal Garnians—if she was just a batty old lady who liked to make up numbers—Josette would be hard-pressed to find safe harbor before the sun came up.

She tapped on the door.

Footsteps sounded inside—slow, cautious, unfriendly footsteps coming down the stairs. A face appeared at the window. It moved back too quickly for Josette to identify it, but she was sure it wasn't Mrs. Turel. She signaled the others to find cover, but they had hardly moved an inch when the door opened and a head stuck out.

"Good God, is that you, Josie? I thought Nadia was imagining things when she told me. Get inside before anyone sees you." It took a moment for her to recognize the man as Mr. Turel. The pistol clutched in his whitened fingers was discordant enough, but what was truly off about him was his size. Mr. Turel had been a robust man even in lean years, but now his frame was gaunt.

They rushed inside. Mr. Turel took a last look up and down the street, then shut the door and barred it. There wasn't much light inside the cramped first floor of the house, but in what little there was, Josette noticed that he did not put away the pistol.

"Who is it?" Mrs. Turel's anxious voice came from upstairs.

"It's Josie," Mr. Turel said, "and a couple of foreign-looking fellows."

"I'll have you know," Bernat said, with a level of volume and indignity that made everyone jump a little, including himself, "that I am as Garnian as the Chikyun Sword, and that Sergeant Jutes is as Garnian as . . . as . . ." He looked over the sergeant's square Brandheimian features and white complexion, and waved a dismissive hand about. "He's been naturalized, in any event."

"They're with me," Josette said, putting a hand on Bernat's shoulder to calm him. "We're here to organize a resistance within the city."

Mr. Turel laughed, and Mrs. Turel joined in as she came down the stairs. Good God, she was thin as a rail, too. Josette hadn't noticed it the day before, in all the commotion.

Mrs. Turel reached the bottom of the stairs and said, "Josie, we've been fighting the Vins since they got here. Sit down, sit down. No, no, away from the window, you damn fool." This last comment was directed at Bernat, who had no sooner collapsed into a chair than Mr. Turel grabbed it by the back and tried to dump him onto the floor.

Bernat stood, grumbling about his sore leg, and moved to another chair, while Mr. Turel leaned in to whisper to Josette, "You sure he's not a foreigner?"

"I believe his family is from the south of Garnia," she said.

"Oh, them," Mr. Turel said, as if it explained everything. "That's hardly Garnian at all."

"I am the son of the Marquis of Copia Lugon," Bernat insisted, as he set his sore leg up on the Turels' dining table.

"I can trace my lineage back to the ancient Tellurians, with ancestors from every duchy in the country. How can anyone be more authentically Garnian than that?"

Mrs. Turel clapped her hands to her cheeks. "Arthur, I think he's the man Elise talked about."

"Him?" Mr. Turel asked, leaning over to study Bernat. He huffed. "I thought he'd be taller. And less foreign-looking."

"If anything, it's you, sir, who are—"

"Bernie, shush," Josette said, stopping him before he got them thrown out onto the street and left to the sparse mercy of the Vins. She would have to explain later that these people had probably never been south of . . . well, south of Durum, now that she thought of it. They didn't realize just how foreign-looking the majority of their countrymen were, nor how manifestly Vin-like the features of a typical Durumite would seem to the rest of the country.

They did have a tinge of Vin in their accent, for one thing. She had never noticed it while growing up here, nor had she ever heard it mentioned until Roland's comment, but now that it had been pointed out to her, it was unmistakable. It was hardly surprising, however. Durum had once been a jewel of Vinzhalia, long before it was conquered by Garnia and went into its centuries-long decline, as lucrative trade withered under the strain of near-constant warfare.

When Josette last lived in Durum, there were still families who—with broadly varying degrees of secrecy—blamed Garnia for Durum's plight and longed for a restoration to Vin rule. No one knew just how many of them had taken their discontent to the level of spying for Vinzhalia, but there were enough of them that the city's half-hearted counterespionage efforts uncovered a spy or two every generation.

A hollow boom sounded outside and all five heads turned to the west, just in time to hear the following crack. In the morning light, the Garnian artillery was firing again.

Josette asked Mr. Turel, "How do we signal the resistance fighters?"

He looked confused at the very question.

She clarified. "Do you place something in a window, to signal the need for a meeting? Leave a bucket upturned at the well? Or is it a certain pattern of hammer blows at the blacksmith? There must be something. How do you pass messages?"

Mr. Turel looked to Mrs. Turel, who shrugged her shoulders and said, "Usually I just go down to Heny's, on the excuse of needing a remedy for ladies' troubles."

Josette blinked twice while she worked out the obvious in her head. "You mean to say Heny the midwife is leading the resistance in Durum?"

Mr. Turel scowled at that. "Not leading it," he said, sharply.

"More at the center of it," Mrs. Turel added. "It only makes sense. Every woman in town has one excuse or another to visit her, and not the Vins nor their informants would ever think twice at our comings and goings. So she just sort of turned into the, uh, what do you call the bit at the middle of a wheel, Arthur?"

"Hub."

"She turned into the hub. Is it a hub? No, that's not right. The part at the middle of the wheel."

"It's called the hub, Nadia."

"No, that's not it. Whatever it is, though, Heny's that."

"It's a hub."

"No, you're thinking of something else."

Josette interrupted before things became too bloody. "Can you visit Heny today, and get us in touch with her?" The cannons went off again, all four of them in a rippling fire running north to south.

Mrs. Turel looked down at her nightshirt. "Just let me dress, and I'll go right now. While I'm out, try to remember that word, will you?"

"It's a hub!" This time it was not just Mr. Turel, but Bernat and Jutes who all said it together.

Mrs. Turel paused a moment on the stairs, thought it over, and shook her head. "No, that ain't it."

Josette stopped Bernat from giving any further thoughts, then asked Mr. Turel, "Do you have someplace to hide us for the day?"

Mr. Turel nodded and led them down to a root cellar. The floor down there was surprisingly comfortable, as it was amply padded by empty sacks, and had hardly any food in it to get in their way. Once she was situated, Josette retrieved her rifled pistol, fit a percussion cap into the slot ahead of the hammer, and cradled it on her stomach as she closed her eyes.

And, though here it was merely chill and humid, rather than freezing and wet, her mind went back to the roof of that goat shed, where flint scraped against frizzen, and icy wind blew the sparks into her face.

ENSIGN KEMBER WAS still standing watch when the siege guns began to fire in the morning light. Lieutenant Hanon had assigned her the night watch as soon as Captain Dupre was off the ship, had left orders not to wake him, and was still asleep in his berth. She wasn't sure what she was supposed to do in such a circumstance, so she remained on watch into the morning.

She might have argued with him in the first place, citing the regulations which forbid auxiliary officers from standing watch at night, but those regulations were habitually ignored in the signal corps, and the same regulations forbade her from firing the cannons, so that would never do. So she'd gone on watch, and remained on watch, and now she was stuck on watch, for the crew of the morning relief had already come on duty, and she'd look a mercurial fool if she suddenly decided to take Corporal Lupien off the rudder and give him the deck. The entire situation from top to bottom was perfectly absurd, of course, and yet perfectly in keeping with her experience of the army.

What would the captain do?

The captain would walk back there and kick out the supports on Lieutenant Hanon's berth, to let him either tumble onto the catwalk or fall through the ship's thin outer envelope, as his reaction speed and airman's instincts dictated.

Then again, the captain didn't seem to care what people thought of her. If the captain had Kember's scar, she'd wear it openly. She wouldn't cover it in concealer, even if it made her hideous, even if the sight of it made that Roland fellow scorn her. And even if he scorned her, she'd never let anyone know. Inside, she might be hurting, but it would never show on the surface. In fact, you might not even know they'd split up.

Whereas Kember's reactions to her very few, very short courtships had been the exact opposite. She had never worried when they ended. In fact, she was usually relieved—but she always took care to show pain on the surface, lest anyone think her unusual.

At noon, Hanon was still in his berth. Kember used the excuse of the changing watch to give Lupien the deck, but at least one officer had to be awake and ready to take command, so she took up the station of the deck lookout, though it had been over twenty-four hours since she last had a wink of sleep.

This was why, after the fog burned away and was replaced by partial cloud cover, she passed it off as mere imagination when she saw a flash of white tailfin disappearing into a cloud to starboard. It couldn't have been another ship, after all, since what she thought she'd seen was a tail that tapered smoothly into the frames amidships, the way *Mistral*'s did. With her sister ships still under construction, *Mistral* was the only rigid airship in the sky with a design like that. And hadn't Kember closed her eyes to rest them, and only opened them when her drooping head startled her awake? In that moment, she must have dreamed of her own ship—she'd done it before—and woke with an image of it reflected in her mind's eye.

She returned her attention to Durum, watching for any of the prearranged signals from the captain. Her eyes went over it, street by street. But at the end of each circuit of the town, her gaze turned back to that one patch of sky, where lay the great billowing cloud that her dream-conjured ship had disappeared into.

"I REMEMBERED WHAT that word is," Mrs. Turel said, as she came down the steps to the root cellar. "It's 'axle.' And all of you thinking it was something else. Heny and me had a laugh about that, let me tell you."

Bernat sat up from his resting spot on a pile of lumpy burlap and shielded his eyes against the light coming in from upstairs. Jutes and Josette stirred in the gloom of the root cellar.

"Will Heny be coming?" Josette asked.

"She's sending an escort after dark, to smuggle you to her place," Mrs. Turel said, with an odd sort of impish delight in her voice.

Bernat had to wait all afternoon and half the evening to find out what that delight meant. Throughout his forced quiescence, he occupied himself in alternately napping, listening to the cannons, being shushed by Josette for trying to talk, and trying to feed a scrap of rotten turnip to the cellar rats. None of them would approach him, though, preferring instead to scratch around near the walls at the opposite end of the cellar, occasionally getting into fights or engaging in licentious acts.

The Turels were meager entertainment. Of their scant conversations, only a word here and there could be understood through the floorboards. He gathered that their farmland lay outside the walls, and the siege had denied them their occupation. Unaccustomed to being shut in and idle during the day, they sat at opposite ends of a table through entire hours of unmoving silence. It must have been the most dreadfully awkward day—though Bernat had to admit, as he rolled rotten turnip between his fingers and listened to rats fornicating in the dark, his own day was in the running.

And so it was the purest joy he felt when, at about seven in the evening, he heard a knock on the door. It might have been Heny's man, or it might have been the Vins come to hang them all. Either way, it would be a relief.

The little door at the top of the steps opened. "Bernie?" a voice asked.

"Elise?" He squinted into the light. "Elise!" He leapt up, ignoring the brutal soreness in his injured leg. He was in such a hurry, he hit his head on the floorboards, not just when he stood, but again when he was going up the steps.

It was worth it, though. It was worth all the suffering in the world to wrap his arms around Elise and kiss her with such a force of burning desire that the rats would blush to see it. He could hear the Turels making indelicate comments to each other, and Josette clearing her throat with great force and frequency, but he ignored them. His beloved was safe and alive, and he was in her arms, and that was all that mattered.

Together, they fell into a wonderful sort of timelessness, in which the comments and throat-clearing faded away to nothing, and all that existed in all the world was Elise and himself. He couldn't have said how much time passed before they finally leaned apart. He only knew it was long enough to get the beginnings of a cramp in his tongue, but not quite long enough for Josette to douse them with the pail of water she'd fetched from somewhere.

"Hello, Mother," Josette said as she set the pail down, a hint of disappointment in her eyes.

"Josie?" Elise said, noticing her for the first time. "What are you doing here?"

Josette was about to speak, but she appeared to think better of her first choice of words. She sighed and said instead, "Just tagging along on Lord Hinkal's mission."

Elise let him go and took a couple of steps toward Josette. Josette took a couple of steps toward Elise as well, but they did not embrace. For a moment, Bernat thought he might be treated to the absurd sight of mother and daughter shaking hands, but they only stood there at a respectful distance, and nodded to each other.

"You're looking well," Josette said.

"And you . . . the same."

Josette looked at the front window, then at her feet, then seemed to suck on a tooth behind tightly closed lips, and finally said, "Heny's got you running errands for the resistance, eh?"

"She has." Elise looked at the back window, then at her feet, then fiddled with the collar of her chemise, and finally continued, "We better get moving. It'll be curfew soon. I'd put those bags of yours in a laundry basket, so you don't look quite so much like soldiers on the march."

The Turels volunteered their laundry basket and the luggage was stuffed into it, after Bernat retrieved his cane from Josette's bag. Elise and Josette carried the basket between them, while Bernat and Jutes walked slightly ahead, keeping an eye out for Vin patrols.

"Shouldn't be too many of the bastards in this quarter of town," Elise said as they walked. "Bernie, what's happened to your leg?"

Bernat wasn't sure it was wise to chat while sneaking through the streets of occupied Durum, but he supposed Elise knew what she was doing. "Hurt it in a crash, near Kuchin."

He glanced back to see equal parts pity and anxiety written on Elise's face. She said, "Those ships aren't safe, Bernie. I wish you wouldn't go up in them. You're not in the army, are you? Not officially?"

"No," Bernat said. "I offered to join, but they told me I was too pretty."

Elise laughed. "That was never a problem for Josie."

Josette interjected a deep sigh, which shut them both up.

Apart from a few faces pressed to windows, they didn't see another soul through ten blocks of walking. Near the north gate, with the daylight nearly gone, they came to what seemed less a house than a cottage, fronting one of Durum's many urban gardens. Indeed, the garden hardly seemed to stop at the house, which had herbs growing out of its turf roof.

"What a delightful town," Bernat murmured, pausing to admire it, while the others shuffled inside. He followed to find the inside of the house just as charming. It was laid out like a country cottage on the inside as well, with one long room tightly packed with hearth, table, and two beds separated from each other by curtains hanging from the bare rafters. The windows were all shuttered.

Next to the hearth sat an older woman, paunchy despite her thin frame, but bearing that paradox of malnutrition quite well. "Make yourselves at home," the woman he took to be Heny said, as she ground away at a mortar and pestle. "Pesha will be back any minute."

"Pesha was Heny's apprentice," Josette explained quietly.

Bernat wasn't sure why an apprentice would still live here after so many years. He began to put together a good guess, however, when he sat down on the bed farthest from the hearth, there being only three chairs in the entire house, and noticed the dust on it. It was only a very sparse layer atop the sheets, hardly noticeable except under prudent snooping, but when he probed the hem of the top sheet with his finger, he saw that the dust did not extend to the lower sheet. That was to say, the bed had been neatly made, and then it had sat with the top sheet undisturbed for long enough to become dusty.

When Heny looked up, he shot her a sly smile, but she only narrowed her eyes back at him as she upturned the mortar into an iron pot, poured water over it, and set it on the hook over the hearth fire.

Turning toward Josette, Heny said, "Get over here, Josie. Let me see you in the light." Josette obeyed, standing by the hearth. Heny poked a finger at her collarbone, then squeezed the flesh on her arm. "Staying healthy. Good. Your mother put a lot of work into you."

"For all the good it did," Elise said.

Jutes, sitting on the other bed, took a sudden interest in the boiling pot on the fire, making it plain that he was most certainly not paying any attention to the abuse his captain was taking, if he indeed had enough attention to spare from the fascinating bubbling in the pot to realize anyone was speaking at all.

And so Jutes was taken by surprise—quite genuine surprise—when Heny pulled him to his feet, poked at him, and looked him over just as critically. When she marched around the bed to Bernat, he saved some of his dignity by getting to his feet before she reached him, and stood with his head held high, his hands doubled on the crook of his cane.

After poking and pinching him, Heny threw her hands in the air and said, less in frustration than despair, "Worst bunch of goddamn spies I ever seen. One of you's the only man under fifty in the whole town who uses a cane, one of you's the spitting image of Elise Dupre, and the most incognito of the bunch is a goddamn Brandheimian who may as well have 'Sergeant' tattooed on his fucking forehead. You could have knocked on the gate and politely asked the Vins to let you have a word with the resistance, for all the effort you've put into subtlety."

Josette, looking every bit the captain despite her peasant garb, said to Heny, "We didn't come here to be berated."

Heny snorted. "Well you couldn't have done a better job of it, if that *was* what you came for."

"We came to liberate Durum," Josette asserted, in a tone so hard it made Heny take a step back. "But the Vins have a larger garrison than we expected, so we need your help to do it. If that doesn't suit you, I'll signal my ship to pick us up, and we'll leave the town as we found it."

"Josie!" Elise snapped.

"Shut up, Mother," Josette said without even looking away from Heny. "My mother will be coming with us, mind you, even if she has to be gagged and stuffed into a gunnysack. So I'll have what I came for, and I won't think twice when I fly away and leave the rest of this worthless town to the Vins."

Jutes went from standing uncomfortably near Heny to looming uncomfortably over her. It was a subtle shift, but Bernat thought he pulled it off well.

"Such a wretched girl," Elise said. "Don't you think so, Bernie?"

"Yes, and not for the first time," Bernat said, turning a pleasant smile on Josette. "Indeed, not for the first time today."

Heny only laughed—rather merrily, considering all the ill feeling going around—and said, "Well, I think she turned out just fine." She put an affectionate hand on Josette's shoulder and squeezed. "You know just where you stand, with her."

"Likewise." Josette relaxed, and Jutes went back to merely standing.

"Mehmed would be proud of you," Heny said.

Josette's mother seemed about to speak up, but decided against it.

As things settled down, Josette noticed Heny's apprentice,

standing just inside the door. Or, she corrected herself, she noticed the woman who'd been Heny's apprentice when Josette left to join the army.

"Hi, Josie," Pesha said, lifting one hand to shoulder level and giving a hesitant wave from two yards away.

Josette returned a respectful nod. "Good to see you again. Stayed on as Heny's assistant, did you?"

Pesha's thin lips twitched into a smile that didn't show her teeth. She gave the smallest of nods, and said in a mouse's voice, "And washerwoman at the town hall." She stood, shuffling her feet and looking anxiously from face to face for a few moments, before adding, "In the afternoons."

Josette was taken aback by how reserved she had become. Pesha was only a few years older than her, but that had been a big difference back then, and Josette always thought of her as practically an authority figure. It was positively unnerving to see her blushing and aloof, and still doing much the same job she'd been at for over two decades.

"Washerwoman, eh?" Bernat asked, with a sly inflection on the last sound.

Pesha's closed-lip smile came back. "They don't know I understand Vin, see. Usually they watch what they say anyway, but every now and then . . ." The smile expanded until a narrow streak of her front teeth showed, which for her must have been like grinning from ear to ear.

"From what Pesha and some others have gathered," Heny said, "the Vin garrison is what's left of the 64th regiment. Started out four thousand strong, we heard, and lost a third of that at the first attack on Arle. They were looking for revenge at Canard, but they got hurt even worse there. Limped back to Durum with around nine hundred men left, stole every scrap of coin from us that some other Vin hadn't already stole, and got put on garrison duty while they reinforced.

Since then they've gotten about a hundred men in from Vinzhalia."

"Mrs. Turel said they had five hundred and eighty-six." Josette tried to hold her temper. "If there are a thousand, we're sunk. Goddamn that old bat."

Heny didn't flinch under Josette's angry gaze. "Mrs. Turel's right," she said. "As of today, there's five hundred and eighty-six of them. And you respect your elders." She emphasized this by sticking a finger hard into Josette's ribs.

"So what happened to the others?"

"Around two hundred and fifty were wounded at Canard so bad they either died later or got sent home," Heny said. "Twenty-four died of typhus. Eight succumbed to flu over the winter. Six were sent home after they got drunk and hurt themselves. One was hanged for striking an officer." Heny shared a conspiratorial grin with Pesha and Josette's mother, before she went on in a sly tone, "And we got the rest."

"Good God!" Bernat cried, loud enough that Josette's mother had to reminded him to keep his voice down.

"You mean to say that the resistance has killed . . ." Josette did the math in her head. "A hundred and twenty-five Vin fusiliers?"

Pesha blushed and looked sheepish. "Not all killed. Some we only wounded or made sick enough that they got sent home."

"We got the most with poison," Heny said. "They made it easy enough, since they stole all their goddamn food from us. We poisoned a couple legs of mutton bound for their stewpots, and we killed over seventy of the bastards in one go. Took hundreds more off their feet for a month, too." She took a deep breath. "Vins hanged two hundred of us for that. An even two hundred."

"That's when they got Audrey, Madeena, and Sibil," Pesha said, naming three girls who'd been Josette's age when she ran away to join the army. "And Mr. Rostom and Kadi Halphin, too, even though they'd both been locked in the dungeon the whole time, and couldn't have had a hand in it. Only two or three who were actually in on the plan got taken and hanged, and I bet that was nothing but coincidence."

"Soldiers make lousy policemen," Josette said. "Good soldiers most especially."

"The other Vins we got one or two at a time," Heny said. "Arranged accidents, ambushed patrols, and that sort of thing. We're having a harder time of it now, seeing how they don't go anywhere in groups smaller than four these days."

As impressed as Josette was with the town's fighting spirit, that last comment made her realize that Durum had cut its own throat. If the town had meekly acquiesced to Vin rule, the 64th would have marched out ages ago, and been replaced by the smaller garrison of invalids and old men Josette had expected to find here. Instead, they faced nearly six hundred of the most experienced infantrymen in the world—men who would be out for blood after losing so many of their friends, hardened by the hell the Durum resistance had put them through.

"And what about our people?" Josette asked, hoping against all odds for some good news to balance out the bad.

"Two of the men from your airship are safe," Heny said.

"Corne and Kiffer," Pesha added.

"You sent them to just the right place, Josie. Anywhere else and they'd be dead twice over: once from the putrid rot in their wounds, and again from the Vins catching 'em. And there's some folk from the signal base still alive, too."

"Where?"

"Just under your feet, of course. Oh, I forgot!" Heny's voice became suddenly cheerful. "You haven't been back since we made a proper room out of the cellar. Oh, you have to see it, Josie. It's lovely."

Pesha nodded along, her enthusiasm turning her from quiet to chatty in an instant. "It really is lovely. Had it done over about three years back. It's got brick walls now and a carpet and everything. You wouldn't even know it's a cellar, except there aren't windows. It's like having a whole other floor. You have to see it."

"We use it as a day room during the summer, because it's nice and cool down there," Heny said, her voice bordering on boastful. "You just have to see it."

"It's lovely," Pesha added.

"We disguised the stairs when the Vins took over, so you can't even tell it's there if you didn't know already." Pesha pointed to a spot on the floor near the back corner of the cottage, but Josette really couldn't tell where it was, even when it was pointed out.

"Why don't you stay down there?" Heny said. "It's the safest place in town, and I'm sure they can make room for you."

"Oh, yes!" Pesha said, clasping her hands. "You'll love it. I'd take you down now, but it's a pain to get the boards back in place."

Josette sighed. "On the subject of the Vin garrison . . ."

Heny looked disappointed at the change in topic, and Pesha even more so.

"I'm sorry to say that our battalion is no match for them," Josette said. "We couldn't beat them even if we faced off on an open field, let alone with the Vins on the walls. And we don't have the time or supplies for a prolonged siege." She paused to let that sink in. "However, if we can gather a force inside the town to spike the guns on the wall, or attack the garrison from inside, or just stir up enough trouble to keep them looking over their shoulders, then we have a chance. I dare say you have your own ideas about that."

"One," Heny said, nodding slowly. "The gunpowder."

"Blow up their powder magazine?" Josette grinned at the idea.

"Nothing like exploding a powder magazine for taking the fight out of defenders," Jutes said. "It's bloody brilliant."

"Only," Heny said, "they've moved their gunpowder storage from the east side of town to the west, closer to the guns that face Garnian territory. The problem is, their new powder magazine's underground, with tunnels leading to the wall."

Jutes was the first of them to figure it out. "And you don't know where the magazine is," he said.

Heny nodded. "Not a damn clue. We been trying to find it for months, but we can't get anyone in there without being spotted. Half the people that tried are rotting on the ends of ropes in the town square."

"Perhaps *Mistral* can see where it is from above," Bernat said.

Heny shook her head. "We managed to get a shrine maiden up to the top of the pagoda to look for it, which took a damn lot of tears and crying out to God, let me tell you. The Vins suspected she was up to something, those heathen bastards. But when she finally got up there, she couldn't see squat. Wherever they put the magazine, they've left no sign of it aboveground. There's only one way to get the location, but we never had the right mix of talent for it, until now."

Josette thought she knew what Heny was getting at, but wasn't quite ready to accept it. "What do you mean?"

"Right now, in this very room, we got two expert poachers," Heny said, nodding to Josette and her mother. "And an experienced hunter," she went on, looking at Bernat. Then, pointing to Jutes, she added, "And some good old-fashioned army muscle."

Josette closed her eyes. "You want us to take a prisoner?"

"You were always a clever lass, Josie."

"Jutes?" Josette asked.

"Risky. Prisoner snatches are as likely to get the snatchers taken prisoner as the snatchee." Jutes's face hardened. "But I don't see another option."

"And, assuming this can even be done, where do you plan to interrogate the prisoner?"

Heny only pointed at the floor.

"Oh, it's just lovely down there," Pesha said.

11

BERNAT HAD DARED to believe he was past spending the night atop piles of garbage, but the needs of Durum's resistance compelled him to take up the habit again. At least, he consoled himself, it was very old and very dry garbage which had lost most of its smell over the years.

He was inside one of Durum's many trash houses. They were buildings left abandoned—some over a century ago— then used as convenient neighborhood refuse dumps until they were filled to the rafters.

Until this night, he hadn't believed they existed, despite Josette's insistence. Now that he could hardly deny the proof, he decided that their presence reflected no shame on Durum, but rather a resourceful ingenuity.

He only wished that Durum's ingenuity was less lumpy, and that it didn't still smell faintly of rotten cabbage. There were less-lumpy patches here and there, and of course one could always lie on the house's exposed rafters rather than directly on the trash, but the choices were limited by the surprisingly good condition of the roof. There were only a few places, here and there, where a gap in the beams and shingles provided a space wide enough to shoot a rifle through, and even fewer that pointed along the street they were interested in.

Elise was the only one of them who got to lie on a rafter beam, at the mutual insistence of Josette and himself. He had further insisted that Josette take the least lumpy, least aromatic patch of garbage to make her sharpshooter's nest in, even though she assured him that he'd come to regret it.

"I'm used to this sort of thing," she'd whispered, and even in the pitch dark, he could tell she was staring off into space and remembering another time. "You'll be fidgeting all night, and moaning about the discomfort within an hour."

He had insisted, nevertheless, and was proud to have proved her wrong, for the pagoda's bell had rung out the hour twice before he started to moan about his discomfort.

"Hush," Josette said, from the darkness to his left. "The Vin patrol's coming around again."

It was a few minutes before he could see them from his vantage point, through an inch-wide vertical crack in the roof which offered little visibility to the sides and could only let him look directly up and down the avenue ahead. They were the same four patrolmen he'd seen twice already, softly illuminated by lantern light as they made their circuit through the southwest quarter of town. He sighted along the barrel of his rifle, keeping it dutifully aimed at the rightmost man and ready to bring him down at a moment's notice, though the ambush wouldn't be sprung for a while yet, unless something went very wrong.

If, on the other hand, everything went to plan, the patrol would go off-duty about half an hour before daybreak. According to Heny, who had the information from watchers about town, the men on this patrol route always stopped to clear their muskets by firing into the soft earth by the side of the street. At that moment, when the sound would disguise their own fire, the party in the trash house would shoot three of them. Then all Sergeant Jutes had to do was leap from the nearby house he was hiding in and knock the fourth man on the head. Pesha had also hidden herself somewhere along the street and was ready, at Josette's suggestion, to provide a distraction if anything went wrong.

But surely nothing would. In fact, it all seemed so easy that Bernat was already thinking of the bon mots he would throw at Josette, to tease her for being so worried. He already had a good one in mind, but it would only work if she made some reference to the cock spring of his rifle, so he'd have to devise some method of maneuvering her onto the topic.

It was while he was contemplating this that things went wrong in the absolute last way he could have imagined, when a Vin officer strolled down the street from another direction entirely, and stopped to contemplate the very house Bernat was hiding in.

The man had come from his right, and he wondered just how long he'd been over there, standing in the open in the middle of the street, but entirely hidden from the ambush party's view. Long enough to hear Bernat's complaints, or Josette's admonition that they might be overheard? The Vin was intently interested in the house, in any event, and too damn close for Bernat to point the rifle down at him without sitting up and giving himself away by the sound of rustling garbage.

Worse, Bernat realized with dawning terror, neither Elise nor Josette could see the man from their hiding places. If either of them spoke, or merely shifted to a more comfortable position, it would remove whatever doubt remained in the Vin officer's mind.

In the darkness, the officer's eyes were two shadowed sockets, but it seemed to Bernat that they ran upward to the roof, scanned along it, and settled right onto the very hole he was watching through. He told himself that his fear was lying to him. But if his fear was lying to him, it was assisted by his imagination, which told him the Vins would burn the house down to root him out, that he'd die in agony, hearing his lover's screams above his own.

A second officer came from the right and stood next to the first, and he too seemed to stare up at the roof, and seemed to see straight through the darkness, and to look directly into Bernat's eyes, now watering from being held open so long.

The second man flicked a fire striker. The sparks fell into a fold of charpaper held in his other hand. Bernat—seeing visions of a house aflame—jerked up into a crouch, aligned the rifle as best he could in his shaking hands, and was just about to pull the trigger when the officer's charpaper caught the spark and ignited, and in the light from that small flame he saw that it was Major Dvakov, an unlit cigarette hanging limply from his mouth.

In that new light, he saw both officers' eyes jerk over to fix on the hole he pointed his rifle through. Their eyes had not, it seemed, been on him before, but they certainly were now, and they were straining to identify the source of the disturbance above them.

He could hear Josette breathing to his left, and he was more afraid of the spiteful things she would say to him while they all burned to death than he was of the prospect itself, and even as his heart pounded so hard that the force of the blood hurt his ears and his eyes felt like they would burst, he was made half giddy at the thought that his greatest fear was not a fiery demise, but Josette's disapproval. He had to bite down on his tongue to keep himself from laughing.

The Vins laughed for him. "Goddamn saboteurs have us jumping at rats," the officer he didn't recognize said, speaking Vinzhalian. "What a couple of fools we are."

Dvakov lit his cigarette and gave the charpaper a flick to put it out. He replied in the same language, "Better to jump at the little rats and be a fool, Colonel, than to not jump at the big ones and be a dead man." They both had another good laugh at that, which gave Bernat the courage to take a shallow breath. "Then again, sir, if you'd only let me loose on the big ones, perhaps we wouldn't have to jump at all."

Bernat couldn't tell if the comment was friendly or resentful.

However it was meant, the colonel responded by giving Dvakov a good-natured slap on the shoulder and said, "The last time I let you loose, Nuri, you hanged half the town."

"Surely not *half,* Colonel . . ."

"And what would you do if I let you loose again? I suppose you'd want public beatings and executions for the top names on the suspect list?"

"Not at all, Colonel, not at all," Dvakov said. "Public beatings and executions for *every* name on the suspect list. Then you can be certain the guilty party has been dealt with."

"Along with more than a few innocent souls."

"If there is such a thing as an innocent soul in this demon's ass of a town. And if there is, will their god not take care of them, in due course?"

The colonel chuckled at that, and by now Bernat had recovered enough of his wits to marvel at how very civil they were in debating the points for and against mass murder. "No, no, Nuri. There are rules about this sort of thing, and we have them for a reason." He looked down the street, to where the patrolmen were just going around the corner and out of sight. "Best not to tempt fate by lingering here in the dark, though."

"Indeed. Some innocent souls might come along and slit our throats."

They both had another laugh at that. Bernat, clammy and uncomfortable with sweat, his nerves still on edge, was getting rather tired of having to listen to their merriment, and so was glad when they disappeared from view and their voices receded down the street.

After a long time spent in silence, Josette hissed from the darkness, "Who the hell were they?"

"The colonel of the Vin regiment, I think, and Major Dvakov."

"What were they talking about?" Elise asked.

"Just routine beatings and murders."

"Then for God's sake shut up about it," Josette said. "Another word from either of you, and I'll creep out quietly and give you away to the Vins." Bernat hadn't formed a reply, wasn't even sure he would reply, and certainly hadn't uttered the slightest sound, when Josette pre-empted him with, "I said, shut up."

So he sat calmly for the rest of the night, watching the patrol appear periodically as it went around and around its route. In the times between, he reflected that all that nonsense about fearing Josette's judgement was just that: nothing more than another freak symptom of his soldier's heart. Nothing to worry about, outside of the broader problem.

It must have been an hour before dawn when Elise reached over to wake him. At first, he didn't realize he'd been asleep, but a look at the lightening sky left no room for argument. He only hoped he hadn't snored.

Mistral was just visible to the west of town, her envelope minutely brighter than the charcoal gray of the sky. He had to search to find her again every time he looked away, but even so, her presence bucked up his courage. The patrol came around again, and the dawn crept closer.

Shortly after, four flashes spaced two seconds apart lit *Mistral*'s envelope and the cloud cover alike with orange-yellow light. Seconds after the last flash, the sound of the first Garnian cannon reached them. The Vins' cannons returned fire, but were slower by far.

The patrol came around for the last sweep of their watch, if Heny's reports had any truth to them. Bernat trained his rifle on the rightmost man. He aimed for the head, a risky shot, but one which would prevent any call for help. And now the patrolmen stopped and lingered several blocks away, their nightly duty finally over.

But they didn't clear their muskets. They only stood there, stretching and gabbing at each other, until the relief patrol came down the street to meet them.

Now there were eight Vins on the street. Eight Vins with loaded muskets, where there were supposed to be four with empty ones. After a few minutes spent chatting with their relief, the night patrol left by the same street the day patrol had arrived by, but that changed nothing. If Bernat fired now, they'd be back before he could reload.

"Don't," Josette whispered. Bernat noticed that she didn't even dare to add the word "fire," lest speaking it cause confusion. The precaution wasn't necessary in his case. He might be new to this, but even he could see that to act now would be disastrous.

But Pesha was even newer to it than Bernat, and didn't possess the natural aptitude for all things that his noble blood had granted him. She emerged from the front door of a house as the patrolmen passed by, and walked toward them from behind.

"Oh hell," he heard Josette mutter.

Pesha had a basket in her arms. She nearly dropped it when Jutes came out of his hiding place and tried to drag her silently out of sight. She pushed him away and they scuffled in such a subdued and stealthy manner that it was surreal to watch. Bernat set his entire mind to willing the Vin patrol to keep looking forward, to not look back, to not detect the faint sound of feet scraping on cobblestones behind them.

Jutes must have decided that he'd tempted fate long enough, for he ducked into the space between two houses and left Pesha to the fruits of her choices.

The inevitable finally happened, as one of the Vins looked over his shoulder. He spun around and pointed his musket at Pesha. The other three, having just begun their day and still quite sharp, took one look at the girl and instantly dropped to kneeling positions with their guns pointed in different directions. Their heads swung back and forth as they scanned the houses and street for signs of an ambush.

Pesha was twenty feet from them, an easy shot even with a musket. She threw her arms in the air, her basket falling. It landed, bounced, and fell on its side, whereupon a dozen furry lightning bolts shot out of it and scattered up and down the street. "My kittens!" she shouted in Garnian. Without seeming to think, without any apparent cognizance of the fact that there was a musket aimed at her, she ran after the nearest cat.

By the time she scooped it up and was running after the next, the discipline of the Vin patrol had evaporated. The man who had been pointing his musket at her now dropped the weapon so he could make a grab for a kitten that ran between his feet. The man next to him was scarcely more sensible, only slinging his musket before he gave chase. Another patrolman kept his gun in one hand and scooped up a kitten in the other, but finding himself unable to keep a hold on the mewling little fugitive, leaned the musket against a nearby house so he could use both hands.

Only the fourth Vin had the presence of mind to keep his gun in both hands, and to watch for signs of ambush instead of running after a bunch of cats, and his cool professionalism sealed his fate. Pesha came at him from behind. She dropped her kitten and took a foot of gleaming steel dagger from her blouse. She brought the blade up, and hesitated. Even from this distance, Bernat could see the glint as it shifted in the morning light, shaking in her hand. But despite her reservations, when she struck, she struck with the precision of an anatomist. She slid the knife into his neck and stuffed her other hand into his mouth to stifle the scream.

"What do we do?" Bernat asked. When he received no

answer, he looked to his left and found his companions missing. He looked out of his embrasure to find them running down the street, already halfway to Pesha. Jutes was closer still, having leapt from his hiding spot as a patrolman ran past. Now Jutes had a wooden bludgeon out and, just as the Vin turned around to see what was behind him, Jutes shattered his face. The patrolman went down like a barrel of nails, hitting the cobblestones so hard that some of his blood splashed on a wall ten feet away.

One of the surviving Vins, the youngest, still didn't seem to understand what was going on. He saw the facts of the events. He couldn't have missed them. Indeed, he was looking right at Pesha as she pulled her dagger free of a man's neck. But he kept running after one of the kittens, staring moonfaced at Pesha until the kitten went through the space in a slatted fence, which he then ran headlong into.

His inattention damned him, even as attention had damned the first man to fall. He crashed back from his impact with the fence and landed in the street. Pesha walked up to him in a halting stagger, holding her bloody dagger at the limit of her arm's length, as if trying to keep it as far away as possible. She stood over him and grasped the handle in both hands.

"Not that one!" Josette cried. "That's the one we want!"

It wouldn't have been too late, if Pesha weren't in such a daze. She must have heard Josette's warning, but was too addled to understand it. She knelt down and drove the dagger through the young Vin's belly and up under his ribs.

That only left one, who had by now unslung his musket and was aiming from the hip at an onrushing Sergeant Jutes. But Jutes was charging like a goddamn rhinoceros, and didn't even flinch at the point of the bayonet. He was upon the man in an instant, heaving his bludgeon at the bayonet to knock the musket aside and then using his entire body as a battering ram.

He hit so hard that neither of them could pick themselves

up for some time after the impact. But Elise was there to help Jutes up, while the surviving Vin got the butt of Josette's rifle for good measure.

She looked back along the street and called, "Wake up, Bernie, we're leaving!"

12

JUTES AND BERNAT shuffled into Heny's cottage, carrying the Vin fusilier between them. Josette went down the stairs first, and Bernat heard her say from the bottom step, "Oh, it is lovely."

Manhandling their dazed, barely conscious burden down into the basement, Bernat saw that it was indeed lovely down here. The stone walls evoked an old country home, the wine-colored carpet lent the simple elegance of a hunting lodge, and the warm lamplight made it all feel so very welcoming. The sight and smell of five bedraggled Garnian fugitives detracted considerably from the effect, but this only made Bernat wonder at just how lovely it must be without them. He already wanted to visit in the summertime.

He recognized some of them, despite their greatly reduced frames and lean faces. Private Corne, who had lost one hand and most of the other to a premature cannon discharge, rose from a bed of old blanket and squinted bleary eyes to see what was happening. When he spotted the prisoner, he grabbed a pair of pliers with the three remaining fingers of his good hand and showed his teeth in an eager grin. The man next to him was Private Kiffer. Bernat also recognized three of the fellows from the former air base, all staring like jackals at the helpless prisoner.

Josette was not pleased. She stared hard at the men and said, "You may put away those goddamn pliers, Private Corne, if you find that they are impeding your ability to salute an officer."

The others got the message immediately, snapping into their own salutes. Corne lagged behind, looking first surprised and then indignant, but he finally tucked the pliers into the crook of his left elbow and saluted with his right hand.

Bernat thought it in rather poor taste, for Josette to single out the man who'd lost so much in service of her ship, but he understood her reasons when she barked, "I see that some of you are very eager to torture this man. It pleases me to disappoint you. You will not harm the prisoner unless I tell you to. You will not threaten him. You will not even attempt to interrogate him except on my order." Only then did she return their salute, allowing them to relax.

She motioned to Jutes, and the Vin was handed over to the men from the airbase, who carried him away to be tied into a chair behind a delightful little writing desk in the back corner of the room.

With the enlisted men out of earshot, Bernat said to Josette, "That was disconcerting. By comparison to the norm, I might almost call you timid in your concern for that prisoner."

Elise finished securing the trapdoor from the inside and came down the steps to join them. "I think it was admirable," she said. For the first time Bernat had ever seen, Elise smiled at her daughter. She put a hand on Josette's shoulder. "I was worried you'd lost all your principles when you joined the Garnian army."

Josette put her back to the room. "Principles? Hell, I'm just trying to salvage something from this fiasco. Take a good look at that man."

Bernat did. As Corne wiped his face clean, it revealed a marbled network of previous scars on his left cheek, all older than the bruises and broken teeth he'd received from Josette's rifle butt. The Vin spat blood on the table and returned Bernat's gaze, his eyes blazing with defiance.

"That man," Josette continued, "has been in the thick of two of the bloodiest battles in this war. He's marched into musket and cannon fire, charged bayonet to bayonet, been wounded, seen his friends die in front of him—three of them this very day. And you see the green sash on his shoulder? He's in the light company—the *elite* company. That means he's one of the hardest goddamn bastards in a regiment that's nothing but hard goddamn bastards. Do you think an evening with a pair of pliers is going to break him?" She shook her head. "We should have taken the stupefied boy. I'd wager he was a replacement, and he had the look of someone we could break quickly."

Elise's proud expression was beginning to fade, the corners of her lips turning down twitch by twitch.

"You were in the infantry," Josette said to Jutes. "How long do you suppose a man like this one can hold out?"

Jutes didn't have to think. "I've seen his sort last months, and that's when you got ways to confirm what they're telling you. Without that, we could work on him for years and never hear a single word of truth."

"Well, we have days, and not many of those," Josette said. "Any ideas?"

Jutes thought about it. "Always surprised me how often, if you got to 'em just after they were snatched up, they'd be rattled or confused enough to spill everything without even thinking." He looked across the room, into the Vin's defiant eyes. "Not sure that'll work on this one, though, and asking about the magazine so soon will tip our hand. Mayhap we could play on his passions, instead. I've seen that work pretty fast."

"You mean, promise him a woman?" Bernat asked.

"Not that sort of passions. Back in the Halachia campaign, we caught this little lieutenant, just promoted from ensign, who'd stayed to fight after his captain was killed and the rest of the company ran."

"Commendable," Bernat said.

"Yeah, well, this commendable little shit told us exactly where his company was retreating to. Showed us on a map where they'd fortified some farm houses. And you know why? 'Cause some handsome, quick-thinking Brandheimian corporal told him we'd give his company a fair fight, a chance to redeem their honor, if only we knew where to find 'em."

"And you gave them a fair fight?"

"Hell no. We barricaded the houses in the night and threw burning carcass shot on the roofs. The Vins all burned alive."

Bernat was about to make a delightfully witty comment about roast dumplings, but thought better of it when he saw Elise's disapproving expression.

"Another time, our captain got a Vin prisoner to tell us where an ambush was laid, by convincing him we had more men than they thought. As soon as he thought his friends were doomed to be killed by our counterattack, he told us where they were, thinking he was saving 'em."

"And this one?" Josette asked, looking at the infantryman in the corner. "What do you think he'll respond to?"

Jutes shrugged. "Gotta feel him out first. Might be best if Lord Hinkal does it, sir. The Vin ain't gonna be so inclined to believe the sincerity of someone who beat him over the head, or who was about to go at him with pliers." He looked at Bernat. "You'll have to be real nice to him. Be his one friend down here, and you might just find his soft spots. Even the hardest man's got 'em."

Judging by the disapproving look that Elise shot him, Bernat had not done a good job of hiding his disappointment at being called upon to treat the Vin so respectfully. Indeed, he'd been looking for some Vin bastard to paint his frustrations on for some time now—even before he saw what they'd done to the people of Durum—and what better canvas than a prisoner meant for interrogation? If he'd known he was going to have to make friends with the son of a bitch, Bernat wouldn't have left the damn ship.

Josette must have read his true feeling as well, for she said, "Be subtle."

Bernat did not resist for long. He nodded and said, "Subtlety is one of my favorite middle names."

She put a hand on his shoulder, and spoke as if consoling a dispirited little child, "Listen, once we get the location of the magazine, you can torture him to your heart's content, with whatever time we have left over, okay?"

He beamed a smile at her and said, "Yours is a generous soul."

He tried to give Elise's shoulder a squeeze, but she shrugged his hand off and shot him a nasty look. As he walked away, toward the Vin fusilier, Elise said in a whisper, "This war's twisted you, Josie. Into something unnatural."

At least she hadn't said it to Bernat, but he would have to tread carefully if he wanted to stay in Elise's good graces. After he finished getting information out of the Vin, and after he finished rearranging the man's various organs into the most painful configurations possible, Bernat resolved to put all of his energy into his relationship.

He stepped up to the table, where the Vin watched him warily. "Someone untie him, please," he said to the room, generally. When that was seen to, he took a chair and carried it around to sit next to the fusilier. The pliers lay on the table in front of him, placed there by Corne. Bernat handed them back. "Take these away, please. And bring a cup of wine, or whatever is on hand. Oh, and bring whatever Heny uses to soothe extracted teeth."

"They just got the trapdoor closed," Corne said, neither taking the pliers nor moving from his spot.

"Then get it open again."

Corne still didn't move, even as Jutes walked up and crossed his arms. "She can't tell us what to do now," Corne said to Bernat, "and you never could anyway." Only then did Corne notice Sergeant Jutes looming over him.

Bernat leaned toward Corne and said, in a smooth and genteel voice, "I will certainly remind the sergeant to take that into consideration when he decides what to do with you."

Corne hesitated a moment, then snatched up the pliers and left. What a wonderful thing leverage was. Bernat wished he'd appreciated it before now—though in fairness to himself, it was only quite recently that he'd ever had any.

"I must apologize for my associate," Bernat said in Vinzhalian. "It's only that you fellows took his hands and killed a fair number of his friends, and he's somewhat resentful of the fact." The Vin stared back and said nothing. Fresh blood trickled from his swollen left eyelid, the wound having re-opened while he was being restrained. "Which is no excuse for his boorish behavior, of course, but I do offer it by way of an explanation."

Silence still. So Bernat only sat and shared in that silence, and kept an impassive face until Corne returned. The private slapped a mug on the table, spilling some of the cider inside. He then retrieved a small ointment pot, which he'd tucked against his side, and threw that down as well.

"Thank you." Bernat offered the ointment to the fusilier, and spoke again in Vinzhalian, "Do try it. I'm sure broken teeth must hurt quite a bit."

It took some convincing, but the Vin finally took the ointment and applied half the pot to three pulpy stumps which had once been his upper front teeth. When he was done, he swallowed the cider in one long gulp.

"Would you like another cider?" Bernat asked, and then held up his hands with a smile. "I don't want you to think I'm trying to get you drunk, though."

"I can hold my liquor," the fusilier said. His words were reedy, coming through the gap in his teeth. Every head in the room turned toward him, for these were the first words the man had said.

"Cider is not actually a . . ." Bernat checked himself. "But let us never mind that." In Garnian, he said to Sergeant Jutes, "Would you mind fetching another?"

"And I can hold my tongue, too," the fusilier said.

"I don't doubt it." Bernat made a sorrowful face, then flashed a conspiratorial grin at him. "You're one of the hardest goddamn bastards in a regiment that's nothing but hard goddamn bastards. These buffoons couldn't break you if they had years."

The Vin's face twitched momentarily, to show the slightest hint of pride.

"Which makes what these animals wanted to do to you all the more unforgivable. You've been through so much already, and then to be treated like this? I can't imagine how angry it would make me. Ah, here's that cider."

"WAR HAS TWISTED you, Josie, into something unnatural," Josette's mother said, when Bernat walked away.

Josette ignored the comment and set to work laying the party's three rifles on the carpet. She blew the priming out of their pans so they wouldn't fire accidentally, then repeated the operation with her pistol. That finished, she began unpacking the bag she'd brought with her.

Her mother was silent so long that Josette had to look up to confirm she was still there. Elise shook her head and said, "I'm glad your father didn't live to see what you've turned into. He always worried you'd be . . . corrupted, things being what they are in Garnia, but he never could have imagined this."

"Good God," Josette said, pulling signal flags and flares from the bag and arranging them in rows. "I wonder, in the time since Father died, how many times have you called up his ghost to testify against me? I ask only because I fear he must be growing very tired of it. Though, I suppose the round trip between Durum and hell isn't so far as to be an inconvenience."

"You're trying to make me cry," her mother said, but her eyes were dry.

"I have never *tried* to make you cry." Josette took the cutlasses, all of them bundled in linen, and began unwrapping them. "I'm just naturally good at it, is all. Can't imagine where I got that from."

"When your ship picks you up . . . they are picking you up before the attack, aren't they?"

"Yes" was all she said. She had swords to unwrap.

"Bernat's going, too?"

"Yes."

"Before the attack?"

"Yes!" She looked up from one of the cutlasses, which had acquired a few nicks on the edge, and would need a good honing. "*Mistral* will pick us up prior to the attack. Where is the confusion?"

"No confusion. Just making sure." Her mother took a breath. "I'd like to go along with you."

Josette couldn't help but laugh. "You'll go because he's going? Not because I'm going, but because he's going?"

"Because both of you are going."

"You'll be pleased to learn that I was always planning to take you with us. The extra ballast will allow us to drop that many more muskets to Heny and her men. So you'll actually be useful for something. Who says you can't try new things, later in life?" She withdrew the last item from the bag. It was an infantry musket, brought along as an example piece, so that at least some members of the resistance could familiarize themselves with it and be taught the basic principles of combat musketry.

But her mother's eyes had fixed on another weapon. She knelt down and picked up Josette's rifled pistol. "This is beautiful," she said, smiling with admiration. "Whatever you may think of Bernat, you can't deny his good taste in firearms."

Josette snorted. "That pistol's mine, Mother. How the hell would it be Bernie's?"

Her mother stared at her, confused.

Suddenly, Josette struck upon the reason. "Good God, you think he's rich, don't you?"

Her mother's cheeks turned red, but she offered no reply.

"He's the second son, Mother. Which means—yes, I did look into it—he's really only a commoner with a fancy name. He's a 'lord' in the same way that I'm a 'captain.' It's an empty title given to the younger sons of a marquis, as nothing more than a courtesy. When his father dies, it's the oldest son who will get the real title, the real land, and all the real money, unless you can manage to poison the poor bastard first."

Only at that moment did she remember that she was talking about Roland. For the first time, it occurred to her that his coming inheritance and succession was a point in favor of sending him the more propitious letter. Or, now that she thought on it further, was it a point against? She wasn't sure, and realizing that she was contemplating her affection for him in those terms made her feel a little sick.

"So, is the wedding off?" she asked her mother. And after another nasty look, corrected herself. "Sorry. I didn't mean to be rude. Is the fling off?"

"No," her mother said, but she had to think about it first. "It was just a surprise, is all. I suppose I let myself get used to the idea of a more comfortable life."

Josette thought of advising her to get used to diplomatic

visits from limber Sotrian officials, but that might be a cut too many, and she wasn't sure her mother would care in any event.

Her mother looked across the room, to Bernat flashing his slick smile at the Vin fusilier, and laying into him with specious charm. She said, "And used to the idea of a more compassionate man. Which he was before you got at him. You let the war break him."

"Let's not get melodramatic." Josette carefully removed the rocket flares from the pack, but left them in their oilcloth covers, lest too much manipulation generate a static spark that could set them off.

Her mother shook her head. "Minimize it all you like, but he wasn't like this before he fell in with your crowd. He was good-hearted."

Josette unpacked the cartridge boxes and began going through them one by one, lifting the lids and standing the paper cartridges upright wherever they'd slipped. "Before he fell in with my crowd, he was conspiring to wreck my career and have me shipped to the Utarman fever swamps. Do you know what happens to people in the fever swamps, Mother? If you think carefully, you'll find there's a hint in the name."

"Yet you seem fond of him now."

Josette laughed. "Yes, well, perhaps such a venomous person reminds me of home."

13

Though her eyes were open and pointed across Heny's lovely basement room, Josette saw none of it. She looked instead across the roof of a goat shed, as her rifle's frizzen sprang back, the flint sparking across it. The wind picked up the exposed priming in the pan, sending stinging grains of gunpowder into her eyes and nostrils. She held them open despite the pain, and kept the wolf in her sights.

Someone coughed, and in the next moment she saw her locale for what it was. A single lantern burned in the corner nearest the Vin fusilier, who had been separated from the rest of the room by a paper screen. Apart from her, only Kiffer was awake, taking his turn at guard duty.

Josette brushed the wrinkles out of her uniform and went to sit next to him, waving him back into his chair when he attempted to rise on his one remaining leg.

"How's life in Durum?" she asked Kiffer.

"Haven't seen any of it past this ceiling," the private replied. "But what I hear ain't good, sir. Vins have been cracking down real hard, hanging rabble-rousers by the score." He grinned. "But for every one the Vins hang, another three rise up. Seems to be a certain . . . ornery streak to people from Durum, if you don't mind me saying so, sir."

"Not at all." She looked over the men sleeping on the floor. One of her former crewmen, though offloaded in Durum, was not among them. "Is Private Hermant still alive?"

Kiffer looked at his foot. "No, sir." He took a deep breath.

"Resistance made use of him, seeing how his wound wasn't too bad and he was good with a gun. Vins caught him and a dozen others, when the resistance was trying to ambush a party of fusiliers cutting firewood. After that first big success with the poison, it seemed like the Vins were reading our minds. We never did pull off a big operation after that—not without costing a lot of blood on our side. Lost the signal-base lieutenant and half his men, across three or four foiled ambushes. So now they stick to the smaller stuff. Like nabbin' that piece a' trash." When he hooked a thumb to indicate the Vinzhalian, Kiffer finally seemed to realize that he was rambling, and quieted down. "Sorry, sir."

She waved the matter away. "I'm sure it must be difficult, to be stuck down here."

"I'm not saying it takes the same kind a' fortitude as going out to ambush Vins, sir, but it takes some kind of fortitude." He shifted in his chair. "It takes some kind of fortitude."

A most uncomfortable silence followed, which Josette broke with, "Heny took good care of your leg, though?"

"Wonderful care, wonderful care," Kiffer said. He thumped his thigh, just above the fold in his pant leg. "Hardly even hurts anymore. The shoulder, either, though the ball's still in there."

"Heny does good work."

"Better than the town surgeon, and that's a damn certainty, sir. You know the Vins hanged him, after two of them died when he operated on them? Townsfolk all said he didn't kill them on purpose, he was just a lousy surgeon. Bloody-minded Vins never listened. Hanged his wife, too, on account of there was two of them dead, and so there ought to be at least two of us. Pardon me, sir. I meant two folk from Durum."

"I think you've lived here long enough to claim that dubious honor, Private, if you want it."

Kiffer grinned and said, "Thank you, sir. And I would want

that honor, sir, knowing the tenacity of these folk. No dis-respect intended, sir, but I'm surprised you're so disparaging of it, considering the exploits of your own mother."

Josette arched an eyebrow, but said nothing.

Kiffer seemed to realize that he was sailing into dangerous waters. "Though of course, sir, not sure it's proper for me to recount them, if she didn't already."

Josette still said nothing, but only stared at the man.

"Then again, mayhap she's just too modest, and would pre-fer it this way." He swallowed hard, leaning out to see if any of the slumbering bodies nearby were secretly awake and eavesdropping. Elise, at least, was not in the room, having left early in the night to run messages for Heny. "She joined up just after the poisoning. She had a natural use, you see, sir, 'cause she'd been kicked out of her house and was sleeping wherever she could beg a bed for the night. So it didn't raise any suspicions to have her carry messages from house to house. She went along on an ambush, too. Heny said she was too valuable as a messenger, but your mother wouldn't take no. Good thing, 'cause the Vins smelled the trap and turned it around on us. If your mother hadn't been there, the whole ambush party would've been killed, but she got nearly half of them out alive, on account of her knowing the forest so well. That's the time Private Hermant died, now that I think of it. But there's another four men from that party that owe her their lives."

Josette was about to make a snide remark, but thought better of it and said, "Let's be thankful the Durum resistance has people like her in it."

"Fewer and fewer. But . . ." Kiffer paused to kick the Vin in the side, but the man only wobbled on his chair, and didn't even look up. "Soon we'll pay the bastards back tenfold."

A line of bright light appeared on the ceiling, as someone

above removed a plank from the false floor over the stairs. Josette tensed.

"Only Pesha checking in, sir," Kiffer said. "Must be morning, up above."

"I'll just go and see how things stand on the surface."

Things stood rather well, by Pesha's reporting. News of the coming uprising was being spread to select, trustworthy citizens, who stood ready to recruit their neighbors when the moment arrived. Scenting their coming liberation, no Durumite had argued against an uprising.

"What about the breach?" Josette asked.

Pesha shrugged. "Vins won't let us near enough the walls to see. But the fog looks like it's burning off, if you want to try talking to your ship. I mean, if you think it's safe."

It was certainly not safe. And yet . . .

"FLARE!"

Kember was at the rail in a second, telescope in hand. "Where away?"

"Six points to starboard," the lookout said, pointing with his flattened hand. The sky was overcast, but the cloud ceiling was high, and there was excellent visibility between clouds and earth. "Middle of the northwest quarter. Garden behind the cottage. The one with the funny roof."

She trained her telescope on it. The captain was kneeling on the ground, partially concealed from the street by a pile of unmelted snow that must have been deposited there during the winter.

Kember lowered the telescope and looked back across the hurricane deck, to the steersmen. "Swing the elevators up and down twice, to acknowledge."

The steersman did it, and the whole ship angled slightly as

the elevators moved. On the ground, the captain quenched her flare with dirt and snow. She retrieved signal flags and, not daring to stand up for signaling, lay with her back on the ground and swung the flags in a wig-wag code. It looked absurdly like she was trying to make patterns in the dirt, but absurdity was nothing next to to being caught by the Vins and hanged.

She reported the situation in Durum, asked *Mistral* to look for signs of a new gunpowder magazine, and asked for news of the siege. Kember responded by ordering *Mistral*'s control fins waggled in a pre-arranged alphabetical signal. It was a slow method, but had the advantage of not broadcasting to the Vins that *Mistral* was in communication with someone in the town. Kember used it to report that Garnian artillery had breached the wall, and were now making it more practical to assault. As if to punctuate the message, the four guns of the Garnian battery fired into the collapsed section of Durum's wall, in their continuing effort to widen the breach and flatten the rubble within it.

When the captain asked about obstacles being built in the breach, Kember replied, *None. Twelve shells dropped on work parties last night.*

Ensign Kember wasn't sure, but she thought she sensed a hint of pride in the captain's acknowledging signal. Then the captain signed off and scurried away into the cottage, before the Vins could catch on to their means of communication.

"You dropped a dozen what, Ensign?" Lieutenant Hanon was awake and standing over her. He must have crept up while she was looking through the telescope.

"Shells, sir. Four and one-half inch spherical explosive shells." When he didn't answer, she went on, "To keep the Vins from laying mines or obstacles in the breach. We heard work parties moving in the dark, and dropped twelve bombs at staggered intervals, to make them think twice. It's all in the log, sir. I would have sent for you, sir, but you asked to not be disturbed." Had he not heard the shells going off? Or had he heard them and immediately started devising a means of using the situation against her?

"And who actually dropped the bombs in question?"

"Private Tanaka, sir."

"Have him brought to the hurricane deck."

After a moment's uncomfortable silence, Kember pointed to the lookout with her nose and said, "This is him, sir. He's a cannoneer, sir, but he has lookout duty in the morning watch, except when we're rigged for battle."

Lieutenant Hanon was thrown off, but he recovered himself and said in twice as pretentious a voice, "I'm afraid, Private, that as I gave no order to bomb the breach, I will be forced to stop the cost of those shells out of your pay."

The private was appalled, as was every man and woman on the deck. Twelve shells would cost over a lira, representing several months of Tanaka's pay.

"You should count yourself fortunate," Hanon continued, smugly pleased with the reaction he'd caused, "that we are filled with inflammable air, or I would have to account for the loss of ballast, and its equivalent cost of luftgas."

That was an even more ridiculous notion, and Kember thought Hanon should count himself fortunate the crew didn't decide as one to toss him over the side.

But the bastard had waited until the captain signed off, so there could be no countermanding the order, no chance of appeal or argument. He'd timed it so that his was the only opinion that mattered, regardless of how ridiculous and ill-informed it was.

Still, she had to try. "I'm the one who gave that order, sir."

Hanon made a huffing sound. "But I can't stop it out of your pay, can I? You're an officer, however lowly. Yet the cost must be recovered somehow. We can't simply drop the king's ordinance over the side because we feel like it—because we saw shadows in the night. Not while I'm in command. And whatever you may think, Ensign, I am in command." He smirked and lowered his volume, until only she could hear him. "And I will continue to show you that I am in command, until the lesson sinks in. Walk with me, Ensign."

He went up the companionway steps, without leaving anyone else in charge of the deck. Kember wasn't even sure he knew he was supposed to. She gave Lupien a nod as she went past, though, and the alert corporal got the message.

She caught up to him in the keel, just out of earshot of Private Davies, stationed as relay at the top of the companionway. Lieutenant Hanon turned to her and said, "I understand that this ship constitutes the pinnacle of your meager ambitions, but it's merely a stepping stone for me. I volunteered for the signal corps because I have no influence, and so cannot gain promotion. Other men in my position might hope for a lucky stroke in battle, but . . . I have had bad luck, in that regard." His eyes stared through her, unfocused. "Extremely bad luck. You can't imagine. I joined the air corps because it's the only chance I have left to make major." He refocused and looked hard at her, raising his voice so that it might just be heard by the crew. "And I'll be damned if I'm going to let you make a damn cock-up of it. Do you understand?"

"Yes, sir," she said. "Next time, I'll wake you up when such a decision has to be made."

That was a tactical mistake, and she knew it as soon as she saw the angry look on his face. "You'll do no such thing," he said. "Unless we're under attack or the goddamn sky is falling, you'll stand your goddamn watch quietly, as ensigns are meant to."

"Respectfully, sir, in my opinion—"

"Ensigns aren't meant to have opinions, either! They're

meant to shut up and pay attention, so that when they're lieu-
tenants, they can make decisions without the council of some
goddamn child."

She couldn't stop herself shaking, or stop her cheeks from
burning with anger, her scar from throbbing with pain, but
at least she managed to hold her answer to, "Yes, sir."

Hanon turned back to the hurricane deck. Private Davies
saluted respectfully as he passed, and then as Hanon started
down the companionway ladder, Davies lifted his foot to kick
the lieutenant the rest of the way.

Kember was already running for Davies, and reached him
just as his foot was flying out. She grabbed him from behind
and wrenched him back. Both of them struggled to remain upright, to not fall against the catwalk or over the edge of it, and
so plummet through the envelope. And every moment, Kember
prayed that the lieutenant would not look back, would not
hear the commotion behind him.

Hanon was halfway down the ladder when she saw his face
begin to turn back. She gave up on balance and wrenched on
Davies again, pulling the both of them down to the catwalk.
They landed together on the wicker, which creaked under the
strain of the impact.

Their eyes—and the eyes of everyone forward of the
boiler—were locked on the companionway hatch, waiting for
Lieutenant Hanon to pop his head up, and so catch the spec-
tacle in flagrante.

But he didn't. The steamjack whined on, the wind whistled
by outside, and the lieutenant remained safely below on the
hurricane deck.

Kember let out a breath she hadn't realized she was holding. She disentangled herself from Davies, and Private Grey
came over to help them to their feet. "That was harrowing,"
Grey said, in a voice so small it could hardly be heard.

Davies was not pleased. "Sir, he disrespected you, and him not knowing a damn thing about how to run a proper airship. We can't just stand by and—"

He was silenced by a smack across the head from Private Grey, which seemed as much a shock to her as to her target. "Ensign Kember just saved your life," she said, though it was nearer a hiss. "The least you could do is shut the hell up."

Only then did Davies remember himself. He nodded and said, "Sorry, sir. Thank you. It won't happen again."

Kember nodded and went aft, Grey following. "He's not wrong, though," she said privately. "If we see combat, that man is going to get us all killed."

"We won't see combat until the captain's back," Kember said, giving Grey a reassuring nod. "Captain wouldn't have left him in charge if there was a chance of that."

BERNAT SCOOPED A spoonful of watery stew and sipped at it, draining the broth to reveal a gobbet of meat. He looked on it with suspicion. Apart from the dried rations Josette brought from the ship, it was the first meat he'd seen since entering Durum, and he wondered at its origin. He slipped it discreetly back into his bowl and looked across the table to Private Khirklov. "I was at Canard, you know. Did I mention that?"

The private, who had no qualms about the ingredients of the stew, swallowed a spoonful and looked surprised. "With the Shark?"

Bernat grinned and nodded.

"I thought you was just a passenger. Did you fight?"

Beaming with pride, Bernat said, "I made an adequate accounting of myself, though I confess that I'm no warrior. Who knows? I may have even taken a shot at one of your officers."

"Ha!" The fusilier stuffed another spoonful of stew into his mouth. It dribbled through his missing front teeth as he spoke. "Wouldn't mind thinking that, Bernie, but you probably didn't. We were held in reserve for the first attack, and way over on the left for the second." He wagged his finger in front of Bernat, and gave a gap-toothed grin. "We would'a had you, too, if the guard regiments on the right flank hadn't collapsed just when they did. Guardsmen are overrated—I'll tell you that for free."

Bernat grinned back. "But the right flank wouldn't have collapsed if the Shark wasn't there, overrated as guardsmen may be. So I'd say we both did a good and honorable day's work, eh?" He held up a mug of cider by way of salute.

Private Khirklov did the same. "Aye, we did." He took a deep draught, finishing off the mug, while Bernat drank half a mouthful from his cup. "What's the Shark like, anyway?"

Bernat had to look over his shoulder, to confirm that Khirklov was looking at Josette. The Vins seemed to use "Shark" to refer interchangeably to both the airship and its captain, as if they were two facets of a single entity.

The predator in question was currently leaning against a wall by the stairs, staring into space with a vacant look in her eyes, as she'd been doing since she returned from her brief trip aboveground. Most likely she was mooning over Roland, but he didn't want to contemplate that horrible probability, much less confess it to Khirklov.

"She's the purest warrior I've ever met," Bernat said, in soft and reverent tones. "Lives only for combat, only to kill Garnia's enemies. She takes no joy in sport, food, dance, music, and certainly not in men. She ignores them all, thinking only of bloodshed and the cacophony of battle. She lusts only for that, pursues her enemies relentlessly, shows no mercy once they've attacked her beloved Garnia. She won't countenance the slightest whiff of criticism of her army, her faith, her nation, or the nobles who rule over it. Speaking as one of those very nobles, I have often tried to convince her of my own inadequacies, but she won't hear a word of it, so passionate is her love for her country's protectors. But I can assure you, it is a chaste love. She remains a maiden, despite no end of potential suitors."

The comments had the intended effect, inspiring a deeper respect from Private Khirklov. It was the last bit that clinched the matter. The hoi polloi simply adored the notion of a warrior maiden, and though Bernat couldn't possibly imagine the appeal, he appreciated its utility. "And how did you come to fly with her?" Khirklov asked.

Bernat smiled. "Like so many others, I was drawn into her sphere like iron filings drawn by the invisible force of a lodestone. Just after I met her, I begged General Fieren to allow me to go aboard her ship, as one of her personal bodyguards. I even refused payment, though the general offered me ten florins a week out of his own pocket. That is the depth of inspiration she kindled in me—in both of us. Indeed, in the entire army!"

Though impressed, the fusilier was also growing somewhat confused. He dared to glance at Josette again, though only for a moment—lest he be accused of impiety, perhaps. His forehead and nose wrinkled as he asked, "And . . . how come she keeps staring at nothing?"

"Meditation," Bernat said, without delay. "She spent five years at the top of Mount Unmae, you know, training with the warrior monks."

"Really?" Khirklov asked.

"Look at her brow," Bernat said. "See the discolored bump there? It's from breaking wooden planks with her head. Part of her morning exercises. Astonishing to watch."

"Wish we had someone like that," the fusilier said, swallowing hard.

"Alas, not every nation can be so lucky."

* * *

THE PRIMING CAUGHT a spark and the flash spread back to ignite not just the powder in the pan, but the powder the wind had blown into her face. It singed her cheeks and burned in her nostrils, filling them with a rotten-egg stench. The rifle kicked hard into her shoulder.

Out in the darkness, the crack of the rifle was answered first by a shrill yelp, and then by the echo of both sounds off the town wall.

"Josie? Are you all right?"

Josette looked up to see her mother's head poking down from the false ceiling. She smiled and said, "Quite all right. Just having memory problems."

"Forgot something?" Her mother came down the stairs and stopped to help Heny replace the false ceiling.

"Remembered something," Josette said. She thought of offering the details, but her mother was barely paying attention, and a glance at Jutes dissuaded her entirely. Her sergeant gave every appearance of dozing against the wall, but she suspected he was wide awake and listening to their every word.

As if he could read her mind, Jutes's eyes slipped open and he looked up. "Sir," he said, as he rose to his feet.

"How are the men coming along on the musket?"

"Just fine, sir. All of 'em can explain the operation good enough to teach someone who already knows the workings of a rifle or a fowling piece, which, as I hear tell, ought to be most of the town. Won't be no three shots a minute drill, to be sure, but they'll do well enough."

Josette nodded and looked to her mother. "Will the town be ready? The assault will come at dawn tomorrow, if it's to come at all."

"The town'll be ready," her mother said, as she guided a plank into place. "Do we know where they'll be going?"

"Bernat's working on it. If he can't wring the powder magazine out of the Vin, we'll attack the east gate, instead."

The last plank was in place, and her mother came down the stairs. "Better if it's the magazine. Safer for the townsfolk, too."

Josette smiled. "I agree."

The smile seemed to disagree with her mother. "What the hell is wrong with you, Josie? And don't tell me you're all right. I know you better than that."

Josette gave a little shrug. "I'm just finding it hard to believe that you're really working with the resistance, is all."

"Well, of course I'm working with the resistance!" her mother said, flustered. "What the hell else would I be doing here?"

"It's just, you always hated the army. When Father was conscripted, you screamed yourself to sleep every night for a month."

"That was different! That was . . ." Her mother hesitated, seeming to catch herself before saying something hurtful—or, at least, something more hurtful than her next words. "The army's just pointless brutality. Here, we're actually fightin' for something."

Josette felt the old urge to draw her mother into an argument, but she fought against it. "I only mean to say that I've held an unfair opinion of you, for a very long time." She gathered all her strength to say the next words. "I'm sorry."

"Well, it's about damn time," her mother replied. "After all I did for you, after all I sacrificed, after all you stole from me, it's a blessed relief that now, after all these years, you realize you've been treatin' me unfairly."

Josette had been in so many battles that she would have had to stop and count them, if asked to give a number, but she had never felt so heroic as she did now, when she resisted the urge to shout profanities. "It's either theft or sacrifice," she said in a calm, even tone. "It can't be both. That money was either meant for me or it wasn't."

"It was meant to buy you a future," her mother said, staying calm through what seemed an equally heroic effort of will. "Not so you could run off and buy a commission in the goddamn army. That money could have made you something, gotten you started somewhere."

"It did exactly that, so bravo. I'm afraid you've made the classic mistake of parents everywhere: burying your own aspirations for the sake of your child, then digging them up and expecting her to take them secondhand."

"Oh, very clever, Josie. You had years and years to think of that. No wonder it's cutting."

"You had years to think of a rebuttal, which I eagerly await."

Her mother looked at her feet, then up, not quite meeting her daughter's eyes. "You were smart."

"Still am, I flatter myself to think."

"With a nice wardrobe and a half-decent wig, you could have gone to a university somewhere."

Josette ran fingers through her unruly hair, frowning when they caught in a tangle near the back. "A realistic plan, except for the prickly fact that Garnian universities don't take women."

"I know that! I meant studying abroad! Somewhere like . . ." She was silent for an unusual length of time, considering all the years she'd had to think of someplace. "Like Sotra or someplace like that. Someplace civilized."

It took everything Josette had to keep herself from picking a hurtful comment from all the candidates that sprang to mind. She was on the brink of failing, when Bernat walked over and provided a blessed interruption. He wrapped her mother up in his arms, and they embraced for such a long time that Josette had a chance to cool off.

When they released each other, Josette leapt immediately into questioning, in case a lack of employment should tempt them back to distraction. "How's our honored guest doing?"

Bernat smiled with pride, and perhaps with other emotions better left unspoken. "I have him convinced of the hopelessness of his regiment's situation. In his mind, several experienced battalions have joined the 132nd since he was captured, so that now there are thousands of frothing berserkers at the gates of Durum, inspired by a sort of demigod, who refrains from retaking the town single-handedly only out of politeness. All that remains is to work out a way to broach the subject of the magazine without raising his suspicions."

"Work it out soon," Josette said. "The 132nd must attack tomorrow morning, so we must be out of here before dark."

"Today? We're leaving in broad daylight?"

"Whatever the dangers involved, it's safer than doing it at night. Going down is easy. Coming back up is a great deal harder. Doing it in the dark would be suicide."

Bernat narrowed his eyes. "I've noticed that, whenever you dismiss a course of action as being suicidal, we often end up doing it anyway. Half the time you make fun of me for being worried about it, after the fact."

Josette narrowed her eyes to match. "Nonsense. I don't do that. Sergeant Jutes, do I do that? You can answer honestly. You know I won't hold it against you."

Jutes seemed to know no such thing. "I wouldn't say *half* the time, sir. Perhaps . . . ehh . . . a quarter of the time?"

"Come on Jutes," Bernat said. "It's at least three-eighths."

Jutes stood ramrod straight, looked directly ahead of him, and said, "Never was any good at fractions, sir."

Josette threw up her arms and heaved a defeated sigh. "Very well. In the future, I'll try my best not to make fun of you for questioning my riskier plans. Satisfied?"

Bernat replied with a smile and a little bow.

"Now get back to work on that Vin."

He bowed again, and without a word returned to the table, where the fusilier was probing around inside his mouth with a finger. Once Bernat sat down, and his rear end was finally out of view, Josette's mother regained her focus and said, "Weather's clearing up. Should be a lovely day."

"Then you should stay nearby," Josette said. "We'll want to take advantage of the favorable weather to get out of Durum, as soon as Bernat gets his information and we can put a plan in place."

Her mother looked at her for a long time, as that hint of a smile became more and more explicit. "Thank you, Josie," she said. "Thank you for doing this."

Josette, not knowing what else to say, took a step forward and gave her mother a short and rather awkward hug.

ABOARD *MISTRAL,* THE rumor took less than a minute to travel the length of the keel and spread to the entire ship's company. Canvas hatches were thrown open all along the starboard side, and each had at least one face peering from it.

Kember was peering, too, out of a large ventilation hatch beside the condenser, with Private Grey on one side and the chief mechanic on the other.

"Where the hell did it come from?" the chief mechanic asked, as if the thing they were all staring at might have sprung out of thin air.

"It was there all along," Kember said, barely keeping hold of her nerves. "It was there all along, hiding in the cloud cover."

"How do you know?" Grey asked.

Kember didn't look at her. "Gut feeling, I guess."

The object of their anxiety was an airship—a chasseur with the very same sardine shape as *Mistral,* the same four-airscrew configuration, and the same two bref guns on the hurricane deck. A few of the crewmen who hadn't had a look through a borrowed telescope still insisted that she must be the *Levant* or *Ostro,* somehow hurried out of the construction yards in Kuchin, rather than believe the Vins had a ship so indistinguishable from *Mistral.* And indeed, she might have been *Mistral*'s twin sister, except for the Vinzhalian winged horse painted on the tail and the name *Ayezderhau* on the bow.

She must have had a sharp captain, to escape detection until now—a sharp and patient captain, willing to wait days for the perfect ambush opportunity. She would have still been lying hidden in the clouds even now, if the midday sun hadn't burned them off in an unexpected change from the usual weather.

"So how do we support the assault, if we have to fight that thing at the same time?" Grey asked. "And us with a bum steamjack, and bags ready to explode the first time a shell hits us?" It was not, apparently, a rhetorical question. She actually expected Kember to have the answer.

"I . . . I don't know," she had to admit. "The captain will know. Once we pick up the captain, she'll work something out. She always has an idea, doesn't she?"

That thought gave a boost to morale, at least. Grey nodded, and a sly grin grew on her lips. Chief Megusi nodded, too, though he could not have acquired his confidence in the captain except by secondhand account.

"What'll we do until then?" the chief asked.

"Just circle on opposite sides of the town, I expect. Neither of us wants a fair fight, so we'll give each other a wide berth."

"Until someone sees a chance for an unfair fight," Grey said.

"Right. So make damn sure nothing goes wrong with our steamjack. We can't let them know our condition, or they'd come down on us in an instant."

Grey nodded and went to her post.

Yet it was not *Mistral* that gave the first sign of engine trouble. A quarter of an hour later, it was the Vin chasseur spouting black smoke from her keel, amidships. Soon it was pouring from the seams of the hatches along her length, and even rising from the top of the envelope at the aft crow's nest. The *Ayez-derhau*'s hurricane deck grew more crowded, as men left the keel to keep from being suffocated.

The predatory side came out in most of the crew when they heard about this, or saw it for themselves. Kember felt it as fiercely as any of them, and wondered what was keeping Lieutenant Hanon from coming about and charging for them at full steam.

It's what the captain would do, she thought. But as soon as she came to that conclusion, she paused to examine it and found it wanting. No. No, the captain would smell a trap. The captain would question the unlikely and convenient happenstance of the Vin airship suffering such a disaster at just this moment. "Chief," she said, keeping her eyes on the other ship through the open hatch, "what would a bucket of tar look like, if you tossed it into the firebox and left the inspection hatch open?"

She turned to see his expression shift from sanguine to anxious. "About like that," he said.

No sooner had the implications sunk in than the crewman at the companionway relayed the order, "Steamjack to half power!"

"Oh, hell," Kember said. She was on the hurricane deck by the time the order was carried out and the ship coming about.

"Sir," she said, close to Hanon's ear, and just loud enough to be heard, "I think we should remain on station."

Hanon turned to her, wearing that smug look of his. "Not that I have to explain myself to you, Ensign, but we won't be gone long. I've already signaled the regiment and received permission to give chase, so long as we return by nightfall. A quick aerial kill, which you should count yourself lucky to share in the glory of, and we'll be back here in a flash." He looked forward and laughed. "Look at her turn to run! Limping along like that, we'll be on her before the hour is up."

"It's a ruse, sir. Think about it."

Hanon's smug look turned sour. "Are you suggesting I haven't, Ensign?"

"No, sir. Of course not, sir. Only, I don't think we'll catch her so easily. It's only a bunch of harmless smoke, see? It looks bad, but there's no sign of fire and the airscrews are still turning. What sort of steamjack failure could cause that?"

"I'm not interested in the mechanical details, and neither should you be." He turned forward again. "So rig the ship for action. I'm going to make you eat your words, Ensign."

BERNAT BROKE HIS last ginger cake in two, and offered half to Private Zeren Khirklov. The Vinzhalian fusilier accepted readily, and bit into it. "Wish we had these back home," he said, his words muddled not just by a full mouth, but because he was trying to keep the spicy cake away from the exposed pulp in his cracked teeth.

"I have another bag aboard the airship," Bernat said, feigning distraction. "I'll send you home with it, when this is over tomorrow."

Khirklov paused in mid-chew, and spoke with such force it blew gingery crumbs across the table. "Tomorrow?"

Bernat met his gaze, but still stared through him and into the middle distance. "We attack the breach tomorrow at first light. I expect the whole thing will be over by breakfast."

"Won't be that easy." Khirklov set down the rest of the cake, and stared hard at Bernat's unfocused eyes.

Bernat looked away. "Not easy, no, but it will be quick. I have no doubt that your boys will fight valiantly, that they'll inflict dreadful casualties on the besiegers, but the besiegers will win. It's not your fault. It's only a matter of numbers."

Private Khirklov folded his hands on the table, humbled. "And the Shark," he said with a resignation.

"And the Shark." Bernat offered the poor man a wan smile.

"Your fellows will fight well, I have no doubt. Honor will be satisfied. But you'll lose—if not by breakfast, then at least by lunch." He reached out and patted the fusilier on the hands. "There's no shame in it. No dishonor. It's a simple matter of bad luck, and nothing can change it now."

Khirklov was silent.

"What we can change, Zeren, is what happens next—what happens after. That is the moral dilemma that has weighed heavily on my mind. Because, you see, as it stands now, your entire regiment is apt to be turned over to the newly restored authorities in Durum, to stand trial for . . ." Bernat made a show of searching for the most diplomatic way of putting it. "For what they perceive as crimes against them."

"Now hold on," Private Khirklov began, before Bernat quieted him with another pat on the hand.

"I know. It's going to be a sham." He looked over his shoulder, at the men napping or sitting idle in the basement room. "They're only out for blood, but they'll get it. Those of you who aren't executed outright will go home without teeth, without eyes, and probably without genitals—which will be a damn awkward conversation to have with the wife."

Khirklov took his hands from the table and placed them in his lap.

Bernat gave it some time to sink in, and then continued, "I have an idea that might prevent it, however. They might turn you all over to me and my men, for interrogation, if my methods can provide a few morsels of information . . ."

The fusilier's contemplative expression immediately turned to stone.

"Nothing sensitive," Bernat said, holding his hands out in a placating manner. "Nothing that amounts to anything, really. Just a few irrelevancies and confirmation of things we already know, to keep the worst from happening. Such as, you're from the 64th, right?"

Khirklov said nothing.

"I'll write down that you said yes, for your sake. And there are about five hundred and eighty men remaining in your regiment, right?"

This time he nodded.

"See? Nothing we don't already know. And you fought in the battle for Arle, and at Canard, right?"

"Right."

"Which is of no import to Garnian intelligence, such as it is, but should dazzle them just the same. When your army retreated from Canard, did your regiment participate in the rearguard action?"

"Yes," he said, and smiled with pride. "The 64th was at the back of the retreat, 'cause we was at the front of the attack."

"How many attacks did you fight off from the rearguard?"

"Maybe a score."

"And what sorts of forces attacked?"

"Cavalry. Mostly dragoons, I think."

Bernat jotted it down, and made a show of comparing it to a separate, already-prepared list, which was actually only a list of sexual positions he'd copied out of a book. "Good, good. And how many battalions were left in Durum, initially?"

"Just ours."

"And how many reinforcements did it receive, between then and now?"

"A score or so."

Bernat looked up and arched an eyebrow, looking across the table more in alarm than anger. "This can only work if you tell the truth, Zeren. If they catch you in a lie, they'll say my methods are useless, and leave you to the tender mercies of these brutes." He indicated the men behind him. "Do you really want me to write down that it was only a score or so?" He kept the pencil poised over his sheet, ready to record the damning lie.

"Might be my memory lapsed for a moment there," Khirklov said, swallowing. "I think it was closer to a hundred."

Bernat let out a sigh of relief. He wrote the figure down, then waggled the pencil in a chiding manner. "You had me worried for a second, Zeren. Now, the night you were captured . . ." He unfolded a map of Durum, laid it on the table, and handed the pencil over to Khirklov. "What was your patrol route?"

The fusilier hesitated, until Bernat helpfully turned the southwest corner of the map closest to him, as if he already knew exactly where the route was, and meant to make that area easily accessible. Khirklov nerved himself and traced a roughly square path through the streets.

While he did, Bernat hardly paid attention, and instead gave the appearance of being absorbed in his own document. Given the nature of that document, this did not require much in the way of acting. When Khirklov was finished tracing, Bernat glanced up briefly, gave a cursory nod, and went back to his reading.

Only this time, Bernat's attention to it truly was an act, and what he actually contemplated was the patrol route. The circuit Khirklov had drawn surrounded an area that would be ideal for a powder magazine. The center was far enough from the wall that an accidental detonation wouldn't damage it, but close enough for efficient transfer of cartridges. But was that the magazine? Or did Khirklov's route only interlock with others, the lot of them surrounding the magazine only when taken together?

He called up the image of the map in his mind, so he wouldn't have to look up again and betray his thoughts. A wide, straight avenue cut through the very middle of Khirklov's patrol route from east to west, and kept going right across the town. A street that wide could easily accommodate supply wagons coming from the east. Not only that, but a tunnel could have been made to the west by cutting a trench down the center of the avenue and then simply covering it over.

His gut told him that it was the place, and with time running out, he decided to risk everything on one toss.

"So, you were just making a simple circuit around the powder magazine, here?" Bernat leaned over the map and pointed vaguely toward the center of the patrol area, his finger far enough from the map that he could be indicating any number of buildings.

Khirklov nodded. "Right."

"Go ahead and mark it, then, in your own hand. They might recognize mine."

Without a second thought, Khirklov circled a building.

Bernat smiled. "I think that should be enough." He folded up the map, tucked it into his coat, and reached across the table to shake Khirklov's hand. "I believe you've just saved your entire regiment, Zeren."

The private looked down, suppressing his pride. "Thank you, sir," he said, and the poor bastard really seemed to mean it.

The gnawing desire to see Zeren suffer, the impulse Bernat had suppressed through the long interrogation, now told him that this was the time to stand up and casually announce that anyone could do as they wished with the Vin bastard. It was so perfect, and would make such a perfect story, that he nearly went through with it despite his better judgement, if only for the sake of showmanship. When would a better time arise? He imagined himself walking triumphantly to Josette, not even looking back while the others closed in around the Vin and pummeled him into a bloody mess. To slap the map into her hand while that went on behind him would truly be a crowning moment.

"Sir?" the Vinzhalian said.

Bernat smiled, or rather smiled sincerely, where before it

had only been an act. "Thank you, Zeren," he said, and turned about.

To hell with it. There would be other people to beat the shit out of. There always were. Besides which, it now seemed that this was a test put before him by some greater force. Perhaps it was a chance to prove he was not beholden to the urges brought by his soldier's heart, a chance to show that he was their master. And perhaps there would be other tests like this—indeed, the more he thought of it, the more certain he became—and with each one he would prove himself again, until in the end he was afflicted no more.

As he traversed the room, the others seemed to recognize, despite Bernat's practice at bluffing, that something had changed, that the interrogation was finished. They rose in anticipation, Corne all but drooling at the prospect of having a go at the Vin.

Bernat stopped in front of Corne, looked him hard in the eyes, and said, "Not yet. We may need to question him further. Patience, man, patience."

He might as easily have let the others make up their own minds, and held himself blameless. But might that temptation not be the next test, in some ways more difficult than the first? If it was, then he had passed again, and was well on his way to regaining himself.

He smiled at the thought.

"You have it?" Josette asked, when he came near.

He took the map out and, careful to keep his back to Private Khirklov, so the man wouldn't see what Josette was so interested in, laid it out over the steps of the stairs. Josette, Elise, and Jutes gathered round as he pointed out the building.

"That's poor Mr. Uche's dairy warehouse," Elise said. "You remember it, Josie?"

Josette nodded, and went up the steps to knock on the

false floor panel at the top. No answer came, and Josette seemed hesitant to knock again. "What's taking them so long?"

"Hope it ain't a Vin patrol outside," Jutes said, staring up and trying to see through the gaps in the planks.

"More likely an afternoon liaison," Bernat said, which was met by a scowl and a punch in the arm from Elise.

"A liaison?" Josette asked. "I hope not. At this time of day, any resistance activity is likely to be spotted."

Elise blushed and cleared her throat, and Jutes only stared at his feet, while Bernat tried several times to say something. He finally managed to spit out, "Oh. I thought you knew, or I wouldn't have mentioned it."

"Knew what? Mentioned what? What's going on here? If there's a resistance operation taking place, I damn well need to know about it!"

"No, it's . . ." Bernat sighed. "Heny and Pesha. They're, you know, an item."

Josette blinked several times. "What kind of item?"

"For God's sake," Elise broke in. "They're lovers."

But Josette was no closer to enlightenment. After seeming to run the possibilities around in her mind for a while, she asked, "With whom?"

"Each other!" Bernat said.

"What . . . but . . . how is that even possible?" Josette asked. Bernat had never seen so much confusion written on her typically stony face, not even during the most chaotic and bewildering moments in battle.

Elise patted her daughter's shoulder and said, "Oh, Josie. Don't be such a bumpkin."

"You knew?"

"Everyone knows, Josie. Everyone in town knows. Everyone's always known."

"Save one, apparently," Bernat said.

"But . . . no . . ." Whenever she was on the verge of under-standing it, Josette's mind seemed to eject the possibility with ballistic force. "That doesn't happen!"

Jutes had been skootching backward, so slowly that it was hardly noticeable, but he was now far enough away to turn and walk briskly to the opposite side of the room, where he sat down and pointedly looked in another direction.

"You've been in the army for how long, and this is the first you're hearing about this sort of thing?" Bernat asked.

"Of course I've heard of it! I've known dozens of . . . *them*. But they were all men. That's different!"

Elise only sighed and shook her head.

"Heny can't be . . ." Josette's expression shifted from skep-ticism to horror. She leaned forward, saying in an alarmed whisper, "She's seen . . ." She swallowed hard. "She's seen *inside* me!"

"Well, if it's any consolation," Bernat said, stroking his chin, "the event couldn't have been half as erotic as I'm imag-ining it. Ow!" He reeled from being hit by Josette and Elise at the same time. He rubbed both his arms. "So why was she looking in—"

"None of your goddamn business."

Bernat put his hands up in surrender. "We shall speak of it no more. At this rate, I'm not sure I'd survive the conversa-tion, anyway." He retreated from Josette and Elise, and sought comfort next to Jutes, saying, "There are days, Sergeant, when I wish I were not half so observant as I am."

Jutes looked up and took a deep breath. "But in, eh, light of yer being so observant in, eh, this particular area . . . I was wondering if I could ask the favor of, eh . . . I mean to say, sir, assuming you know that I'm . . ."

Bernat put a reassuring hand on the sergeant's shoulder and said, "I won't tell a soul." In truth, he hadn't even been certain about Jutes until that moment. "Though—and I'm sure this is none of my business, but when has that ever stopped me?—I must ask if you and Gears . . ."

"Were just friends," Jutes said.

"Right." Bernat sought in vain for another topic of conversation. When he couldn't find one, he despaired, and was only saved from having to die of embarrassment when the false panel opened and Pesha stuck her head down.

JOSETTE'S SMILE NEVER deviated, never even twitched, as she explained the plan to Heny and Pesha. The Durumite uprising would attack the magazine from several directions, splitting the mob to make it easier to handle. Once the guards were killed or captured, the various mobs would form a perimeter and hold off the Vins until the magazine could be breached and a fuse set. Tools and muskets would be dropped to them at the beginning of the operation, and *Mistral* would stand by to provide support and covering fire as needed. With muskets in their hands and an airship over their heads, even the untrained mob would make an effective fighting force. Or, failing that, at least an effective distraction.

With tomorrow seen to, Josette turned her attention to today, handing out weapons to her mother, Jutes, and Bernat. "We have to be clear of the cottage before we signal for our lift out," she said to them. "It might be several minutes before *Mistral* can turn and come to us, so be prepared to hold off a patrol or two, and to get onto a roof if necessary. When *Mistral* comes in, we're going to lash ourselves together, Bernie to Jutes and Mother to me. The ship will have to pull up hard as soon as our weight is on it, so we have to go together, and anyone who isn't on the ladder when she rises will be left behind."

They all nodded.

"If anything goes wrong," she said, to Bernat and her mother in particular, "hold on wherever you can, and trust the line to do the rest. There may be shooting as we go up. Ignore it. There's nothing you can do about it anyway. Just hold on, follow my instructions without hesitation, and don't look down. Understand?"

Bernat gave another stiff nod, and her mother hugged her. Josette wasn't sure how to respond to the embrace—even when her father was alive they hadn't been the sort of family that went in for that kind of thing. She returned only a light squeeze and tried to pass off her impassive expression as intent focus for the task at hand.

She went to the back door and stood by it. She put her hand on the knob and took a deep breath. "Okay. This is all going to happen very fast. Stay together and be ready for anything." She opened the door and sprinted out, stopping in the garden to establish a bearing on *Mistral*.

But when she looked up into the clear blue sky, there wasn't an airship to be seen.

"WHAT DOES IT mean?" Bernat asked, when they were back inside, the door barred and the curtains drawn.

"It means we're buggered," Jutes suggested.

"Perhaps the steamjack gave out and they were blown off station," Josette said, more to herself than in answer to Bernat. "Or they were forced to land. I can't think of any other reason *Mistral* wouldn't be visible." She could think of several other reasons, in fact, but didn't want to entertain them. So many of them involved her ship exploding.

"So what do we do now?" Bernat asked.

She didn't have to think. "I worked out signals with Emery. An orange rocket will inform them that we've made contact with the resistance. Depending on their response, we'll know whether *Mistral* will be here to support the attack."

Bernat asked, "And if *Mistral* isn't going to be here, and there isn't going to be an attack, what's the plan to evacuate us from the town?"

That question brought on a snort from Heny and a nasty look from Pesha.

"We don't have one," Josette said. "All we can do is hunker down, wait for the Vins to drop their guard, then sneak out and make our way home." She was speaking to Bernat, but her eyes flicked to Pesha, who couldn't have looked more betrayed. "And we'll lend whatever support we can to the resistance, while we're here."

"I'll have someone set off your rocket," Heny said, looking equally betrayed, but resigned to the situation.

"Someone has to watch for the answering rocket, too. Someone with a pocket watch, so they can note the time."

Heny nodded. "It'll be done. Now you lot better get below. The Vins have been on edge since we snatched that prisoner. If a patrol comes by and sees the shutters closed, they'll break down the door to see what we're hiding, and then you'll have gotten us all killed for nothing." As she stooped to lever up the trapdoor, she added at a mutter, "For nothing."

M ISTRAL WAS JUST outside effective cannon range and closing slowly on the Vin ship. An atmosphere of breathless expectation and anxiety permeated the air around exactly one person aboard: the acting captain, Egmont Hanon. The rest of the crew were quite subdued, for *Mistral* had been just outside effective cannon range for the entire goddamn afternoon, and no one but Lieutenant Hanon thought they could bring the *Ayezderhau* to action before nightfall.

The chase had begun auspiciously enough, with *Mistral* narrowing the gap to only two miles during the forenoon watch, then to one and a half in the next hour, and to one and a quarter in the next. Yet every time it seemed that victory would soon be within reach, the Vins squeezed a little more power out of their supposedly damaged steamjack. Every time they gained, Hanon had ordered a little more power from *Mistral*'s steamjack—just enough to close on them—and every time the mechanics had tried to talk him out of it. But he'd stood his ground, or only compromised a little, until they were at full power—full power from a steamjack that could barely be trusted at half.

Ensign Kember had reported to Hanon four times since

Mistral rigged for action, and each time he seemed even more confident than before, until his conviction bordered on lunacy. Now, from her station aft, she heard an order being sent up from the hurricane deck. She couldn't make it out with the noisy steamjack in between her and the relaying crewman, but she got the gist when the steamjack's whine rose to a higher pitch.

"Goddamn him," Kember said as she went forward. She knew she ought not to disparage her commander in front of the crew, she knew the captain wouldn't, but she also knew that Ensign Kember would go on doing it, however bad an officer it made her. "Goddamn that man."

She came around the boiler to find Private Grey stepping up steamjack output by the unusual method of running a relay between the turbine inlet and the governor assembly. Grey ran to the aft end of the engine and her wrench flashed out to adjust the bristling array of steam nozzle chokes, then she dashed forward—a dash made particularly speedy by virtue of mortal dread—to adjust the coil-spring pressure on the governor. On a healthy steamjack, she could make one adjustment to each and have the leisure of entire seconds to spare in between, but *Mistral*'s jury-rigged turbine would tear itself apart if not carefully shepherded through the operation.

With her attention fixed on that absurd dance of impromptu engineering, Kember didn't see Chief Megusi until she almost tripped over him. He was crouched between boiler and turbine casing, his hands moving around steam manifold pipes as he muttered to himself, "Goddamn solder's gonna melt at this rate, and then where'll we be? In goddamn pieces." He looked up. "Sir! Beg your pardon. Didn't see you there."

"What the hell's happening?" Kember asked.

In the brief time he'd looked away from it, the pipes between boiler and turbine had begun to clank, and he swore furiously as he fixed his attention back upon them and set to his adjustment. "Sorry, sir," he said, making some small effort to speak in an even tone, but not daring to look away from his work again. "Lieutenant Hanon ordered 'halfway between full and emergency power.' He thinks it's something in the way of a compromise, sir, though of course I would never presume to know what's in my captain's mind."

"Certainly not," Kember said. Except, perhaps, in this case. In this case, that was most certainly what was in Hanon's mind. It violated one of the first rules they'd taught in her Principles of Aerostatic Engineering course: that no compromise can be struck between reality and what you'd prefer reality to be.

"It may not seem it from the difference in airspeed," Chief Megusi went on, "but at this power the blades are spinning twice as fast as at full power, and the steam pressure's that much higher, too. I wouldn't even care to put a figure on the extra wear to the engine, but it's a hell of a lot, let me tell you. We already ran her harder than we ought to have, for so long that I'm surprised she hasn't gone up already."

He was interrupted by the steamjack itself. It made a peculiar, lilting whine that rose in volume and ended in a sharp pop. Everyone along the keel, mechanics included, froze in place, expecting that the whole thing might explode at any moment. When it didn't, but only resumed its already troubling sounds, they all took a collective breath—a breath that might have been more soothing, if it hadn't consisted of the noxious air which the steamjack was now continually venting into the keel.

"Engine needs a rest," the chief said, "not more of this. If she catches fire, with our bags full of inflammable air . . . Well sir, I'd say we're doing the Vins' job for them."

Kember nodded and said, "I'll see what I can do about it."

She went down the companionway ladder to the hurricane deck and lowered her goggles against the chill wind. Ahead, the Vin ship was right where it had been, steaming straight into Vinzhalian territory with a tailwind to help. Which meant *Mistral,* when she finally gave up the chase, would have to run against the wind to return to her station. So for every hour she spent in this futile chase, she wasted two more on the return—more than that, actually, because they would have to reduce power. Remaining at present power wouldn't get them home any faster, since being on fire tended to slow a ship down.

She stood beside Hanon and saluted. "Sir. The mechanics have concerns about the steamjack at this level of power."

He didn't return her salute. "If the Vins can take it, and their engine belching black smoke, it's all the more harmless for us." When she didn't answer back, he looked at her and grinned, or at least forced a grin. "No cause for alarm, Ensign. In my old blimp, we opened the throttle all the way, from the moment we unmoored until the moment we landed."

"Respectfully, sir, *Mistral* is not a blimp. And apart from the danger, we're needed at our assigned station. The battalion must either attack or march home tomorrow morning, and if these winds hold, we may not return in time to support them. It doesn't . . . it doesn't look good, sir."

"And what would it look like, if we spent that much time off station, and returned with nothing to show for it?"

Kember wanted to say that if they didn't turn around now, it would look like a bunch of dead infantrymen, but she restrained herself.

"No, we must press on," Hanon said, staring at the enemy as if he could slow them down by force of willpower. "We must press on, and we must come home with a kill. An aerial kill forgives all sin. They don't teach that in any classroom, Ensign, but it's a fact."

Indeed, that had been the reasoning at every stage of this idiotic chase. The farther they followed, the greater the need to come home victorious, and the greater the justification for following farther still.

"I don't mean to harp on the matter," she said, in her best effort at diplomacy, "but the mechanics are very doubtful of the steamjack's ability to tolerate the strain for much longer."

"Well of course they are," he said. "Mechanics are doubtful of every damn thing that threatens to give us an advantage over the enemy. But you must risk something to gain something. Come on, now. I'll just have a word with them, if you can't keep order in the keel by yourself."

"Sir," Kember said, and followed him up the companionway.

Lieutenant Hanon walked as far as the condenser assembly and stopped, seemingly waiting for the mechanics to salute him. The chief did so without looking away from his work, but Grey could only spare the attention to nod her head respectfully as she ran back and forth.

"Ensign Kember tells me you've got a case of nerves," Hanon said, and smiled amiably. "Take heart. If our engine is this strained, their engine must be rattling itself apart by now. Just a little longer and we'll find them at a dead stop, ready to surrender at our first gun."

Kember looked to the mechanics, both of them grave and pessimistic, but neither willing to contradict a superior. "We'll do our best, sir," Chief Megusi said.

Megusi's tone should have conveyed what his words could not, but it was lost on Hanon, who smiled and said, "That's the spirit, Gears!"

Though the turbine shook, and the boiler roared, and the airscrews buzzed, it somehow seemed that the entire length of the keel had gone deadly silent at this last word. All the crew within earshot stared at him. Even Chief Megusi looked up, staring with wide eyes, until an ominous sound from the unattended boiler drew his attention back to it.

Hanon, for his part, noticed nothing amiss. Indeed, he seemed rather proud of himself for knowing the correct nickname for a chief mechanic aboard a chasseur. "Well, carry on," he said, then turned and went back to the hurricane deck, whistling a merry tune as he trotted down the companionway.

Kember watched him disappear below the keel catwalk, and knew that someone would try to kill him.

THE VINS KICKED in Heny's door in the afternoon.

The inhabitants of the basement froze where they were, every eye raised to the ceiling. Above, furniture was pushed over with enough force to dislodge streamers of dust, and boots stomped from one side of the cottage to the other. There were more than four Vins, Bernat thought. Perhaps as many as ten, and they were searching every square inch.

The Garnians in Heny's basement had not been prepared. They were less prepared, indeed, than they had been at any other time since Bernat and his party arrived, for everything had been set for them to return to *Mistral*.

Their rifles were unprimed, unloaded, and bundled tight in canvas, in the perfect order for travel, and in the absolute worst order for fighting the Vins. They couldn't even be unwrapped now, let alone loaded, without risking a sound that would carry through the floor and betray them.

Josette had quietly freed a cutlass from her bundle, but that was the group's only viable weapon. Bernat didn't even have his cane. When it happened, he'd been talking with Zeren— talking in quite a friendly manner, in fact. Now he stood frozen in place, looking across the writing desk that separated them. The prisoner was tied to his chair by his ankles, but the chair wasn't restrained at all, and could be clattered about on the floor. None of them had thought of that, until the danger made the oversight both too obvious to miss and too late to correct.

One of the men from the signal base had stuffed a rag into Khirklov's mouth and was now leaning on his shoulders to hold him down, but Bernat didn't think either precaution would keep him quiet, if he was determined to give them away. And so Bernat implored him to silence with nothing more than a mute expression. Zeren didn't meet his eyes—a bad sign.

Suddenly, Bernat felt cold steel on his shoulder, and whipped his head around so fast that he almost cut his own throat on the cutlass Private Kiffer was trying to give him. It was the one Josette had retrieved, and must have been quietly passed from man to man across the room.

For a moment he believed that Josette only meant to arm him in case the Vins upstairs broke in.

No, that was a lie. He didn't believe that was her intent for even for a moment. But perhaps for a moment he wished that he believed it. Of course the sword was not being given to him for his defense, which would be pointless in any case if the Vins stormed the basement in force. The sword was being given as a tool of murder—cold-blooded murder—in case Zeren tried to make a sound.

Now Zeren met his eyes, and though the prisoner could hardly shrug with someone holding him down, his resigned smile had much the same effect.

Bernat despaired. Not two minutes earlier, he'd been chatting amiably with the man. And it wasn't only that he'd been chatting amiably, but the fact that he *could* chat amiably—he had conquered the urge to violence, and never more would that urge rule him. Here was this man whom Bernat had once wanted to beat to death, for no other reason than he was the enemy. If he was being honest with himself, Bernat knew even then that he wouldn't really have done it. He'd known, as soon as Josette forebade him to harm the man, that while he would struggle with the order, he would not struggle in vain.

He had always believed—believed on a level so deep that it went unquestioned by dint of never being noticed in the first place—that just such a test would be put before him. Now he clung to that buried idea, that God or fate or some other force had brought him to this moment and put the very sword in his hand, so that he *wouldn't* use it.

Questioning it now, he found hope, for he knew that this was the final test, that he only had to hold out for a few seconds longer, and the trapdoor would open, and Heny would stick her head through to tell them the Vins were gone, that they were safe, that Bernat was free again.

But the trapdoor did not open. Heny did not stick her head through.

Zeren—his friend Zeren, his private struggle Zeren, Zeren the final test before Bernat could mend himself and become a whole person again—Zeren spat out his gag and drew in a breath.

Bernat's cutlass was up and clean through Zeren's windpipe before a single syllable could pass the man's lips. He stared back at Bernat, eyes wide with the most genuine surprise, breath escaping from around the steel blade in a hiss punctuated by soft gurgling.

Bernat held it there while Zeren's life drained away, down the front of his uniform. He held it there until Josette finally walked up behind him and, with exquisite gentleness, took the blade from his hand. At some point in between—he couldn't say exactly when, but far too late in any case—Heny had stuck her head through the trapdoor to tell them the Vins were gone.

WORD SPREAD QUICKLY through the ship: they were gaining.

Well, of course they were gaining. The Vin captain was sharp enough to remain at full power, and not be baited into overtaxing his steamjack. If he was committed to teasing *Mistral* along, he would steam at full power until *Mistral* was just on the edge of cannon range, then take his pick from any number of sound gambits. He might match her speed then, or pull away under proper emergency power, confident that *Mistral* would by then be too overstrained to keep up. Or he might simply stay at full power, risking a few cannonballs at long range until the onset of night gave him a brand-new range of options with which to amuse himself.

Even if he wanted to fight, he'd certainly let *Mistral* damage her own engine for a while longer before he came about, for why not take every advantage that his enemy freely offered?

Kember had not voiced these thoughts, not least of all because she could be hanged for doing so. But she had seen networks of whispered words, centered on the more experienced crewmen, and could only assume that they'd all come to the same conclusion. This concerned her almost as much as the tactical situation, for a crew that understood the magnitude of their commander's stupidity might embark on any number of rash endeavors.

She worried even more when their whispering stopped, and changed to short, silent, meaningful glances between crewmen, with an occasional eye cast on her. Something was brewing aboard her ship, and it could only end in a gallows yard, if it didn't end much sooner in a fireball.

She didn't know what to do, and despaired for want of any viable option. She had always known that she might be called upon to help restore authority during a mutiny, but it had never occurred to her, even in her most pessimistic daydreams, that she'd have to stop a mutiny of good men against a rotten officer. When she thought of mutiny at all, she always imagined herself in a band of upstanding officers and loyal crew, bravely facing off against a pack of brutish, frothing malcontents with no motive nobler than mere anarchy.

She never thought she'd have to put down a mutiny against a man she'd like to do away with herself, a man whose removal from command might well be worth the price of a hangman's noose.

No solution had yet occurred to her when, a quarter of an hour later, the order came back: "Increase steamjack to three-quarters between full and emergency power." The order alone was worrying, but the lack of an answer was more worrying by far. There was no acknowledgement, nor did the turbine's speed increase by the slightest.

This was mutiny already, and it could cost Private Grey and Chief Megusi their lives.

And there was Lieutenant Hanon, up from the hurricane deck, coming around the port side of the steamjack to shout at the mechanics. To shout at them from a predictable place on the catwalk—from a spot that could be marked out ahead of time.

With Kember's attention drawn that way, she noticed something even more peculiar. No one except Hanon had their safety lanyard clipped to the overhead jack line on the port side of the keel. She looked up to double-check her own. Starboard side.

She unclipped herself, and reached over as if to shift her lanyard to the port line. The crewmen working nearby froze instantly when she made the motion, their eyes going wide with alarm, then darting away when she noticed. Ensign Kember decided that it might be safest to remain unclipped for the moment, and tucked the lanyard under the shoulder strap of her harness.

She went forward, still not knowing what to do, but knowing she must do something. She came around the left side of the boiler and saw Private Davies above her, sandwiched between two gas bags, hanging in the spiderweb of lines and cables stretching across frame five. He was adjusting the tension on one of the lines, using the ship's tension gauge to do it.

That was another oddity. Experienced riggers didn't use the gauge. No one had taken the heavy steel tool into the rigging since the ship's flight trials, and only then because the trials called for precise data. A good airman didn't need the gauge for routine adjustments; they could read the tension on a line by flicking it and listening for the pitch of the twang.

She tried to meet Davies's eyes, but the moment she looked up, he was already looking away, giving his most rapt attention to the rigging. She thought of ordering him down, but it would be such a strange thing for an ensign to do, with her commanding officer just steps away, that it could only draw more attention to whatever plot was afoot.

She ducked under the end of the turbine and gasped when she saw Hanon. The man looked like he was in the third day of trench fever, pallid and sweating buckets. He wasn't yelling, as she'd expected. She didn't think he had the spirit left for yelling. He could only plead, barely audible above the steamjack, "You don't understand. If I come back alone again, what will they think of me?"

"Alone, sir?" Megusi asked.

Hanon turned even more pallid, and shone with a fresh gleam of sweat. "I mean, if I come back with nothing." He steeled himself, and recovered some semblance of focus. "If we come back with nothing, what will it look like? With more power, we might catch up to them before nightfall, and the wind often shifts in the night. We might be back in time to support a morning attack. And the glory will be as much yours as mine. I'll see to it that you all share. I'll note every exertion in my report. You've done a heroic job of keeping the engine going, Gears . . . Chief. I'll make sure that's known. But what good is it all, if we come back with nothing?"

Kember wondered if her presence was even necessary, for who could think of hurting a creature as pathetic as this?

But Davies must not have had a clear view of Hanon's pleading face from high in the rigging, for in the next moment the tension gauge fell and cracked against Hanon's skull.

The lieutenant crumpled. He reached out to grab Chief Megusi for balance, but Megusi stepped briskly out of the way, as if he'd been primed to do so, and Hanon toppled over the edge of the catwalk. The overhead jack line should have stopped his fall, but instead it tore clean out of its anchor point aft, and Hanon fell through *Mistral*'s thin canvas skin.

If Kember had planned to catch the safety line as it whipped past, she could have never managed it, but pure reflex accomplished a feat that preparation never could have. She snagged the line with one hand, and got the other around it before it went taut with Hanon's full weight and yanked her off her feet.

The keel became a confusion of shouts and streaking motion as she fell. Her chest thumped painfully against the catwalk, then her belly. Her vision resolved into the image of Lieutenant Hanon staring up at her with equal parts entreaty and panic, his face streaked with blood.

He had the jack line firm in both hands, but it wasn't secured to anything, and Kember wasn't strong enough to make up the difference. It slipped, inches at a time, through her hands, and she would have lost it entirely if she hadn't landed atop it and pinned it to the catwalk. She fumbled with her feet until she managed to tangle the slipping line around her leg. It cinched up, squeezing with excruciating force, but it stopped the line from playing out.

Stopped it, that is, until Hanon started to climb up, and the force of hauling himself hand over hand dragged Kember right over the edge of the catwalk. They would have fallen together if someone in the keel hadn't thrown their body over her legs. Still, it wasn't enough. Kember slid toward the edge until she was bent at the waist. She felt a thump above, as another airman added their weight to the pile, and finally her slide was arrested.

Hanon was frozen below, no longer trying to climb. She saw his grip relax, as if he meant to let himself fall to save her life. He only held firm again when he saw that she was no longer slipping.

Not that her position was at all enviable. She was doubled over with her hips and legs on the catwalk, and her head and torso stuck through the bottom of the ship, hanging inverted in empty space. But she was anchored above, and once Hanon saw that, he began climbing the rope again, until he came within arm's reach of her. He reached up, one hand closing around her right harness strap, and then he used that to haul himself high enough to grab the left strap with his other hand.

She let go of the line, and it slipped easily through her fingers, through the clip of his lanyard, and fluttered away below the ship, dancing in the wash of the airscrews.

Hanon made the mistake of looking down, at the forest a thousand feet below him, and when he looked up again, his eyes were filled with panic. He tried to climb up her, his grasping hands battering her about the head as he struggled to hold fast against the buffeting slipstream. "Stay calm!" she shouted over the wind, but had to repeat it three times to get both words out without an intervening punch to the side of her face. If he could only control his panic, she could help him up.

And he would return the favor by putting a noose around half the necks on the ship, wouldn't he? Davies, Grey, and Megusi would be just the start of it.

While he struggled, she forced herself to think clearly, despite the wind and the thrashing and the sight of the ground so far below. She had seen the captain do this, pausing in the

midst of a crisis to consider every angle of the problem with
that keen, quick insight that airship officers either acquired,
or perished for want of.

Her eyes refocused on Hanon. She reached to her left side
and unhooked the clasps securing her harness. They popped
loose, and the shoulder strap on that side slipped an inch. The
thigh strap on the right side dug into her leg as it took up
Hanon's full weight.

As she reached for the clasps on the right, Lieutenant
Hanon looked up at her and opened his mouth to speak, but
she never heard what he said. The right clasp popped open and
her harness slid over her head as easily as a dressing gown
coming off.

Lieutenant Hanon still had his hands around the straps as
he fell. His knuckles were white, grasping her harness all the
tighter despite the futility of it. She watched him, not blinking
despite the wind in her eyes, as he receded away. His features
blurred with distance, his body grew smaller and smaller, and
finally it disappeared against the background of the forest
canopy. Whatever disturbance he created there, it wasn't even
visible from this height.

And then she was being hauled up by strong hands, turned
upright and set on her feet. By instinct, she reached for her
lanyard to clip onto the jack line. After the fourth try, she
looked up and found it missing, remembered what had happened to it, and burst into absurd, braying laughter.

She stopped herself only when she noticed the crew looking at her. All of the crew. Not just the mechanics and riggers
in the keel, but the deck crew as well, crowded onto the companionway ladder with their heads sticking up over the lip of
the catwalk. None of them said a thing, nor moved to return
to their stations. They only stared at her, waiting.

She stared back for several seconds, then closed her eyes,

and willed her lungs to take a breath. "Reduce steamjack to three-quarters power."

Chief Megusi didn't say anything, but when she opened her eyes again, he was shaking his head.

"Three-quarters power until dark, Chief, unless you want that Vin up our ass." She turned forward. "Come about and steer west northwest. And somebody sew up this damaged fabric." She looked back to the crewmen around her, and found them still frozen in place. "Stop your goddamn gawking and put this ship back on station."

They leapt to work.

IT WAS EARLY morning, just after dawn. She was not atop the goat shed, nor even in sight of the town. She stood at the end of a mile-long trail of blood leading from the shed into the woods, more blood than she ever thought a single wolf could hold, yet the stuff still oozed fresh from the beast's hip, where Josette's rifle bullet had passed through.

The two cubs, drawn from the nearby den by the scent of their mother, but equally wary at the sight and scent of a person, stumbled clumsily in the snow a few feet ahead. They first advanced and then retreated, tripping over each other or their own fuzzy legs, and always whining for their mother's attention, trying to draw her to them. But the wolf lay unmoving where it had collapsed, and its fresh blood was the only sign that the carcass still held some tenuous spark of life.

"The hell of it is, I thought I'd be the one to save him from these damn brutes."

Her eyes shot open. She was sitting upright against Heny's basement wall, near the blocked stairs. On the other side of the room, the body of the Vin fusilier was wrapped in linen and set in the corner. There was no offensive odor yet, or at least none that made itself known over the odors of habitation already permeating the basement.

"Oh, pardon me," Bernat said. "I didn't realize you were asleep."

"Only resting my eyes. What were you saying?"

Bernat looked to the writing desk, where Josette's mother was having a subdued game of cards with Jutes, Kiffer, and Corne. "Nothing that seems worth saying, now that I reflect on it."

Ordinarily, she would have leapt at the chance to escape an uncomfortable conversation before it began, but perhaps remembering the wolf cubs had made her sentimental. "You did what you had to do, to keep us alive," she said. "If the cost is you don't like who you are anymore, then ask yourself if that's such a bad trade, after all."

He was quiet a moment, and then said softly, "You've had this conversation with yourself before, haven't you?"

"A hundred times or more," she said, pulling her knees to her chest and resting her chin on them. "Anyway, if it wasn't you, it would have been someone else."

Bernat laughed. "And they'd probably just muck it up?"

She couldn't help but laugh with him. "Yes. Unless it was me."

"Oh, without doubt." He looked again at the card game, his eyes settling on Josette's mother. "And if it had been you, do you think she'd ever forgive you?"

"For this? I don't imagine she'd see anything that called for forgiveness. She knew as well as any of us the necessity of silencing that man."

"It's only that she hasn't spoken to me since."

"I'm sure she's just a little rattled. My father was in the army, remember." Josette took a deep breath. "How she screamed at him, the day he got his conscription notice, saying we all ought to run away together somewhere, instead of letting him be pulled into 'someone else's war.' She forgave him in the end, though. She understands, even if she doesn't show it."

Bernat sat higher against the wall. "You've never told me what he did in the army. Was he in the infantry?"

Shaking her head, Josette said with a proud little smile, "Aerial Signal Corps, as a balloonist. They wouldn't put him on an airship, because his luck was so bad. Three times, he lost his tether and crash-landed behind enemy lines. Got the Spear of Garnia for bravery, though I've always wondered whether he didn't cut his own tether, so he could sell liquor to the Vins."

At half past nine, the trapdoor opened and Heny brought the announcement, "Won't be able to do anything about that body for a while. The Vins are out in force tonight. The silver lining is, you won't hardly notice the smell of it, seeing as how I can't risk emptying your chamber pots. The other bad news is, we ain't had a chance to sneak any extra food in, so tonight it's gonna be dinner for two, split eleven ways."

As the rest groaned, Josette jumped up and asked, "Did we get the signal off?"

"We did," Heny said, taking the last few steps down to the basement. "Which is a big part of why the Vins are in such a stir."

"It couldn't be helped," Josette said.

"Aye, everything you lot did here couldn't be helped and had the best goddamn intentions, I'm sure, but that don't mean it's caused any less trouble for us, and for what?"

Josette didn't shy away from Heny's scowl, but neither did she offer an argument. "Has the battalion signaled in return?"

"One blue rocket, just a few minutes ago."

Josette eyeballed her. "That can't be right. Who'd you hear it from?"

"Hear it, hell, we could see it from here." She turned to shout up the stairs, "Pesha, what color was that rocket just now?"

"Blue!" came the answer.

"One blue rocket?" Josette asked. "And *Mistral* still missing?"

"Still missing," Heny said.

"You're sure of that?"

Heny gave her a scornful glance. She took a deep breath, apparently ready to shout up the stairs again, until Josette held up a hand to stop her.

"So what the hell's it mean?" Heny asked. "They gonna leave the plague behind when they go? Oh wait, I forgot. You are stayin'."

And as much as Josette worried that the 132nd was making a terrible mistake, she took some pleasure in Heny's startled response when she announced, "One blue rocket means they'll attack at dawn."

Now Josette had everyone's attention, and most particularly her mother's. Cards scattered in her wake as she ran to the stairs. "Dawn tomorrow?" she asked.

"Dawn tomorrow," Josette said, "and it's unlikely we'll get muskets from *Mistral*."

By now, Pesha had come down the stairs, drawn by the commotion. "We should get someone making pikes," she said, "for anyone who doesn't have a weapon of their own."

"That's a hell of a lot of pikes," Josette said.

"Then we'll get a hell of a lot of people working on them," Heny said.

She nodded. "Good. Who gets the message out? It'll be a dangerous job, with the Vins alert and on edge."

"I can manage that," Josette's mother said, taking a step forward as she spoke. "And I'd best start now. Only so many hours before dawn."

Josette's first impulse was to stop her, and she had her arm halfway to barring the way when she realized there was no point. Even knowing it would do no good, she said, "It doesn't have to be you."

"It does, actually," her mother said, but not harshly. "Anyone else would caught on the way. And hardly anyone else knows who can be trusted, and who might still be spyin' for the Vins. Send anyone but me and you're doin' worse than sending no one at all."

Josette shared a look with Bernat, then said to her mother, "As soon as the battalion masses to attack in the morning, the Vins will all go to the wall. The streets should be clear of patrols and guards. That'll be the signal for the mob to gather in the square. And tell them to get a hearty breakfast and empty their bowels."

Her mother's eyes opened wide, and she said at a whisper, "I can't tell them *that*, Josie."

"Trust me, you'll be doing them a favor if you do."

Bernat managed a smile and said, "And do come back safe."

Josette's mother looked at him, seemed on the brink of throwing her arms around him, but in the end only turned her head away and went up the stairs without another word.

THE SUN HAD been down for hours, but a clear sky left faint starlight as *Mistral* went dark and altered course, coming into a sweeping curve which, if followed to its end, would bring her around behind the *Ayezderhau*. *Mistral*'s sharpest lookout, carrying the best night glass they had, said she thought she'd seen the *Ayezderhau* adjusting course in response. She thought, but she wasn't sure in the faint light.

The moon would rise in a few more hours, illuminating both ships, so Ensign Kember had a decision to make. Her intention had not been to carry through with the ambush, but only to give the appearance, and so bait the *Ayezderhau*'s cautious captain into countering the maneuver, and in doing so allow *Mistral* to keep ahead of them.

But what if the Vins hadn't taken the bait? What if she'd overestimated the night vision of their lookouts? If the *Ayezderhau* flew straight on, she'd pass them in the night, and the rising sun might find her bombing Garnian infantry, with *Mistral* lagging hopelessly behind. In that case, Kember's only chance was to follow the feint through, lie silently across the *Ayezderhau*'s path, and put two into her steamjack as she went past.

What would Captain Dupre do?

"Sir," a crewman said, whispering despite the mile or more of sky between them and the Vins. "Private Grey thinks we need to shut down the steamjack for at least half an hour, to repair damage to the manifold pipes."

She wanted to scream, but she swallowed it down and said, "I'm going up there. Lupien, you have the deck."

She made her way in the dark by rote, climbing the companionway steps, dodging around the relayman, and heading straight for the steamjack. She found Private Grey lying under an oiled tarp, only the faintest light peeking out from under it.

Kember wriggled under the tarp, and once her eyes adjusted to the lantern light underneath, she shot Grey a nervous look and began to inspect the solder joints of the manifold, looking for the damage.

"Are you okay, Sabrine?" Private Grey asked, just loud enough to be heard.

As always, it took her several seconds to figure out who the hell this "Sabrine" was, and remember it was her. It took her even longer, so long that her face flushed hot with embarrassment, to realize that there was nothing wrong with the steam manifold.

"No," she said, and wanted very much to cry, to start blubbering right there in front of a subordinate. The rush of despair came on so suddenly that it was all she could do to keep her voice down. "I'm not sure I'll ever be okay." While the space beneath the steamjack of a signal corps chasseur is not in any aspect ideal for the giving or receiving of hugs, Private Grey did her best, putting a supporting arm around Kember and squeezing.

"Thank you, Miriam," Kember said, and wiped at the snot dribbling from her nose.

"You'll be okay," Miriam said. "You'll be okay as soon as you convince yourself that you saved everyone aboard this ship. The ledger comes out in your favor, by a big margin."

"Sure, but . . . I just don't know if I'm cut out for this. Look at me, cowering under the steamjack and whimpering."

Unlike the case with hugging, the space under a steamjack is ideal for punching, if only because the victim can't get out of the way. Miriam demonstrated this by hitting her in the arm. "Are you kidding? You're one of the toughest people I know. You got shot in the neck and went back on duty! The only other people I know who could do that are the captain, Sergeant Jutes, and maybe my mom."

"Yeah, but how many of them have killed in cold blood?"

"If I had to guess, two out of three, but I bet Sergeant Jutes is capable of it, too." She put a hand on Kember's shoulder. "Listen, I may not know much about killing, but I'm pretty sure it's not *supposed* to be easy, so there's no shame in having a hard time of it. No shame in finding someone to talk to, either. About that, or anything else that's eating at you."

Kember smiled. "Hey, Miriam. I have to pick between trying to ambush the Vins, or making a beeline to Durum. What do you think Captain Dupre would do?"

"She'd try to ambush them," Miriam said, without hesitation.

Kember sighed. "Yeah. She would, wouldn't she?"

Miriam grinned, the lamplight bright in her eyes. "Undoubtedly, but what would Captain Kember do?"

Kember frowned. "First, she'd blubber under the steamjack."

Miriam nodded. "Check."

Staring into the pipes just over her head, Sabrine Kember thought for a moment and said, "And then she'd head for Durum."

"There you have it."

15

It was before dawn on the day of battle, and Durum had overslept.

Or so it seemed. Josette entered the town square at a trot, and came to a clomping halt when she saw it empty, save for a brigade of decaying bodies hanging from nooses.

"Where in hell is everyone?" Heny asked, as they picked their way through the dark forest of gallows.

"Perhaps 'fashionably late' has finally made it out here?" Bernat answered. Josette could just hear his cane clicking against the paving stones as he slowed to a walk.

Heny made some reply, but her whispering voice was drowned out by another furious cannonade from the west. The artillery, Vin and Garnian alike, had been going at it hammer and tongs for the last half hour. The square was clear of Vin fusiliers—presumably they were all at the wall, staring into the dark in anticipation of an assault.

Which was fortunate for Josette's war party, for at their current strength they'd be hard-pressed to fight off a pack of stray dogs, let alone a detachment of infantry. The sum total of the resistance forces consisted of Heny, Pesha, and the people who'd been living in their basement, less Private Kiffer.

"You don't suppose Elise was captured, do you?" Bernat asked privately, as he came forward to stand next to Josette.

She couldn't make out his expression in the pre-dawn gloom, but she heard the worried tremor in his voice. Indeed, she heard it in her own when she answered, "Maybe not.

Maybe the Durum resistance simply isn't quite what was advertised."

They advanced toward the stone pond at the center of the square, whose population of frogs was unusually silent this morning. The party clustered there, at least two sets of eyes watching every approach, and waited.

In a minute, shapes loomed out of the shadows at the edge of the square. They came near, were challenged, and one of them replied in Garnian, "We ain't early, are we?"

"Early?" Josette asked. "We ought to be assembled and moving by now!"

"Josie?" the voice asked, quite pleasantly. "Your mum told us to come here after the airship showed up."

Josette sighed. Her instructions had been misunderstood. There was no point in getting mad about it now, but that had never stopped her. "*Mistral* is delayed, but we have to start on our own, or the men going into the breach will be slaughtered. I need each of you to run and gather more people. Anyone with a gun or a pitchfork or a goddamn sharpened stick, understand? And anyone with crowbars and tools for getting into the magazine."

In the next quarter of an hour, the resistance began to trickle into the square in varied states of preparedness, until there were two or three score gathered under the lightening sky. About a quarter of them had hunting rifles, another quarter fowling pieces, and the rest were armed with makeshift pikes and a diverse array of firearms. One had a great hand mortar, which was as apt to kill its user as the enemy. Another had a pair of tiny pocket pistols that might penetrate skin if the target didn't have too many layers of clothing on. Two men had arquebuses, both with broken flintlocks, so they could only be fired by touching a burning match to the pan. One man even had an ancient blunderbuss whose muzzle flared open at the end, as wide as a bell. Until that moment, Josette had half-believed such firearms to be the fanciful invention of engravers and illustrators, rather than actual weapons of war.

"Doesn't anyone in this town have a musket?" she asked. "Something that doesn't take an age to reload?" Between all of them, the only musket she could see was the demonstration piece now wielded by Sergeant Jutes.

"What the hell has this town ever needed muskets for?" a man answered. It was Mr. Turel. "Ain't no damn use for hunting, and nobody ever warned us we'd be on the front lines of the damn war. We weren't prepared for this!"

Mr. Turel was not the least prepared of the townsfolk, however, for he did have a pistol and was fully dressed. Some of Josette's impromptu army had been roused straight from their beds, and ran into the square dressed in nightshirts, with clothes and boots tucked under their arms.

Her mother was still missing. The last time anyone had seen her was three in the morning. She asked everyone entering the square, until enough resistance fighters were now gathered that Josette began dividing them into their own little platoons of half a dozen or so. She gave one platoon each to Heny, Bernat, Jutes, and the surviving men from the signal base.

Private Corne cast angry, troubled eyes on her when she didn't give him a platoon, and for a moment she wished she'd left him behind with Kiffer. A glance at his mangled hand softened her attitude. He'd been brave enough to come along, when he might have stayed back without anyone thinking less of him. "I bear some responsibility for your injuries," she said, stepping up to him. "Perhaps I even bear as much as you think I do. But that's the way of the army. We all have to eat shit and pretend we like it, you understand?"

Corne didn't say anything.

"Here are some more coming," she said, looking to the edge

of the square, where another group of ill-armed, half-dressed rabble were running toward them. "Take command and get them organized."

"Yes, sir," Corne said, and now all but a small residue of the hate was gone. "You can count on me."

She nodded, and once the little platoons were in some semblance of order, she gathered their leaders together and gave them their instructions. "But your most important job," she added last, "is not just to give your platoon commands, but to remain steady before them. If you're ever in doubt, you can't go far wrong if you keep advancing on the magazine by any street that's open to you. That will give our boys the best chance in the breach. Above all, remain steady. There's going to be a lot of smoke, and a lot of noise, and people you know are going to die, but you must remain calm. Is everyone ready?"

The question was answered with a cheer, which spread instantly to the townsfolk, and grew into a roaring war cry.

BERNAT HAD ONCE been offered command of a thousand fighting men, that he might have the honor of leading them in pitched battle. Now he was leading half a dozen irregulars down dirty side streets, toward an enemy of unknown force, emplaced behind unknown fortifications. But for all that, he would have only just traded these half dozen for the thousand— which is to say, he was sentimental but not a goddamn idiot.

Though, now that he approached his target and looked back at his little band of amateur warriors, he saw that it was closer to a full dozen now, its numbers swelled by men who'd joined along the way. There were three more a block behind, running to catch up. And when they came even with the rest, Bernat saw that they were not men, but women. It shouldn't have surprised him, he knew. When the women of Durum saw that something needed doing, they came out and did it, whether it was expected of them or not.

It made him think of Elise, who might even now be locked in a jail cell, or tied to a chair in some barracks house, watching the morning light grow brighter as she listened for evidence of the insurrection that would liberate her. That thought drove, if not the fear, then at least the doubt from his mind. He would fight, and he would command his party well, for to do otherwise was to take an unacceptable risk with his lover's life.

He rounded the last corner, facing a long, narrow street leading to the magazine. There were at least eight fusiliers guarding it, formed up in a disciplined line behind a movable barrier. This barrier was no makeshift obstacle, but a sheer-faced wall made of sturdy wooden planks blockading the street.

His directions were to charge headlong into whatever defenses he found, but considering how well the Vins had prepared, he considered ordering the riflemen among his company to pick the Vin fusiliers off from here, beyond the range of their muskets.

No, it would never do. The Vins would simply duck below their barricade, hide behind its heavy planks, and perhaps amuse themselves with a game of cards until Bernat's rabble expended their ammunition.

If he wanted to take the barricade, he would have to charge it. To charge that obstacle, with those skilled musketmen behind it, was true stupidity, but at this moment it was Bernat's assigned task to be stupid, and to inspire his war party to equal heights of idiocy. And when he put it like that, he knew the feat was well within the scope of his talents.

"Charge!"

He'd forgotten to draw his sword, and only realized this as he leapt into a run ahead of his troops. Indeed, he'd forgotten to order his small force to ready their melee weapons. And as he fumbled with the hilt of his sword, he dropped his cane. But it was a bit late to stop and tidy up, so he only went on running and screaming.

Ahead, he saw smoke rise in puffs, and heard the crack of musketry. He shut his eyes, anticipating the volley, but when he opened them, he saw that the Vins had disappeared from the barricade. The fighting was on the far side of it. One of the other companies had reached the magazine before him.

Despite his aching leg, he pushed all the harder and reached the wall yards ahead of anyone else. He gave one last battle cry and jumped at it. He pulled himself over hastily—so hastily that he fumbled and fell in a heap over the fire step, his rifle coming off his shoulder and skittering away across the cobblestones. But he leapt to his feet with admirable dexterity and pulled his sword free of his scabbard, ready to face any number of Vin defenders.

He looked about, searching for his first victim, and saw Josette leaning casually against the barricade. She smiled pleasantly at him and asked, "So you didn't have any trouble finding the place?"

16

Josette watched Bernat try to pick up his rifle in one hand while simultaneously sheathing his sword with the other, which went as well as such an operation possibly could. Yet the dozen-odd people climbing over the wall still looked to him for guidance when they reached the other side. She had to admit he'd performed admirably, fixing the Vins' attention on his charging platoon, while her platoon and others attacked from behind.

She made a quick assessment of their situation inside the barricade. The Vins had movable barriers on every street leading out of this intersection, forming an impromptu redoubt. Heny and Pesha were in one corner, tending to the wounded. Five townsfolk had musket balls in them—only one or two of those could hope to survive—and another dozen were down with broken limbs, fractured skulls, and contusions from hand-to-hand fighting.

"Good God," Bernat said, when he took it in.

"The people we're fighting know their business, and that's a goddamn fact."

He was still looking about the redoubt. "Where did you put them? The Vins, I mean."

"We didn't get any of them," she said. "They retreated into the magazine in perfect order and barred a foot-thick iron door behind them. We'll have to dig down to the powder tunnel to get to the magazine. Like I said, they know their business."

The layout of their redoubt proved it. The buildings over-looking the approaching streets had their doors and ground-floor windows bricked up, and their second-floor windows barred. If the Vins had more men available, those buildings would have each become its own formidable bastion, bristling with muskets that could shred any war party foolish enough to approach the magazine.

Jutes approached. "Magazine might be connected to these buildings," he said, pointing along the streets. "And I don't like the looks of those second-floor windows." He looked not at the windows, but at the street, enclosed by barriers but growing more crowded by the minute as straggling war parties and new recruits joined them. "It'd be like shooting cattle in a stockyard."

"Put them in order, Sergeant," she said.

Jutes went to work organizing the mob, sending some to dig and arraying others behind barricades, but even as he put platoons into position, more would appear and set themselves up wherever they pleased, until the bustling mob outside the magazine resembled nothing so much as a disturbed anthill.

Josette went to work with a shovel alongside half a dozen men, prying up cobblestones. It was a familiar activity, dig-ging in the streets of Durum, and she had to remind herself that she was searching for the tunnel leading from the maga-zine to the cannons, and not for the foundation of a long-forgotten city wall.

As she worked, she searched the mob with her eyes, hoping to find her mother's face among them. She wasn't there, of course, and it was becoming harder to escape the conclusion that she'd been captured—captured while skulking about the night before an attack, which gave the Vins every right to line her up against a wall and shoot her.

She tried to put it out of her mind as she scanned the upper windows along the street again, half expecting to see muskets pointing out of them. There were none, but she dug all the faster at the thought that there might be, the next time she looked.

When the excavation was waist-deep, her shovel hit a timber beam. "It's the tunnel!" she called. "Hatchets, over here! Work fast!"

She climbed out to make room for others to chop and hammer at the planks that made the roof of the powder tunnel. As they worked, she looked anxiously up to the windows again, and this time there really were muskets pointed out of them.

Too many. So goddamn many that she thought she must have seen it wrong, or been mistaken about the situation, for the Vins surely wouldn't have spared this many men from the walls to guard a magazine they had no reason to believe was in danger. There were at least forty fusiliers up there, kneeling two to a window.

"Get down!" she screamed, in just enough time for the few veterans among her party to drop swiftly to the ground, and for the greater number of inexperienced insurrectionists to turn and look at her quizzically.

The muskets above fired together, so loud and so concentrated in this narrow space that the sound of it stabbed into her ears, producing a pain so sharp that for a moment Josette thought she'd been hit in the skull. It was hard to see through the tempest of roiling smoke, but she knew that her mob must have suffered dearly.

And the hell of it was, the damned hell of it was, there was nothing to be done. All her mob could do was stay where it was, or scatter over the barricades and be cut down by the Vins stationed in the buildings flanking those slaughterhouse streets. "Stay down!" she called, hoping the smoke might offer some small protection. But she could already hear some of her people stomping down the surrounding streets. As they ran, muskets fired in ones and twos, and with each shot the sounds of running feet diminished by one pair, ending in a thump.

Some of her riflemen were returning fire, but it was a wasted effort. Their only hope was to break into the magazine and occupy it. Only inside those walls would they find anything like safety, and anything like a fair fight. She took up the hatchet of a fallen man, leapt back into the excavation, and began hacking with a fury driven by pure desperation. Men emerged from the smoke to join her, Jutes among them.

"Corne and Heny are alive," he said as he drove a crowbar into a gap Josette had hacked between two planks. "Not sure about the others." He levered his crowbar hard, putting all his weight into the motion.

The plank beneath them creaked, then groaned, and the tunnel roof gave way with a crash. The whole work party fell into the void, along with half a ton of earth and cobblestones. Jutes lay still and half-buried, and she desperately wanted to check on him, but people were dying and there was no time. She clambered up the slope of debris, stuck her head above street level, and called out, "To me! To me! Everyone into the tunnel!"

BERNAT WAS ON the ground, trying to piece the last several seconds of his memory back together. He'd seen the muskets, heard Josette call out, and dropped just in time. He couldn't remember the moment the Vin fusiliers fired, only that the air was suddenly filled with smoke and the street with blood.

And now Heny was kneeling over him, squinting into his eyes. She drew her hand back and slapped him. He was accustomed to having women slap him, but few had ever done so with such force.

"Yer just dazed." She gave him a reassuring nod. "You'll be fine."

He blinked up at her, his head clearing. "Is Pesha . . ." He couldn't finish the question.

Heny shot him a sour look. "How come every time something goes wrong, everybody just assumes that one of the two of us must be dead? That the only right and proper outcome is fer one of us to cop it?"

"I, uhhh . . ."

"Idiots," she said, and disappeared into the smoke.

And now he heard a crash and a rumbling noise to his right, and soon Josette's voice was calling the mob to her.

"This way!" Bernat said as he went, adding his voice to hers. "Everyone follow me! If you want to get out of here, follow me!" As he passed survivors in the smoke, he grabbed them and pushed them along, until he was close enough to leap down into the excavation.

He saw Jutes lying unconscious—he hoped only unconscious—and caked in dust. "What the hell happened?"

"Just the usual, for us," Josette said, bitterly.

The mob was pouring in now. Bernat borrowed a tinder pouch from one of the townsfolk and lit the end of a frayed length of rope, which burned with a reeking flame, but lit the murk of the tunnel. To the west, it continued on as far as he could see, its wooden trolley tracks disappearing into subterranean darkness. To the east, it ended abruptly in a dead-end made of planks.

"Railway ties!" he said. They'd stopped up the entrance with goddamn railway ties, and it would take a quarter of an hour to cut through them. "How the hell were they planning to move powder through here?"

Josette looked like she might burst from the rage building up inside her. "They weren't," she said. "They knew we were planning to storm the magazine, so they made other plans and set an ambush. Someone talked. Someone talked, and when I get my hands on them, they will beg for death."

Above, the sporadic musket fire slackened, even as the flow of refugees into the tunnel slowed. There were six dozen already crowded in.

Corne was one of the last down the hole. "Where's Heny and Pesha?" Josette asked him.

"Stayed behind to look after the wounded. Said even the Vins wouldn't shoot a couple of healers."

She made a skeptical grunt and said, "See to Jutes, will you?"

Bernat crept over. "You don't suppose Heny and Pesha are the informers?"

"I don't know," she said. "Believe that I'm going to find out."

He froze when he heard the sound of boots hitting cobblestones, somewhere above. "Are the Vins coming over the walls?"

"How the hell should I know?" Josette asked, with irritation. "Why don't you pop up and have a look?"

He peered up at the pale blue sky showing through the excavation, and said, "Because I like my head to not have bullets in it."

"We don't have time to break through those railway ties." She looked west and took a breath. "So the tunnel into ominous darkness wins by default."

Bernat put a hand on her shoulder. "What about Jutes?" he said, quite softly.

She looked at the sergeant, still unconscious, his breath shallow. By way of answer, she only shook her head.

As she pushed through the mob to lead the way to the west, Bernat dragged Sergeant Jutes away from the opening, so that at least no further rubble would fall on him, and perhaps the Vins wouldn't trample over him as they stormed in.

THERE WAS A strangely calming simplicity to this tunnel. Josette had no idea what waited for her in the darkness, but there was only one way to go, and she must either lead her little mob down it or watch them die. There was no chance of making the wrong decision when there was no decision to make, no need to weigh the balance of risks when there was nothing to weigh them against.

None of which changed the fact that she was scurrying through an underground tunnel when she ought to be flying an airship. This was the opposite of her job. This was the exact goddamn opposite of her job, and she tried to work out how the hell she'd arrived at this state of affairs. In the stress of the moment, she couldn't remember, though she was reasonably sure it was somehow Bernat's fault.

Ahead, the tunnel curved right and straightened again, ending in a point of light where the tunnel sloped gently up and opened onto . . . somewhere.

She looked back, and could see the vague shapes of her mob in the torchlight. "Stay here. Pass the word back to hold them at the bend with steady fire. Calm, steady fire, now."

Ten paces from the opening, she could see the city wall stretching away in the distance, aboveground. The tunnel ran parallel to the wall here, opening into the pomerium, an open space between it and the city. If her reckoning was correct, the west gatehouse was somewhere behind them, and the breach beyond that.

She crept back, even as rifles began to fire behind her, their muzzle flashes casting a series of grotesque shadows on the tunnel walls. The riflemen fired not in the steady, controlled rearguard action of trained soldiers, but in a panicked volley. The men near her were peering back to see what was going on behind them.

"Ignore it," she told them. "We have our own fight. When we come out, the gatehouse will be behind us. That is our objective. We rush out, take the gate, and open it. Understand? We head for the gate. No matter what else happens, we head for the gate."

She could only hope the focus on that order would give them some semblance of cohesion. So far, her mob was unbroken only because there was nowhere to run. Once they were in the open, only a blind fixation on the objective could hold them together.

"The gate," she said one last time, turned, and ran the remaining length of the tunnel.

She emerged into the light of morning, the sun risen but not yet showing over the top of the eastern wall. Even this meager light was enough to dazzle her, after the relative darkness of the tunnel, so she had to run blindly along the wall until her vision returned.

She could see the gatehouse emerge from the brightness ahead. Just before it, stretched across the pomerium a hundred yards away, were three companies of Vinzhalian fusiliers in three ranks, advancing steadily toward her with their bayonets gleaming in the morning light.

"Forget the gate!" she called behind her. Her saboteurs needed no further encouragement, once they saw what lay between them and their target. Trained infantry would be hardpressed to break that line, let alone her pathetic little mob.

She swept her eyes in a full circle, weighing the various ways she could get her people killed. The pomerium was clear in the opposite direction—the direction an undisciplined force would naturally run toward. Which meant it had to be a trap.

To her right was the wall, and all routes into its bastions or up to its walk undoubtedly closed off. And finally, to her left, on the inner side of the wide grass pomerium, there lay a long line of houses built tightly against each other, side by side with their neighbors and back-to-back with the houses behind them, with only a few widely spaced streets cutting across the blocks. Getting past those houses would not be easy. It was not meant to be easy. They had been laid out with the express purpose of slowing any attacker who managed to get over the walls.

She turned to her band of insurrectionists. Though only moments had passed during her calculations, one would think from their worried expressions that they'd been standing under enemy observation for hours. She made her own expression as unconcerned as she could and said, "Go for the houses!"

As she dashed for them herself, the Vins halted and began to fire by platoon. A third of their number fired, and while that third reloaded the next third fired, and while they loaded the last third fired, and by then the first were loaded and ready to fire again. Taken together, their disciplined volleys came every five seconds, and only the long range saved Josette's force from complete annihilation.

Between the third and fourth volley, she reached the nearest house and flattened herself into the hollow of the front door. Only a score of men had followed her across the pomerium. The rest were hiding in the false safety of the tunnel, running for the false safety of the opposite direction, or had knelt in the open space to return a pitiful, sputtering fire against the Vins.

"To me!" she called. "Goddamn you all! To me!"

But they didn't come. She'd lost them. All she could do was take the handful she had left and try to keep them alive. She smashed in a window with the butt of her rifle, climbed through, and unbarred the heavy front door from the inside.

The house had only been abandoned recently, most likely after the Vins took over, so it was blessedly free of trash. "Axes and crowbars to the back room. Cut through the rear walls and make a passage into the house behind us. Riflemen upstairs. Two to a window. One man fires once the other is reloaded. Aim well and don't hurry your shots. We only have about as many bullets as there are Vins, so every man you miss is someone I'll expect you to kill by hand."

She stepped back outside, putting herself in plain sight of the enemy as she urged the stragglers to run for the houses. Someone pulled her back, and she was surprised to see it was Mrs. Turel, who scowled and said, "What kind of fool are you, Josie, to stand where they can shoot you?"

As annoyed as Josette was, she had to admit that she was also a little touched. "It inspires confidence," she explained.

"Whose confidence?" Mrs. Turel asked. "Ours or theirs?"

By way of compromise, she stood in the doorway, half shielded from the Vin musketry that pockmarked the house, and from there urged the others to join her. She thought her efforts had succeeded when the tunnel erupted with Durumites, but then she heard Sergeant Jutes's roaring voice shout, "If any of you dumb bastards still ain't out of this tunnel in three seconds, I will skewer you myself and save the Dumplings the trouble!"

He emerged aboveground last of all, covered in dust and as angry as a badger.

JUTES GOT THEM moving, but most of the insurrectionists were running not for the houses but directly away from the Vin infantry. Even Bernat could see that it was a trap, but the mob apparently believed the Vins had been courteous enough to leave a convenient escape route, from which the would-be saboteurs could melt away into the town and tell anyone who asked that they'd slept late this morning.

He tried to keep himself between the mob and that dubious escape route, threatening his own people with his sword when necessary. Many still ran past, or ran toward the houses just far enough to angle past him.

Private Corne took station to Bernat's left, scooping up the rifle from a fallen saboteur and holding it with the barrel steadied across his forearm, threatening to shoot anyone going for the street, and doing so to much better effect than Bernat. It was amazing what value a grievous wound had in convincing people that you meant business.

The Vins fired again. Bernat flinched, wondering if the next moment would bring oblivion. It didn't, but he had precious little respite, for the next volley was only seconds away, and between the second spent realizing that he was still alive and the few seconds spent steeling himself for the next volley, there was hardly a moment in which he could think clearly.

Rifles cracked from the second-floor windows of the mob-occupied houses, but on the Vin firing line, only one fusilier fell. It was entirely possible, even likely, that he was the very first Vin casualty in this entire affair—that while Durumites died by the dozen, and were even now dying under those maddening staccato volleys, the Vins had paid for it all with the loss of a single man.

Bernat wondered why the hell he had ever left Kuchin, to come to the edge of Garnia and help lead a ragged band of amateurs in a fight against some of the finest infantry in the world. In the din of the volleys, he couldn't remember what had brought him to this moment, but he was fairly sure it was Roland's fault.

Jutes came by with two long rifles slung around each shoulder and one in his hand, and they ran together for the nearest house, diving through the door just as a volley pitted the brickwork with dozens of musket balls. They rose to find Josette taking aim through the only downstairs window. She grinned as she sighted, and without looking up said, "Apologies if our noise woke you, Sergeant Jutes." She fired and, without looking to see the effect of her shot, began reloading.

"I was just getting up anyway," Jutes said, and began handing out rifles to those who had none. "Got work to do."

Without a word of instruction, Bernat went to the window, unslung his rifle, and looked out. The Vins were advancing now, coming on at a quick march, and it took an effort of will to not estimate how long it would be before they reached the house. He picked his target from among their front rank, aimed carefully, and fired.

Josette was still reloading, putting her weight on the ramrod to push the tight-fitting bullet down the rifle barrel. Bernat knelt, pulled his hammer back to half cock, tore open a paper cartridge with his teeth, and tipped a few grains into the priming pan. By the time he had charged the rifle and was ramming the bullet home, Josette was only just taking up a firing position.

"Excuse me, sir," Jutes said, edging Bernat aside as he piled furniture behind the barred door.

Josette fired, then tapped Bernat on the shoulder and said, "Get ready."

As he pulled his rammer free of the barrel, he looked up to see the Vins practically upon them. He had only gotten one goddamn shot off, and as he fumbled to slide the rammer back into its slot, he thought for the first time in his short military experience that he would gladly trade in his rifle for an inaccurate but fast-loading smoothbore musket.

Josette had flattened herself against one side of the window, so he flattened himself against the other and drew his sword. Outside, the fusiliers were trying to break down the front door with their feet, shoulders, and musket butts. Somewhere in the back of the house, he could hear Durumite axmen breaking through the rear wall. "Who the hell builds a house without a back door?" he asked.

"Someone anticipating this precise situation, but with the sides reversed," Josette answered.

He was about to make an insightful comment about civic planning when a bayonet-tipped musket was thrust through the open window. The point was aimed at his belly, but the fusilier who wielded it was not eager to make himself an easy target, and so stabbed blindly from relative safety below the sill. The fusilier's prudence cost him his weapon, as Bernat grabbed the musket and yanked it right out of his grasp.

"Ha!" Bernat said, letting the gun fall to his feet so he could jab at the man with his sword. "I was just thinking we could use a musket, and now we have one, thank God."

Josette was hacking with her sword at the point of a second bayonet thrust through the window. "And what do you intend to load it with?" she asked between swings. "Or do you think God will make a second trip to deliver the correct caliber bullets?"

Bernat glanced down at the bore of the musket, which was so wide that his rifle bullets could get lost in it. "Things never go quite right, do they?" He brought his sword down and drew blood from the hand of a fusilier trying to climb through the window.

"Things were going just fine until the day I met you," Josette said, leaning around the window to stab at a fusilier, then hastily ducking back when another took a shot at her.

"I object to that," he said. "Not only on the grounds that it is a very hurtful thing to say . . ." Here he had to pause to pin a thrust bayonet against the windowsill, lest it skewer Josette. "But on the grounds that it must be a lie, because things were going fine for me until the day I met you!"

One of the growing number of Vins on the other side managed to trap Josette's sword against the jamb of the window. With Bernat's own sword pinning a bayonet, he couldn't help her, and with both of them occupied, a third fusilier flung his musket through the window and heaved himself nimbly over the sill to land on top of his weapon, inside the house. The Vin rose into a ready crouch, musket retrieved and already in hand, and from there lunged for Bernat.

Bernat could not use his sword unless he released the bayonet stuck through the window and let Josette be skewered. As the Vin inside barreled on, his own bayonet leveled at Bernat's belly, he could do nothing but feebly bat at the point with his free hand. Between that and squirming out of the way at the last moment, Bernat managed to save himself. He heard the bayonet hit the wall next to him, but the fusilier was no fool. He kicked at Bernat and put him off balance, pulling the musket back for another lunge.

And just when it seemed that Bernat must either die on a Vin bayonet or let Josette die on another, a rifle crack filled the house and the Vin fell, the momentum of his last lunge carrying his lifeless body to the foot of the window. Private Corne looked over the barrel of a smoking rifle, steadied on his stump. "Sir," was all he said to Bernat, with a respectful tip of his head.

In the back of the house, a wall gave way and Jutes's voice boomed through the rooms and hallways, "In good order now! One at a time! Keep a rearguard, goddamn you! And if any of you bloody bastards runs into the streets and leaves the rest of us to the Vins, know that I will survive, and know that I will hunt you down."

"If it weren't for the difference in rank," Josette said, and grunted as she finally managed to get a good angle on the fusilier threatening her outside and put her sword through his neck, "I would kiss Sergeant Jutes."

Bernat wanted to make a comment on Jutes's preferences in such matters, and silently cursed the promise that stopped him. "His loss" was all he said.

"Go," she said, and whipped her head toward the back of the house. "I'll be right behind you."

JOSETTE RETREATED JUST inside the house's back room, knelt in the open doorway, and drew her pistol. Behind her, the fugitives filed through the hole in the wall with none of the efficiency of professional soldiers. She could hear their clothes catching and ripping on the splinters around the hastily cut passage, heard them trying to push their way through the narrow passage two at a time, blocking the way until Jutes could sort them out.

Her eyes stayed on the window, not fixed but held loose and barely focused, in case a fusilier appeared from an unexpected angle. The top of a fusilier's shako cap showed over the windowsill, but there was something off about the way it moved. She waited. Another shako appeared next to it, rose until she could see the barest line of forehead under the visor. It blurred slightly as she focused her eyes at the muzzle of her pistol to aim, then it leapt back in a spray of red when she pulled the trigger. Both shakos fell back simultaneously, along with the stick one of them had been perched on.

She retreated quickly around the doorjamb and signaled to the others to stay low. True to her expectations, one of the Vins held a musket over his head, pointed it through the window, and fired blind into the house. The flash was still a blotch of purple in her vision when a second musket was blind-fired in the same way, and another, and another.

"I think you've made them a little angry," she heard Bernat say from behind her, as she reloaded her pistol and fitted another percussion cap.

Mrs. Turel replied, "Josie's always had trouble making friends."

She looked back. Only five or six Durumites left to evacuate, Mr. and Mrs. Turel among them. "Come on, move while we have them rattled," she said. "They're going to unrattle as soon as they remember what they're up against."

She looked back to the window, only to see a fusilier's musket pointed directly at her, and a finger pulling back on the trigger. As the gun fired, she saw but did not hear it going off, and felt a hot pressure on the right side of her face, followed immediately by a strange, chill numbness. She stared into the smoky blur of the room, finally knowing what it felt like to be shot in the head. She had shot so many that way, and thought she was doing them a kindness, but this was horrible.

She saw the unformed shape of a person in front of her. No, above her. When had she fallen to the floor? She heard Bernat telling her to hold still, his voice strangely distant, though he was only inches from her face. Jutes was there, holding her down, and only then did she realize that she'd been trying to push him away. Her vision darkened, and pain returned to her world as Bernat pulled something out of her eyelid. Her vision sharpened slightly, despite the warm liquid filling her eye, and she could just see Bernat holding a three-inch-long, bloody wooden splinter from the bullet-shattered doorjamb.

"Just missed the eye," he said, as he flicked it away. "Best leave the rest for Heny to sort out. Don't worry, your cheeks were never your best feature."

Jutes let her go, took up her pistol, and fired at something toward the front of the house. She sat up and saw that more time had passed than she realized. Everyone was through except the three of them. She looked through the ragged hole in the back wall and could see someone dragging Mr. Turel out of the way on the other side, his hip bloodied by the same bullet that had grazed her cheek and showered her face with splinters.

Jutes helped her up and they retreated together, Bernat firing his rifle before he backed through the impromptu back door himself. As soon as he was clear, a pair of Durumites began piling old timber across the hole, while two more stood guard with makeshift pikes.

For just a moment, she was thankful that they'd come out into a house that just happened to have a stockpile of timber, albeit a bit on the moldy side. But when she saw one of the townsfolk stuff a cracked cooking pot into the hole, her optimism wavered, and when she saw the other toss the ancient, mummified body of a cat on top of it, she groaned.

"We came out in a goddamn trash house?"

"Hardly used," said a man she recognized but couldn't quite place. "The front room is only filled to about waist height."

She took her pistol back from Jutes and stumbled through the short hall leading to the front. She nearly fell, but Bernat was there, and stuck a hand out to hold her in place. "I'd like you to sit down for a bit," he said.

"And I'd like to be back aboard my ship with a nice cup of tea," she answered, pushing past him.

She emerged into the front room and swept her eyes across it. Two windows. One door. No stairs. Three men at each window, kneeling in trash and firing at something across the street. More huddled in the corners and along the wall, packed in, terrified, not running only because there was nowhere to run. Corne performed the act of a brave leader admirably, though he too seemed on the edge of despair.

As she picked her way over the shifting, unstable terrain of garbage, one of the men's rifles hung fire—the priming powder ignited but the gun didn't go off. He ought to have known to hold the weapon steady, but he desperately pulled at the trigger over and over, always expecting the next pull to produce a different result, and when after ten tries it didn't, he began thrashing the weapon about, as if he could shake the bullet free.

"Remain calm," she said. Her thick voice drew their attention to her bloodied face, and had rather the opposite effect than what she'd intended. "Focus on your targets. What are we firing at?"

"Company of Vins occupying the house across from us," one man said, then flinched as the rifle which had hung fire suddenly discharged, flew out of its owner's hands, and landed behind him.

Josette laid belly-down in the trash to count the puffs of smoke from the windows on the other side of the street. There was certainly not a company over there. At most, it was a dozen men. "Patience and calm," she said. "Keep up a steady fire while we get organized and prepare to sally."

They should have sallied already, up against that meager handful of fusiliers, but they were no longer a fighting force. They had barely been one to begin with, and now the morale shock of so many dead friends, and the grating fear of their precarious situation, had turned them all to water. She had to restore them to some semblance of fighting spirit before she could take them out of here, or they'd run at the first opportunity, and whatever hope remained would be lost.

Rifles fired in the back room, painting even more fear onto the faces in the front. "Private Corne, keep them spitting, keep them steady."

Corne nodded to her, appearing somehow relieved to have a direct order telling him to do exactly what he'd been failing to do already, and the mob seemed relieved to hear him get that futile order. Battle did curious things to the mind.

She returned to the back room to find Mr. Turel still quiet, but sweat soaked, ashen, and gritting his teeth with the pain. Bernat and Jutes were firing into the half-clogged passage between the houses, and a couple of fusiliers were firing back. No one was hitting anything, which was hardly surprising. The cover was good and the angles bad.

She was worming her way around the room when the gap in the wall erupted in flame. A piece of burning wadding paper had landed in the hole in the wall and set their makeshift barricade of desiccated trash on fire. The way her day was going, how could it not?

On the other side, the Vins fired through the flame and smoke, making no effort to extinguish it, for they could run away if it got out of control.

Without a further word, Jutes pulled off his deel and began beating at the fire with it

"Bernie, you too!" Josette cried, as she pulled a piece of rotten burlap from the trash and went to work on the flames.

Bernat took off his coat, a fine green affair with embroidery on the breast, and looked at it with lamentations swelling in his eyes. Then he took off his shirt and put the jacket back on. "It's the best I can do," he said, as he joined them.

Amidst the cracking muskets and the roaring fire, Josette became aware of a strange musical sound. She'd had enough time to make several swings with her makeshift fire blanket and dodge two bullets before she recognized it as laughter. It took her another bullet, barely avoided and zinging past her ear, to realize it was coming from Jutes.

"And what the hell is so funny, Sergeant?"

Jutes ceased laughing, she thought, not in response to her question, but because he'd simply run out of breath. He gulped air and said, still wheezing with mirth, "I was just thinking how boring our lives were, before we met Lord Hinkal."

The warped lumber stuffed into the passage caught flame now, and the fire roared up to blacken the surface of the wall, threatening to spread to its timbers as well. Despite it all, as he stared into the inferno, Bernat laughed as well. "If you can find any thread of logic that ties me to this monumental degree of misfortune, I will gladly remove myself from society to save its people from my curse, and take up vocation at the most secluded monastery I can locate."

"No, sir!" Jutes roared. "I beg you to stay. Those poor monks never did anything to you." And at that, the three of them laughed so much it drew the baffled and alarmed stares of everyone else in the room, the stricken Mr. Turel among them.

The wall itself caught fire now, the flames reaching the ceiling and flattening against it in curious, ever-shifting whorls of light. The Durumites were scrambling out, dragging Mr. Turel and crowding into the relative safety of the front room. The Vins weren't even shooting now. They must have evacuated the house behind. The three Mistrals backed away, but kept swinging at the fire with their makeshift fire blankets.

"Private Corne, you better be ready to leave in a hurry," Josette shouted down the hall, "because we're not staying long." The intensity of the fire had her backed against the wall next to the short hallway, and the smoke had her coughing for breath.

"Corne? Are you ready?" There was no answer from the front room. "Goddamn it, Corne, answer me." No answer still. "Corne, you had better be dead out there, or you'll wish you were."

"Captain," came the reply, finally. It was Corne, but there was a resigned tone to his voice that she didn't want to identify. "It's over."

"Like hell it is," she said, unslinging her rifle and charging down the hallway. She emerged from the smoky twilight to see the front door hanging wide open. Through it and the windows, she could see a line of fusiliers that stretched left and right as far as she could see.

She brought her rifle up, and a dozen muskets were raised to match it. She cursed, threw the weapon down, and said, "Get the wounded out first. Quickly now, before this place comes down on our heads."

17

"At least this is a new experience," Bernat said, and received a sour look from Josette. "What? I've never been a prisoner of war before. I don't imagine anyone back at the palace has, either. They'll be so jealous!"

Their pen had been hastily constructed in the street, fenced off with cheval de frise—tree trunks studded with wooden spikes, old swords, and any other convenient, sharp object. A few blocks over, the fire was spreading, and the only thing the Vins had done to fight it was to bring down the houses on either side with gunpowder charges.

As he looked around the pen, it seemed to Bernat that there were more prisoners now than there'd been insurrectionists at the outset. Despite the terrible casualties their force had taken, even more had emerged from their homes to join the mob, and had been captured at one point or another.

Only half a company of fusiliers guarded them. The rest of the Vins were back on the wall, though an assault today seemed increasingly unlikely. The 132nd had never committed to the attack, and for all the mob's effort and sacrifice, they might as well have slept in. Bernat would have to remember that the next time someone criticized his own sleeping habits.

The sun wasn't yet over the rooftops, which added to the subdued atmosphere pervading the prisoners. Most sat, a few stood, but no one spoke above a whisper, except some at the edges of the pen who were pleading innocence and ignorance to the guards. Even the wounded were quiet, some utterly silent, others speaking softly to anxious wives or husbands.

"Ever been a prisoner, Captain?" Jutes asked. Of the three of them, he alone was standing, studying the guards as if waiting for his moment.

"Not in connection with the army," Josette said, without looking up. Her voice was more slurred now, the left side of her face swollen terribly.

"Well, it's hardly even a fuss," Jutes said. "A few days in the pen, a week at most, and they'll have us all paroled. We only have to swear to stay out of the fighting until Garnia's captured enough prisoners that we can be formally exchanged."

"Which, the way this war is going, might take an age," Josette said.

Bernat brightened. "Meaning we'll be free to do as we wish?"

"As long as we don't contribute to the war," Jutes said.

"Then we should take a vacation! We can summer at my family estate in Copia Lugon, take a carriage tour of Ortus. Have you ever traveled through Ortus in the fall? It's beautiful. Does your mother enjoy fishing at all? There are such lovely little streams. And if not, the hunting is excellent as well."

"If she's still alive by then."

"Pish," he said, genuinely optimistic. "I doubt they've even captured her, or she'd be in the pen with us. She must have been driven to ground during the night, and is only waiting for this to blow over."

Josette only sat with her eyes on the ground, occasionally trying to pick a splinter of wood or bone out of the oozing, bloody mess of open flesh on the right side of her face, and doing more damage than good with her blind probing.

Bernat looked for Heny in the crowd, but thought better of calling her over when he saw her speaking to Mrs. Turel.

Mr. Turel was on the ground between them, unconscious and still bleeding. "Help him," Mrs. Turel said. "Help him, please."

Heny chewed something Bernat could not identify, spat, and said, "I can help him die slower, or I can help him die faster. Which do you want? Choose quick. I got others to help." Bernat didn't catch the rest of their conversation, and was quite sure he didn't want to catch it.

They all mused silently for a while, until Jutes narrowed his eyes at something outside the pen. He said, "Something's happening, sir. Vin colonel's coming over. And he's got . . . oh hell."

Bernat stood and looked over the heads of the other prisoners. He saw Elise walking just behind the colonel and his aides. He swallowed and said, "I'm, uh, I'm afraid they have caught your mother, after all."

Josette didn't stand, didn't even look up, but only shook her head. "She wasn't caught."

"What do you . . . oh hell." Bernat looked between them several times. "You can't mean that . . . Surely you don't think . . . For God's sake, Josette, she's your mother!"

"They're coming to the edge of the pen, sir," Jutes said, in as even and toneless a voice as was humanly possible. "They're waving us over."

Without a word, Josette lifted herself up and pushed her way through the prisoners. Jutes followed, and Bernat took up the rear, kindly apologizing to all the people she'd knocked around on her way forward.

When they reached the edge, and Josette and Elise stood across the cheval de frise from each other, Bernat steeled himself for the coming explosion. He had known Josette angry before, but this would be a haranguing for the history books.

But Josette only stared at her, and said in her still-slurred voice, "You evil bitch."

Elise flinched, looked at the ground, then at Josette's wound.

She finally met her daughter's eyes, and spoke as if she'd been rehearsing her words all night. "Josie, you remember those stories about what Durum was like, before the Garnians came? Durum was powerful. It was wealthy. They had to move the walls out six times in as many generations, to account for the growth. Then Garnia took over, and turned it into the trash heap it is today."

Josette took a deep breath. "The Vins aren't going to change anything, Mother. Somewhere deep in your heart, you know that. So why didn't you leave? Why didn't you just leave? Move to Vinzhalia? Breed horses? Or maybe just horseshit, which you can obviously produce at will and in great abundance. If Father saw this, it would break his heart."

"Your father was the one who turned me to it." Elise took no satisfaction in her daughter's surprise. "He was Vinzhalian."

The chill was so sharp following those words that it spread outward from Josette through the nearby prisoners. They began to stand, a few at a time, and stare silently at Elise on Josette's behalf.

"The Dupres fled Durum when the Garnians invaded, but your Grandma Dupre came back with Mehmed, back to their ancestral home, after her husband was hanged for stealing, and your Grandma Sargis hid them in her attic until they learned to hide their Vin accents, and could tell everyone they were from out west."

"My God," Josette said. "My entire family has been spying for the Vins, since before I was born."

Elise shook her head. "No, not that long. We were only planning to sneak away to Vinzhalia after we were married. Mehmed still had family there, and we thought they might hide us 'til I could get rid of my accent, the way we hid Mehmed. But then you came along, and I couldn't see myself trekking that far through the wilderness carrying a baby, and so the move kept gettin' put off and off. We were almost ready, and you was almost old enough, when your father got conscripted. If it weren't for that, you would've been raised in Vinzhalia, and you being so young at the time, you'd hardly even remember being Garnian after a while."

Bernat thought that if the first row of prisoners threw themselves onto the spikes of the cheval de frise, the next row might be able to clamber over them and tear Elise to pieces. He thought they might just do it, too.

Elise took a small step back, but went on. "When he didn't return, I thought of taking you to Vinzhalia myself, but you never would have taken to it. You were always your father's daughter. So I stayed here. I stayed here for your sake, but I had to have some kind'a plan to ensure your future . . ."

"You evil bitch," was all Josette said in reply.

"It did ensure your future, though, didn't it? Ensured your future, and kept me fed after you left, 'cause you sure as hell wasn't sending any money home, was you?"

Josette shook her head, and even that small movement seemed a wild gesticulation, in comparison to her former rigidity. "Are you trying to tell me that I bought my commission in the Army of Garnia with money you made by spying for our enemies? You should have told me. You should have told me when I was a girl. Everyone could have avoided a fair bit of trouble, that way."

Elise shrugged. "Your father always wanted to tell you, but I knew it'd be a disaster if we did. You never did understand, about doing the things that had to be done. You sure didn't when you left. You remember when you came home crying over them wolf cubs you couldn't bring yourself to finish off?"

Josette looked up. "How did you even know about that? I never told you."

" 'Cause I followed you." Her mother laughed. "I followed you and finished the job you couldn't finish yourself. All this time, I thought you knew that, thought you must'a seen my footprints next to yours on your way back. But I suppose you never could track worth a damn."

"She makes up for it with other qualities," Bernat replied. "Not being an evil bitch, foremost among them." There was a short pause, in which Josette could almost hear the gears turning in his head, before he added, "Not by this day's standards, at least."

"You never thought with your head, never took a clear view of things." Her mother frowned. "You know, that wolf was the best thing that ever happened to us. Price of meat more than doubled, on account of that wolf. I even stopped passing things on to Vinzhalian scouts. Didn't need to, with the money I was bringing in from hunting. That wolf was a godsend, and you shot it. You killed it, and for what? Duty to the town? Loyalty to a bunch of jackasses who, like as not, would have strung you up with the rest of us if they'd known where your father really came from?" She laughed. "Ain't that just Garnia to a tee? And that's why I could never tell you where you really belonged. There was too much of where you didn't belong already baked into you."

Josette flashed an ironic smile. "You're one to speak, Mother."

Elise only shook her head. "Last year, I got you out of here before the Vinzhalian army came, didn't I? As much as it hurt—and it did hurt—to treat you so bad you wouldn't stay. And I tried to make sure you'd be out of here this time, too."

Bernat nearly exploded. "Wait a minute. You didn't try to get *me* out last year! You told me to stay! You tried to keep me here!" He gasped as the facts of the matter finally dawned on him. "You were going to take me hostage and ransom me to my family!"

"No!" Elise said. "I mean, not this time. I really did want to go away with you, this time. We could have lived wherever you wanted. And maybe later on . . . well, lots of countries take in expatriate nobles, don't they?"

But Bernat was having none of it. He screamed out, "You bitch! You evil, evil bitch!"

Josette only had to clear her throat to stop him.

"Sorry," he said, pushing the word out in a resentful puff of air. He took a moment to calm himself. "This isn't about me. I realize that, and I apologize."

The Vin colonel, who until now had been standing silent and awkward alongside his aides, took advantage of the lull to step forward and ask Elise in perfect Garnian, "I take it these are the two you'd like us not to shoot?"

If there was a single person in the pen uninterested in this conversation, they were interested now. A murmur spread through the mob, as those who hadn't heard asked about it from those who had.

"You can't shoot prisoners," Josette said, flatly. "Not unless you want Garnia to start shooting yours."

The colonel turned to her and bowed. "You are indeed correct . . . Lieutenant, is it? Or Captain? I can never remember how the ranks in your aeronautical corps work. I cannot shoot prisoners. But I can shoot rebels, insurrectionists, and spies. I see no uniforms, and so I necessarily see no soldiers. I may shoot or spare whomever of you I please. Be happy that we have a deal with your mother to spare you."

"All of this was your idea?" Josette asked her mother.

The colonel answered before her mother could. "No need to blame her. Major Dvakov had the honor of conceiving the plan. Nuri? Step up, now. There's a good man. He's been our liaison with Mrs. Dupre."

Dvakov stepped forward and gave Josette a crisp bow. She noticed that he had her pistol tucked into his sword belt. "I can take but half the credit. The plan was conceived jointly." The major grinned, clearly aware that he was destroying any deniability that her mother might still retain. "And I must congratulate Mrs. Dupre for her part. She assured us we would destroy the entire resistance in one swoop, but in my wildest imaginings, I never thought it would be this easy."

Josette sucked on her front teeth and said, "We're having an off day."

Major Dvakov tilted his head to the side, studying her as a bird studies a worm. "I should think you are. Your ship, your mother, and your battalion all failed you today, and the sun not even full in the sky. I think it will come as a relief, when we shoot you."

"We're not shooting her!" her mother cried, loud enough to echo off the nearby houses.

Major Dvakov turned to his colonel, eyes wide, and spoke like a little child imploring his father, "Oh, but we must, Colonel. Do you not recognize her?"

The colonel had been appraising Josette since Dvakov mentioned an airship. "Is it really her?" he asked. "I thought she was taller."

Dvakov grinned in reply. "I met her earlier, when she was in uniform. And what will our country say of us if we have the Shark, the bane of balloonists, the very witch of the sky, held firmly in our grasp, with an ironclad pretext on which to execute her, and we let her go?"

Josette's mother looked as if she was trying to turn Major Dvakov to stone with her gaze. "You told me I could pick any two of them. These are the two I pick."

The major laughed at her and threw his arms joyously into the air. "Yes, but you didn't say it was *her*! You never even told us she was in the city. All this time, we thought she was in the sky above us, and she's been right here. Oh, you have been a bad, bad little spy, Elise. So bad that I think our deal is forfeit. Is that your opinion as well, Colonel?"

The colonel replied in Vinzhalian, and only then did Josette appreciate that Major Dvakov had carried on the conversation thus far in Garnian—no doubt so that Josette would understand every goddamn word.

Her mother joined the discussion in what seemed equally fluent Vinzhalian, until she was silenced by the major casually shoving his palm into her face.

When the argument between the Vin officers died down, the colonel turned to Elise and said in Garnian, "I'm sorry. If I had the least doubt about who she is, I could grant your request. As it is, I cannot in good conscience allow her to go free."

Her mother, voice quivering, never meeting her eyes, said very softly, "I'm sorry, Josie." She looked next to Bernat, expectantly.

Josette turned to see Bernat staring absently at the sky, his chin held in his hand. After a moment, he looked at Elise as if just now noticing her, and said, "Oh, are you waiting for me? I'd prefer to remain where I am, thank you. I'll not walk away, arm in arm, while you put your own daughter in front of a firing squad."

Her mother's eyes were swimming now. "But I love you," she whispered.

"You only wanted me for the ransom!"

Major Dvakov interjected in whining Garnian, "Can we please get this finished? I haven't had breakfast."

"YOU CERTAINLY NEVER struck me as a Vin," Bernat said to Josette as they were marched away with hands bound behind their backs, alongside Jutes, Corne, Heny, Pesha, Mrs. Turel, and a couple others that Major Dvakov took to be high-ranking co-conspirators. Elise was nowhere to be seen, having fled under the force of Bernat's glare, and disappeared down a side street while Dvakov was collecting the prisoners.

"That's because I'm not a Vin." Josette said it forcefully, more frustrated than depressed.

"I know, I know," he said. "But, if not for a conscription, you might have ended up a filthy royalist. It makes my stomach turn."

"Monarchist," Josette said, hardly paying attention to him. She was looking about, her eyes cast slightly up.

"Come again?" Bernat asked.

"The Vins are monarchists," she said. "We're royalists."

He frowned. "Are we? Yes, yes, of course, that's what I meant: a filthy monarchist." He meant to go on, but their march was rather shorter than he'd expected—just around a corner, so the prisoners in the stockade couldn't see. As a boy, he'd watched one of his father's tenant farmers do the same while slaughtering pigs.

As the fusiliers lined them up against a row of houses, with Josette's eyes still darting about, Bernat finally realized what she was watching for. He wasn't sure whether it was folly or tenacity to believe that *Mistral* would swoop in and save them all in the nick of time, and he didn't suppose he had long enough to figure out the answer.

Whichever it was, he found himself sliding his eyes back and forth across the crest of the wall. He was still at it when they lined him against the wall next to Jutes, who leaned over and whispered, "That was a bloody stupid thing you did."

Bernat found that it took force of will to take his gaze off the sky and its slim hope of salvation. "You're going to have to be more specific," he said, sparing only a glance.

"I mean, saying you'd stay with us," Jutes said.

Bernat unwound by degrees, returned a wan smile to Jutes, and shrugged. "I listened to my heart. Shame it's even less practical than the rest of me."

Jutes looked at his feet. "Well," he said, and did not quite sigh, but let most of his breath out. "Thank you."

Bernat grasped for words to adequately answer Jutes's gratitude, and despaired of finding them in the little time he had.

Dvakov made his way along the line, an orderly following close behind, until he came to Bernat. He searched him for intelligence and found none—a state of affairs which Josette, in the ordinary course of events, would not hesitate to make a biting comment about. But she made no such comment now, so at least there was a silver lining to all this.

The major moved on to Josette, and had more luck. He found, in a patch pocket sewn on her trousers, the two separate letters she'd been writing to Roland. Dvakov read first one, then the other, and stood perplexed by their contradictory messages. Eventually, something seemed to dawn on him, and he handed them both to his orderly, saying, "They must be in code. After breakfast, we'll see if anyone can decipher them."

His nine men were already lined up against the opposite wall, musket butts held at the hip, muzzles pointed at the sky. Dvakov drew Josette's pistol and cocked it, ready to finish off anyone the fusiliers failed to kill outright.

"I just want you to know," he said to Josette, "that it's a real honor to kill you."

"I'm sure your family will be proud," she answered. "The whole burrow will be all atwitter about it."

Dvakov eschewed a biting response, but simply grinned and said, "Aim."

It occurred to Bernat that, as biting responses went, it was hard to beat a volley of musket balls. He took one last look at the crest of the wall, thinking that this time he would really see *Mistral*'s envelope coming over the top like a rising sun, and save them all at the last possible moment.

But there was nothing there.

He closed his eyes.

He never even heard the order to fire, or perhaps he didn't

have time to comprehend it. He heard only the bang, felt only a lurch—no pain except in his ears—and then he was falling.

He landed on his feet, then collapsed to the ground.

And realized that something wasn't quite right about that order of events.

He opened his eyes to see a column of smoke and fire rising above the city in the direction of the gunpowder magazine. Already, it was a quarter of a mile high and beginning to pillow out at the top. The ground still shook from the colossal, literally earth-shaking force of the blast, but Bernat had acquired some modicum of an airman's balance, and so he was back on his feet in moments.

The other airmen were even faster. Josette not only had her feet under her, but had brought her bound hands to her front by swinging them under her legs as she ran slantwise toward Major Dvakov.

The major and his fusiliers, however, were creatures entirely of the land, and now the land in its upheaval had forsaken them. One fusilier managed to come unsteadily to his feet just as Jutes barreled into him, shoulder foremost, with so much force that he was thrown against his neighbor, and all three of them smashed with brutal force against the wall behind. Bernat followed the sergeant's example as best he could, running hell-bent for the nearest fusilier.

He could not replicate Jutes's performance, but Bernat and the Vin went to the ground together in a disorderly heap. Bernat's time aboard *Mistral* showed again as he disentangled himself and rose before the Vin could, despite having his hands free. Bernat used the only limbs available to him, kicking at the fusilier's face until it was a bloody mess and the man stayed down.

He straightened up to see Jutes already going after another fusilier. That one recovered his musket just in time, however, aiming the bayonet at Jutes and bracing himself. Jutes had to twist aside at the last moment, missing his target and barreling past.

But now the rumbling of the ground was fading, the unwounded Vins were all rising at once, and the advantage swung to them. One raised his musket and aimed at Bernat.

"Bernie, duck!"

He responded instantly, and heard Josette's pistol crack behind him, so close he could feel the heat on his back. The man threatening him fell like a sack of beets, a bullet through his skull.

Glancing back, he saw Josette holding her pistol in her bound hands, Dvakov in a heap behind her. She didn't tarry, but threw herself on the fusilier who had Jutes up against a wall, and sent him sprawling. Bernat thought better of attempting such a feat, and knelt down astride a dropped musket to cut his bonds on the bayonet.

It was an inelegant operation. The bayonet was not sharp along its length, as he'd expected, but only had a dull edge within half an inch of the point. He worked the bindings across that half inch with all the force he could muster, and managed to jab himself in both wrists. The warmth spilling over his hands only encouraged him to work faster, for if he was destined to bleed to death from his own carelessness, he was determined to do some good before the end.

His bonds came free in a blood-soaked mass, and without checking the extent of his self-inflicted punctures, he snatched up the musket and brought the butt to his shoulder. He looked out to see Josette and Jutes still harrying the single fusilier and doing quite a professional job of it, while three fusiliers together fought off the rest of their party, and had already killed or wounded two of them.

Without a second thought, Bernat shot the man threatening his friends, and didn't waste any time trying to convince himself that the decision had any tactical reasoning behind it, or served any purpose but keeping them safe. As he bent to pick up another musket, one of the fusiliers, a man he might have killed instead, shot Mrs. Turel in the gut, and bayoneted her for good measure.

Bernat aimed his fresh musket at the man, eager to take retribution. But just as he put pressure on the trigger, Josette called out, "Bernie, left!"

With an impulse that carried from his ears to his arms, with barely a stop in his brain, he swung his musket to the left. He saw a fusilier taking aim and, in the same motion he'd already begun, Bernat pulled his trigger to snap off a shot.

As he peered through the smoke to see the effect, Josette yelled again. "Behind you!"

He swung around to see Major Dvakov and one of the fusiliers Jutes had tackled, each scrambling to find dropped weapons. Bernat leveled his musket's bayonet at the fusilier, and was working up the courage to charge at him when the man went down with a bullet in his chest—shot from where, Bernat did not stop to ask, for Dvakov had by now found his sword.

Bernat charged him, but Dvakov parried the bayonet with ease, engaging it with the flat of his sword and then flinging it aside in one fluid, graceful motion. With the bayonet safely out of the way, Dvakov twisted his wrist to bring the blade into Bernat's path, where his momentum would carry him onto its point with only the smallest effort from the major. Bernat brought the butt of the musket up to crack it across the man's skull, a move that would have surely earned him unkind words from his old fencing instructor, but which turned out to be fantastically successful in a street brawl. A splash of blood painted the cobblestones, some of it Dvakov's and some Bernat's, flung from his wrists by the swift motion.

He spun around. Josette was holding the last two fusiliers at bay with an empty pistol, which they would surely come to realize at any moment. He ran, dropping his musket and scooping up another on the way. He halted in front of the Vins, screaming that he would send a bullet into the groin of the first man who moved.

They threw down their arms, whereupon Heny piped in with, "Any o' you wanna tell me what in the hell just happened?"

18

Josette loped over to Major Dvakov, answering Heny as she went. "Someone blew the magazine." She retrieved both her letters.

"And someone was shooting," Heny said, as she looked over the wounded. "Same person who blew up the powder, I'd wager. A damn good thing, too, or we would'a been stuck pigs for certain."

Josette looked for evidence of rifle fire from the direction of the magazine, but any puffs of smoke were lost in front of the larger plume. "Who it was, and why, I can't even imagine."

Bernat looked up from pressing his wrists together to stanch the bleeding. "Then your imagination must not reach very far."

She narrowed her eyes at him.

"Oh, sorry," he said. "I'm sure the magazine was so impressed by our valiant efforts that it exploded out of sympathy, and the rubble decided to take up sport shooting."

She did her best to ignore him, peeking her head around the corner to look back at the prisoner pen. As she'd hoped and expected, the guards there were standing their ground, either unwilling to leave the bulk of the prisoners unguarded, or—in all the confusion of the blast—unaware that something had gone wrong with the execution.

But passivity was not one of this regiment's flaws. They would work out the situation soon enough, and Josette's present position would be swarmed by Vin infantry. That meant she had to move fast and leave the wounded behind, which struck her as an even greater injustice when she heard the too-familiar sound of Private Corne screaming.

"Not the leg," he said, when he'd caught his breath. "Not the leg, too."

She looked over her forces. Corne had suffered a bayonet wound in the thigh. A townsman she didn't recognize had been pierced by a musket ball high on the right side of his torso, and Pesha was attending to his wound. Jutes was tying linen around Bernat's perforated wrists, which oozed crimson into the bandages.

And then there was Mrs. Turel, awake but completely silent despite her painful mortal wound. The bullet had gone in over the kidney on her left side, and the bayonet a few inches below her sternum. If there was any goddamn mercy left in the world, she would soon bleed to death, and be spared the lingering agony of a gut wound.

More pertinently, the pace of the cannon fire on the walls had picked up, which could only mean the Garnian 132nd was massing for an attack. Even with the magazine gone and the Vins rattled, it would be a tough operation with the sun in their eyes.

Josette found an unlocked door along the street and said, "Put the wounded in here, bar the door, and hope for the best. Everyone who isn't staying, grab two muskets and a cartridge box each."

Bernat had his coat off and was examining it. He asked, "Do we have time to soak these bloodstains?" When he received only a nasty look in answer, he said, "No, no, of course not. I realize that. It's only, they'll be so much harder to get out, once they dry." He waited a moment more, in case that additional fact might sway the company. "But of course, we're in a hurry. I know, I know."

"And what about them, sir?" Jutes asked, still looking at the fusiliers.

Major Dvakov was just coming to, or perhaps ceasing to

pretend unconsciousness. Once he had a grasp of the situation, he only looked at Josette expectantly.

She kept her gloating to a minimum, despite herself. "Aren't you going to tell me I'm not allowed to shoot prisoners?" she asked.

He returned a little sniff, almost bemused. "I would if I thought it would help. I'm a pragmatist, you know."

She glanced at the house where her own wounded would hole up, and called to the others. "If there's a cellar in there, we'll lock these prisoners in it. If not, we'll slit their throats."

She knew for a fact that all the houses on this street had cellars—she'd played in some of them as a child—but she didn't like Major Dvakov's smug little face and wanted to see some anxiety on it.

Heny and a townsman stayed behind to tend the wounded, while Pesha armed herself and followed Josette. The party ran toward the wall—any attempt to free the Durumite prisoners would be futile. Halfway there, they heard a crisp bang from above, as the Vin fusiliers unleashed their first volley into the Garnian battalion's forlorn hope. The volley trailed off into the crackle of independent fire, and the Vin cannons joined in, throwing grapeshot into the mass of attackers. "Faster!" Josette called.

It was Bernat and Pesha holding them back, and now both did their admirable best to get a move on. As fast as they ran, however, they arrived at the line of houses behind the breach to find that someone had beaten them there.

Josette spent a precious quarter of a minute just studying her mother's face. All the while, her mother only looked back at her with a little smile, and not even a sad one, as she stood in the middle of the road, hands up.

"Was that you shooting?"

Her mother only nodded.

"And you blew up the magazine?"

Another nod.

"How?"

A shrug. "I walked in, put a slow fuse in a cask, lit it, and walked out. The lieutenant in charge of the guards knows me. Knew me, I mean. Told him I needed powder for my rifle."

"This doesn't change anything," Josette said. "I hope you know that."

Her mother replied with a little laugh. "It changes one thing, Josie. You're alive."

"Oh, very touching. Very touching indee—"

She was interrupted by another blast of grapeshot fired outward from the wall.

"Sorry, Mother. We'll have to finish this later. Between now and then, I suggest you work on a better story." She turned to Jutes. "Tie her up and throw her in one of the trash houses. There should be a few along here."

Pesha caught her breath and asked, "Are we not beating her to death, then? Why not?"

"We don't have time to do it properly," Josette said, looking directly into her mother's eyes all the while. "This way, if we win, we can come back later. If we lose, the Vins will get her, and do the job as well as we ever could."

WHILE JOSETTE CLIMBED onto a roof to study the disposition of the Vin defenders, Bernat snuck away to make sure Elise wasn't treated too inhumanely. He found to his relief that Jutes had had the same idea. He'd tied her bonds as comfortably as he could and made a dry platform atop the garbage, out of a door torn from its hinges.

"Do forgive Josette's spitefulness," he said to Elise. "She becomes irritable when she has to give up a fight, and when she's nearly been executed, and when her mother betrays her, and when her life and allegiance turn out to be a lie, and when . . . The point is, she's having rather a bad day, and a certain amount of malevolent wrath is to be expected."

Elise clasped her hands in a manner that would have seemed penitent if they weren't already tied together. "You'll talk to her, though? You forgive me?"

Bernat had to stifle his laughter, lest it attract too much attention. "Hell no," he said. "What in the world ever gave you that idea? No, my dear. When they hang you, I'll volunteer to tie the noose."

She looked at him for a long time, then turned her eyes away and said, "She made you like this."

"No, she didn't. It's simply becoming more difficult to avoid the resentment of the people one betrays when one commits treason, these days. I read that in a newspaper."

She said nothing more, and kept her eyes downcast. Bernat waited awhile, hoping she would say something more. For, though he'd gone over in the first place to see to her comfort, having once embarked upon browbeating, he now didn't wish to stop.

"Better be going," Jutes said, in short order.

Bernat nodded and set out, but as he turned to take a last look at her through the window of that garbage-filled house, he saw her looking back at him.

They continued on, stopping ahead of the nearest cross street leading to the pomerium. Josette pressed herself against the wall and peeked around the corner, then made room for Bernat and Jutes to do the same.

The Vinzhalian defenders stood loosely spaced on the firing step, protected from above by their improvised wooden roof and from the front by stone merlons. They crouched behind these to reload, popping out just long enough to shoot down at the attacking Garnians.

"We'll split in two," Josette said. "One party on each side of the street. If we can keep up a brisk fire, we may give the appearance of a larger force and draw their attention away from the boys in the breach."

Jutes pondered a moment, then said, "You can do a poor impression of a musket volley by throwing a handful of cartridges on a fire. If we manage to hit at least one of them to drive home the illusion, they might pull a company off the wall to come and kill us."

"I do so love our little schemes," Bernat said. He looked to Josette. "I'll stay next to you. That way, if you die, I can console myself with your rifle."

"Good thinking," she said with an approving nod, which made Bernat glad to learn that his suggestion was born out of sound tactical instinct rather than petulance, as he'd originally thought. "Can you still run on that leg?" she asked.

"Perfectly well, if I ignore the excruciating pain."

She nodded gravely and set everyone to finding wood for making a fire, which the party gathered primarily from splinters torn from window transoms. They piled it up, covered it with a dusting of loose gunpowder, and lit it with a musket's flint.

With the fire going, Bernat glanced around the corner, then motioned Jutes and Pesha to make their dash across the street. He took a last look at the defenders before yielding the position to Josette.

Josette steadied her rifle against the corner of the house, while Bernat stood by with a double handful of cartridges. To take his cue, Bernat didn't watch her trigger finger, nor the lock of the rifle, but her nearer eye. When he saw in it that she was about to shoot, he tossed the cartridges onto the little fire, and her shot came just in the middle of a sputtering series of bangs. Without pausing to admire his timing, he took her empty rifle and clapped a musket into her hand. He loaded while she aimed, pausing only long enough to trade another loaded musket for a spent one each time she fired. By the time she expended their supply of muskets, he had the rifle loaded, and handed it over.

From the quick glance Josette cast back along the access street, he guessed this would be the last shot before they retreated, so he gathered up their arms. The moment she fired, she called out, "Fall back!" and turned to run down the street.

The Vins burst onto the street in a mass, at least a dozen of them crowding into the lane and pounding down it with a whooping battle cry. Bernat ran faster than he had ever run before, injured leg or no.

THIS WAS EXACTLY what Josette had planned, and represented the best success she could have hoped for. She repeated this to herself over and over again, as she ran frantically down the street, legs pumping for dear life. The company of Vinzhalian fusiliers chasing her meant one less company on the wall.

But really, why did her best plans always end with someone trying to kill her? Bernie had a point about that. It was a mystery she would have to contemplate—provided, of course, that she lived out the minute.

Ahead, Jutes had nearly reached the safety of the next corner. She glanced back to make sure Bernat was running in the right direction. He was, thank God, but Pesha lagged far behind. The Vins were only twenty yards away from her, and in a boiling rage.

At an order, they halted and put themselves into a firing line. They raised their muskets and took aim. "Find cover!" Josette cried.

Jutes spun on his heel and dove out of sight, around the corner. Bernat skittered into the space between two houses, while Josette pressed herself as flat as she could into a doorway. Pesha kept running, either not hearing or not comprehending in the confusion of battle.

"Get down!" Bernat screamed after her, and that finally got

through. Pesha threw herself flat just as the volley went off, and for a second it seemed she had escaped its wrath.

Even she seemed to think so, for in the next instant she tried to push herself to her feet using an arm that was missing a musket-ball-sized scallop of flesh halfway between shoulder and elbow. She only appeared to understand when she saw white bone sticking through her skin, and the blood sopping her shirtsleeve and pouring onto the street. Bernat leapt out of his hiding place and ran to her. Josette joined him, and together they got her up and helped her around the next corner, where Jutes was waiting to fire a covering shot at the Vins.

Josette tried to clear her mind and think of her next move. This deep in the city, the defensive civic planning of the outer blocks gave way to an older, less coherent urban landscape. Durum's streets had the usual quirks of their era: blind alleys, constricted avenues, and side streets which split off or looped back on themselves for some obscure purpose, lost to time.

She remembered a blind alley nearby, with an old, long-abandoned blacksmithy at the end of it. From the street, it gave every appearance of a dead-end, but in fact the wall behind the blacksmith's forge had been dismantled, its bricks stolen and sold off, and now a person could duck under the forge's hood and step out into a hedge behind the building, and so escape pursuers. Josette knew this because, as a teen-ager, she was the one who'd dismantled it.

She led them down a street, around a bend, and into the alley. And there was the smithy, its front wall long since cut down for firewood, its anvil long since sold for scrap iron, but its forge standing cold, dark, and inviting.

They had to get through fast, before the first Vins looked into the alley, or the deception wouldn't work. "There's a gap in the back of the forge," she explained as she ran, counting on instant comprehension for the plan to go off. She ducked under the hood and saw light showing mottled from the other side. Thank God no one had patched up the wall in the intervening years.

But neither had anyone trimmed the goddamn hedge on the other side, as she soon discovered while pressing her way into it. It had grown thick and sturdy since the last time she had to squeeze through, and pushing through the tangled mass of branches and creeping vines slowed them down.

"Just leave me," Pesha said, as the others struggled to drag her through.

"No" was all Bernat said, and they finally pushed and pulled, leaving her much the worse for wear.

Jutes shook his head on the other side and said, "They saw us."

Of course they had. Josette was beginning to think her mother's sabotage of the magazine had used up the very last allotment of the luck her family possessed. She looked over the field behind the smithy, which was much as she remembered it: fallow, flat, with no cover, and surrounded on three sides by open street. Perfect for target practice, which might well have been its original purpose, and would soon be again if she didn't think of something. The Vins would be coming around the long way any minute.

"You don't suppose there's another cache of gunpowder someone could blow up, do you?" Bernat asked.

She hushed him with a hand held up, palm forward. "Do you hear that?"

No one else did, and perhaps it was only her imagination. But at this point, it would hardly hurt to indulge it. She looked up at the hedges, which had grown quite high since she was a teenager.

"You could get away if you leave me behind," Pesha said.

Bernat shook his head. "We've settled that question already."

"No, she's right," Josette said. "We'll hide her in the hedge and climb to the roof."

Bernat didn't look happy, but he didn't have a better plan,

either. They shoved Pesha into a hollow at the base of the hedge, doing yet more damage to her arm, and covered her with vines—a camouflage that might fool the half-blind or anyone who didn't look at it very hard. They left her to bandage her own wound as they made their ascent.

Josette shot quickly up, heaving herself from hedge to vine to masonry and grabbing whichever made the best handhold with hardly a second thought. At the top, she threw her rifle around the forge chimney, then swung herself up and over the edge. Sergeant Jutes was not far behind her, and Bernat came last, grumbling and muttering the whole way. They sheltered together in the shadow of the chimney.

While Josette and Jutes reloaded their weapons, Bernat was picking over his jacket. It was severely torn and scuffed, in addition to being covered with his blood, Pesha's blood, ancient soot from the forge, and residue from the hedges. "How many suits must this damnable war take from me," he asked no one in particular, "before it's finally sated?"

While Josette was ramming a ball down the muzzle of her rifle, she stretched to look out at the field below and scan the horizon. She grinned at what she saw. "The Vins are coming cautiously, ducked behind the fence over there," she said, pointing with her nose. "Must still think there's more of us. Hard to shake off a notion like that, once it's firmly in place."

She took a shot at them, and the party of fusiliers answered her with a full volley. She ducked back as they fired, their bullets plinking against the stone chimney, or sending puffs of splinters flying from the roof.

"Just hold out a little longer," she said.

"What, do you think they'll get bored of us?" Bernat asked, glancing around the other side.

By way of answer, she only pointed him to the east-southeast, where *Mistral* was coming toward them, her envelope gleaming bright orange in the morning light.

ENSIGN KEMBER STUDIED the situation through a telescope, and found it grim.

The Garnian battalion's forlorn hope was being pinned in the breach, raked by grapeshot and musket volleys, and cut to bloody ribbons. The supporting companies—the companies that were supposed to exploit the hope's sacrifice—were formed up in the rear, and showed no sign of advancing.

The column of smoke rising over the city said that the captain's mob of townsfolk must have had some success, but the penned-up mass of civilians said that their career as a fighting force had been short-lived. She hoped the captain herself wasn't stuck in that pen, or worse.

"Sir, there," the deck lookout said, pointing two points to port. "There's a couple score of Vins chasing after a small group." He leaned forward over the rail, as if being a foot closer would make all the difference in resolving pertinent details. "They've got the Vins hopping mad."

Kember nodded. "That must be the captain. Pass the word to rig signal lamp." She went to the taffrail to look aft. The *Ayezderhau* was still about a mile behind, but now several thousand feet above them and still climbing. She would follow *Mistral* and set up shop, no doubt, so that if *Mistral* came in to give close support to the assaulting 132nd, the *Ayezderhau* could fire shells at her from the safety of altitude.

And so *Mistral* would have no choice but to stand safely

away and watch the men of the 132nd die in the breach, or spend precious time matching *Ayezderhau*'s altitude, while the men of the 132nd died in the breach. She could see no other options.

But the captain would know what to do. The captain always had an idea.

The signalman, Private Turk, called from the forward rail, "Signal lamp rigged, sir."

She stepped back to the commander's station, ahead of and between the steersmen. "Signal, *enemy of greater force in pursuit, request orders,* then repeat it."

"Captain signaling," the lookout said. "Wigwag. Message reads, *Maintain course and speed, rig ladder for one pickup. Bernie and Jutes will remain to aid resistance.*" He looked back, lowering his telescope. "Ladder for pickup? That can't be right. Want me to ask her to repeat it, sir?"

Kember took a good look at the man, while most of the deck crew snickered. He was one of the replacement crew, and hadn't been with them during their actions the previous year. "No need," she said. "Secure signal lamp. Pass the word to rig ladder."

It wouldn't take long to close on the captain's position, but even that short time seemed to go by at an accelerated rate, for Ensign Kember had still come up with no possible explanation or excuse for Lieutenant Hanon's death. None that could reasonably be believed, at any rate. Whenever Kember tried to imagine a way out, it always ended with her running to the rail and jumping overboard.

It wasn't just that. It was that she'd never killed anyone before. Well, she'd killed people with a cannon, now that she thought of it, but that didn't count. They were so far away.

"We're coming up on the town, sir."

The lookout's warning snapped her out of her reflections

and cut off any hope of developing a better plan of action. When the time came, she would just have to jump overboard and hope things worked out somehow.

She heard the horsefly buzz of a bullet passing by her head, and though she tried to remain steady, she couldn't help but look to her left, where the Vin fusiliers on the wall were shooting at *Mistral*. Another bullet hit the envelope above her, sending a puff of its borate doping jumping from the fabric to be swept back by the slipstream.

The captain was below and directly ahead, standing astride a sharply slanting roof, with Jutes and Lord Hinkal sheltering behind the chimney. The ladder was lined up on her, but the slightest change in the wind, if not immediately corrected, would yank the ladder and pitch even the sure-footed captain over the edge, and it wouldn't take much more to drag it over the roof and knock Bernat and Jutes over as well. If she thought Hanon's death was hard to explain, it would be a hell of a thing to account for that sort of massacre.

"Reverse!" Kember called, then ran to the rail to keep the captain in sight even as the hurricane deck passed over her. The steamjack turbine groaned as *Mistral*'s airscrews came to a bouncing halt, twisting clockwise and counterclockwise a few times before springing into reverse and nearly blasting Kember off the rail with their wash.

The ship slowed, came to a full stop with the tail above the captain's head, and the ladder dipped just far enough for its lowest rung to touch the roof. All the captain had to do was step onto it, and they had her.

AN AIR OF anxiety and guilt filled the ship. As Josette went forward through the keel, there were no warm faces or welcome-homes, only grim countenances, stiff salutes, and eyes fixed on the wounded side of her face. She stepped down the companionway to find that the unpopular Lieutenant Hanon was nowhere to be seen, and knew instantly that something had happened here. Something damn ugly.

She forced herself to ignore it for the moment, while she assessed the tactical situation. Kember seemed quite relieved to describe it to her, treating the task as a condemned man would treat a stay of execution. But for all that, Kember had made the right decisions. She was gaining altitude and in the meantime staying out of the firing arc of the Vin ship. Still, *Mistral* was out of the fight until she could claw her way up to the enemy ship's lofty altitude, or until Josette gained the power to change the fundamental realities of air combat.

And so she had time to get some answers. "Where the hell have you been, and where the hell is Lieutenant Hanon?"

"Well, sir . . ." Kember began, then stood with her mouth open, at a loss for words.

Josette gave up on Kember, and looked to Lupien at the rudder. "Corporal?" she asked. "Anything to say about this?"

"No, sir," he said, never meeting her eyes.

"Corporal, I assume you steered *Mistral* off station. Was an order given to that effect, or was that your own initiative?" She stepped up to him and put her face an inch from his, though his eyes never flinched, never pointed anywhere but directly ahead. "Perhaps you were bored with the view over Durum? Perhaps there was a lady you fancied aboard the Vin airship?"

"Lieutenant Hanon ordered it," Kember said.

Josette turned to her. "Found your tongue? Good. Where is he, so that I may solicit an explanation? Quickly now, Ensign. There's a battle on, and it would be embarrassing to miss it."

"He's dead, sir," Kember said, and looked again at the rail.

That's what she had thought. There was some bitter story behind those three little words, but it was a story she'd never hear, even if she lived to be a hundred. Given time, the account would coalesce into something the whole crew agreed on, and it might even bear some small resemblance to the facts, but the real truth would never come out. "It's a loss to the service," she said, knowing better than to squeeze a stone, "but we must carry on. What's the disposition of the Vin chasseur?"

Kember turned her head from the rail and stared at Josette for a while, eyes wide.

Josette leaned over and whispered, "Don't embarrass us in front of the Vins, Ensign."

"She's . . ." Kember's voice broke, but she swallowed and went on, "She's the *Ayezderhau,* a two-gun chasseur, sir, of our design. I mean, sir, that she's our *exact* design. The Vins must have gotten hold of the plans."

Josette's face contorted into a snarl so wretched that it invented its own special category of anger. Ensign Kember ceased prattling, took a step back, and tensed as if she expected to be struck.

"Goddamn her," Josette muttered. "She couldn't even leave me my ship."

"Sir?"

"You're certain?" Josette asked through clenched teeth.

"She's *Mistral* to a tee, sir. Except she's got to be full of luftgas, right? And have a healthy steamjack. And us with inflammable air and a steamjack that's . . . that's been sorely overtaxed. I mean, sir, one good shot with shell or carcass, or if our engine catches fire again, and we'll be done for!"

Josette only shook her head and considered her options. "If we do climb to engage her, do you have an idea of how she'll react?"

Kember didn't have to think long. "She'll decline action, if she can. She's not here to sink us, I think, and her captain doesn't want to risk an engagement on even terms. She's here to support the city, or at least preserve the garrison. I think that's why she drew us off station in the first place, sir. She doesn't want a fight. She just wants us out of it."

"Well, I want us in it," Josette said. But how was she supposed to kill a ship that was four thousand feet above her, when merely shooting off her own guns could blow *Mistral* to hell, never mind enemy fire? "We'll steer a wide circle around the city, and watch for a chance to slip in. Elevators, level us off at one thousand feet, just high enough to offer support to our forces on the ground, should the opportunity arise."

As Kember turned to go up the companionway, Josette said, "Remain here, Ensign. I may require your council."

ON THE ROOFTOP, Jutes was staring up at the Vin airship and cursing up a storm. "It's the bloody cheek of it," he said.

"Uh-huh," Bernat said, traversing Elise's rifle over the field and streets below, watching for movement.

"They couldn't'a changed it just a little? Just to set themselves apart? No, they had to copy it all exactly. The bloody cheek of it."

If the Vin detachment had returned after scattering at *Mistral*'s approach, it had returned with damn good hiding spots. "I think it's safe to climb down."

"Bloody cheek."

"I said, I think it's safe to climb down."

They descended to find Pesha alive and, if not well, then at least far enough from exsanguination that she wouldn't die within the next hour or so.

At least, that's what Bernat told himself, as he followed Jutes back toward the prisoner pen. As he went, he looked off to the southeast, where *Mistral* was still orbiting well away from the Vin airship, having already steered half a circle around the town. "The Shark doesn't seem very hungry today."

Jutes looked at the sky and grinned. "She's workin' up an appetite."

THE AIRSHIPS CIRCLED in concentric orbits, *Mistral* on the outside, her course describing a circle that stretched well beyond the walls, and *Ayezderhau* in a tighter circle, always over the city. *Ayezderhau* could merge into *Mistral*'s orbit and bring her to action on highly favorable terms, but the Vin ship had no incentive to do so, as it already held the position most favorable to its mission. *Mistral* could not at once fight an engagement a mile in the air and support the assault at ground level. And even if *Mistral* did bring the Vins to action, she would be drawn into a long, tedious turning fight rather than the short, decisive engagement Josette desired.

She turned to Kember and said, "You know this captain's habits. What's he hoping we'll do?"

"He'll be happiest if we try to support the infantry. That way, he can lob shells down on us from the safety of altitude. And I bet he's itching to pull some ruse to trick us into doing just that, but he's worried we won't be fooled again. Besides which, he probably knows our reputation, and figures he only has to wait and we'll try something, despite the risk."

"We'll try something despite the stupidity, you mean?"

Kember only cleared her throat and looked forward.

Certainly, Josette wanted to try something, but what? Apart from *Mistral*'s bum steamjack and inclination to explode at the merest spark, the two ships were evenly matched in almost every way. From her current unenviable position, how could *Mistral* sink a ship with all the same strengths and weaknesses?

A grin rose slowly on Josette's lips. All the same strengths and weaknesses.

"Ensign," Josette said, "what do you suppose was the greatest flaw in this ship's original design?"

Kember spoke without hesitation. "The goddamn tail nearly came off in a turn." She became excited for a moment, but it shifted to anxiety just as quickly. "Oh, but sir! The *Ayezderhau* hasn't got the yard design. That had six airscrews and she has four, like we do now. So we don't know which set of plans she's built from."

Josette snorted and took a calming breath. "I do."

Kember just stared at her, confused beyond the capacity for speech.

"I ran into the bitch who stole our plans while I was in Durum. *Ayezderhau* is built according to our first redesign, and we've improved the tail since then, haven't we?"

Kember looked no less confused, and rather more alarmed. "But sir! We never tested it!"

"Ensign?" Josette asked.

"Yes, sir?"

"I'll have less pessimism on the hurricane deck, please."

"Yes, sir."

Josette turned to Luc Lupien, on the rudder. "You understand what we're doing?"

He answered her with a nod and a sly grin.

"A little more right rudder, then, easy at first. But we'll maintain this inferior altitude. We make a more tempting target, all the way down here."

She went to the rail to watch the other chasseur, but couldn't see it around *Mistral*'s own expansive superstructure. She had to climb onto the port rail, planting her feet on it and leaning out at a forty-five-degree angle, with a thousand feet of empty air below her, before she could see the enemy ship. She hung with one hand gripping a diagonal martingale line, the wind in her face. The chill blast hurt her wound at first, but the pain was soon numbed by the cold.

Mistral turned inward, cutting across the wide circle she'd been steering. "Come on, now," Josette said, whispering to the enemy captain across half a mile of sky. "If you can out-turn us, you get a free shot. If you can't, we're too far below you to shoot back. So what's the risk?"

But the Vin captain didn't seem to hear, or at least smelled something fishy in her invitation to battle. He maintained his slow, easy turn around the city. Kember must have read it in Josette's face, for the girl leaned over the rail and called, "Perhaps if we threaten the garrison, he'll have no choice."

Josette grinned. "Lupien, bring us right in line with the breach and then hold steady on that course." That would allow the Vin a nice, clean shot at *Mistral*, if he turned just a little.

And he did, cutting a straight line across the edge of his orbit. High above, he was lining up his shot, and *Mistral* was steaming right into the line of his guns.

Josette watched for the moment they would fire, eyes not on their guns but on the motion of their tailfins. "Left rudder!" Josette called, and a second later the Vin chasseur fired her first gun.

Her eyes widened. As the second gun fired, she watched the first shell descend through the sky, trailing wispy smoke that glowed orange in the light of the morning sun. It exploded above them at the perfect altitude to set *Mistral*'s envelope aflame, but fifty yards to starboard—the exact distance *Mistral* had shifted by virtue of her last-second maneuver. Smoking fragments of shell casing tumbled into the streets below.

The second was lined up right along *Mistral*'s line of flight, and so near that Josette ducked her head at the sight of it. It burst above her, sending red-hot debris into the forward frames.

"Fire in the nose!" she called. "Get to it quick, please, 'cause we're not slowing down! Steamjack ahead, emergency power! Rudderman, resume our turn!"

And as *Mistral* entered a tighter orbit of the town, turning to keep out of the arc of *Ayezderhau*'s guns, the Vin captain turned to follow. And why not? He had the height of them, and in the ever-tightening, converging circles of a turn-fight, he could keep her away from the Vin infantry on the city wall.

She looked to *Mistral*'s nosecone. The fire up there was still small, but it wouldn't take much. The number nine gas bag was less than a yard behind the flames. Worse yet, the fire stoked in the wind, growing larger in proportion to their increased speed. A flame-ringed hole opened in the envelope, and if a single ember went through it . . .

The fire hissed and steam swept aft along the outside of the envelope. An extra bucketful of water—two, actually, and now three—poured from the hole in the nose, as the riggers wisely squandered ballast to make damn sure the fire was out.

Above, the *Ayezderhau*'s orbit was a quarter turn behind *Mistral*'s, her orbit tightening, so that just a few circles would bring them far enough into *Mistral*'s turn to take another shot.

Which meant Josette had succeeded in convincing the Vin captain to kill her, as she hoped she would. No matter what else happened, no matter her shortcomings, she could take pride in knowing this was one thing she was good at. "Another turn on the wheel, Luc!" she called to Corporal Lupien. *Mistral* eased in, her circle matching *Ayezderhau*'s, but the Vin ship turned tighter still.

"Half a turn more," she called, not quite so loud this time, as if reducing the volume of the order might create a compromise with its effect on the airframe. She could feel the stress on the superstructure already, as little pops and sprangs traveled down the keel and out through the longitudinal girders, and from there along the martingale in her hand.

The *Ayezderhau* turned tighter still, so tight that another circle would bring her guns to bear.

"Give the wheel another half turn!"

That was too much damn strain on *Mistral*'s superstructure, but she had little choice if she didn't want to spend the next few minutes on fire. Corporal Lupien had to put his weight onto the wheel to hold it there. At the tail, the rudder shivered against the rush of wind over its surface, doing all it could to resist the turn, as if it knew what a terrible idea this was.

And above, the *Ayezderhau* matched *Mistral*'s turn with only the slightest effort. It seemed the Vin captain was even cleverer than she'd thought, for he'd made his own modifications to his ship's tailcone.

"As hard as she'll go, Luc!" There was no going back now, so why the hell not?

Lupien hesitated for a moment, until she shot him a look that made him think better. He put both hands on the wheel and pulled so hard his feet lifted off the deck. Kember ran over and pushed upward from the other side, to help him.

Mistral's tail strained against the turn, the wind so hard on it that ripples ran across its fabric, pressing in and outlining the girders beneath. The entire airframe bent like a macaroni noodle. *Mistral* made her pain known, crying out all along her length with a sound like the crackle of musketry, as slivers of wood flew loose from overstrained box girders. In frame two, a bracing cable parted with such force that its end whipped back and cut through the envelope. Keel girders groaned, on the edge of snapping. A few more moments in this turn, and *Mistral* would break her own spine.

And then, standing out even amid that cacophony, there came the piercing, cracking sound of a keel girder snapping in half. Josette swept her eyes along her ship, looking to see which frame had failed, which girder had given way.

She couldn't find it.

Daring to hope, she looked up at the other ship and saw its tail kinked, its keel askew. It was the Vins who'd lost a girder. And yet the Vin chasseur still turned with *Mistral*, and came far enough over to line up the perfect shot. If *Ayezderhau* shot now, both ships would die together, *Mistral* by fire and *Ayezderhau* by the fury of her own guns—her damaged keel torn apart by their recoil.

Josette watched without blinking, her eyes watering from the blast of wind against them.

And *Ayezderhau* fell off from her turn, and came out of it without firing a shot.

"Rudder amidships!" Josette called. Corporal Lupien only had to let go of his wheel, and it spun back through two turns by itself. The strain came off *Mistral*'s frame as the rudder swung back to its amidships position.

Another loud crack drew Josette's eyes up to *Ayezderhau*. A second girder had failed aboard her, but the Vin ship was still in the sky, and still steaming forward with a strange placidity.

She could picture the Vin captain racing back through the keel, arriving to find mangled girders, and calculating the forces in his head. She could picture it far too easily, for she had once done it herself, and saved her ship from destruction only by the quickest, most decisive action.

But the Vin captain was not quite so quick, nor so decisive. A third girder snapped aboard *Ayezderhau*, its broken ends whipping out through her envelope near the tail. And then, a heartbeat behind, her keel tore itself apart. Josette saw it before she heard it—saw a rift opening on *Ayezderhau*'s underbelly, halfway between airscrews and tail, and then the envelope doubling up on itself as the great airship folded into a pathetic, V-shaped mass.

It fell, keel still twisting around the break, objects tumbling out of it and coming down faster than the ship—mere dots at this distance. Equipment and sandbags, she hoped. Someone on *Ayezderhau*'s hurricane deck had the presence of mind to pull the emergency ballast ropes, and great gushes of water streamed from the underside of her envelope. She fell through three thousand feet in mere seconds, but grew lighter as she went. By the time she sank past *Mistral*, her fall was nearly arrested.

She was still losing gas, however, and whatever crew remained were running out of ballast to throw overboard. And so *Ayezderhau* floated on the wind, drifting lower and lower, falling toward the city at a gentle pace.

20

"WELL THAT'S A stroke of good luck, isn't it?"

Bernat looked at Jutes, and found him grinning at the sky. "Ain't so much luck, I think. Come on. We got an army to break outta jail."

There was no blind approach to the prisoner pen, so they had to advance on it right out in the open. But *Mistral* was driving down upon the Vin guards, filling more and more of the sky as she approached, which had a rather distracting effect on them. One rifle shot from the airship was all it took, and a dozen hardened fusiliers were begging Jutes and Bernat to accept their honorable surrender.

And yet, even after the Vins dropped their muskets, and even with *Mistral* keeping a sharp-eyed overwatch, Bernat felt hopelessly exposed as he rounded up his prisoners. After all, might one of these fearless men not think it a worthy exchange, to trade his own paltry life for the chance to kill a nobleman of Bernat's renown and importance?

Luckily, the fusiliers were but crude accountants, and none of them tried anything. If Bernat hadn't been occupied in freeing the Durumite prisoners, he might have been thoroughly insulted. With the pen open, townsfolk were spilling out with such vigor that they threatened to turn into a rampaging mob. The Vin airship's destruction had restored their spirits, while the humiliation of the pen had brought their blood to a boil. Only Jutes's sheer force of personality kept angry townsfolk from beating the helpless Vin prisoners to death.

The crush to get out of the pen, the eagerness of the Durumites to take their revenge, was so great that many were pushed up against the cheval de frise, and cut their hands trying to keep off the blades. It was so bad that, above their heads, Josette began shouting at them through a speaking trumpet. "Mr. Kemal, you want to turn this into the same goddamn mess that got you caught in the first place? Mrs. Boyev, what would your late husband say if he could see you acting like this? Pierre, you have some sense. Get your brothers into line! Marcel, the Dumpling bastard who killed Madeena is on the wall, not there! Mr. Niyazi, would you sacrifice our chance to retake the town, just to lash out at a handful of the bastards? If we win, they'll still be there! You can kill them later!"

She went on like that, calling them by name and imploring them to order. And it worked. Her targets fell shamefacedly into line, one by one. Some even took it upon themselves to bring their fellows to order.

"Sergeant Jutes," she called down, pointing to the south, where the Vin airship had dipped to below the height of the town walls. "I want whatever luftgas is left in that ship. She hasn't surrendered yet, so take as many men as you need to storm her. The others will go with Bernat and attack the breach."

Jutes gave an acknowledging signal and saluted. *Mistral* sprang to life, steaming for the western wall, where the sound of musketry was intensifying. "She knows we don't have any weapons for these people apart from the few muskets we took from the Vins, doesn't she?" Bernat asked.

"She knows," Jutes said, as he split his team off from the others.

"Then what are my chances of taking the breach?"

Jutes looked at him with an odd expression. "Zero," he said.

"Then what's the point?"

"General hellraising," the sergeant said with a grin. "Don't worry, sir. You'll do great." And with a bellowing war cry, Jutes charged toward the Vin airship, two dozen townsfolk on his heels.

Bernat looked to those who were left, numbering several score at least. "Rar, grr, and such things!" he called, and hobbled toward the breach as fast as the pain in his leg would allow. When he dared to look back, he saw with relief, and no small measure of surprise, that they were all following.

JOSETTE LOOKED BACK over the taffrail until she was certain the mob was following Bernat, and then returned to her station.

"Sir," Kember said, leaning toward her, "you should really have your face looked to."

Josette made a point of ignoring her. "Rudderman, steer to cross the wall, then turn us parallel to it."

"In front of the wall, sir?" Luc Lupien asked. "Not behind it?"

"Between our men and theirs," she said, "to give them an example to follow." After a moment's further thought, she added to the elevator steersman, "But do keep us above the arc of their cannons. We needn't get carried away."

As *Mistral* came up on the wall, Josette took the opportunity to get a couple of shots at them with the bref guns, but the Vin fusiliers again showed their steel, staying calm despite their peril. If they'd tried to rush out of the way they would have surely bunched up, and Kember's well-aimed blasts of canister shot would have killed a score of them. As it was, the Vins laid flat on the wall, and as the smoke of the shots cleared aft, it was impossible to say what the effect was. The Vins' makeshift wooden cover had two wide gaps in it, certainly, but no more than a handful of fusiliers were killed, if even that many.

Josette shook her head. "Give me ten regiments like this one, and I'll conquer half the world."

"Only half?" somebody asked as *Mistral* passed above the wall. She couldn't make out the voice, for at that moment the fusiliers rose and fired a full volley into the ship's underbelly. Apart from the crack of the discharge, there was the sound of snapping plywood along the keel, and the ping of bullets hitting the steamjack, but blessedly no screams.

She ran her eyes over the hurricane deck. No one hurt. "Anyone hit?" she called up the companionway.

Private Davies, at the relay position, answered her, "Grey's hit in the arm—not mortal—and Chief Megusi has a graze. They were aiming amidships, at the steamjack, the clever bastards."

"Damage?" she asked, going halfway up the companionway ladder to look along the keel.

Megusi's voice came back, shaken but in control. "Most of them hit the boiler or the aft end of the turbine." His face appeared around the trumpet flair of the turbine, soaked with condensed steam. "No damage to the boiler, but until I can patch the turbine, I can only give you about a quarter power, and even that's more risk than I like."

"One-quarter power, then. Carry on."

He saluted, which was absurd at a time like this, but she returned it out of habit before stepping back to her station.

"Riflemen: steady, aimed fire on the wall. Steersmen, swing us in front of the Garnian companies assembled toward the rear."

Below them, whatever was left of the forlorn hope was still pinned in the breach. They hid behind any fragment of rubble large enough to provide protection from the murderous fire pouring into them from the jagged edges of the wall on either side of the breach. Some of them fired back, to little effect, and others simply huddled on the unstable scree slope, waiting for a miracle.

A Garnian company had now advanced to within three hundred yards of the wall and was firing by platoon—though with none of the crisp, highly drilled efficiency of the Vin companies. Their muskets were worse than useless at that range, and such an ineffectual, amateurish fire would only boost the defenders' morale. As near as Josette could work out, they'd been brought up to provide cover and allow the forlorn hope to retreat from the breach, but the men of the forlorn hope were smarter than their officers, and they knew the gambit wouldn't work. Or perhaps it was simply that the men of the hope were frightened beyond the ability to act, which still put them well ahead of whatever idiot had ordered platoon fire at three hundred yards.

She ordered a turn that would bring *Mistral* around in front of them, went to the rail with speaking trumpet in hand, and shouted down at the captain of the company, "What the hell are you doing back here?" She took great care to give her words the form of a question, but the tone of a relayed order. "The fight's that way!"

The Garnian infantry captain, no doubt thinking he'd missed an order, and that he'd be in a great deal of trouble if he didn't show willing and advance with gusto, ordered his company into a quick march. It took some additional motivation from their sergeants, but the company was soon on the move.

"It's amazing what the fear of being thought afraid will do to an ambitious company captain," Josette said. She looked over the rail, to the companies still formed up in the rear. "But if they don't join the fight, I'd say I'm in rather a lot of trouble."

"Nothing like what those poor bastards are in for," Ensign Kember said, looking over the opposite rail, where that single company of Fangless Fops, outnumbered five to one, were charging into the breach.

Despite being slowed by his stiff leg, Bernat's little militia couldn't quite keep up with him. They followed several paces behind, which was either an odd sort of politeness or a conscious effort to ensure that Bernat alone bore the consequences of first contact with the enemy.

He rounded a connecting street and could see the breach ahead, the broken edges of the wall flanking it, and two hundred and fifty fusiliers stretching out on either side. Gunsmoke drifted up and to the south, the puffs of independent fire mingling in odd patterns with the longer, unbroken lines of smoke from volleys, and forming an odd sort of recording of the regiment's musketry.

Bernat's group spilled out onto the pomerium. Behind him, he heard gunshots. He turned to see that his little militia had grown yet again during the trip, and many of the new recruits had brought rifles or scatterguns. But, along with his few musketmen, they fired their shots the second they were on the pomerium—too great a range for effective fire from such an unsteady force—and so not a single Durumite bullet hit. Other townsfolk had picked up whatever makeshift weapons they could find along the way, and were now armed with pitchforks, threshing flails, rakes, cobblestones, and in one case even a saucepan.

The Vin fusiliers answered this cosmopolitan array of weapons in the same familiar way: with a thunderous volley of musketry. At orders barked above, two hundred of them ceased their platoon fire, loaded, turned crisply on their heels, and fired together into the town, aiming for the densest part of the mob, as they came into effective range.

A pitiful, pained, collective groan rose from the Durumite

mob. Those who didn't fall checked as one, mere yards from the breach. Bernat knew they were stalled even before he looked back at them. He was only surprised at how far behind they were. He found himself very much alone, and very much a target, standing halfway between the bulk of his force and their objective.

"Come on!" he screamed, flecks of spittle flying from his mouth, despite how goddamn dry it was. "Those boys out there—" He was interrupted by the boom and clatter of the cannon in the nearest bastion firing grapeshot down at the 132nd. Even though it wasn't aimed at Bernat's mob, that grapeshot seemed to freeze them more firmly in place. "Goddamn it," he begged, "just give me a few more yards!"

The mob did not advance a few more yards, did not climb into the breach, but neither did they run away. His words had stopped a full rout, but Bernat had achieved the worst possible compromise, for now his people stood under enemy fire while accomplishing nothing. As much as he cursed them for it, as much as he wanted to call them fools as well as cowards, he was gripped by the same idiotic impulse to freeze where he was. He knew he had to move or die, and yet he stood rooted to the ground, half wishing that a bullet would cut short his failure as a military leader.

And a bullet granted his wish.

It came not from the wall but from directly above, and was accompanied by the report of a Brewer rifle, distinctly louder than the fusiliers' muskets. More to Bernat's interest, it did not hit him, but plucked a Vin defender off the wall and sent the man plummeting fifty feet to the pomerium below. Bernat looked up to see *Mistral* rising over the wall, and heard more fire from the ship's Brewers. He turned, made a bellowing war cry, and stormed up the inside slope of the breach. "Follow me!" he screamed.

His fighting mob followed.

* * *

"Reverse engine! Left hard rudder! Elevators down five degrees!"

The captain's orders brought *Mistral* into a downward, twisting turn as the ship slowed, so that her length came parallel to the wall, her bref guns pointing down at it as she drifted with her remaining momentum.

Ensign Kember was behind the starboard gun, eyes on its forward sight and hand clenched around its lanyard. The gunsight slid over the slanting wooden roof atop the wall. She couldn't see them, but underneath that roof were men. Men she hated—no goddamn Dumpling sympathizer she—but men whose pain and fear were not diminished because of her hatred. In her head, the face of Lieutenant Hanon stared up at her, imploring.

"Ensign!" the captain barked. "Quit fondling that gun and shoot!"

Kember pulled the lanyard without another moment's thought. The morality of inflicting pain and death was one thing, but having the captain mad at you was another entirely.

Canister shot exploded from the muzzle, a fanning arc containing a hundred and sixty lead balls that tore through lumber and flesh with equal ease. The protective roof was blasted apart. Pulped bodies flew over both sides of the wall. Even at the edges of the canister shot's destructive cone, splinters of wood flew fast enough to maim.

The Vins' composure once again limited their casualties to only a few, but of the men who were killed, the sheer volume and force of musket balls reduced them to mere scraps of meat. Kember didn't let her thoughts dwell on the sight of it, only because her duty called her to the port bref gun. This one was loaded with ordinary round shot, the least remarkable of all *Mistral*'s armament.

"Elevators up!" the captain called, her order bringing the ship closer to level.

She gave the elevation screw a single turn, sighting on the far edge of the hole she'd already blasted in the Vins' protective roof. She pulled the lanyard, stepped out of the way of the recoil, and peered into the smoke.

She couldn't see the shot's effect. The roof blocked the view. But she could hear it. She could hear the cannonball ricocheting inside that tight space, could trace the flight of the ball by the crunching impacts against stone or wood as it bounced right down the line of the wall. A hundred yards away, it hit a merlon and ricocheted out into the town. As the smoke cleared and *Mistral* steered to come behind the wall, she could see the effect on the Vins. But she only saw it for a moment before she closed her eyes.

"DAMN FINE SHOOTING, Ensign." Josette clapped the girl on the shoulder as she looked forward.

The cannonball, fired at an acute angle into the space between wall and cover, had bounced between them, killing and maiming as it went, before skipping out and falling into the town ironmonger's scrap yard. It left a dozen Vin infantrymen dead and twice as many missing arms or legs.

Taking a rifle, Josette went to the taffrail and looked down into the breach. She spotted Bernie by his stylish jacket, now tattered and caked with mortar dust from the rubble. The Durum mob was behind him, struggling up the unstable inner slope of the breach, scrambling on hands and knees, sliding two yards down for every three up, while the single forward company of the 132nd was climbing the outer slope. The Vins, meanwhile, fired down from the wall on either side. There was only room for one or two men to stand on the jagged edges of the wall, but each fusilier took his shot and stepped aside to let another through, so that together they kept up a continuous fire. Garnians were being slaughtered on both sides of the breach, but even by dying they were doing the work of a forlorn hope, occupying the defenders' attention and giving the 132nd a chance to advance in force.

And they were advancing. All the reserve companies were moving forward at double time, and at that speed might arrive just in time to see their friends routed and fleeing the breach, for the renewed forlorn hope was itself wavering. Josette could see it in the way they picked their way through the rubble, not bounding up the slope but crawling on their bellies from stone to stone, always looking for some outcrop of rubble to keep between themselves and the nearest Vin fusilier. Only Bernat climbed the breach with vigor, and that was about to get him killed.

"Steersmen, come into the wind and keep us directly over the breach. Riflemen, fire at the Vins on the edges. Deliberate, careful aim, please."

Below, a fusilier fired his musket and turned to make room for the next. Josette took aim and quite deliberately shot him in the ass. As his comrades came forward to carry him away, she took a fresh rifle and shot one of them in the ass as well. As cathartic as this was after the morning she'd had, her real purpose was to block up the edges of the wall with wounded men who couldn't get out of the way to let new shooters through.

And it worked. Bernie led the Durum mob up the slope, toward the battered edges of the wall flanking the breach, and faced only scant musket fire as he went. Indeed, more fire was aimed at Josette, but she stood her ground, hoping the distance and elevation would protect her, and that the screams of their wounded comrades would unsteady the fusiliers' aim.

Bernat crested the rubble heap in the middle of the breach. At the top of it, with nowhere to go but down, he turned left and futilely kept trying to go up, climbing hand over hand on the steeper slope leading to the lip of the wall, where the Vins were shooting down at them. This made him a very stupid man, but Josette couldn't help but grin at the audacity. It must have amused the advanced company of the 132nd as well, for the Garnian infantrymen rose off their bellies and bounded up the slope, sending loose rocks tumbling behind them, to be dodged by their comrades farther down.

And why wouldn't they race up the rubble? After all, there was a gentleman like them at the top, climbing to attack the Vins without so much as a sword or bayonet, and townsfolk swarming behind him, including one member of the Durumite mob armed only with . . . was that really a saucepan? And higher still there was a mere woman standing stalwart in her airship, half her face ruined, but proving by her accurate rifle fire that Vinzhalian asses bled the same color as anyone's.

The Fighting Philosophers stormed the breach, shouting themselves hoarse as they went. Under the cover of rifle fire from *Mistral,* they followed Bernat's example, climbing to the top of the rubble and then dividing outward to climb to the very top of the wall. The Vins replied with bullets and bayonets, and even loose stones tossed from above.

Not one of the 132nd made it to the top of the wall, though a score died trying. But they had done their work nevertheless, for they were in the breach in force. Men from the companies behind them finally arrived, funneling into the breach, and went up the slope in a wave, spilling over the top of the rubble and into the town. The Vins saw the danger and sent companies down the bastion stairs, aiming to form a second defense in the pomerium below, but wherever the stairs opened onto the pomerium, there were townsfolk waiting in force, and they were out for blood.

And so, on the pomerium behind the wall, with not a single Vin on the ground to trouble them, the men of the

132nd were being organized into a firing line, in whatever order they came through the breach and by whatever officers were nearest. They fired one volley at the wall—such a nervous, ill-aimed volley that several shots hit *Mistral*'s envelope by mistake.

The effort was all but useless in its physical effect. A hundred or more Garnian muskets had slain one or two Vins, if that many.

Yet, for all its pitiful effect in drawing blood, that was the volley that won the battle. For it convinced the Vins that they would soon be facing an overwhelming force inside the town, and that there was nothing they could do to change that fundamental reality, no matter how stubbornly they clung to the high ground, no matter how many Garnians they managed to kill in the meantime.

And so, rather than inflame the passions of the victors with a futile effort at holding the wall, they threw down their arms.

"Send a bird," Josette said. "Message to read, *Durum is ours.*"

21

THE CITY'S CANNONS fired in celebration now, and the concussion of every shot sent a pulse of pain through Bernat's aching leg. "I have never done so much walking and running in my life," he said, leaning heavily on his cane, "as I have while recovering from a leg wound. In all seriousness, do you think God hates me?"

Beside him, Josette looked at the town through the west gate, where they'd stopped to let him rest. She shrugged and said, "I'm not a theologian, you know. I can't speak on such matters. I can only say that, if I was God, I would certainly hate you."

He snorted. "Yes, but you could say that about everyone you know."

"Nonsense," she said, sticking her nose in the air. "I'm quite fond of Sergeant Jutes."

He was about to probe for her current attitude toward Roland or her mother, but thought better of it. "Why don't you go on ahead?" he asked instead. "I'd like to see how Pesha is getting on, and I expect you'd prefer to go straight to your captured airship."

"I admit that I'm eager to see how much of their luftgas Jutes managed to save."

An avaricious thought which had been bubbling in the depths of Bernat's mind finally broke through to the surface. "Does this capture fall under prize law? Does it legally belong to us? The ship and all that luftgas . . . Why, we'd all be rich.

Even the crewmen. And where do supernumeraries fall in this regard?"

"The same as a warrant officer," Josette answered. "So, according to prize law, you split an eighth of the total value with Chips and Chief Megusi."

Bernat's eyes widened. "So, between ship and luftgas . . ."

"And bref guns, powder, shot, cordage, goldbeater's, instruments, chronometers, not to mention head money. I'd say that your one twenty-fourth share entitles you to something in the nature of twenty thousand liras, if not more."

Bernat stumbled backward as he imaged the possibilities.

"Or it would," Josette added flatly, "if naval prize law applied to the aerial corps—which, of course, it doesn't."

The shock of it sent him stumbling farther back, right against the thick stone wall of the gatehouse. "You let me think we were rich!"

She only grinned.

"You spiteful bitch!"

After a moment's thoughtful reflection, she nodded in agreement, then said, "Meet up at the pub later?"

"Yes, yes," he said, waving her away.

She turned and walked off, whistling a jaunty tune and picking at the fresh bandages on her face.

Bernat rested a while longer at the gatehouse, watching townsfolk, soldiers, and officers as they came and went. More townsfolk going than coming, he noticed, and he finally stopped a group of them to ask about it.

"Headin' to the fields," a grizzled older man said. "Plantin' season." He led a dozen grizzled middle-aged men, several of whom bore hastily bandaged wounds from the morning's battle.

Bernat was taken aback. "But surely you should spend today in rest and celebration?"

The old man would have none of it. "Planting's gotta be

done, my lord. We're a week behind on account of the siege, and low on food on account of the granaries getting burned last fall, and on account of what the Vins ate, and if we don't get seed in the ground fast, we'll have nothing left, long a'fore harvest comes."

Bernat wondered if they knew that the 132nd had eaten their plow oxen. But as the farmers walked off to their fields, Bernat was sure they'd manage. They still had their plow horses, didn't they? And though it was unlikely anyone had thought to feed those horses since the siege began, the people of Durum were a resourceful people, and would surely find a way to plow, and to harrow, and to do whatever else was involved in planting—probably something to do with rakes, he imagined.

When they were past, he set off for Durum's town hall, where the gravely wounded were being tended to. It took him a while to find Pesha, for this was a town hall in the old sense—a single hall, large enough to hold a significant fraction of the populous. Indeed, a significant fraction of them were laid out in it now. After a quarter hour's search, he found Pesha in a distant corner, lying with a tourniquet twined tight around her upper arm and a bandage wrapped around the stump below it.

She was still sweating from the pain when he knelt beside her and asked, "Was it Heny who amputated?"

Pesha answered in a voice exhausted from the intensity of her ordeal, and hoarse from the intensity of her screaming. "She didn't trust anyone else to do it. The battalion doctor offered." She smiled as she stopped to catch her breath. "She told him to go to hell."

"Good, good," Bernat said. "You never know, with these army doctors. Most of them are half mad and half drunk. Still, I can't imagine having to do that to someone I . . ." He trailed off.

"Hurt her more than me, I think," Pesha said. "Still, it'll be a story to tell the grandkids, won't it?"

This comment garnered some odd looks from the patients around her, and Bernat didn't think she would have dared to say it if she were in a more balanced state of mind. "You know," he said, grasping for anything to distract from that careless comment, "we thought for a time that you and Heny were the turncoats, that you'd given away our plans to the Vins."

Pesha didn't even bother to call him an idiot, though her face said quite enough.

"Well, I . . . I think I'll just see about . . . I'll leave you to your . . . Best you get some rest." He patted her on the head, which did not improve her disposition. Indeed, quite the contrary.

He left before he could dig himself into a deeper hole, and nearly stepped on several wounded townsfolk in his hurry to get out the door.

Outside, the Vinzhalian fusiliers were being gathered up into a pen in the town square—a little larger and more exposed than the one the Durumites had been herded into, but otherwise similar. He spotted Major Emery among a group of Garnian officers, and went over to shake his hand.

"Damn fine work, damn fine work," Emery said. "You led the force that blew the magazine? Damn fine work! Made all the difference."

"Well, it wasn't just me, you know." It hadn't been him at all, but long experience had taught him that he should never stretch modesty to excess, when one could make a fair compromise with reality. "The townsfolk and Captain Dupre did their part."

"Dupre did admirably," he said. "Damn shame about her mother."

Bernat had been wondering how he was going to work up

to that, and was relieved that Emery broached the subject first. "Has she been found yet?"

"The mother? Oh yes, of course. We learned her location from that woman with the arm wound . . . Pika?"

"Pesha," Bernat said.

"That's the one, poor soul. She told us where to find her. She's in the town dungeon now—can you believe they still have one?—and she'll hang in the morning. So will some of this lot, if we can find an eyewitness."

Bernat followed his pointing finger to three Vin captains, their colonel, and Major Dvakov—his face swollen from the wound Bernat had inflicted.

"There are reports that one or more of them was planning to shoot the prisoners," Emery said, "but no one can agree on which of them it was, or if they really did it. You don't know anything about that, do you?"

Dvakov was currently arguing with Colonel Okura, demanding his full rights as a gentleman and a prisoner of war, to parole, to lawyers, and to due process. Bernat walked up to him and grinned, which shut the bastard up in an instant. A silence settled across the gathered officers of the 132nd Garnian and the 64th Vinzhalian alike. They all seemed to know what was coming, and that Bernat would damn Major Dvakov with a word.

Major Dvakov stood with slumped shoulders, waiting for the hammer to fall. Bernat just grinned viciously, stuck out his hand, and said, "Lord Bernat Hinkal, sir. Your servant, and an honor to meet you, after you fought so bravely. Have you had a chance to have breakfast yet?"

Dvakov tried to speak, but it only came out as a jumble of subvocal sounds and unconnected syllables.

Bernat turned to Colonel Okura and shook his head. "Do you mean to say, it's after lunch, and you haven't invited these gentlemen to breakfast? I'm surprised at you. War is no excuse for incivility."

JOSETTE DIDN'T HAVE to ask where the *Ayezderhau* came down. She could see the enormous envelope over the rooftops from the moment she went through the gate, and could see as well that it was securely moored, and still buoyant with at least some of its luftgas.

She took the long way getting to it, so that she could walk past the crater of the Vin magazine and see whether it had revealed the foundations of one of the old city walls—of which she'd found four out of a fabled six when she was a girl.

As she got closer, the evidence of the explosion grew. Five blocks away, bricks and clods of earth lay scattered in the street. Four blocks now, and larger stones had punched holes in roofs or buried themselves in gardens. Within a few blocks of the now-simmering plume, so close that the heat of the blast still soaked the cobbles underfoot, once-subterranean boulders had been flung outward in radiating lines. Along these lines, there was nothing but razed buildings, each tipped with the offending missile, wherever it finally came to rest.

Within a block of the explosion, the neighborhood was a smoking hellscape, and she had to slow down to pick her way through the buckled, unstable streets. She reached the lip of the crater and peered into it. No hint of an ancient wall could be seen in the wide swath of Durum the blast had excavated. But as she stared into it, it occurred to her that the crater might prove a boon for the town, if they took to discarding their trash here, instead of stuffing it into neighboring homes. She made her way around it and onward toward *Ayezderhau.*

When she came into the shadow of the great airship's envelope, she found Jutes perched on the hurricane deck, holding tight to the rail to keep from sliding off the steeply angled wicker. The deck had wedged between two buildings when it came down, so that a person could now walk from the roof-top of one building, cross the inclined deck, and go through the second-floor window of the building across the street. This second-floor window was how the townsfolk were getting on and off the ship, as they carried loads of miscellaneous ballast to keep it weighed down.

She went up that way herself, to the second-floor room that served as a gangplank onto the captured ship. A townswoman sped past her carrying a basket of cobblestones, handed them through the window to another townsman on *Ayezderhau*'s hurricane deck, and then saluted Josette on her way out. Josette returned the salute out of habit.

She stuck her head out the window to find *Ayezderhau*'s bref guns well secured, some of the crew and an ensign sitting with their backs against the far rail, and Jutes standing at the companionway, shouting directions to his ad hoc prize crew about where they should place ballast.

"Well in hand, Sergeant?" she asked.

Jutes grinned back at her, not bothering to salute. "Well in hand, sir. We're secure fore and aft, and I'm re-ballasting to keep her from settling against any of these buildings and doing herself more damage."

"The luftgas?"

"Saved almost everything from bag five forward, and maybe half the gas in bag four. Looks like their steamjack's near enough to ours, too, that we can finally get the parts we've been needing. 'Course we'll have to tear their steamjack apart to get at those parts, which means we'd actually come out ahead if we just renamed this ship *Mistral,* and passed the real *Mistral* off as the capture." There was a sly twinkle in his eyes that confirmed he was joking.

Good thing, too. That twinkle might have saved his life.

"I'm going to forget you said that, Sergeant, since I could never forgive it."

He smirked and said only, "Sir."

"Their captain?"

Jutes shook his head.

She looked at the Vin ensign, the only officer among the prisoners huddled on deck. "The captain was in frame two when the tail went," the young ensign said, speaking in thickly accented Garnian. "He was first to fall, because he rushed back there trying to save us."

Josette swallowed, her throat suddenly dry. "I'm sorry."

"I was on an airship at Canard, too," the Vin ensign said, her eyes burning with hate. "So that's both my captains you've killed."

Josette was silent for a while, as Jutes looked to her for permission to quiet the ensign. She shook her head at him, then met the girl's eyes, saying, "It's no easy business we're in." She looked at Jutes. "Make sure they're not mistreated."

She was downstairs and nearly out the front door, when she heard her sergeant's boots coming down the stairs. "Wanted you to know, sir," he said, lowering his voice when a townswoman passed with a basket of cobblestones, "just on the off chance that you didn't already, that I ain't gonna tell anyone about your . . ."

"Dumpling heritage?" Josette asked, quite loud enough to be overheard. "Thank you. I don't think we can keep a lid on it, but I appreciate the sentiment."

"Do you need, uh . . . That is to say, is there . . ."

Josette couldn't find the words to Jutes's question any more than he could, but she knew the question nevertheless. "Someone once asked me why I do this job," she said. "I've thought back on it from time to time, but I never could come up with a good answer."

By the look in Jutes's eyes as he cast them up at the envelope of the *Ayezderhau,* she could see that he was familiar enough with the feeling.

"Today, I've been asking myself, 'If I'd known I was a Vin, would I be doing it for them instead?'" She took a breath. "I wish the answer was as elusive. My mother was wrong about me. I would have ... understood, whatever that means. I idolized my father. If he'd told me he was from the moon, I'd probably call myself a Moon-Woman. If he'd confessed to being a Vin, it wouldn't even be a question."

Jutes hadn't been expecting that. His eyes whipped down, and studied her face for some time before finally accepting the truth of her comment. He grinned with a nervousness that was almost entirely affected—almost. "I saw some spare Vin uniforms in ship's stores," he said, pointing a thumb at *Ayezderhau*'s keel. "I could put a couple of their airmen to work at tailoring 'em for you."

She made a real effort to not smirk, but in the end it was futile. "I don't think it will be necessary. I swore an oath to Garnia, and I'll honor that oath until I die. Still odd to think that it could have just as easily been to Vinzhalia."

"Loyalty's a damn peculiar thing," Jutes, the only Brandheimian in Durum, said softly.

"A damn peculiar thing," Josette repeated. She was just heading out the door, and he heading back up the stairs, when she spun about and asked, "Jutes, do I have any Vin in my accent?"

Jutes looked genuinely surprised by the question. He shook his head and said, "A touch of Durum, sir, which I've always found quite pleasant, but no Vin that I've noticed."

She gave him a nod and headed straight for the tavern. There, she ordered ale in the largest mug they had on the premises, laid her two letters to Roland out in front of her, and drank until she didn't care who saw them.

Soon enough, she knew what to do. It was all very clear cut.

There was only one viable path forward when it came to Roland, and all she'd required to see it clearly was four mugs of beer, a crushing betrayal, and decades of lies—it was a wonder she hadn't tried that earlier. It all came down to the moment when he let slip that he'd fallen in love with her. The fact of the admission was not the issue, for by now she was convinced of its sincerity. It was the theatrics of it, timed to best throw her off balance, and so allow him to capture her. It had almost worked, but she now realized that she'd had quite enough of that sort of thing, and so took up the letter that began, "Roland, I am sorry to say I don't love you," and finished writing it.

She hardly had it signed when a score of young soldiers burst through the door and claimed this tavern in the name of the king. They were checked only briefly by the chagrin of the tavern keeper, and checked not at all by the presence of an airship captain who could have them all arrested.

Indeed, Josette's presence only inspired more enthusiasm. One young man sat down in the chair next to hers and asked, "How many women aboard your ship, ma'am?"

Before she could answer, another sat down on the other side of her and said, "I was going to volunteer for the air corps, myself, but I have this weird shoulder." He demonstrated what seemed to her a perfectly ordinary shoulder in every respect, by holding his arm in the air and stretching it until the joints popped in an entirely typical manner.

A third man sat down opposite her on the bench, set another mug of ale in front of her, hunched forward, and pushed it until it nearly fell into her lap—all the while staring silently. While he was at it, a fourth sat down and asked, "Does your face hurt, ma'am?"

Josette folded her letter, slipped it into her jacket pocket, and said, "All right then, who wants to get a game of catch ten going?"

Over the next several hours and dozens of hands of cards,

Josette took a fair amount of the men's wealth. They didn't seem to resent it, however, or perhaps even to notice it in the midst of their revelries. They behaved rudely, got drunk as fast as they could, made inappropriate advances, and invented all sorts of improbable stories that exaggerated their own personal heroism. In other words, they had at last become proper Garnian soldiers.

Bernat came in as dusk approached, just ahead of another two soldiers from the 132nd. He leaned across Josette's table and said, "You seem to be enjoying yourself."

"What's not to enjoy?" she said, and stuffed a handful of pine nuts from a nearby bowl into her mouth. Speaking around them, she said in a voice quite loud enough to be heard from one end of the tavern to the other, and perhaps even from the street outside, "I've liberated a town I hate, I've made a bunch of university brats into killers, it turns out I'm a Vin Dumpling, and in the morning they're going to hang my mother." At the last item, she swallowed and pointed at him. "Bernie, I've been waiting ages for someone to do that."

At this, the soldiers at the table set down their cards, stood, and shuffled away.

Josette looked sourly at their backs. "What? You don't wanna play anymore, just because we're celebrating my mom gettin' hanged?" She threw her hand of cards at them. "To hell with you."

Bernat sat down opposite her, tilted his head to the side, and asked, "How much have you drunk?"

"Well, there's these two here," she said, gesturing at the empty mugs in front of her. "And one or two others that fell and rolled under the table. That's all." Under his withering stare, she added, "Since the last time the bartender came around."

Bernat took a mug and sniffed the dregs. "Thank God the ale here is watered down, or you'd be dead."

She gesticulated at him. "Bernie, I don't need weak ale to not die. I not . . . die . . . every . . . all of the . . ." She trailed off, puzzled for a way out of the grammatical maze she'd become lost in.

Bernat patted her hand consolingly and said, "Some day, great men will discover how words fit together. For now, my dear, don't trouble yourself with such inscrutable questions."

After a few more moments searching for a breakthrough, Josette nodded her agreement.

"The question foremost on my mind," he said, leaning in and lowering his voice, "is how many more drinks you'll need—if indeed any, and if indeed there's anything left that you haven't already drunk—to help me break into the dungeon and set your mother free."

Josette laughed, only stopping when she realized he was serious, and then she took a breath and laughed for a while longer. He sat quietly through it all, elbows on the table and hands folded in front of his chin. When it was clear he wasn't going to offer anything more, she said, "We'd never get the door open."

He tossed something onto the table. When she managed to focus on it, she found that it was a key.

"Where did you get that?"

"I stole it, of course."

"Even with a key, she'll be guarded."

Bernat pointed to the two men he'd come in with, now playing nine-pins. "Those are the guards over there. There won't be anyone else along to replace them until two in the morning."

She was quiet for so long, she worried Bernat might think she'd fallen asleep with her eyes open. But if he did, it didn't change his countenance. He only sat there, wearing a placid, concerned look on his face. Finally she said, her voice a great deal more stern and sober than the last time she spoke, "Then why haven't you done it already?"

"Well," he said, his eyes darting away and then back to her, "it's the look of the thing, isn't it? The job wants two."

"She betrayed the town."

"Yes."

"Twice."

"Yes."

"And she gave the Vins the plans for my airship."

"She did."

"Airmen may die because of that."

"Yes."

"People have already died because of her treachery."

"I know. I was there, if you recall."

"And it doesn't bother you?"

"It bothers me a great deal. Perhaps more than anything has ever bothered me, in what I can now see was a rather sheltered life. Yet none of that will be changed by a hangman."

She looked away. "So do it yourself. I won't stop you."

"The job wants two."

She rolled her eyes up to the ceiling, and kept them there. "How does it take two people to break someone out of an unguarded cell, when you already have the key?"

"The job wants two" was all he said.

She looked back at him and put on the widest, best smile she could manage under the circumstances. "Then it won't be done," she said.

He sat and watched her for a little while, then picked up the key and slipped it into a pocket. "Very well," he said. "That's something of a relief, to be honest. That is to say, I could never escape suspicion if she turned up missing. Not after we made love."

Josette maintained her composure.

"And not just once, but over and over again."

She chewed on a pine nut and looked away.

"And in such depraved and degrading positions. Yet so inventive! I can see where you get your sense of innovation."

His only reaction when she threw the bowl of pine nuts at him was to close his eyes. As he opened them again, he remained stone-faced as the nuts scattered all about him.

"May we change the subject?" Josette asked, quite mildly.

"By all means," he said, rubbing the spot where the bowl had struck his forehead.

She picked a loose nut from the table. "So," she said, nibbling on it, "what else has occupied your day?"

"You'll be pleased to know that Pesha will live," he said, likewise picking and nibbling a nut. "And it looks like Corne will keep his leg, as long as infection doesn't set in."

"Heny's damn good with that sort of thing, whatever one may say about her other predilections."

Bernat snorted. "Whatever some may say, you mean."

"Some, indeed," she answered. "By my accounting, the defenders of that unnatural predilection are made up of a turncoat and the foppish lover of a turncoat, neither of whom I'd call a good character witness."

"Then I suppose you don't realize that Jutes—" Bernat stopped cold, as something went on inside his head. It was some internal struggle that Josette might have been able to piece together, if she'd only been a touch closer to sober. "Jutes admires them both very much," he finally finished.

"Sergeant Jutes admires them?" she asked. That threw her. "Well, if someone as upright and above-board as Jutes has that opinion . . . Perhaps I'll have to think a bit more about it."

"Perhaps you should, regarding this and other matters," Bernat said. And if he'd left it at that, she might have convinced herself to go with him and free her mother. She'd half talked herself into it as it was, when he dashed his own hopes with his eagerness to manipulate. "You'll be happy to know, too, that I have my soldier's heart well in hand. I didn't condemn Major Dvakov, when I easily could have."

"Oh good," she said evenly. "I was hoping you'd get that sorted out. And that certainly is the accepted means of curing soldier's heart: saving the life of a smug little shit who deserves to die a dozen times over. That, or bathing in the sacred waters of the spring of Atbok, but that's such a long trip."

His face went indignant, bordering on petulant. "You're making fun of me."

"Thank you for noticing," she said. "In my defense, you're begging for it. More so than usual, even. Do you know why they call it soldier's heart, Bernie?"

He perked up a little. "I had wondered."

"It's because they used to think it was caused by being away from home." She leaned back in her chair and smirked. "Well, I say they used to think that, but I don't think anyone ever did. I think it was just one of those little fibs that high-ranking officers tell themselves, along the same line as, 'I got this job by merit.'" She tried to find a mug that had more than dregs in it, and grew grim when her search came up empty. "It's an excuse, of course. It's a way for the generals to believe it's not their fault. That they didn't do this to the men under their command, that it wasn't their orders, and certainly not their negligence. It's only something that would have happened anyway, the first time the men were away from home. But the fundamental thing about soldier's heart, Bernie . . . Are you listening very carefully, now?"

He was, but he leaned in closer, and she did the same, until their foreheads nearly touched across the table.

"The real, core thing that you have to know about soldier's heart, Bernie, the thing about soldier's heart that you want to remember . . . is that you don't have it, and you never have."

Judging by his expression, that was the very last thing Bernat expected to hear. He rocked back as if she'd just struck him in the face with something quite a bit heavier than a bowl of nuts.

Josette continued, "What you have is something we in the army—those of us who've been in the army long enough to know, I mean—it's what we in the army call, 'being an asshole.'" She smiled reassuringly and made an expansive gesture with her hands. "Don't worry, it's a common condition."

Bernat pondered this while the barman put a fresh mug of ale before each of them. "But my recent tendency toward destruction, this drive to solve every problem by beating the hell out of people . . ."

"Hasn't a thing to do with soldier's heart," Josette said. "I've seen soldier's heart cause anger, Bernie, I've even seen it cause rage, but it doesn't cause violence. That's you. That's something you chose to do, from almost the moment you got a taste for it. Tell me, how often do your bouts of violence actually follow a bout of anger? How often do you panic about something in the past, instead of something in the present?"

He swallowed and said nothing.

"You get panicky when your life's in danger. That ain't soldier's heart, or anything at all, really. That's as ordinary as ordinary gets. And if you suddenly find that you're solving your problems with violence, it's because you damn well taught yourself to solve your problems with violence." She drained her mug and added, "I'm proud of you."

When she reached for Bernat's drink, he handed it over without argument.

"But there's nothing peculiar about the way you are." She looked him up and down. "Not in the military sense, anyhow."

He was silent for so long, and stared so forlornly at the wall, that she thought he might cry. But then he only nodded. "So

I don't have soldier's heart? This is just who I am? That's a sobering thought."

"Well, I got good news on that front," she said, raising her mug to him in salute. "There's nothing so sobering you can't outdrink it."

"I'm not convinced of that," Bernat said. They were both silent for a while, and then, after a few false starts, he asked, "Have you been home yet?"

Josette didn't answer, but Bernat's half smile showed that he knew the answer in any event.

"You should drop by." He stood and turned to leave. After a step, he looked back to add, "Visit Duchess Prettyheart. See what she's been up to since you last spoke." As he left, Josette wondered if there was enough ale in the tavern to make sense of that comment. She suspected there wasn't, but resolved to make the attempt, out of courtesy.

The question was settled a little before midnight, when the tavern keeper tipped the last keg and a corporal—newly promoted out of the forlorn hope—paid him half a penny to suck it dry.

It was then that Josette finally recognized the wisdom in Bernat's advice. Yes, she would visit her childhood home, because Vin soldiers might have quartered in it during the occupation, and in that case there would be alcohol hidden there. The effects of the tavern's watered-down ale were waning, after all, and sobriety simply wasn't an option after the day she'd had.

So she walked, thinking of the foundations of ancient walls, and of the making of soldiers, and of the business she was in, and of two tiny wolf cubs crying in the snow, and arrived so suddenly at her destination that it seemed she could hardly have passed through the space between.

She stood at the end of a narrow lane in front of a brick-and-stone house. She stood there for some time, though she couldn't have said quite how much, before trying the door and finding it locked. But when she heaved up on the handle, she found that, even after all these years, doing so made enough space between the door and the doorjamb that she could work the bolt back with her fingers and unlock the door without a key.

It was pitch black inside, but the curtains were permeated with the smell of smoke and human gas—which meant Vin soldiers had, indeed, been quartered here. She found her mother's oil lamp not where it had been, but sitting at the center of the dining table, and struck a light with steel and flint left carelessly next to it. By the pale yellow light of the lamp, she put the flint back into the drawer under the window, where it belonged.

The lower room was much as she had last left it, minus the loom, but plus several stereoplate illustrations of buxom women in various states of undress. She looked into all the likely hiding places, and found a small bottle of Vinzhalian arkhi hidden inside a hollowed-out nook in a ceiling beam. This intensely alcoholic Vin delicacy was made from fermented mare's milk, smelled like paraffin fuel, tasted like rancid butter, and was gone far too soon.

By reflexive impulse, she left the empty bottle by the door for the rag-and-bone man to collect in the morning—never stopping to wonder who would let him in, or if he was even still alive. From just inside the doorway, she looked across the room to the stairs. She took the lamp and went up to the second floor, calling herself a fool for ever hesitating, and for doubting the snow-white purity of her own motives in going upstairs only to search for alcohol.

Upstairs, the ancient bed that had once dominated the room was gone. In its place were four portable cots lined in front of the fireplace. In between, the floor was dusted with unswept gray soot. The windowsill was similarly covered, where the

Vins had carelessly tossed ash from the fireplace out the window. But not with any regularity, judging by the unsightly gray mound piled under the grate.

She searched the room from top to bottom, looking in all the secret hidey holes she knew well, and all the likely spots a newcomer might think of. She left the loose stone under the window for last, not because that was where Duchess Prettyheart had been hidden—what an absurd thought—but because it was the last hiding place the Vins were likely to discover.

The loose stone fit perfectly into its mortar. Only someone lying belly-down on the floor was apt to notice the worn bottom edge, where little hands could slide a knife under the stone, and lever it up and out of its hollow.

Somewhat larger hands did the job now, remembering the trick of it after a few failed attempts. Holding the lamp next to her head, Josette peered into the space inside. There was something in there, hopefully something better than that godawful arkhi the Vins had stashed downstairs.

She reached in, but what she pulled out was Duchess Prettyheart, wearing the same summer dress she'd worn to the prince's ball, the last time Josette had seen her. That had been a heady time for the young duchess, what with having to find something to wear at the last minute after Mr. Skender's goat ate all her clothes, and having her first kiss with the prince at midnight under the sparkling light of a golden chandelier— albeit a golden chandelier that looked rather like candlelight reflected off the polished side of a brass teakettle.

It was a wonder the rats hadn't gotten to her. It was rats that had made the hollow behind the stone in the first place, she always thought, chewing their warrens through the older, softer daub plaster the house was originally made of, before the stone and brick facings were added.

How had the rats not found her?

But the rats had indeed found her, Josette saw as she held

the doll up to the light. And not just found her, but torn her to pieces. And not just once, but over and over again. Somewhere in the walls of this house, there must have been rats' nests made from three or four dolls' worth of Duchess Prettyheart.

But someone had cared for her all these years, taking her from her hiding place at intervals to patch her up. Every reparative stitch had been made with precise attention, every patch matched as perfectly as possible to the material, every bit of wool and sawdust stuffing replaced and pushed carefully into place—with never a hollow in the doll's stuffing, and never a spot too dense. And then the mender had returned Duchess Prettyheart to the same hiding place, for reasons as irrational as they were obvious.

Josette nearly fell down the stairs in her haste to reach the street. She ran to the end of the lane, tripping frequently but never falling. She tried to think of where Bernat might be, if not the tavern she'd just come from.

For, if she couldn't find him, all was lost.

BERNAT STOOD SHIVERING in the chill of the night, fingering the ice-cold key in his coat pocket so frequently that in time it warmed to his body temperature. He checked his pocket watch again, but still couldn't read it in the feeble starlight.

He was beginning to think Josette must have passed out inside the house, when finally he heard unsteady footfalls coming down the lane. Flickering yellow light lit the street in front, and then Josette came racing round the corner, carrying a lamp in one hand and a doll in the other. She had so little notion of where she was going that she didn't notice him there until he said, "There you are."

She stopped in front of him, began to speak, then turned away to throw up into a nearby flower box. After wiping her mouth on her sleeve, she said, "I thought I'd have to run all over town to find you."

"Nonsense," he said, handing his handkerchief to her. "Knowing where to be is one of my qualities."

"Oh, what's the other one?"

"Ignoring comments such as that." He checked his watch by the light of the lamp. Half past midnight. "Shall we go, or is there more to disgorge?"

She looked as if there might be, but after a moment's consideration she said, "Let's start out and see how it goes."

"Best, then, if we set our pace on the brisk side."

Brisk they were, arriving at the dungeon in only fifteen minutes. But then, "dungeon" was coming it a little high. On his first visit during the afternoon, he was expecting dripping walls, row upon row of barred cells, and never a sign of the sky. The Durum dungeon, on the other hand, was composed in its entirety of two spacious cells built into the basement of the town hall and a comfy nook for the jailer, each with a fine view of the square through a grating set at eye level within and street level without. In central Kuchin, such rooms would rent for ten liras a month.

Cell walls and cell doors alike were made from ancient timber and rusted iron. When they opened Elise's door, she was standing at the grating, staring at the stars, sucking whatever juice she could from the last hours of her life.

She turned when they entered, looking from one to the other with eyes that wouldn't dare to hope. They looked evenly at Josette, and Elise asked, "So what's it to be, then?"

"Three nooses between us, if we don't hurry," Josette said. "Come on, Mother. We'll have time for nostalgic melancholia once we're out of the city."

Elise was released and stepped toward Bernat. He recoiled, worried she might attempt to embrace him. If that had been her plan, she thought better of it when she saw his reaction.

"Open the other door" was all she said, ducking into the jailer's nook and coming out with a foot-long wooden tipstaff.

There was a creaking from the other cell. Major Dvakov stepped out of shadow and into the lantern light, his face stoic and stern. He said nothing, but only stared into Bernat with eyes that seemed to dissect him, cutting him open to discover the very root of his every weakness.

"But how—" Bernat began.

"I sent a runner to Major Emery, after you left the tavern," Josette said, answering his question before he could finish it. "Told them to hang the son of a bitch."

He swallowed hard, unable to look away from Dvakov. "Well," he said, his voice faltering only a little, "I suppose, as long as I'm not the one who doomed him . . ."

"Open the door," Elise said, arms at her side, staff swinging gently back and forth in one hand. Josette drew her pistol and held it ready.

Dvakov even stepped politely back when Bernat turned the key in the lock, giving the door room to swing inward. The Vin major didn't flinch when Elise's first blow hit him in the gut. Her second took out his knee and sent him to the floor. She hit him no higher than the shoulders, raining blows on his kidneys, his extremities, his groin, until finally his pain outran his stoicism and he cried out. Only then did she send a crushing blow against his windpipe that muffled the screams.

She had turned his body to jelly before she began to tire, but he still lived when she started on his head, retaining enough strength in her flagging arms to make his face into an unrecognizable jumble of bruises and blood.

Bernat looked away, meeting Josette's eyes. "We are in a bit of a hurry, Mother," she said.

Elise dropped the staff and leaned against the dungeon wall, gasping for breath. Bernat thought he heard sobbing mixed amid her heavy breaths, but by the time he looked, she had wiped her face clean, removing the spattered blood and any tears that might have wetted her cheeks.

On their way out, they left the lantern and dungeon key at the bottom of a rain barrel. They threaded their way through the streets of southwestern Durum. It was easier going than when the Vins were in charge, since the 132nd had few patrols out. At least, it had few patrols that hadn't noticed suspicious activity at the tavern much earlier in the evening, and decided it was their sworn duty to investigate.

There were guards on the wall, but they were looking outward. The escape party slipped into the breach and picked their way over the rubble, worried now about tumbling rocks that might give them away, rather than Vin bullets. From there, it was only a matter of following the circumference of the wall to the woods.

"Get off the road before dawn," Josette said from somewhere to Bernat's left. It was so dark on the edge of the forest that he wouldn't have known she was there if she didn't speak. "You know the woods, so the search parties won't find you. Just make sure you keep moving east and stay off the road until you're deep into Vinzhalia. Don't turn around. Don't ever come back here. Those are the terms of your release."

The only sounds in reply were croaking frogs and chirping insects. It was quiet so long, Bernat began to wonder if Elise had slipped away unnoticed. And then, finally, she said, "You're the only good thing I ever did with my life, Josie. That's why I've hated you so much, these past years: for getting away from me."

"That's, um, that's very sweet, Mother."

He thought he heard them embrace, and then heard Elise shuffling about in the dark. "Still there, Bernie?" she asked.

"I'm here" was all he said.

She found him and put her arms around him. He returned

her embrace, but not for too long, nor too tightly, lest she get the idea that he still loved her. He did love her, for all that, but he could hardly let her know it.

"Here, take this to keep you safe," Josette said.

There was some fumbling in the dark before Elise gasped and said, "I can't take your pistol, Josie. The king gave it to you."

A moment of thoughtful silence, and then Josette said, "Good God, you're right. I would never have offered if I'd had less to drink. Here, give it back, and take this instead."

The subvocal sounds Elise made during the exchange were at first indignant, but quickly turned to a soft coo. "Duchess Prettyheart," she said. There was an unnerving sort of softness in Elise's usually strident voice, and it underlay a barely detectable tremor.

"She's better off under your care, I think. And she always did like dumplings."

Again, Elise was so perfectly quiet for so long that Bernat thought she had already snuck off. Then she broke the silence with, "You ain't the same girl who cried over those wolves. I'm sorry I said you were."

"Be safe, Mother" was all Josette said in reply.

"You know, you'd fix a lot of your problems by settling down with a nice man."

Bernat could sense Josette struggling to keep her voice low as she said again, "Be safe, Mother." She then heaved a defeated sigh and added, "I love you."

But this time, Elise really was gone, having disappeared into the woods with a hunter's silent stride. Bernat fumbled through the dark until he bumped into Josette, who was not searching, but only standing stiff and still.

"It's all right," she said. "I'm sure she heard me. That's the important bit, isn't it?"

Bernat wasn't sure it was, but he said confidently, "Yes. Yes, it is."

"I was going to let her die," she said, barely audible now.

He laughed, but not cruelly. "No, you weren't."

They walked toward Durum. The top half of *Ayezderhau*'s vast envelope was visible over the city wall, lit from within by her keel lights.

"What'll we do with her?" he asked.

"In the morning we'll patch and mend as best we can, refloat her, and Kember will take a skeleton crew back to Arle, with *Mistral* following. The sooner we can get out of here, the less likely it is we'll be arrested for breaking Mother out of jail."

"Is Kember ready to command a wounded ship all the way back to Arle?"

He could hear the strange little smile in her voice. "No, but she'll be closer to ready once she's done it."

"That seems backward, somehow."

"Welcome to the world, Bernie." She stopped, seeming to sense without being told that he needed to rest his leg. "I really don't regret it, you know. That I no longer cry over wolf cubs and suchlike."

"I know," he said, leaning over to rub the muscles in his calf. "But there is a bit of you that regrets it." Before she could deny it, he went on. "A little shard of something different, that doesn't quite fit with the rest, and sometimes it gets into the gears and messes up the works."

She hesitated before saying, "Maybe."

He'd been hoping for more, after deploying such a lovely metaphor, but he supposed it would have to do. "You know," he said, "I've been thinking of you and Roland."

"So have I," she said.

"And what's your letter going to say?"

There was no crinkle of paper, and no light to read by in

any event, but she spoke her next words as if reciting them off the page. " 'Roland, I am sorry to say I don't love you. But if you will resolve to not blurt out any more declarations of love meant to sway my heart in spite of myself, or attempt any other silly gambits aimed at my heart, I am open to the possibility that my feelings will change, and I am willing to spend time in your company in the interim.' "

"Well," he said, trying to find something to compliment, "it's a good thing that 'most romantic thing you've ever said' is not a terribly competitive field."

She snorted in the darkness. "And what have you concluded, about me and Roland?"

"I've concluded that I've been right all along. You ought to write to him and break it off. Not only for your own sake, but so he'll be as miserable as he plainly deserves to be."

The smile was gone from her voice now. "What epiphany led you to believe that this ought to be the edict of my heart?"

He frowned. "Oh, it's not your heart that I look to for guidance. It's mine, and it's the heart of a malevolent bastard, as you so kindly reminded me earlier. So I'm compelled to stand by my original advice." A pause. "You don't have to listen to it, of course."

"That's very gracious of you."

After due consideration, Bernat said, "It is, isn't it?" He looked for *Mistral*, moored somewhere out there, but her keel lights were out and he couldn't find a trace of her in the night. "Think you can find your way in the dark?"

"I always have," she said, as they began the long trip home.